Sweetheart
Deal

ALSO BY CLAIRE MATTURRO

Bone Valley

Wildcat Wine

Skinny-dipping

Sweetheart
Deal

CLAIRE MATTURRO

wm WILLIAM MORROW   *An Imprint of* HarperCollins*Publishers*

SWEETHEART DEAL. Copyright © 2007 by Claire Hamner Matturro. All rights reserved. Printed in the United States of America. No part of this book may be used or reproduced in any manner whatsoever without written permission except in the case of brief quotations embodied in critical articles and reviews. For information address HarperCollins Publishers, 10 East 53rd Street, New York, NY 10022.

HarperCollins books may be purchased for educational, business, or sales promotional use. For information please write: Special Markets Department, HarperCollins Publishers, 10 East 53rd Street, New York, NY 10022.

FIRST EDITION

Designed by Kara Strubel

Library of Congress Cataloging-in-Publication Data

Matturro, Claire Hamner, 1954–
    Sweetheart deal / Claire Matturro.
        p. cm.
    ISBN: 978-0-06-077325-0
    ISBN-10: 0-06-077325-1
    1. Clearly, Lilly (Fictitious character)—Fiction. 2. Attorney and client—Fiction. 3. Women lawyers—Fiction. 4. Sarasota (Fla.)—Fiction. I. Title.
    PS3613.A87D95 2007
    813'.6—dc22   2006047088

07 08 09 10 11   ID/RRD   10 9 8 7 6 5 4 3 2 1

To Della Johnson Hamner,
and in memory of Ada Bell Taylor Johnson

acknowledgments

My cousin, Paige Johnson Hodo, and her husband, Dr. David Hodo, were a tremendous help to me in writing this book, and I wish to thank them. Paige and David read an early draft, and then we sat together and brainstormed until we had collectively improved the heck out of the story line. David Hodo, a brilliant and compassionate psychiatrist, also generously shared his expertise with regard to psychogenic drugs as used in the Willette subplot. With regard to his help on the pharmaceuticals and the tox screens, let me say this: if I rounded off a sharp edge, or otherwise made a mistake, that was me—Dr. Hodo knows his stuff. He also loaned me his name for one of the characters.

As with my previous books, this one is a team effort with all the fine and talented folks at William Morrow. My editor, Carolyn Marino; her assistant, Wendy Lee; and the copy editor all made this a far, far better book, and did so with grace and patience and a good deal of creative energy. My agent, Elaine Koster, was the calm voice and the steady hand and the interpreter of the fine print. And my publicist, Samantha Hagerbaumer, remains unfailingly energetic, supportive, creative, and unnaturally well organized. Thank you all to the William Morrow/HarperCollins family.

And, speaking of family, two things: first, lest there be any doubt or questions about this, let me remind the readers, this book is fiction. None of Lilly's fictional family is based upon my own, though my two grandmothers were wise and all-loving and welcoming and strong, like Lilly's fictional grandmother.

The second thing about family is this: As I said, this book—any book, really—is a team effort, and my family is a supportive and essential part of that team. Bill, my husband, retains his uncoveted spot as The First Reader (of all ten to twelve drafts, all four hundred pages of every one of them). On book tours, he is the steady hand and the support that makes it not just possible, but fun. My brother, William D. Hamner, remains the police and forensic expert, a key sounding board and brainstormer, who often writes my male dialogue. My parents and my cousins are the support team, fact-checkers, dialect coaches, and unpaid publicists. My friend Mike Lehner, family by choice if not blood, is my Spanish translator, another of the unenvied early readers, an unpaid publicist and editor of great skill.

Thank you all.

For anyone interested in reading further about the smuggling of endangered and exotic animals, reptiles, birds, and plants in violation of national and international laws, I highly recommend Stan Zimmerman's fascinating book *A History of Smuggling in Florida* (The History Press, 2006). Chapter 6 has a great overview of the subject, including the probable extinction facing sturgeons due to the continuing illegal market for its roe, otherwise known as caviar.

And, finally and especially, thank you to my wonderful nephew, William Robert "Billy" Hamner, for writing the lyrics to Lonnie's hit song, "Sweetheart Deal."

Sweetheart Deal

chapter 1

Your cheating mind will tell on you.

  I, Lilly Belle Rose Cleary, attorney-at-law, so thought as I glared at my own client. Not only was this man attempting to defraud the legal system, he was not listening to me, his defense attorney. Thus, I was engaged in a wrangle of wits with an idiot.

  And I was not winning.

  This is, of course, not that unusual in the larger scheme of things; one has only to look back at some of our recent presidential debates to see other shining examples of battles of the wits won by the witless.

  Still, it didn't happen that often to me, and I was irritated, and wondering if I was losing my stomach for my line of work, which was defending doctors, lawyers, and other professionals against the costly and insulting burden of malpractice lawsuits brought by their former patients and clients.

  I balanced myself for my next verbal thrust, reducing it to the direct order and not the rationale. "You cannot respond to a motion to produce the relevant medical records by providing the plaintiff's attorney with altered medical records. Absolutely not."

  "Why not?" my idiotic and wholly charmless client asked, in his personal quest to ruin what was otherwise, so far, a seemingly pleasant morning in Sarasota, Florida.

"Because it is unethical, it is illegal, and it is a fraud upon the court, which will subject both you and me to sanctions." Then, getting to the real crux of the matter, I said, "You can't get away with it. It's obvious. You changed the information in a blue pen; the original text is in black ink."

"But it won't matter when it is photocopied," my idiot client replied.

I sighed. Could anyone be that stupid and allowed to live outside an institution? "It will still be obvious. You've scribbled over half the notes. Besides, did it ever occur to you that the plaintiff's attorney might demand a look at the original records?"

Henry Platt, my sweet, pink-cheeked claims adjuster, the very man who had referred this case to me and who was now present to protect his company's interest and offer me moral support, took up the challenge. "Besides, if you use . . . that is, doctor the, er, I mean, alter the . . . I mean, falsify, er . . . engage in a fraud, then we, your malpractice insurance company, can deny coverage."

Excellent point for Henry. I liked this man more and more over the years that we had worked together. "And if Henry's company denies coverage due to your, er, fraud, since they've hired me to represent you pursuant to the terms of your policy, I would no longer be your attorney. The insurer will not pay any of your legal expenses. You will be totally on your own."

"About those original records?" Idiot Client asked.

"Yes," Henry and I said in concert.

"You mean the plaintiff's attorney could look at them? The real ones? I mean, the original ones?"

"A request to review the original records would not be out of line in a medical malpractice case," I said, using my most lawyerlike tone of voice. The one that said I'm in charge, you're not. "Especially in light of the fact you've scribbled over a number of words and written in different ones.

In fact, I would consider it legal malpractice on the part of the plaintiff's attorney if she did not inspect the original medical records."

"But . . . these are the original records."

Henry and I rose out of our chairs and glared down at Idiot Client, a chiropractor who had been treating a man he had diagnosed with spinal subluxation. Unfortunately, what the man actually had was a cancerous tumor of the spine, which had not much improved under Idiot Client's spinal manipulation. Only the intervention of the patient's daughter had gotten the patient appropriate medical attention, and led to a malpractice suit against this man, this client, this idiot, this would-be fraud, this chiropractor to whom Henry's liability-insurance company had the grave misfortune of having sold a malpractice policy.

"These are the originals?" I asked. Sometimes stress blocks my ears.

"Yes," Idiot Client said.

"You took a blue pen and changed things on the original records, which were in black ink? And you didn't—what? Think this would be noticed by anyone?" I struggled to keep from yelling. I noticed Henry's cheeks were splotching red.

"I didn't think anybody would look at the originals. Everything photocopies black and white," he said. "I . . . I panicked."

Henry and I looked at each other across the top of this man's head as we continued standing and the idiot between us remained seated.

"Settle?" Henry said, a little squeak in his voice. "Lilly, can we settle it? Quick?"

"Henry, a word. Outside," I said.

We stepped out into the hallway, out of the earshot of our hopefully soon-to-be Not Client. I paused, waiting for Henry to read my mind as I could not suggest that he take a course of action detrimental to my client, the chiropractor, even if I couldn't as of this minute personally stand that client. "Henry?"

"He clearly, er . . . that is, he committed a fraud, and there's an unambiguous provision in our policy for"—Henry paled and gulped air—

"denying coverage in that event. My company owes him nothing," Henry said. "Not even a defense."

I nodded, careful not to encourage Henry in the path I would have demanded in a heartbeat if I was not ethically charged, at least for the time being, with protecting my client's interests. "You tell him. You know I'm still his attorney until the court grants my motion to withdraw."

"Could we get Bonita in here to, er, er . . ."

"Witness it?"

"Yes."

Technically, Bonita, my long-suffering and unnaturally calm legal secretary supreme, widow, mother of five headstrong children, and the object of Henry's great affection and three-year quest to marry, was not needed as a witness and would have been suspect in any event, seeing where her loyalties lay. But I nodded. Henry was always more forceful around Bonita. If he needed his sweetie by his side before he could act boldly, this was fine with me. "Go get her," I said.

A few moments later, the three of us slipped back into the room. Idiot Client looked at the ever-lovely Bonita, stood up and puffed out his chest, sucked in his belly, and offered his hand. Henry marched between them quicker than a bull moose on the make. Over his shoulder, I could see a small smile flit about Bonita's face.

"On the basis of the fraud you have committed, my company will be denying coverage. And since we have hired Ms. Cleary to represent you pursuant to your contract, which is now nullified by your fraud, she will, pursuant to my instructions, file a motion to withdraw as your counsel. I'll get the paperwork started," Henry said, clear, straight, and without his usual faltering. Bonita beamed.

"You can't do that," the man said. "I'll sue you. I'll sue you both."

"Well, as your attorney at least for the next couple of minutes, I would advise you to please consider what an interesting witness Mr. Platt would make. And these"— I held up the altered records—"interesting evidence, wouldn't you agree?"

Idiot Client jumped up, snatched his records out of my hands, growled at us, and dashed out the door. Bonita hugged Henry as if he had cured cancer. Hugging complete, Henry turned to me and offered his hand, and we shook as if he and I had won a huge defense verdict.

Just as Henry and I finished shaking hands, the phone in the conference room rang. I let it ring. I had left clear instructions not to be disturbed.

While I was grinding my teeth, the phone stopped ringing. But soon enough, my law firm's receptionist's voice chirped over the phone intercom, telling me, and not incidentally Henry and Bonita, that my brother needed to speak with me and, honest, she wouldn't have interrupted but he insisted it was a family emergency, and Bonita didn't answer my office phone.

"Which brother?" I asked, knowing my two brothers—mad hatter, Pentecostal, pot-smoking Delvon and steady-as-a-rock-in-a-still-lake Dan—have vastly differing concepts of an emergency.

"Dan."

Uh-oh. Dan's the normal one. Dan's the one who could properly define emergency, the one who doesn't have emergencies like other people have supper.

I snatched up the phone and waited for a series of clicks, and then Dan's voice came over the line, and he said, "Lilly Belle?"

"Dan, it's me. What's wrong?"

"Well, we got us a problem here."

He paused and I inhaled, imagining the dead or maimed bodies of people I loved. "What, Dan?"

"My momma, I mean, our momma, has been ... she's ... they've arrested her."

"For what?" I said, eyeing Henry and Bonita, and wondering in one part of my brain how to get them out of the room without seeming rude and with the other part of my brain wondering what in the hell my mother could have done to get arrested. I mean, the woman never left the house. Hell, the woman never got out of her pajamas.

"The police chief saw her shoot a man."

"She shot somebody," I said, too loudly and in a complete abandonment of proper office decorum. Henry and Bonita were most definitely paying attention. I also noticed they were holding hands. "Is she all right?"

"She's fine, but they got her in the hospital instead of the jail. The doctor, you remember Dr. Weinstein? He's treated her before. Moved here from up North about, oh, almost a couple years ago?"

"No, I don't know him. I haven't been there in twenty years, remember? And how did he treat her? He does house calls?"

"Oh, no, nobody does house calls. Mom coughed over the phone for him, and he wrote out a scrip for some antibiotics. Cleared her right up."

"She coughed over the phone for him?" Yeah, that was the standard of care, all right.

"Sure did. Fixed her right up. Well, he's a good doctor, and he has her pretty well sedated in the hospital now."

Oh, and that'd be different, I thought, but caught my tongue in time to avoid saying so in the presence of Henry and Bonita.

"When did this happen?"

"Last night. But we decided to wait a bit on calling you, see if anything . . . you know, changed."

Changed? As in she un-shot the man? Or as in she was un-arrested? Or maybe changed as in the man was treated and released? Or died.

"Is he"—*dead* was the word I wanted, but the rapt stares of Henry and Bonita made me wordsmith a tad—"in a state where his prognosis is clear?"

"Lilly Belle, she shot that man to death."

My mother had killed a man?

As I tried to process the notion that my reclusive mother, who was inclined toward serious inactivity, had finally actually *done* something, however bizarre and troublesome, Henry tilted forward in his chair as if to hear Dan's end of the phone call.

"Lilly, we need you. We need you to come up here. Can you come help?"

Damn, Dan didn't ask much of me. He was my brother, and he was strong, and if he needed me enough to ask for help, then I had to go. It was that simple.

"Let me call you back in a few minutes," I said, and gently put down the phone.

"Do you want me to, er . . . get . . . er, call someone, Lilly?" Henry the Sweet asked. His face was bunched up in what I knew was genuine concern for me. Bonita rose and stood beside me, her hand lightly on my shoulder.

"No, I . . . I guess I better go. I mean, go to Bugfest, to help Dan." So saying, I trotted out of the conference room with Henry and Bonita in tow. Around the corner we went, and down the hall to my office, where Bonita pulled out my calendar. "I can cancel or reschedule everything for the rest of this week," she said, after a quick glance.

While Henry patted my arm to the point of irritation, I made a hasty mental list of instructions for Bonita on top of canceling appointments and such things. My key instruction, though, was to be sure to prepare a rough draft of a motion to withdraw as counsel for Idiot Client, and get a couple of ace law clerks started on the supporting memorandum of law on the off-chance the man would oppose my motion.

"I can drive you to the airport if you want to catch a plane," ever-helpful Henry chirped.

My hands started sweating at the mere mention of *airport,* with its treacherous terminals, running sidewalks, luggage conveyer belts, security checkpoints, and hordes of people from places with different and horrid diseases to which I had no immunity.

"Airport," Bonita whispered, and shook her head at Henry, who looked immediately abashed.

"No, driving, driving is . . . better," I said. "It's only a five-hour drive."

"Sorry, I forgot about your . . . airport phob—er, er—"

"Lilly, do not worry. Henry will help me, and we will hold down the fort," Bonita said, interrupting quickly enough to show not only her tact and mastery of American idiom, but knowing precisely how to make Henry look up and beam again.

After leaving Henry and Bonita to make goo-goo eyes at each other, I sped home as fast as my faithful little Honda Civic could hurl itself across the numerous speed bumps erected by overly protective local powers-that-be that thought knocking out the undercarriage of automobiles would somehow preserve the quaint neighborhood quality of the homes in the Southgate Community.

And found Armando, the squat and obviously unhappy son of Bonita, camped outside my front door, waiting. Wrapped around his thick, brown neck was Johnny Winter, the ferret that once saved my life but who still spat at me every time I got near him.

Unlike the rest of Bonita's five children, Armando had always acted like he didn't much care for me. But then, he acted like he didn't much care for anyone. I would have blamed it on his adolescence—he was sixteen now—if I hadn't known him as a child, when he had that same belligerence, his own extreme leave-me-alone thing going.

So, yeah, I was surprised to see him waiting for me. Surprised and disturbed, since I didn't have time for him.

But I didn't have the heart to say so.

"So, hey, Armando. What's up?" I said, putting on my chipper voice as a hopeful antidote to his grim face.

"Can I stay here? For a while?" he asked.

Oh-oh. Not good. Not good in general, and especially not good timing. I glanced at my watch. "Your mom know you're skipping school?"

"She doesn't care. She's so . . . wrapped up in Carmen and Henry."

Ah, jealousy. Carmen, being Bonita's only girl and the youngest, naturally got a lot of extra attention, plus she was sweet as a clean puppy and four times cuter. And Henry was gaining rapidly in his three-year quest to become part of Bonita's family.

"You know your mother cares about you, and she won't like you skipping school," I said, in a textbook example of lame responses. But hey, I haven't had much experience in raising children, okay? And so, spank me, but what I was thinking about was how to get rid of him. "Armando, why don't I drop you off at your home in a few minutes. I've got to pack, pack really quickly. My mother is in the hospital, and I've got to go to Georgia."

"Cool. I can come with you," he said, and jumped up, an eager smile on his face. But then Bonita's good raising made him duck his head, no doubt a bit aghast at his own bad manners. When he finally looked me in the eyes, he said, "I'm sorry, *Tia* Lilly, about your mom, I mean. Is it real bad?"

"I don't know yet. That's why I have to hurry. And I don't think this is the trip to take you with me. My youngest nephew is your age, and I'd be glad to take you to Georgia another time, and y'all could meet each other, but, Armando, there's just too much going on right now. Do you see that?"

He stared over my shoulder, gazing into the distance and utterly refusing to meet my eyes.

"Armando, is everything all right?"

At that moment, the formerly sleeping ferret, Johnny Winter, the albino polecat cousin draped about Armando, woke up, oonked at me as a warm-up to spitting, and then spat until I backed up.

"Can I house-sit for you, while you're gone?" Armando asked. And gently brushed Johnny out of his face.

"It's all right with me, if your mom agrees. Tell you what, you call her while I pack, and put her on the phone with me. If she says you can stay here, you can stay."

As we went inside together, I realized this boy—this young man—had never in the many years I had known him ever called me *Tia* Lilly before, though his siblings had done so for years.

I wasn't sure there was going to be anything in the whole damn town of Bugfest that I could eat. While I wasn't changing time zones, I was traveling to the land of pig-out-and-slaw-down, where barbecued pork reigned supreme, edging out fried chicken only by a slice of Texas toast, and I was a vegetarian, whole foods, organic only, tofu eater, convinced the secret to a healthy, happy life lay in fueling it properly. That is, I didn't eat barbecue or fried chicken.

So, yeah, food was going to be an issue. But after settling with Bonita that Armando could house-sit, and giving them both my brother Dan's address and phone number, I crashed through the Granary on my way out of Sarasota and grabbed the obvious: organic apples, bottled water, yogurt, kefir, organic fair-trade coffee, and all the boxes of Save the Forest Organic Trail Mix Bars that the store had in stock.

I was already on I–75, near the Gainesville exit, when I realized I should probably mention to Philip Cohen, my persistent lover/boy-friend/beau/alleged-fiancé-to-be, that I was going to be out of town for a few days, in case he should miss me. Philip is the best relationship I've ever had, though he keeps trying to ruin it by insisting we get married. Even with that major flaw, he's a keeper, so I pulled out my cell phone and got him on the line.

"Something's come up," I said, skipping the usual intro. I was driving too fast to absorb the tiny flicker on a tinier screen, which would tell me whether my cell was charging me roaming fees or not, and I wasn't chit-chatting at an unknown cost per chit.

"Busy," Philip said, instead of hello. "Trial. Next week."

Yeah, I knew that, but figured he'd want to know I was out of town, even preoccupied as he was preparing to defend a man indicted for commercial espionage. His client, who was Cary Grant debonair, had been breaking into businesses, homes, briefcases, and computers to steal corporate secrets, patents, client lists, proprietary info, the real account-ing records, and just about anything else anyone would pay him to steal. Philip insisted this man could do things with computers the FBI only wished they could. This client had been making a lucrative living stealing information, and probably would have continued to do so, but his wife discovered him with his girlfriend and tipped off his next target.

This Cary Grant–cool guy, who posted his own bail in an amount well beyond most people's projected lifetime earnings, always flirted outrageously with me when our paths crossed. Yeah, he was tempting. But he had a wife, a girlfriend, and an impressive list of criminal indictments that made the usually unflappable Philip blanch, and the IRS was sniffing around. Plus, if I dated his client, Philip would probably break up with me.

Anyway, as Philip had been hyperventilating about for weeks, this case was going to take lots of trial prep time, so I hit the punch line in a hurry. "I'm going to Bugfest to visit my brother a few days. Everything is cool. Call you when I'm back."

Philip muttered something that loosely translated into "Okay," and I hung up. If I hadn't been a trial attorney myself, I'd have been grievously offended by his lack of concern or curiosity. But I knew the days before any trial were precious, and preparation trumped everything short of nuclear terrorist attacks, and I put up my cell and hummed on down the highway.

My five-hour drive took me from the autumn in southwest Florida, where fall isn't much different than summer, to Georgia, where I could feel a coolness in the breeze that wafted into the open window of my car. The fields along the sides of the road were filled with purple wildflowers and goldenrod so tall and thick you would have thought it was planted and cultivated, like cotton. And already, in the bay and sweetgums, yellow, gold, and red touched the leaves.

Given my mission, I had driven like a bat out of hell on my way to Georgia. One can do that on I–75 north, and not stand out at all. But on the last lap of the trip, on Meridian Road, the famed canopy thoroughfare out of Tallahassee that crossed the Georgia state line right in the middle of a plantation that reeked of old money and landed gentry, anything faster than forty was difficult.

At an ancient white church in the wildwoods, I turned off Meridian onto Hadley-Ferry Road, and slowed down even further when I hit the city limits. Having nearly completed my drive north from Sarasota into the deep south of southwest Georgia, I was hoping to un-spasm my neck by the sheer force of my own willpower as I coasted past the courthouse square and stared up at the Mule Day banners hanging pillar-to-post on every block, as bright and happy as the Christmas decorations that would hang there in another month.

Mule Day?

Yeah, this Saturday would be the first Saturday in November, which meant the annual Mule Day Festival.

A part of me suddenly wanted to go to Mule Day. After all, my mad hatter brother Delvon and I had had some good times at the Mule Days of our weird little childhoods. But a bigger part of me hoped that before Saturday I would be done doing whatever it was Dan wanted me to do, and I'd be home in Sarasota.

About the time I stopped oohing at the thought of Mule Day, I saw the old Zebulon, the town's movie house, an old-fashioned Art Deco palace with elaborately decorated walls and the balconies where the local teenagers had learned to make out. As I drove by, I was glad to see obvious signs of renovations, including a beaut of a bright, new marquee.

This weird urge to see a movie at the Zeb caught me off guard, and briefly I wondered if I'd have time to catch a Saturday-night show.

But mostly I was too hungry to plan much beyond eating a healthy, organic snack to fortify myself for whatever was coming my way. Having skipped lunch in my haste, I worried with the wrapper of a trail mix bar, driving one-handedly. As I jammed the trail mix bar in my mouth, a mosquito flew in from the netherworlds to torment me.

Four blocks past the intersection that marked the end of downtown, and nearly at my mother's house, a quick and bright blue something big ran out slap-dab in front of my ancient Honda.

Busy as I was with the trail mix bar and with slapping at the mosquito, I lost a second or two in dodge-time.

Slamming on my brakes, I felt the car skidding west into the oncoming lane, which, unfortunately, was already occupied by a late-model Ford pickup. I spun the steering wheel madly, but my front bumper caught the truck's bumper and we careened off in a sort of low-end auto dance toward a shallow ditch, but not before an old Thunderbird, whose driver had dodged toward instead of away from the melee, clipped the rear of the truck.

The three of us spun through the ditch and into a front yard, my Honda narrowly missing an ornate blue birdbath. When we had all come to rest, the man in the truck scrambled out, ran to my door, and yanked it open. "You all right, ma'am? You aren't hurt or nothing, are you?"

The mosquito sharing the front seat with me took the lull in my frantic hand-waving as a prime opportunity and bit me in the middle of my forehead. Oh, great, a car wreck and a red welt. This was going well, I thought, then wondered exactly what I had expected. After all, there'd been plenty of reasons why I had left this town right after high school graduation night.

"I'm all right. How about you?" I asked the pickup man.

"Oh, takes more'n a little fender bender to do me in," he said. "I'm a veteran of the Great War."

I climbed out of my car and together we walked back to the Thunder-bird, where another older man pushed himself out of the driver's side and got to his feet. He looked me up and down, then grinned. "Why, I'll be doggoned if it isn't Lawyer Cleary's gal. That photo in the paper your brother Dan had 'em run when you won that lawyer partnership thing hardly did you justice," he said. The old man stuck out his hand, and I took it.

After shaking hands, the three of us circled the vehicles, none of which appeared much improved by the experience but certainly not disabled.

"Reckon we don't need a wrecker," the Thunderbird man said. "My car'll drive. I can sure knock that bumper back right on your car, ma'am, that way we don't need to swap insurance."

I figured that meant I was the only one in the group who actually had auto insurance. As this little wreck was technically my fault, I nodded, thinking the less my company knew about it the less high my rates would go.

"Good, good," Thunderbird Man said, and kicked on my bumper until it was more or less in the traditional place for a bumper.

"I can get my son-in-law to fix mine," Great War Veteran said. "He ought to be good for something."

The large, blue creature that had caused all the commotion let out a loud, unworldly scream, pulled up a bug in the dry grass of the ditch, and flew in a perfect blue arc toward the front porch of the house in whose yard we were all more or less parked. A woman came out on the porch.

The Thunderbird man shouted at the woman: "I told you, you ought to keep that bird penned up. That peacock nearly caused us to wreck out here."

Ignoring him, the woman studied me. I studied her back, something familiar in her face. About the same time I recognized my middle-school English teacher and my mother's only known friend, Eleanor Spivey, she must have recognized me.

"Well, Lilly Belle Rose. It's about time you came back," Eleanor said, "now that your mother needs you, accused as she is of killing that bill collector."

"That was your momma?" Veteran Man asked. "How come you go and let her live like that?" He took a step away from me, creating extra air space around me, which was immediately filled with a swarm of gnats.

"Well, as long as you all are here, you might as well come in. I have some fresh iced tea and ice-box cookies. You too, Lilly Belle Rose, come on in."

"I go by just Lilly now. You can drop the Belle and the Rose. And thank you, Miss Spivey, but I'm not thirsty and I need to get on over to Dan's."

My former English teacher opened the door, the two men walked toward her, and the peacock ran past them into the house. "Not you, Free

Bird, no sir, I do not hold with animals in the house." The peacock came trotting back out, while I thought, *Free Bird*? Funny, Eleanor didn't look much like the Lynyrd Skynyrd type, and for a moment I flashed on the summer Brother Delvon and I had listened to a purloined cassette with Skynyrd's "Free Bird" over and over. It wasn't our generation's song, but we took it to heart anyway.

"Lilly, call me Eleanor. Dan won't be home until after five-thirty, and you can sit a spell, and I put fresh mint in the tea." Eleanor smiled at me as if she were glad to see me.

My grandmother used to grow mint and crush the leaves in our tea. I was suddenly thirsty, and I smiled back. "Is the tea organic, by chance?" I asked.

"It's Luzianne. Same as your grandmomma made. You have consumed your own weight ten times over in Luzianne iced tea." There was a snip in her voice when she added, "Do not get above your raising on me now."

Great. Already my former English teacher was fussing at me. I slapped at another mosquito, but not before it bit me. Free Bird flew up to the railing on the porch, uttered a couple of *pluck-pluck* noises, and stared at me, a long bug dangling out of his beak.

After twenty years, I was home again.

chapter 2

Ah, the sweet, green grass of home, I thought, and looked down the street to assure myself there was no prison wall at the end of it.

Still itchy, I walked up onto the front porch of my brother's house, which is a tad too close to our mother's house for my personal taste, and I kicked at some sawdust gathered in piles under the eaves.

A towheaded teenager with freckles and blue eyes opened the door and said, "Aunt Lilly?"

I wasn't sure what to make of his tentativeness. I wasn't sure if I could hug him, or if, at sixteen, my nephew had reached an age where that wouldn't be tolerated. I wasn't sure what I was doing, standing in front of my brother Dan's house.

Kicking the sawdust out of my way and making a little shower of pale dust, I stepped toward my nephew.

"Damn carpenter bees, they been eating on the porch since spring, like to give Daddy a fit," he said.

"Bobby?"

"Yes'um, it's me."

"Are you allowed to cuss?"

"I didn't cuss, I just said *damn*. *Damn's* okay. You got to watch the f-word, and you can't be taking the Lord's name in vain."

Okay, that laid some ground rules I might need to remember if I was going to stay more than the night.

While Bobby was staring at the sawdust, I snuck up and gave him a quick hug, which he accepted without too much wiggling, and Dan came up behind him and bear-hugged me like we'd been best friends forever. We hadn't. Dan, with his red face and his red hair and the quiet Methodist ways he'd adopted from Patti Lea, his wife, never quite approved of me, though he was far too polite to say so. But polite or not, Dan never hid his disapproval of our older brother, Delvon, who had been simultaneously a lay Pentecostal preacher and a local independent businessman in the field of recreational drug procurement before the Georgia Bureau of Investigations put him out of business—at least around Bugfest, that is. Despite the fact Delvon was currently being rehabilitated by the love of a good woman, the mere mention of his name could make Dan spit iced tea, he'd get so mad. But there he was, my brother, dear, sweet Dan, hugging me and saying how good I looked and wasn't it nice I had finally come home to visit.

Come to visit? Like this was Easter. Like he hadn't asked me to come back and help him with our mother, the town's own female Boo Radley but with more attitude and less social value.

"Damn carpenter bees, they been eating on the eaves since spring," Dan said, looking down at the sawdust.

Yeah, okay, I got that—his house was being consumed by bugs. What I didn't get was why my mother was accused of murder. Dan's face didn't suggest now was a great time to ask.

"So?" I said, which is the word I prefer to use on the rare occasions when I can't think of a thing to say. "So."

"So, get in here, Lilly Belle Rose. Want a Coke?"

"I do," Bobby said.

"No, thank you," I said. I was still sloshing from the sweet tea syrup that

Eleanor Spivey had poured over ice cubes in thick brown rivulets after I narrowly escaped killing her pet peacock, and all the while I kept insisting to her I didn't want a second glass of tea and no, ma'am, I never did learn what a present perfect progressive was, but I'd managed to graduate from law school and make a decent life for myself despite this grievous short-coming. "I don't care for a Coke and I'm just using Lilly these days."

"Well, come on in, then, Lilly Belle Rose, we'll get us some Cokes," Dan said.

Okay, apparently I no longer spoke English.

In short order, I was sitting on a plaid couch, with Bobby on one side and Dan on the other, and all three of us had cold Coke bottles in our hands, and Dan was explaining something that was going in one ear and out the other.

Dan has that effect on me. He's a sweet guy, salt of the earth, steady taxpayer, but he's delivered Cokes from a truck on the same delivery route for eighteen years. The only time he hadn't lived in our hometown was the four years he was in the Marines, and even that didn't make any particular impression on him. His politics were limited to considerations of the antics of the high school football coach, and his main economic concern was whether Pepsi was making any inroads in the local Coke consumption. Dan was the boy who always did his homework, Dan is the man who never calls in sick to work, and who will wash the dishes and do a good job, when it is his turn. Dan is the father who actually goes to PTA meetings, and he can sit through a three-hour Easter salvation sermon and not fidget a single body part. His are the mutant genes. I have trouble relating to him. I have trouble sitting still.

So, while Dan prattled, I fretted about assorted professional worries. Bobby poked my leg, and I looked at Dan and had the sudden feeling he had just asked me an important question and was waiting for an impor-tant answer.

So I gave him the perfect lawyer answer: "That depends."

"Well, that's about what I thought too, and about what I told the city attorney, but he sure seems to think it's the best thing. You being the lawyer, I reckon you're gonna have to talk with him. Anyway, I wanted to warn you. Before we get to the hospital. So, Lilly, you and me can go to the hospital soon as you're ready."

As soon as I was ready? Ready to see my mother in the psych ward of the local hospital after she had shot a man? Ready to see the woman who had evicted me at age fifteen and hadn't said two consecutive words directly to me since then? Oh, let's put that *ready* thing down on the calendar for 2015.

We sat on the couch a few more minutes, me wondering what Dan had just told me about the city attorney and what I was going to do with my undrunk Coke that wouldn't hurt Dan's feelings. Before I could decide what trick I might play, Dan got up and went into the kitchen. Being so busy worrying about not listening to him the first time, I hadn't been listening again, so I didn't know why he got up, but I took advantage of the moment.

"Here," I said to Bobby, "trade you." I took his empty bottle in exchange for my full one. "Now what did your dad just tell me about the city attorney?"

"They want to lock Grandmom up in a loony bin instead of jail, only I'm not supposed to call it a loony bin."

Placing Willette Rose Cleary in a mental institution? Well, that's probably the most sensible thing to do, I thought, although in truth, she seemed to do all right on her own so long as nobody tried to get her to leave the house—or at least that was Dan's take on things in the past. I looked at young Bobby sitting attentively beside me, and I asked him, "Have you ever actually seen your grandmother?"

"No, but I've shouted at her through her door a good many times. Momma takes us over there every Christmas to yell through the shut door and leave her presents on the porch, and every Easter to wish her a Happy Easter, and leave her a basket."

"She ever talk back at you?"

"Once or twice."

"What did she say to you?"

"Not so much," he said, and shrugged.

Yeah, pretty much the same conversations I'd had with her as a kid.

"So, Bobby, what's the scoop? Why are they saying she killed that man? Where in the world did she get a gun? I mean nobody goes in or out of that house, and my father never left her a gun."

"Daddy told me not to talk to anybody about it."

"I'm not *anybody*, I'm your aunt, you can tell me."

"Naw, I better let Daddy tell you."

Okay, so the kid could keep a secret. And was a bottomless pit, apparently, I thought as I watched him gulp the last of my Coke. I had a sudden urge to hug him again, but was afraid I'd scare him off.

Dan came back into the living room. "Police chief got our momma under guard at the hospital, but his under-chief says we can go on in, being as how we're family, but you aren't supposed to upset her or anything. They had to have restraints on her when they first brought her in. She was a real mess. Had a whole psychotic fit in the ER and then the next morning."

"She's never been psychotic before," I said.

"She's never shot a man before."

"Well, why'd she shoot this man?"

"Aw, Lilly Belle Rose, it's a long story, and the truth is, we don't know why. Tell you what, you being so sensitive to bug bites—them mosquitoes're tough this time of day even if it is fall—Bobby, son, you wait here with Lilly, and I'll run the car up by the front door."

"Yeah, whatever," Bobby said.

As Dan went off to be chivalrous, I looked at my youngest nephew. He was so cute it was almost unreal. Wavy blond hair like his momma, big blue eyes like his daddy, full lips like me—I had to say, this kid was a heartbreaker. I had that urge to hug him again, but I stifled it in favor of plying him with questions.

"So, Bobby, one more time. I'm your blood aunt. You can talk to me. Now tell me what is going on." Then I remembered where I was, in a family where proper manners were only one rung below God, and I said, "Please."

Bobby, over-sugared by now, twitched a bit, as if needing movement for thought, and then said, "Don't you tell nobody I told you this, but Grandmom shot a man who came to get paid for a deep freeze."

"Willette bought a deep freeze?"

"No, ma'am, that was the problem, see?"

"She didn't buy a deep freeze, a man came to get paid for the deep freeze she didn't order, and so she shot him?"

"Yeah, but there was a voodoo curse on the deep freeze too, how come she shot him."

"She admitted she shot him?"

"I don't think so, but the chief of police saw her do it, that's the way I heard it, but I didn't get the whole story 'fore Momma shooed me out a the room."

My priming him for more questions was cut off by the sound of Dan honking the car horn.

"You be sure, now, not to say nothing about that voodoo curse, you hear? You know how Momma is about stuff like that."

No, I didn't, though I had the feeling I might be about to learn. In the meantime, I promised my nephew I could keep my sources secret, and went outside, wondering, Great, now what?

've never yet been in a hospital that didn't make me want to scream and then shower in Clorox. Staph and other germs, grown wholly immune to antibiotics because we eat penicillin and tetracycline pills like M&M's, are everywhere, leaping from the thin air into my mucous membranes, where they can grow faster than mildew in the summer in my hometown.

Though I shuddered, Dan pushed me on down the hallway toward a room I didn't want to go into.

Standing outside the door was a man in a police uniform. He looked uncomfortable.

As a delaying tactic, I stopped and smiled at him. "Hey," I said in hometown cheerleader fashion. "Could I get you a chair?"

"No, ma'am," he said. "I 'preciate the offer, but I'm on duty."

"On duty?"

"Yes, ma'am, I'm guarding the er, the er . . . the lady prisoner. And making sure nobody hurts her." He stood up a little straighter as he spoke.

"Guarding Willette?" Why? I wondered as I studied the man in what

I hoped was a less-than-obvious way. He was short, rounded at the edges, and at or near retirement age, and not anyone who could deter me from any course of action I chose. I pegged him as a school crossing guard, one much kidded by the students and liked by parents, and wholly without fighting skills.

And a man who very much needed a chair.

"I'm Lilly Cleary," I said, and offered a hand, which he took. "I'm Willette's daughter. Thank you for helping her. And I think you need a chair."

"Rodney Harrelson, assistant chief of police," he said. "A chair'd be nice, now you mention it."

This man was the assistant chief of police? And he was guarding my mother? I turned questioningly to Dan, who had already ducked into the hospital room and come back out to see what was keeping me.

"I'll get him a chair," Dan said, sabotaging my stalling. "You go on in and see your mother."

"I'll get the chair," I said.

"Lilly Belle, it'll be all right. Go on in there," Dan said, his voice softer. "I'm sure she'll be glad to see you. I mean, you know, if she recognizes you."

Ah, Dan the optimist.

I inhaled and walked into the hospital room, and stood, rock-still, just inside the door.

A few inhale-exhale, cool, clean waterfall visualizations later, a Hispanic woman slipped beside me, approached my mother, and spoke something too low for me to hear to another woman standing beside the still life-form in the bed. Then the Hispanic woman put a cake on the bedside stand, knelt, seemed to pray, stood up, made the sign of the cross, and left.

"You can go all the way in," Dan said, reappearing in the doorway.

Step by small step, I tiptoed into the room. It was filled with flowers, and this surprised me. Who sends flowers to a comatose crazy woman who shoots a man?

As Dan took my hand and squeezed it, I peered into the bed. The woman there bore some resemblance to the mother I remembered, except much smaller. She was hooked up to an IV, with a bag feeding something pale yellow and liquid into her veins. Probably a banana bag, I thought, the fluid used to rehydrate drunks, filled with vitamins and dextrose.

My mother lay very still. Her eyes were closed, and her color had a gray tinge that didn't look good.

But it was her jaw and mouth I noticed most. Well, that and the fact there were cake crumbs all over her bed. I brushed these off as I peered closer at her face.

Definitely bruises. Fresh bruises. I leaned even closer over her face and squinted at the blue and purple marks.

"Why is her mouth so bruised up?" I asked, rising up and turning back to Dan.

"Say something to her," Dan said. "Greet your mother."

I glared at him a moment, then spun around and stared at my mother. And said, "So."

"Greet her properly. Maybe she can hear you," he said, the sound of reproach clear enough.

Great, first Eleanor, now my own brother was fussing at me.

"Good evening . . . Mo— Mother." I strangled a bit over that *Mother*. No way I could say *Mom*.

Then I put my finger under her head, moved her chin up as gently as I could, and looked under it. More bruises. In exactly the same spots one might have put one's fingers if, say, one were trying to force her mouth open. Or hold it shut.

"What do you know about these bruises?" I asked.

"Not so much, really. The hospital folks all say she came in with those bruises. The police chief, he's not so sure."

I looked back at Willette, who slept without moving. "What's wrong with her?" I mean, you know, besides the fact she had been basically crazy as far back as I could remember.

"She's doped up. The doctor, Dr. Weinstein, he's keeping her full a Thorazine. She was a real sight when they first carried her in, kept fighting everybody and yelling," the woman standing by the bed said. "Didn't want to be taken out of that house of hers."

For the first time, I turned and really looked at this woman. She was almost plump, broad-shouldered, brightly dressed, and pretty in an everyday sort of way. For a moment I wondered how she got all those tiny beads into her black hair, and then I realized I knew her.

"Lilly Belle Rose," Dan started to say, "this is—"

"Shalonda," I shouted out. "Shalonda Rivers."

Shalonda jumped over and gave me a tight hug, stepped back, and said, "Well, white girl, you sure grew up hot."

We started giggling.

Shalonda and I had spent a large part of our high school experience in after-school detention, because, for reasons the guidance counselor never could pinpoint, neither of us could ever do what we were told to do. I escaped expulsion only because my father was the school board's lawyer, and that, in turn, meant no matter what Delvon or I did, we didn't get expelled. Shalonda never got kicked out of school because she was a gold-star swimmer and everybody figured her for a top-college scholarship and an Olympic medal. She was that good. We could have burned down the gym and still graduated.

What we'd had in common, besides a marked tendency to get into trouble, was a shared crush on Big Lonnie Ledbetter, the boy who was going to go somewhere, a strapping blond with the look of a surfer about him, and a heck of a flirt, who sang a good country tenor and played a seriously mean guitar. In high school, he was always putting on shows attended mostly by the girls, and we all figured him for the next Vince Gill, the country tenor that simultaneously made three generations of women swoon.

Big Lonnie'd actually had a kind of a hit once. Something about lost love and a bad hand of cards. Long before the radio even started playing

Big Lonnie's only hit, I had let go of my crush, had shed it as quick as I'd shed my hometown. But he'd come crashing back into my life, albeit not in person, when he purchased my grandmother's house from my mother a few years back. I hadn't been happy about that then, and, truth be told, I was still pissed that my own flesh and blood would sell that house, sacred as it was to Dan, Delvon, and me, to Lonnie when Delvon and I had done our damnedest to buy it.

Yeah, Willette's betrayal on that still stung. But right now there were more important things to ponder than losing that house. Like the four hundred questions hatching in my head about Willette, and catching up with Shalonda.

"You ever get that gold medal?" I asked, though surely Dan or Delvon would have mentioned this, or I'd have read about it in the papers.

"Naw. Stuff happens, you know? Now come say something nice to your momma. Your brother's right, she may be out cold, but I just bet you she can hear you anyway, down deep where it counts."

With Shalonda tugging at me, I approached my mother again, bent down over her and said, "Hello . . . Mother." My mouth dried up. I swallowed, and bit my tongue. And, finally, got this out: "This is Lilly. How are you?"

Naturally, she didn't move or respond.

"Well, that's all right," Dan said. "She'll come around. You wait and see, she'll be up and glad to see you in no time."

Oh, sweet Danny and his good soul, I thought. After all this time, still thinking Willette would be glad to see me. Warm and fuzzy with my thoughts of my gentle older brother, I started to reach out to Willette, but I felt the first warning nudge of anxiety kicking up inside my stomach.

Making myself breathe deeply, I backed up to the center of the room where there was the most air space, and tried to distract my worry by playing twenty questions. "So, Shalonda, you work here at the hospital, or what?"

"Naw. Your sister-in-law and me are big buddies now, you know that?

We got close volunteering at the library's literacy program. So I'm sitting with your momma to help out, her being under arrest and real upset and confused 'bout where she's at. Ever time they let her wake up out of that Thorazine mess, she has a huge fit. Thought maybe I'd be a comfort to her if I was here next time she wakes up."

A comfort to Willette? That suggested a relationship. Though Shalonda and I had hung out at my grandparents' house a lot, I didn't remember Shalonda ever actually being inside Willette's house. Couldn't even remember if she'd met my mother. "You know Willette?"

"Nobody knows her, you know? But I'm a social worker and I got me some tricks."

"A social worker?"

"Yeah, but I'm kinda between things right now." She looked away from me when she said that, then turned back. "Got Rodney outside the door so she can't get up and run off." Shalonda giggled again, and then apparently she thought maybe she should not have, because she said "I'm sorry," and hushed.

"I don't think she's going to run away," I said.

"Well, she is under arrest. Demetrious thought having a guard would be better than handcuffing her to the bed."

"Demetrious?"

"Oh, he's the police chief," Dan said.

"And my husband," Shalonda said. "It's Shalonda Dupree now." She held up her left hand and showed off a single gold band.

Whoa there, Shalonda Rivers, who had been every bit as wild as she was athletic, had married the chief of police? And didn't I remember some rumors that Shalonda and Big Lonnie had quite the thing going on in college? Obviously I'd missed a few chapters.

I offered a congratulations, and was all set to ask more about this, but Dan stepped up closer to Shalonda, and asked, "Has Willette said anything to you yet? I mean, about what happened."

"Nope."

"She say anything to anybody about what happened?" I asked.

"Nope. Not to me or anyone else. She was a holy terror when they brought her in the ER and they dosed her up so on tranquilizers they 'bout OD'd her. Now ever time she wakes up, she starts pitching conniptions like you ain't hardly heard, and the nurse, she's got her orders—that is, give her another shot."

"Has a psychiatrist seen her?" I asked.

"No, just Dr. Weinstein. He's an internist," Dan said. "I told you, he's her doctor of record, and he came right out to the ER that night."

Yeah, the doctor who prescribed meds to a woman after she coughed over the phone for him, I remembered all right. Let's say my confidence level in this guy wasn't high.

"We need to get a psychiatrist in to see her. Right away," I said, hoping it didn't sound too much like I was giving an order, though I clearly was.

And, having switched on the part of my brain that takes care of things, not giggles with old girlfriends, I said, "And you, Dan, are you by chance her legal guardian?"

"Why's she need a legal guardian?"

Taking that for a no, I sighed. "She does not appear to be competent. Someone needs to be able to legally act on her behalf. It's after five now, but hopefully we can get an emergency hearing tomorrow. We can talk about this tonight, but you need to get it done as soon as possible."

Dan gave me a look that let me know he'd noticed I was giving orders.

While Dan and I glared at each other, Shalonda reached over and stroked the side of my mother's face with a light, gentle touch and then turned back to me. "It's a downright shame, that Ray Glenn scaring her so bad she's gone off the edge. But sitting with her ain't real hard, and there's plenty of pound cake. Want some?"

I looked at the pound cake, a classic Southern comfort food so named because it contained a pound of butter as well as other seductive substances, and I shuddered with a sudden desire to eat a very big piece. But

I shook my head and refocused on the fact that the police chief wanted Willette if not under guard, at least not alone. Being a lawyer and, therefore, suspicious, I couldn't help but wonder if there was more to the story. Let's see, bruises? An OD? And a dead man?

Rodney had said he was to make sure nobody hurt Willette.

Was my mother in some kind of danger?

I needed to talk to the person in charge. And now.

"So you're married to the police chief? Could I talk with him?"

"Sure can." Shalonda picked up the bedside phone, punched in some numbers, and said, "Tell Demetrious to get himself over to the hospital. He's got a visitor at Willette Cleary's room—her daughter the lawyer wants to talk to him."

There was only one chair in the room. Dan offered it first to me, then to Shalonda, who deferred to me and then to Dan, who said, "No thank you, ladies first." Shalonda told us we could sit on the bed, as Willette didn't take up much room, but Dan said maybe we ought not to. So while we were all stuck standing up to show how polite we were, Shalonda and I tried catching up as we waited for the police chief. Apparently, Shalonda hadn't done anything interesting in the last two decades except up and marry Demetrious last year, or else Dan's quiet Methodist ways were inhibiting her free and unbridled expression. Pretty much I figured on the latter and couldn't wait to get her alone.

I edged up toward my mother again, and stared at those bruises. But before I could question Shalonda, someone said, "Knock, knock."

We all turned to the door, and a man came striding in, without, I might add, waiting for anyone to invite him to do so. He had long legs and long arms, which he swung as he loped energetically toward us.

"Simon McDowell, hospital administrator," he said, sticking his hand out toward me. His hands were as big as his arms were long.

I took his hand, squeezed it quickly, and dropped it, and immediately felt the need to go wash my hands. No telling what this man had touched as he went about his hospital duties. I had yet to actually look at his face.

"Excuse me," I said, and ducked into the cubbyhole bathroom in my mother's room. I washed my hands, not once but twice, and came back into the room, all without touching anything except paper towels.

Simon was brushing some cake crumbs off of my mother's bed. "I told you, do not let people eat over her bed," he said, directing his words toward Shalonda.

"And I told you, I don't work for you," she said.

"We are just trying to keep Mrs. Cleary clean and quiet," he said. Then he turned to me and smiled. This time I looked at his face, a long, thin one, saved from homeliness by a square jaw, a dimpled chin, and really big eyes. Not just big eyes, but large gold eyes. Then I noticed his hair was also a golden brown, and he had flecks of gold in his stylish glasses frames. I forgot his face as I traveled down his collection of gold stuff. A light gold shirt. Dark gold pants. Bright gold tie. Okay, somebody needs to tell him monochrome is a boring fashion statement.

"We are a good hospital, a very good hospital," he said. "And we don't let our patients get dirty in bed." And he kind of rose up on his toes, slanting forward toward me as he spoke, and I had a sudden sense of physical power. The man was tall. Not quite giant, but definitely big.

"Very good hospital. Are you the daughter, the Florida lawyer?" he asked.

"Yes." I didn't want to commit to anything else just yet. But Dan stepped in and introduced us, all proper and polite.

"Well, I've heard some good things about you," Simon said. "Very good things." And he eyed me up and down, quickly but obviously. And smiled again in a way that felt more like a wink. "Very, very good."

Okay, vocabulary- and fashion-challenged, both. And I was in no mood to flirt. Still, I couldn't help but notice the man had some potential. Taller than me, which, since I'm six feet, doesn't happen all that much, well-trimmed full head of that golden hair, broad shoulders, flat stomach, and those big hands. I like a big man. I wished that I had changed clothes and brushed out my yard-long hair before coming to the hospital.

"I just wanted to meet you, and to assure you that we are doing all we can to take good care, very good care of your mother." Simon swayed back and forth as he spoke, and started swinging his arms. Then he took a couple steps too close to me, forcing me to jump back. "Very, very good."

No, take back that *potential* thing. The man was irritating.

"Then why did she nearly OD in the ER, and what's with these bruises?" I said.

"I can assure you," he said, sounding every bit the hospital administrator, "we can document that your mother came into the ER with those bruises. And with a nearly fatal level of barbiturates and narcotics already in her system. Only the quick thinking and skills of our ER crew saved her. We have a good crew in the ER."

"Let me guess, a very good crew, a very, very good crew," I said. Shalonda giggled.

"Yes, absolutely," Simon said. "Our records will show they saved your mother's life."

Yeah, I want to see those ER records and talk to a couple of nurses on the sly, I thought. But I smiled like I believed him, like I wasn't a malpractice attorney who had heard similar statements too many times to count. "Thank you for that," I said.

"Here, Lilly, let me give you my card." Simon hopped a bit toward me, and I hopped a bit away from him. "And I'll put my personal numbers on the back," Simon said, pulling out a card and scribbling something. "My cell, my home, and my direct line here." He handed over the card with an exaggerated flourish. "Good, very good."

I took the card, resisting the urge to offer an equally exaggerated bow.

"Would you like to see the rest of the hospital? I'd be delighted to give you a guided tour. Right now work for you?"

A tour of the hospital? Yeah, right, give those staph germs an even better shot at me. "No thank you, I've got family things to attend to right now," I said, using the voice I used when explaining the obvious.

"How about the town? I can get off in a jiffy and give you a tour of the town."

"I grew up here. I know my way around." Around what? Five city blocks?

"Well, back to work. Now, don't you lose that card. And you call me, anytime," Simon said, and bounced his big self right out of the room. Then he stuck his head back in. "Lilly, you and I should get together. Soon. Very soon. Very, very soon. Talk over your mother's care. Get to know each other. Call me." Grin, leer, grin, on his part. Like this was a barroom, not a hospital with a comatose woman on a bed not five feet from him. And he ducked out, without waiting for my response.

Shalonda and I looked at each other and giggled. "Very, very good," we said, perfectly synchronized.

"This isn't funny, none of it," Dan said.

Before I retorted, Demetrious came into the room, kissed Shalonda on the lips, and said, "Hey, Londa, everything all right?"

"Willette hasn't said pea turkey," she said.

Demetrious Dupree filled up the room in a hurry, carefully pressed into his uniform, and with the look of a man that didn't lose any arguments. It took me a minute to realize he was actually rather short and compact. We did our pleased-to-meet-yous, and Demetrious offered me the only chair. Rather than go through that whole stupid chair dance again, I took it.

But when I opened my mouth to start asking questions, I was seized by a physical sensation, like an anaconda was wrapping itself around my chest and cracking my ribs.

chapter 4

No sense beating around any bush just because I was having a panic attack. "So, why are there bruises on my mother's chin?" I asked.

Sitting there surrounded by Shalonda, Brother Dan, and the police chief, in the oppressive air of the hospital, I feared some evil genie with a time machine and malicious intent had swept me backward into the world of Bugfest. My head throbbed. My stomach burned. My gut twisted. My hands sweated. My heart beat so fast and hard my chest hurt. I stood up to flee, knocking my chair back a couple of steps.

But Demetrious said, in a strangely calming tone, "It's all right, Miss Cleary. We understand your mother needs help, not prosecution. Please, sit a moment."

Strangely nonresponsive to my question about her bruises. But more than I wanted to know if my mother had been assaulted, I needed to get outside. Quick. I darted for the door, but Shalonda beat me to it, blocking it with her solid body. She took my hand, and held it. "Don't you worry, white girl." Shalonda turned me around and pointed me back into the hospital room. I saw Demetrious shoot her a look I couldn't quite make out.

"Why don't you sit down, again?" Demetrious said.

I didn't sit, but I didn't run either.

"The city attorney and I have discussed with Dan, and would like to discuss with you, having your mother committed. We are making phone calls to different facilities." Demetrious paused. I took a step backward toward the door out, then froze. "Please, Miss Cleary, have a seat," he said.

"Why don't you tell her what happened," Dan said.

Curiosity slowed down my heartbeat. "Yes, exactly what did happen? And why are there bruises on her face?" I have this theory, not wholly exhausted by years of cross examinations during trials, that a question asked often enough eventually gets answered.

"I was in my police car, nearby Willette's, er, Mrs. Cleary's house, when the dispatcher reported a 911 call about shots fired. I went straight there."

So, okay, either a chronological narrative, or he was ducking the bruises question again.

"When I got to the front door, it was open, and I went right in."

"Uh-huh," I said, and nodded, thinking Willette never left her doors unlocked, let alone open.

"What I saw was your mother, holding a gun, and standing right over Ray Glenn Fussele. I told Willette, er, Mrs. Cleary, to put the gun down, and she did. I got the gun, and checked Ray Glenn's pulse, but couldn't find one, and I called 911 for an ambulance, and then Willette, er, I mean, Mrs. Cleary—"

"You can call her Willette," I said. "I do."

"Well, I don't mean any disrespect by it. Thing is, before I could tend to Ray Glenn, your mother came apart on me, got hysterical. But the EMTs said Ray Glenn was dead right there, and wouldn't have been anything I could do. Your mother shot him at pretty close range."

I studied Demetrious, but didn't see anything in his face that told me any more than his words. "So you didn't actually see her fire the gun?" I asked in my best lawyer get-the-facts-right voice.

"No." The "but" hung in the air.

"Ray Glenn surely broke into Willette's house. That is, since we all know full well Willette, er, Mrs. Cleary didn't voluntarily let anyone inside the house—"

"On the porch was as close as anyone got," Dan said, as if we didn't all know that.

"Yes. And given that, a local jury would probably warm toward a self-defense verdict. Especially in light of Ray Glenn's"—I watched Demetrious grit his teeth and flex his jaw muscles—"bad reputation around the county. That man . . . he was a bad man."

"He had evil in him, that's right," Shalonda said.

"I've been trying to catch him on something for years, but nobody'd ever testify against him," Demetrious said, his voice low and his face angry. "Well, he finally got what was coming to him."

That look, and his tone of voice, made me study Demetrious a bit harder.

"Still, I would urge Dan and you to place Willette in a mental hospital as part of an arranged plea bargain. Involuntary manslaughter."

"Why should she plead to involuntary manslaughter, when even you believe it was self-defense?" Okay, okay, I got it that the police chief was trying to help Willette, but I'm a lawyer and sometimes I can't help saying things like that.

"If she pleads, we can skip the trial and get her placed right away," Demetrious said. "Pending commitment, Dr. Weinstein can keep Willette sedated to keep her quiet. But we should act quickly, for her own sake."

"If you and the city attorney agree it's self-defense, then don't charge her with anything. And if you don't charge her, there isn't a trial, and she doesn't need to plead to anything." When I said this, Dan inhaled audibly. I ignored this. "Maybe a little less Thorazine would be a good idea too," I said, staring at my mother, immobile and expressionless. "She needs to wake up, tell us what happened, and eat."

"Well, I'm not a doctor or anything, but I agree she needs to eat. And a lot. But the doc, he says he isn't giving her that much dope. Just enough to keep her from having those fits," Shalonda said.

"Why hasn't anybody called in a real psychiatrist?" I asked. "I mentioned that we needed to do this, but I wasn't sure if—"

"She doesn't have any insurance," Dan said. "And she isn't sixty-five yet."

"So?" I said. "If she's in state custody, doesn't the state have to pay—"

"There's a man, a psychiatrist, who comes up from Tallahassee, that has hospital privileges and does some contract work for the city and the county, but he hasn't been here yet. And there's . . ." My brother paused, glanced at Demetrious, and stopped.

"Jurisdictional issues," Demetrious said. "We're working out the details of a . . ." And then he puttered out too.

Okay, I get it, I thought, but didn't say. Nobody was going to waste the psychiatrist's time and somebody else's money until the legal processes at play decided whether Willette went to jail, was committed to a state hospital, or one of us could cough up money for a private institution. I wondered who was going to pay for her hospital bills, her or the city? But I didn't ask, because I saw what the real problem was: Nobody really knew what to do with Willette. Which, of course, was not a new problem.

"I'll pay for it, the psychiatrist, if that's the holdup," I said, with an upwardly mobile professional's attitude that throwing money at a problem will zip stalled things right along. "You know this guy from Tallahassee?"

Nobody would look at me.

"What?"

"He's . . . real busy," Dan the Polite said in what I took for nice-guy code for the Tallahassee psychiatrist was not very good.

"What about that guy that was Dad's friend? He still around?" I asked.

"You mean Dr. Hodo?" Dan asked. "Why he's . . . well, you know."

I paused to see what spin Dan might put on the fact that a few decades back Willette had banned Dr. Hodo from our house and our lives for no apparent reason. But Dan didn't say anything more.

"He has an excellent reputation, Dr. David Hodo," Demetrious said.

"Yeah, he's supposed to be the best," Shalonda said. "Got an office over to the Thomasville Road. I've worked with him on a couple cases here at the hospital, so I know he's got privileges here."

I remembered a man with a deep voice and blue eyes who went fishing with my dad and came to visit us a few times when we were children, and then didn't. What I didn't know was whether he was a good psychiatrist.

Memo to mental file, I thought: Get Henry to do an insurance database check on Dr. Hodo's lawsuit status, and if he isn't Dr. Wacko-Sued-a-Lot, call him first chance. But right now I had Demetrious in front of me, and I wanted to learn everything he knew.

"Did she have the bruises on her face when you found her at her house, or did she get them here at the hospital?" I asked.

There was a long pause, and I had the distinct feeling I'd stepped in it.

Finally Demetrious said, with an air of resignation, "Truth is, there is some debate. I do not recall seeing bruising. But the admitting doctor swears there was already bruising on her face."

"Like someone was holding her mouth shut, forcibly," I said.

"Yes." Demetrious walked over to my mother's still body and positioned his hand over her jaw and mouth, but very carefully did not touch her. But we could all see how his hand and fingers fit the pattern of the bruises.

And I could see it would fit either way—to force her mouth open, or to force it shut.

So, the hospital could be covering up for its own lack of gentleness, or Demetrious maybe clamped down a bit rough to shut her up, or maybe Ray Glenn had been trying to shut her up.

Or somebody tried to force something down her throat.

"What kind of OD did she nearly have?" I asked, to everyone's apparent discomfort.

"*What?*" I snapped when nobody answered.

"Tranquilizers, was my understanding of it, plus some painkillers," Demetrious said. "A potentially fatal dose. Apparently she has a pretty high tolerance."

I figured as much about the tolerance levels, since she'd been at the pills since I was a kid, but I decided not to illuminate Demetrious on that score, and stuck with my initial goal.

"And she got it, the overdose of tranquilizers, where? In the ER? Or at her house?"

"Dr. Weinstein says she came into the hospital already doped up," Demetrious said.

Yep, just what Simon said. So, either it was the truth, or the doc I'd yet to meet and the hospital administrator who'd all but drooled on me had gotten their official stories straight.

"But, you know, the plain truth is this, I don't think anybody really knows." Demetrious looked me in the eyes, as if daring me to say exactly what I said next.

"Well, is anybody trying to find out?" This in my best, steely-eyed cross-examination voice.

"Lilly, you need to calm down," Dan said, and stepped up beside me and put one hand on my arm.

By Sarasota courtroom standards, I was calm. By Miami courtroom standards, I was positively passive. But this was Greater Dixie, where one, especially a woman, is expected to have exquisitely good manners even upon finding out that one's mother had nearly died from too many drugs while under arrest in a hospital and no one seemed to know if the OD was accidental or deliberate.

I inhaled. Made words that sounded like a polite apology, waited till Dan took his hand off my arm, and then smiled a let's-start-over smile at the police chief and asked if anyone saw Ray Glenn break in, or saw his car in Willette's driveway.

"Nope, none of the neighbors saw Ray Glenn get in. It was after ten on a school night, and everybody was pretty much in bed, or getting ready. Ray Glenn's car was parked on the street a block past her house, so I guess he walked over, not wanting his car in the driveway to attract attention."

"This is just all my fault," Dan said.

"Nope, Dan, you can't be blaming yourself," Shalonda said.

"Londa's right, that Ray Glenn was a bad man, a downright nasty man," Demetrious said, "but you didn't make him that way."

"What do you mean, your fault?" I asked.

And this time, Lilly Belle, I commanded myself, actually listen to your brother.

chapter 5

All for the lack of a refrigerator.

All those extreme environmentalists who think we should unplug and squat in tiny tents and not drive cars would have loved the fact that Willette was definitely a low user of electrical energy. And that she didn't have a car. But Dan didn't like those facts.

"Refrigerator broke," he said. "And without even a car, wasn't any way she could get to a store to get one, or even get her fresh food."

"So? How did that lead to a fatal shooting?"

"See how skinny she is? She's been living on Coca-Cola, peanuts, and fried pork skins," he said, as indignant as if this were all my fault. "She was drinking all them Cokes hot," he said.

How was it this woman wasn't already dead, I wondered, while Dan kept explaining.

"See, I told them the delivery men had to call me before they showed up with the refrigerator, so I could meet them there. No way Willette's letting strangers into that house."

No way she's letting Dan in, from what I'd heard, but I nodded.

"But it all got screwed up. Nobody called me, and they showed up with a deep freeze, not a refrigerator."

"Uh-huh," I said, still waiting for the proximate-cause connection between the deep freeze and the dead man.

"Naturally Willette wouldn't let them in, so they left the appliance on the back porch," Dan said. "Willette called me, yelling that I had to come over and get the thing off her porch because she had looked in it and it was full of 'jelly eggs' that she thought meant someone was trying to put a voodoo curse on her."

Putting aside for the moment my surprise that Dan actually had real, day-to-day-stuff conversations with the woman, I asked the obvious: "What do you think she meant by that?"

"Who knows? She might've imagined the whole thing."

"But she talks with you?"

"Oh, yeah. She always has."

"Then why won't she talk to Delvon, or me? Or our father?"

"Maybe because none of you tries to talk to her."

Hey, she started it, I thought, but said nothing.

"See," Dan continued, "I took off work to go see about the deep freeze, but when I got to Willette's, the store had either picked it back up or it was never there in the first place. But they hadn't left a refrigerator. I tried to get it straightened out, but the store claimed its records showed a completed delivery of a refrigerator and nothing about a deep freeze."

"So, what happened?" I asked. "How's this end with Willette shooting a guy?"

"Well, no matter how many times I told everybody at the store that no refrigerator had been delivered, the store kept pestering Mom for payment. I reckon that's why Ray Glenn was at her house, that store manager must've finally sent Ray Glenn, their bill collector and repo man, to call on Mom in person, and that's how come he broke in," Dan said.

"You wouldn't believe the things we hear 'bout how that man repos stuff," Shalonda tossed in there.

"And then I asked Mom if anybody had tried to ever actually deliver a refrigerator, and she said no."

What I still couldn't get over was that Dan talked to Willette on such a regular basis. I mean, yeah, I knew from his periodic reports that he kept up with the big-picture stuff, but I hadn't appreciated the amount of routine conversation they must have had—albeit, apparently, only through a closed door or over the phone.

Delvon and I did not talk to her. Even when we tried to buy Grandmom's house after it passed to Willette at our grandfather's death, we had a real estate agent call her with our excellent offer. That having failed, apparently to spite us, Delvon and I gave up any attempt at contact, direct or indirect. Yet, Dan *talked* with her.

And Patti Lea had Bobby talking to her through a locked door.

While I was cogitating on the wonders of my brother's attempts to keep up a relationship with *Mom,* Demetrious agreed that as best as he could figure, Ray Glenn was sent there to collect on an erroneous bill, and possibly got rough with Willette. "Maybe that's where the bruises came from. I don't know. Another thing nobody knows is where your mother got the gun," he said, and looked at Dan for a moment.

"I told you already, twice, I didn't give that gun to my mother," Dan said.

Well, if Dan said he didn't give her the gun, he didn't give her the gun. But before I could open my mouth to defend his honor, Demetrious said, "I know, Dan, I know."

"So who did?" Shalonda said.

That seemed to me to be a minor point, except perhaps that I needed to thank the gun-giver for the gift that saved Willette's life. But more important than a note of appreciation, I was going to have to ask around about this Ray Glenn Fussele thing myself, as I didn't exactly hear things adding up in clear, neat columns of good sense and reasonable reactions.

And even if my mother and I didn't much like each other, I would have to find out if someone had tried to kill her, and I would have to keep her out of jail.

After all, she was my mother.

chapter 6

stood in the front doorway and gulped a breath of fresh air before I peeked inside.

Willette's house.

History was in this house. My history. A history I didn't much enjoy remembering.

I didn't want to be anywhere near that house. But here I was, because Dan had asked me politely, and after all, he almost never asked me for anything.

Just moments earlier, we'd said good-bye to Demetrious at the hospital, and I'd sat in my car with my cell phone, making calls, badgering Henry until he satisfied me that our father's old friend, Dr. Hodo, had never been sued, sanctioned, arrested, or disciplined. Then I had the rare pleasure of dealing with a host of the women who answer phones after office hours until I had extracted a promise that Dr. Hodo would come by the hospital tomorrow "as soon as he could." I'd taken aim for tonight, but he was up-county on a nursing-home run, and physically unavailable. Even getting him there in the morning took a fight. Yeah, okay, I exaggerated the family connection a bit in bending these gatekeepers to my will, but things might be dire with old Willette, I just couldn't tell.

After that, Dan had taken me to our mother's house, where Bobby was carrying trash to a Dumpster on the street, the yard lit by the streetlights and a big moon, what we used to call a harvest moon.

I didn't see any yellow tape, and I asked Dan, "Isn't this a crime scene? Are we allowed to be here, messing around in all this . . . mess?"

"Demetrious and his crime tech spent a good deal of time in the house and the yard right after the shooting. Finally they said it was too big a mess, and they couldn't handle it, and couldn't find anything. Besides, it seemed pretty cut-and-dried to Demetrious," Dan said.

That didn't sound like good solid police work to me, and as much as to avoid having to do anything, like actually stepping inside the house, I said, "I think we should call Demetrious and make sure. Make them come back and . . . I don't know, dust for fingerprints—"

"Lilly Belle, I promise you, they've done all that. I know you need a little time to get used to the idea of being back here. Why don't you walk around in the yard, look over things, and when you're ready, come on inside."

Reprieved, I backed out of the doorway, and stood in the side yard. Shrubs and bushes and weeds and the occasional chunk of rusted metal cluttered the area around the house, and threw off eerie silhouettes. Good thing I wasn't one of those people afraid of snakes or werewolves. Just airports, piles of paper, and unwashed vegetables, I thought, and glanced again at the spooky shadows cast by the big moon as I stomped through some thorny blackberry bushes on my way to the backyard. I wanted to see if our tree house was still there.

It was. Nestled in the branches of a classically huge live oak was a yellow-pine plank tree house that Brother Delvon and I, with the help of our grandfather, had built when we were just puppies, and Granddad was still allowed to babysit us. That this gift from our grandfather still stood was a testament to his skills as a carpenter.

I walked up to the base of the live oak, and positively admired that tree house. From what I could tell, it seemed solid. I turned back to Willette's house, which, even in the eerie glow of reflected streetlights and the moon, looked shabby, beaten-up, and neglected.

My mother's house. After she kicked my father out, he made no further claim on the house, moving northward to a TVA lake community. He apparently intended to stay gone, even now. I admired his resolve, and wished for a moment I'd done better on my own pledge not to return here. Nonetheless, I tramped through high grass and trash, back to the front door of the house. A house I had not been inside of since the day Delvon and I returned from an adolescent rampage across the greater southeast and found our mother had sold our clothes and our bedroom furniture and changed the locks. We only got in that day because Dan was home and had opened the door when we'd pounded on it after our keys would not work. Dan's stuff was gone too, but he had already borrowed a sleeping bag, and told us he hadn't really liked his clothes that much, and he had a job bagging groceries at the Pig and could buy some more, and as far as he was concerned, it was all just a minor inconvenience. None of us ever figured out why Willette sold Dan's stuff too; he hadn't run away. Maybe she was just ready to give that empty-nest thing a try. But Dan wasn't ready to fledge yet. Rather, he had dug in; he intended to stay in that house.

Delvon and I took a different view of the matter.

We left.

We moved in with Farmer Dave, Delvon's friend and, in short order, my first love. Farmer Dave taught us how to run a very profitable home business in growing and selling marijuana.

And, having left, Delvon and I didn't come back.

Until tonight. So, here I was, standing in the doorway. Every light in the house was on, but still a dungeon ambience clung to it all as I glared inside and looked around. Staring into the physical embodiment of some of my worst phobias.

The house was beyond dirty.

Spidery webs of gray and black hung from corners and from the ceiling. Piles of yellowing papers filled every surface, and crowded the floor in bundles. The walls were black and soot-colored with what I took for mold. A stench I didn't want to identify wafted out of the kitchen area toward me.

Garbage. Raw garbage. Mold. Debris. Trash. Dirt.

Germs.

Patti Lea, my sister-in-law, with whom I had a cautiously optimistic relationship, was standing in the middle of the living room, with a mask over her nose and mouth, yellow kitchen gloves up to her elbows, and a pair of coveralls buttoned up, completely hiding her own clothes. Tufts of her thick, blond hair stuck out in wholly untypical wayward waves. Above the mask, I could see her eyes were red.

"I haven't even made a dent in all this . . . this *mess*," she said, by way of greeting.

"Well, don't wear yourself out. We got plenty of time," Dan said. "Maybe we can get somebody in to help us."

"Inside this house? No way you're letting anybody see *in* this house. It's bad enough what they can see from the outside," Patti Lea said, with an edge of what might be the beginning of hysteria in her voice. "I don't want anyone in town knowing we let it get to this, this . . . *all this crap!*"

That was about as close to cussing as I'd ever heard her come, and I nodded toward her, afraid to smile or speak till she calmed down, which she did in an instant.

"Why, hello, Lilly. I'm glad you could come visit. We'll need to catch up. Pardon me if we don't hug, but I'm just a mess."

Mess was quickly becoming both the byword of the day and an understatement.

I nodded again, mumbled something that I hoped was pleasant, but the truth was I was somewhat numbed and muted by the sights in front of me.

After a more controlled visual scan of the room, in case my first look had been some kind of hideous hallucination brought on by too much sugar in that iced tea I'd drunk earlier, I saw things were actually worse than I'd first thought. Gulping, I made myself look back at Dan and Patti.

"Well, it's just got to be done, that's all there is to it," Dan said.

"You are going to help?" Patti asked me, carefully pronouncing each word in a way that warned me how stressed she was. "We need your help. We need . . . Can you help us? Clean this up?"

Though the phrase "Hell, no, that's why I have money, so we can hire this done" sprang readily to my mouth, I didn't say it. This was, as Patti Lea already had indicated, a family matter. It was up to us. We'd let this mess happen, and we had to clean it up. Dan and me. And Patti Lea too, I guess, on the theory that "for better, for worse" included her crazy mother-in-law and all that encompassed.

"So you will stay and help us?" Patti asked again. I had the feeling this was a test.

"Yes," I said, as the muscles in the back of my neck clinched and burned at nothing more than the thought of walking farther into the mess.

We stood for a minute, the three of us, Dan, and Patti Lea, and I, and we each silently contemplated the task of cleaning up Willette's house. Unimaginably, pathologically filthy, moldy, and cluttered with forty years of pure crap. No one would believe me if I tried to describe it.

But hey, who in the world would I admit this to, let alone try to describe it to?

"Come on, I'll show you the bedroom," Dan said.

I followed, holding my breath as long as I could.

Willette's bedroom was in the back of the house, and its only saving grace was a big plate-glass window that looked out over the yard, with a view of the big live oak with the tree house. As a child, I used to sneak into her room and stare out the window at the squirrels and the birds in the live oak—until Willette caught me and banished me from her room.

Still, I had liked that window, unencumbered as it was by any interior wood frame or cross ties, a big, single, sheer piece of glass between the room and the outside. A window I now saw was covered with filthy drapes that might have once been blue. Or maybe that was the mold. I wanted to look out the window, but couldn't bring myself to touch the drapes.

Instead, I studied the room. The mattress where she slept had thin, filthy sheets on it and was indented and stained from use. I could not see the floor for the used Kleenex and trash thrown about. An urge to cry crawled up into my throat, but I swallowed until I could will it away.

"We can't figure out how in the world she didn't set this room on fire," Dan said, bravely digging into the tissues and pulling up a frayed electrical cord to an ancient lamp. "Lord looked out after her, is all we can figure."

But it was the dented mattress with the darkened, stained sheets that got me—why she either couldn't, or wouldn't, buy a new mattress and put clean sheets on the bed was beyond my comprehension.

"It's a firetrap, all right," Dan said, as I held my hands tight against my sides and listened to my heart pounding, *rat-a-tat*, in a chest that seemed suddenly to have a great weight pressing against it. I took to swallowing again.

"I've got to get some air," I said, and literally jumped through the doorway and skidded around the corner, aiming for the great outdoors. In the living room, I bolted past Patti and into the front yard, Dan behind me.

After I gasped a few lungfuls of clean outside air, I asked, "Have you called our father? See if he can help?"

Dan shook his head. "I did, and he didn't want any part of this trouble. Said he couldn't help us anyway."

"What else did he say?"

"That since Willette kicked him out a long time ago he wouldn't be coming down from the lake to help her. We're on our own."

"We always were. On our own, I mean."

"Not while we still had Grandmom," he said. "And Granddad, till, you know, he got too . . . too tired and all."

Yeah, *too tired*. I translated that: Till he drank himself into a man nobody could count on. As I stood there with my brother, I wondered what mutant gene made Dan too polite to speak the truth.

With so much to do, I didn't want to get maudlin or mad, and if our father wasn't going to help, then I wondered for half a second if our brother, Delvon, might come back. Being of strong back and sound stomach, he'd be handy in cleaning out the house.

But quickly I put that thought away as too risky. In Bugfest, there were outstanding warrants on Delvon for things that could put him into jail for a long time. Besides, I didn't want to have to listen to Delvon and Dan bicker, or referee their fight if it came to blows. Delvon was fine where he was, living in Florida with his new lady friend, Lenora the saint.

"You need to get appointed her guardian, as soon as possible," I said, putting away the thought of Delvon. "Do you by chance know a judge? I mean, personally?"

"Nope. Judge Parker doesn't go to the Methodist Church like me and Patti, he goes over to the First Baptist."

I sighed. "Okay, do you know a lawyer? I mean, besides me. I'd do this in a heartbeat but I'm not licensed in Georgia, and a local attorney that the judge knows would probably work better anyway." I'd been away too long for home-court favorite status, and, frankly, I'd never heard of Judge Parker and had never set foot in the First Baptist Church. My guess was that in a formal courtroom, I'd play out before him like a big-city upstart heathen. Dan needed local talent to whip this guardian thing through in a hurry. "Do you know a local lawyer Judge Parker likes?"

"Yeah, I know just the lawyer to call. Bobby's girlfriend's momma is a lawyer, and everybody likes her. She's real nice."

"Go call her."

"What's the hurry? It's after office hours, and, I mean, Willette's in good care, and—"

I felt frustration pinching my trapezius muscles in a spasm that would probably out-twist any Advil. "Go, please, call her. It's important that you—we—act quickly. You need to have that legal authority. To get her the best doctor, to make a deal with Demetrious and the city attorney, to get her into a proper institution, and—" I sputtered out in my fatigue.

After a beat, Dan nodded and started back inside Willette's, and I turned my back to the house and stared out at the street, making mental notes of all the things I had to do. Before I got to the part that included, say, food or sleep, Patti Lea came stomping out of the house, aimed right at me. A paroxysm of pain shot through my shoulders and up my neck when I saw her expression and that she was thrusting something from inside Willette's den of dirt at me.

"You better take this," Patti said, handing me a gray metal box. The lock had been crudely pried open. "It's important papers, some legal stuff, copies of everybody's birth certificates, stuff your dad drafted. The deed to the house, some stuff about your grandmother's place, insurance policies. She had it hid good up in the attic. You wouldn't believe the mold and filth on this box. I figure you being the lawyer, you should look through it."

Mold and filth? I dodged as Patti thrust the box at me.

"Would you just take it?" she said in that at-wits-end tone of voice I'd used myself a few thousand times thus far in my life. "Look at the stuff inside, okay, and let us know if any of it's important."

Yeah, after I sprayed it down with Lysol and boiled it first.

While I gingerly held the box, Dan came trotting back to us.

"Guardianship?" I asked.

"Got the lady lawyer on the phone right off. Going by first thing in the morning to talk with her. She'll get right on it."

"Right on it," in Bugfest time, could mean next week, or next month, so I added *prod Dan* to my list of things to do.

"Look, you've had a long day, what with driving up, and you can't get started on this ... this, er, project until you get coveralls and gloves and stuff, so I reckon the best thing for you to do is to go on back to our house, clean up, and make yourself at home," Dan said. "And take Patti, she's all whipped out. You can take my car. Me and Bobby'll come on later, nice night for a little walk."

Clean up was all that soaked into my brain at the moment.

I stashed the metal box under the front seat of Dan's trusty old Ford for the time being, and watched Patti yank off her coveralls and face mask before she climbed into the passenger side, her movements stiff from work and exhaustion.

Neither of us said anything.

The minutes of non-talk stretched out as I drove. In the silence, I opted for engaging my sister-in-law in conversation about herself, to ease us past the awkward moment. "So, how's the business?"

"Oh, I had to shut it down for a bit, you know, after Willette . . . went into the hospital. Sam, he's a good man, but if he goes off his meds, he's likely as not to scare off the customers and wreck the place, so I couldn't leave him with all that stress, and I called his sister, and she said, sure, she'd invite him over to Dothan to stay with her for a vacation, because if I wasn't around to watch him . . ."

Patti stopped and turned to me. "Sorry. You don't know Sam."

No, I didn't. Instead, what I knew was that Patti Lea was as nervous about being alone with me as I was with her. In all the many years she had been my brother's wife, we'd carefully avoided much one-on-one time. But it was typical of what I knew about her from Dan that she'd hire the otherwise unemployable as help in her small-engine repair shop. I wanted to say something to ease the weirdness between us, but couldn't think of anything. So, okay, failing that, I tried to find out something useful.

"Where'd Ray Fussele work?"

"At Big Lonnie Ledbetter's appliance store. Ray was, I don't know, some kind of assistant manager or something. You remember Big Lonnie, right? Had that one hit song a while back. Pretty good song, you ask me. But now he runs that store and is on the county commission."

Yeah, and practically stole my grandmother's house from Delvon and me, I thought, but didn't say. "So Big Lonnie owns the store where Dan ordered the refrigerator?"

"It wouldn't be Dan's first mistake," Patti Lea said, "but you know they were in school together, and that's how it is."

I sighed, Patti sighed, and we pulled into the driveway. I practically knocked her down in my mad dash to the guest bathroom, where I showered until I ran all the hot water out of their tank.

Then I called Bonita and made sure she'd canceled everything for the rest of the week, especially anything with a judge involved, as I didn't trust another attorney with court appearances, even on paltry motions. After she assured me she had already done that, especially since I had told her to do all that before I even left Sarasota, I asked, "You got a draft of that motion to withdraw done yet?"

"Check your e-mails. It's waiting on you to review, change, print, sign, and overnight it."

"I'll drag out my laptop and do it now," I said. Fast as I could, I wanted to get as far away from the case of the Idiot Client who had altered his records.

Blah, blah, blah, about other legal stuff, and I said my thanks and good-bye.

"You be careful," Bonita said, as if I were in Miami instead of Bugfest, a town of some eight thousand people, mostly of the Baptist or Methodist persuasion.

"Don't worry, nothing much ever happens in Bugfest."

Hey, so, yeah, I got that wrong, but a law degree doesn't make me psychic.

chapter 7

In south Georgia, the earth is lush and never idle, regardless of the time of year.

In winter, the pine trees never drop their needles, and the old-timers have collard patches and cabbages, dark green against the brown and gray fallow fields. Rye grass covers the pastures and hills with rich color that looks like a child dashed a bright green crayon across the landscape. And the camellias, my word, the camellias bloom all winter in a profusion of reds and pinks and whites.

In spring, stand back, nature does this whole baroque thing, showing off with lavender wisteria drooping off the trees, their vines tenacious and hardy. On the sides of the road, crimson clover blooms red, and the landscape is dazzling with jasmine, azaleas, and the snow-white petals of the famed dogwood. And when the honeysuckle and the magnolias bloom, and I stand still and inhale, I know instinctively what heaven smells like.

In summertime, the region has rain-forest-type weather, and vegetation will take over in a season. Kudzu will consume whole buildings, and if you stand still too long, it will shoot a few tendrils up your legs. Bamboo will go from fernlike sprouts to treelike forests in a single season. And poison ivy will replicate exponentially while you stand and watch it.

And in early autumn, all that summer poison ivy turns a glorious red, and purple and yellow flowers spring up from the earth and wave in the cooling breezes.

So, naturally, in a place where the plants never once slow down, rather just trade momentum with each other, Willette's property had the wild look of a place nature was busily reclaiming as her own sole province.

Which was all right by me in a general sense, but as I floated the beam of my flashlight through the lush growth in Willette's backyard, I couldn't help but wonder: How in the world had the neighbors let her get away with this? Didn't they have zoning enforcement? But then I took in the thick hedge of privet around the property. A living privacy fence that protected Willette's yard from prying eyes and the neighbors from the sight of Willette's backyard.

And from the sight of the tree house that had lured me back out in the night.

Moments earlier, in the bed in my brother's house, where I was pointedly not sleeping, I had thought I could somehow conquer the combined pangs of hunger and insomnia by chasing my childhood ghosts across yellow pine planks. So, I had crawled out of bed, dressed, and walked down the safe, quiet streets of my hometown, and had come to my mother's place.

In the beam of the flashlight, I could see a kind of a path I hadn't noticed earlier. Not something anybody had mowed, mind you, but the kind of track that develops from regular foot traffic. A narrow walk right up to the tree house.

Who was I not to follow this inviting dent in the assertive undergrowth?

Mere seconds later, I tugged on the planks nailed to the tree, forming a crude ladder. I gauged the distance I would fall if one didn't hold, and told myself a smart person would wait until daylight. No, a smart person wouldn't climb the tree at all. But I was caught in a web of memories—Delvon and me, and Granddad, hanging around in a tree, hiding from everyone else, playing country music on a transistor radio, Granddad telling us stories and drinking, Delvon and me learning all the words to our grandfather's music, Johnny Horton and Hank Williams, when other kids were learning the Lord's Prayer and the Twenty-third Psalm—and smart had been driven out. I wedged the flashlight into my shirt pocket to free both hands, and, for reasons I couldn't explain, I began to climb.

Once in the tree house, I tested the flooring and flooded the small space with light. The first thing I thought was how much smaller it was than I had remembered. The second thing I thought was that somebody was still using it—oh, like the footpath hadn't hinted at that? A thick sleeping bag opened across the flooring, a cooler sat in the corner, and a trail of unlit candles rested along the railing, heavy, round candles, ones not likely to fall or blow off. I tiptoed across the floor of the tree house, and the bottom felt solid and safe. I peeked into the cooler: junk food and Cokes. I touched the cans—cool, but not cold. Then I picked up the fake-ice pack—still cold, but not frozen.

Somebody had been using the tree house recently.

But how recently?

So, how long did one of those fake blue ice things stay cold, I wondered.

Again, I swept the area with the flashlight until I spotted a small ashtray in the corner, and I went toward it, and sniffed it, and though there was no roach or marijuana joint in it, I could still smell the pungent odor of pot. I poked around under the sleeping bag and, sure enough, found a small metal pipe, and I sniffed it. Pot, definitely. The pipe itself was an ornate little dude that looked costly and well-used. I put it in my pants pocket.

So, Delvon's and my old tree house was now somebody's hideaway, somebody who drank Coke and smoked pot.

Judging from the tales Delvon had told about his thriving home-based business—thriving, that is, until the Georgia Bureau of Investigations and their pot-sniffing dogs showed up and put him out of business—that narrowed it down to about every teenager in town, and a goodly portion of the twentysomethings. Probably a bunch of baby boomers out there, too, who hadn't completely given up the habits of their wild youth.

Maybe the pot smoker was closer to home. The fruit doesn't fall far from the tree and all that—assuming the tree included Delvon and me.

But I had other things to worry about besides whether my nephew was experimenting with marijuana. I turned off the flashlight and sat down on the sleeping bag, so I could be comfortable while I allowed my anxieties to roam free through my mind. In the cool November night air, I shivered, I watched the stars in the clear sky, and I wondered what in the blue blazes was going on.

When the anxiety-produced adrenaline kicked at my heart, my fingers itched to write down and number the things I needed to do. But lacking pen or paper, I started making a mental list to calm myself. Things to do tomorrow, I said out loud: Overnight the motion to withdraw, which I had already read, rewritten, printed, and signed; follow up with Dr. Hodo; clean house for Patti; find something organic and naturally green that I could eat; figure out this deep-freeze thing; make damn certain Dan got the paperwork done to be Willette's guardian; look at the ER records; talk to the hospital nurses; et cetera, et cetera.

My eyes had long become accustomed to the dark when I heard the distinct and unwanted sounds of someone else crossing the lawn and stomping through high grass and weeds toward the tree house.

Just an insomniac neighbor, I reassured myself.

Or not.

Nothing like being in a tree house late at night with no weapon to evoke a certain level of paranoia.

With no way out except the way the intruder was coming in, no place to hide, and the flashlight too small to make any kind of weapon, I looked up.

Straight up.

Into the dark tree branches, as the tree house was roofless.

Yeah, I used to be quite the tomboy.

But I used to be quite young when I was a tomboy.

It'd been twenty years since I'd had my last tree-climbing adventure. One didn't much need to climb trees to be a trial attorney in Sarasota, and I'd been negligent in letting my tomboy skills languish.

I looked down at the advancing shape of a man.

I looked again at the dark green branches above my head, and way, way above the ground.

Hey, tree climbing was like riding a bike, wasn't it?

Thus, with my risk-benefit analysis over, I scrambled up on the railing of the tree house, half jumped and half climbed up on that first limb, found my foothold, grabbed at a branch above it, and started climbing up into the big tree in the dark.

chapter **8**

A **peacock is the** male bird of the species called peafowl; they are kin to pheasants, they hail originally from Southeast Asia, and they happily eat cat food, berries, and cracked corn. Peacocks roost in trees, and you better not wake them up.

Most of this I learned later from Eleanor.

The thing about roosting in trees and not waking them up I learned like I've learned most of the valuable lessons in life. The hard way.

That is, I woke one up. Suddenly.

I was so busy making sure I climbed onto sturdy branches, didn't fall to my death or injury, and didn't make loud noises alerting the man climbing up the plank ladder into the tree house I was a few feet above him, that I just happened to overlook the large, dark shadow of the bird perched on the last limb I climbed onto.

The peacock, however, noticed me. It woke with a loud scream and a great flapping of its big wings, and it aimed its beak right at me.

Naturally, I took quick evasive action to avoid being pecked upon by a large bird in the middle of a tree in the middle of the night.

But ducking and running takes on a wholly different quality in a tree.

Which is why I fell, butt-first, down through the leaves and branches of the great live oak and landed with a thud, not gracefully at all, at the feet of one surprised man. With a peacock right on my tail, chasing me like some avenging angel of the fowl world.

The peacock had an advantage. It could fly.

As it turned out, I couldn't.

Fortunately, I landed on the sleeping bag.

Fortunately, the man was Demetrious.

Fortunately, the peacock respected authority and flew back up into the tree with only minor squawks after the chief of police spoke sternly to it, shooing it with his hands.

And then he knelt over me, and graciously asked, "Are you all right?"

Other than embarrassed and itchy and a tad sore in the bottom, I figured I was okay, and said so.

"Well, don't get up until you're sure you aren't hurt," Demetrious said.

I popped right up on my feet as quick as I could. "I'm fine. Really."

"Are you sure you're all right?"

"I'm fine. Really."

"Well, then . . ." And he paused, and I swear, in the moonlight and the faint reflection of the streetlight, I saw a bit of a grin on his face.

Above us, Free Bird let out another scream, as if to say *Shut up*.

But I had to wonder: was Free Bird, the errant peacock, the physical embodiment of some of my bad karma coming back after me? I mean, the bird caused me to hit not one but two cars my first hour in town and to fall on my butt smack-dab in front of a man I had meant to hide from.

Why couldn't Eleanor just have a pet cat or dog, like everybody else?

chapter 9

Though my experiences in the last few years had taught me that cooperating with law enforcement officers probably is the best way to go when involved in a murder investigation, those old habits of mine ran deep.

Keep your mouth shut around Official People being an old habit.

A lesson learned in the house of my parents and carried over to the years with Delvon and Farmer Dave, when a casual misspeak could have landed Delvon and me in some godforsaken juvenile detention home, and Dave in jail. Of course, Dave ended up in jail anyway, but later on and not because I'd blabbed anything, and instead of juvie hall, I made it out of the back forty of Bugfest and into law school, but I'd still held with that lesson.

So there I was, stuck with it: Keep your mouth shut around Official People.

While I rubbed my butt and scratched a few mosquito bites and kept my mouth determinedly closed, Demetrious asked me a few questions as he checked the cooler and felt the fake ice, just like I had. From his pocket, he pulled out one of those mini-lights and flashed it on the sleeping bag. After studying on it a moment, he picked the heavy fabric up and felt around under it, and put it down.

Finally, Demetrious seemed satisfied, and I was ready to breathe a sigh of relief.

"Somebody's been hanging out here," he said, as if somehow I'd failed to notice that.

"Uh-huh," I said, and scratched some more, for all the good it was doing. Apparently, I was on the local night menu as after-dinner treat for a thousand mosquitoes. I was taking that citronella natural bug repellent I'd dabbed on back to the health food store and getting my money back.

"Got any idea who?"

"Nope, not me. I don't live here. You remember? Only drove up today, to help Dan. That's all."

"What are you doing up here, in the tree house?"

"What are you doing here?"

"Looking around, thinking," he said.

"Yeah, me too. While I got you here," I said, as if I had summoned him to my office, "could you tell me what kind of gun Willette had?"

"Just a .38, a standard, what you could easily call a Saturday night special, unregistered and as far as I am concerned, untraceable."

"You tried to trace it?" Never assume people actually do their jobs being a lesson I'd learned in defending professionals against malpractice suits.

"Yes. I do know how to investigate a crime."

Oops, a tad snippy. Topic change in order, I thought, and asked, "What do you think Willette meant about those 'jelly eggs'?"

"Don't know. She was hallucinating that night in the ER, could be she just hallucinated the jelly eggs."

"Hallucinating? Like seeing things?"

"That's what it usually means."

I never knew Willette to hallucinate before, but then I hadn't been keeping up that closely with her, and I made another mental note to ask Dan about this.

"She say anything to you? At the house? On the way to the hospital?"

"She was hysterical. I think I mentioned that. She screamed a lot."

Demetrious either didn't know any more or wasn't going to tell me any more—I knew that as surely as I knew I was tired, bone-tired. "I think I'll go on back to Dan's."

"I'll be leaving now too."

Like a gentleman, he went down first, then held my flashlight on the crude plank ladder to guide me until I was safely on the ground.

"Walk you home?" Demetrious offered. "Make sure Free Bird doesn't attack you again?"

This time I could see the grin for sure.

"Well, if you hadn't scared me, sneaking up like that, I wouldn't have climbed up the tree."

"I'm sorry I scared you. Really. Now, may I walk you home?"

As it seemed both impolite and suspicious to say no, I thanked him, and side by side, under the streetlights, we walked down the old sidewalk to Dan's house.

"Shalonda thinks the world of you," he said. "I hope you'll come out and visit us, we'd like to show you our place, and you can visit my mules."

"Your mules?" As in, *visit them*?

"Yep, got several mules out at my place. I train them as well as keep them for other folks. Plus I own a couple. My best one, Big Beauty, we call him BB, is entered in just about every category at the mule rodeo, at Mule Day. You did know that's this Saturday? Maybe you can find time to go? See Big Beauty in the rodeo?"

Man, I thought, you need to be fighting crime, not running a boarding school for mules. But I hadn't missed the lilt of enthusiasm in his voice, so what I said was, "I'll sure try."

At the door, Demetrious offered me his hand, and we shook.

Great, the police chief was busy training mules instead of solving crimes.

I added *solve the Willette-shoots-Ray-Glenn case* to my mental list of things to do.

And soon, before my stash of organic foods gave out.

chapter 10

Well, damn.

Someone had turned on a radio, and it was blaring. I opened my eyes and for a moment couldn't figure out where I was and why there was a Georgia Bull Dog flag on the wall, staring back at me.

The radio announcer screamed out the time of day, that being morning, and the station, that being 93.3, its slogan "Real Country for Real Country Folks," and then damned if he didn't play "Sweetheart Deal," Big Lonnie Ledbetter's only hit.

Unable to escape the noise, I rolled over and listened. It was kind of catchy.

On the shady side of Shreveport in a crooked bar and grill
With nothing but a losing streak and a lot of time to kill
A hopeless hand before me and my luck was slipping fast
And I was face to face with the greatest gamble of my past

She laid down her cards like I laid down my lies
Taking all my money and all I had inside

She beat me before but she came back for more
She's winning all my money like I once won her heart
It's a tough game when my Sweetheart deals the cards

My Sweetheart deals again, another losing hand
My Sweetheart deals the ace and I just can't understand
Luck can't be a lady 'cause I'm not lucky at all
Now I've lost it all with the luck of the draw
And now I feel the loss with every hand she steals
I just can't win the game when my Sweetheart deals

"You up?" Patti shouted at me from the doorway, drowning out the deejay's comments when the song finished.

"Coffee," I bleated out, in a begging tone wholly unbecoming.

"On the stove," she said. "Got a percolator with fresh coffee you are welcome to," and she disappeared.

By the time I was dressed and showered and had fixed my own fair-trade, shade-grown organic coffee, Patti was leaving her instructions. "Go through Willette's papers," she said to me. And to my bleary-eyed nephew, she said, "Help your aunt and then get to school. Come over to Willette's after school." She kissed him while he squirmed, then out the door she went.

Not one to shrink from either doing or delegating work, Patti Lea was wildly successful in running her own small-engine repair shop. Still, I made a mental note never to be reduced to being her employee, even if she did hire folks like Sam, the man who went off his meds and wrecked things.

"So," I said, looking at Bobby.

"Whatever," he said.

"You miss your brother, now that he is off at college?"

"Naw," he said. "I got more room."

"Still."

"Whatever."

"So. All right, let's get those papers out of the box and into the strong sunlight."

He shrugged.

Despite his lack of enthusiasm for the chore, Bobby helped me weigh down the papers on the back deck in the bright sun of morning, then we took turns spraying Lysol on them while we held our breath, as I didn't think inhaling Lysol would be any healthier for us than breathing in the mold spores off the old papers.

Patti Lea was right, of course. I did need to study these papers. Why, I didn't know, but that's what lawyers do, study paper. I looked at Bobby. "As the family lawyer, I'm appointing you to be in charge of them," I said. "Turn them over in the direct sun as soon as you get home from school, and wash your hands after you touch them. Please?"

"Yeah. Okay."

My next chore was to check on Willette. But before I left for the hospital, I reached into my pocket and pulled out the ornate marijuana pipe and confronted Bobby. "This yours?"

Bobby gave me one of those perfectly innocent *Who, me?* looks that I had also perfected by his age. "Not mine," he said.

"Ever seen it before?"

Bobby stepped closer, squinted at it, then shook his head.

"Found it in the tree house," I said.

"Yeah? Cool," he said.

After another round of talented denials—I mean this boy could join a Broadway play right now—I told him we needed to have a serious talk about drugs and stuff.

"Naw, Mom and Dad already did that. And the one about safe sex and abstinence and just about everything else." Bobby's tone suggested he was not the least interested in having similar talks with me.

Yeah, trust the good parents to have done all that. But unlike Delvon and me, Dan and Patti could not speak from experience on matters of drugs and sin.

"We'll talk later," I said, and winked like it might be fun. I put the pipe back in my pocket and dashed off to the hospital, where Rodney was sitting in a chair, doing his best to look alert.

"Were you here all night?" I asked, after a proper greeting.

"Oh, no, ma'am. Otis Lee Tate took over the night shift. I had me a good night's sleep. Don't you be worrying none," Rodney said.

"Any problems?"

"Oh, no, ma'am, she's not much of a flight risk." He grinned.

"Anybody bother her?"

"Not that Otis Lee mentioned, nope. But she's got a doctor in there, a psychiatrist."

"Great," I said, and slipped into Willette's room. A man was staring at my mother and didn't look around at me. I greeted Shalonda, and noted the flowers and pound cakes appeared to be reproducing.

"Dr. Hodo," Shalonda said, "I'd like to introduce you to Lilly Cleary."

The good doctor turned around, and I studied him like I would a prospective expert witness. Older, of course, than the last time I'd seen him, before Willette banished him from our house. Slender, wavy white hair. Elegant, actually. I had either forgotten that or it hadn't registered on my child's brain. My father's old friend was an elegant-looking man.

"I don't like this situation at all," Dr. Hodo said.

"Well, me either. So, we agree," I said.

His bluntness actually comforted me. Then I remembered my manners, stuck out my hand, tried to smile, and said, "Oh, how good of you to come. I'd have been here sooner this morning, but I had to disinfect a bunch of legal papers."

The look of scrutiny he gave me suggested I might have been better off not mentioning disinfecting paper.

But what he said was "She is far too sedated. The dose of Thorazine that's been prescribed should keep her calm, not comatose."

"Dr. Weinstein told me he thought she was in some kind of shock, like a coma 'cause she was so traumatized," Shalonda said.

"Yes, he shared that same theory with me," Dr. Hodo said. I was relieved to hear a little tartness in his voice. Tart appreciates tart being one of my theories.

"You actually saw this Dr. Weinstein?" I asked.

"Briefly."

"Me too," Shalonda said. "Real briefly."

"I asked him about her tox screen," Dr. Hodo said, "even suggested running another one. But Dr. Weinstein assured me he was on top of things, and that to tell me anything else would be a violation of her privacy."

"We're the family and we've called you in on a consult. I'll make sure Dr. Weinstein and the nurses know that. Now, can you un-prescribe the Thorazine? She needs to wake up, eat, and tell us what happened," I said.

"I don't like to cancel another physician's orders until I've had a chance to discuss it with him fully. Legally, I have no authority over Willette. But I will call him and initiate further discussion." Dr. Hodo studied me as if he were gauging my inner resources or something. "Did anybody tell you she nearly died in the ER the evening they brought her in?"

"Shalonda and my brother mentioned an OD."

"So the hospital never told you about this?"

"Not the hospital per se, no." Having practiced as a medical malpractice defense attorney for thirteen years, which I hoped wasn't an unlucky, bad-karma-generating time frame, I wasn't surprised that nobody officially connected with the hospital had bothered to mention this. I mean, why highlight your negligence to the family attorney, right?

"Well, we might want to look into it. Those bruises around her mouth, you saw those?"

"Yes. I asked, but no one seems to know where they came from."

"Dr. Weinstein was adamant that your mother came into the ER with near toxic levels of narcotics in her system, and with those bruises."

"I guess his practicing CYA wasn't a violation of her privacy rights," I said.

Dr. Hodo grinned at me then, just a quick flitter of a weary little smile that he quickly controlled, and said, "CYA. Cover your ass. The new guiding principle of medical care." Then he turned back to my mother and measured the bruises with his wide hands. "You see the pattern?"

"Yes. And I've had plenty to say about it, really," I said. "And despite what Dr. What's-his-face said, the police officer that brought her to the ER said he didn't see any bruises on her at her house."

Actually, I think what Demetrious said was he couldn't be sure. I'd have to ask him again. But I didn't mind tossing the conflict into play, because one thing trial attorneys know is that if you pit two sources against each other, sometimes the real facts will emerge from the contest.

"I can't say on that, then," Dr. Hodo said, "since I wasn't there. Meanwhile, would you like to know what I'm thinking so far?"

"Absolutely."

"Your mother is probably a severe agoraphobic, possibly with a clinical depression complication, and suffering from an obsessive-compulsive disorder. I understand she is quite the list maker."

List maker? Uh-oh, was that a gene-pool thing?

"With severe agoraphobia, it isn't unusual for a person to be so afraid of leaving their house that they can't reach outside for the mail, or the newspaper," he said.

Or to take out the garbage, I thought.

"While there are milder forms, where fear of things like malls and airports can cause panic attacks, and a person, with help, can still leave their home, your mother has a more acute case."

Uh-oh. Fear of airports? Panic attacks? Making lists wasn't bad enough?

While I was cursing my DNA, Dr. Hodo scribbled down something and said he had to leave, as he had other patients, but would be in touch if I'd give him a number.

I pulled a business card out of my purse, wrote down my cell phone number and Dan's house phone, and handed it over.

"Take some advice?" he asked.

"Absolutely."

"Offer the pound cakes to the nurses," Dr. Hodo said. "Helps build goodwill, and prevents waste. Doesn't look like your mother is going to eat them." He glanced at me. "Thin as you are, I'm guessing you do not eat much pound cake either. Maybe the flowers too, your mom isn't likely to miss them. At least let the nurses enjoy them." He sniffed at a pound cake.

"Would you like to take one?" I asked.

"No," he said, and patted his flat belly. "Past thirty, you have to be careful about consuming foods like that." But his eyes said he sure did want one of those pound cakes.

Yes, I knew about the seductive evils of pound cake. What I was more interested in discussing was the myriad of things I didn't know. "I don't understand why she is so . . . catatonic," I said. "And Dan said she was psychotic, that's why they're keeping her drugged. To my knowledge, she's never been psychotic before. What would cause that . . . that change?"

"I don't know. Yet. That's what I intend to find out."

With that, the good Dr. Hodo turned and left the room, and I trailed him out to the hallway. Outside of Shalonda's hearing, I had to ask him. "Do you ever hear from my dad?"

"Yes," he said. "We go fishing together on the rare occasion when I can get away. He is doing fine."

"Does he . . ." I started to ask if he ever talked about me, but stopped.

Dr. Hodo gave me time to finish, but then, being a trained psychiatrist and all, I guess he figured out I wasn't going to, and he answered the question I couldn't ask. "Your father is very proud of you, whether he's said so or not. He follows your career."

"How?"

"Through Dan."

Yeah, Dan the good son, the family conduit, the man who continued to insist upon having a relationship with his distant father and his barricaded mother.

"You do know Willette would hate having me on her case, don't you?"

"Yes," I said. "But you can help her, can't you?"

"I don't know. But I will try my damnedest." Then he all but winked at me. "You grew up just fine. I'm glad for you."

With that, Dr. Hodo turned and headed down the hallway, and I slipped back into Willette's hospital room. I stared first at Willette's still form, then at Shalonda. "So?"

"So, white girl, let's talk 'bout something 'sides Willette for a moment. Anybody tell you where I'm living now?"

"No."

"Out on the part of what used to be your grandmom's farm. You know, that sixty acres your granddad sold after your grandmomma passed over. All that pasture land he didn't need since he wasn't going to run cows no more. Went through a couple of hands 'fore Demetrious got it, built himself a pretty little house on the high part, and then he fixed up the barn real good." Shalonda paused and studied me. "I sure do miss your granddad and grandmom. They were good people. I looked for you to be at your granddad's funeral, but you weren't."

"I was in trial. Mid-trial. I asked for a continuance, but the jerk attorney on the other side objected, and the judge denied my motion."

"You couldn't let somebody else take it for a day?"

"No, I couldn't. It was my client and my trial."

"White girl, nobody's indispensable."

I turned away from her and stared down at the prone body of my mother. Willette hadn't gone to her own father's funeral and nobody had raised a hissy fit over that. Besides, it was an important, complex trial, and I was up for partnership that year, and if I'd left matters in the hands of the second chair and we'd lost, I'd've been toast in the firm. But there wasn't any point in trying to explain that to anyone in Bugfest. And for a moment, I thought about how little payment Granddad has gotten from selling the pasture land. When he needed somebody to live with him and take care of him, he didn't have any money left. Those bills had come to me.

But I didn't want my old friend Shalonda thinking poorly of me. "I cared for him when he needed me to, in his life. After he passed, I trusted him to Grandmom."

Shalonda came over to me and hugged me. "I know your grandmomma was waiting there for him, help him cross over. And there's something else I know. I know you loved your granddaddy and your grandmomma. Don't you ever worry 'bout me not knowing that 'bout you."

Shalonda let go of me, and I swallowed a few times, and then physically shook, to shake off that strangling feeling. I needed to get out into the fresh, open air. Right now.

"You good here?" I asked. "I'm supposed to help Patti Lea clean out Willette's house."

"I'm good here, you go on. Not anything you can do here. I'll get the cakes and flowers passed around."

"I'll call you later," I said, "and we'll get together, hang out and catch up." Then I fled out of the hospital. Once outside, in the clean, crisp air of an autumn morning, I stood under a sweetgum tree by the side of the parking lot and called Bonita on my cell to check in. After her multilayered assurances, I put my phone up and inhaled deeply. Then I looked at the hospital again, and shuddered. I needed to go back into that concrete-halled collection of germs and viruses and demand to confer with the elusive Dr. Weinstein, check on those ER records, and corner the nurses on duty the night Willette was brought in.

But I had promised to help Patti.

So, instead of going back in, I got in my Honda and I drove from the frying pan of germs straight into the fire of filth.

chapter 11

Trash. **Piles of** trash.

Moldy, smelly piles of trash.

I actually have nightmares where I am suffocating in trash.

I opened my mouth to explain this to my brother, who is not otherwise a cruel man, but before I could make sound come forth from within me, he thrust a mask, gloves, and a set of coveralls at me, and Patti Lea slammed and banged in another room.

"It's pretty dirty in here," he said, as if somehow I had been deprived of every single one of my senses.

Maybe, I thought as my heart thumped against my rib cage in a lurch that made my stomach nearly heave, I had actually died in that crash with the pickup and the Thunderbird. Maybe I was dead. And this was hell.

"It'll be all right, Lilly. We'll get it done," Dan said, and touched my arm, breaking my rising panic at the thought I might be dead and in hell.

Hell might be where I was going, but no way that's where Dan went.

"Okay, lead the way," I said, and slipped a mask over my nose and mouth. Inside my head, a hundred little people started kick-dancing, and they were all screaming at me to get out of there.

"I promised Patti," I said, "so shut up."

"You say something? Hard to hear you with that face mask on."

I shook my head and followed Dan through a tour of the house, ending in the den.

Every surface was filled with piles of papers in rubber bands.

"Old bills, stuff like that," Dan said. "Why she kept all this, me and Patti Lea can't rightly figure out. Thing is, we'd like to find her bank records. She ought to have some money, maybe some CDs or something. I mean she sold Grandmom's place cheap, but not for nothing, so there's got to be some bank records someplace. Patti couldn't find any in that metal box of important papers she gave you, so keep an eye out for something like that."

Oh, frigging great, I had to look at this stuff? I couldn't just throw it out?

"This den's about the cleanest room," Dan said. "Can you look through it to start, for anything like current bank statements?"

Numbly, I nodded.

"I got to get over to see the lady lawyer—you know, Bobby's girlfriend's mother. Got to see about getting appointed Willette's guardian, like you insisted."

Dan left. Randomly, I picked up a few things. As I looked through the collection of papers stuffed everywhere, I couldn't help myself—I looked for something of mine that my mother might have saved, some token of an affection she had never otherwise voiced. In a pile of other yellowed papers, with a coating of dead insects, I found my old report cards, secured with a rubber band that broke with age when I started to roll it off.

That collection hadn't even made it into the metal box of important papers. Rather, my report cards had just been tossed in next to a pile of old phone bills, dating back twenty years. My report cards were, I realized, not evidence of a mother's pride—my grades had been pretty bad and the teachers had scrawled out notes about my attitude, which was also apparently pretty bad, by Bugfest standards of the day. Rather, the cards seemed to have been, like the phone bills, kept not for any real purpose but some obsessive need to collect such things.

Or maybe, as was surely the case with twenty years of old newspapers, my report cards were just so much trash that no one had ever bothered to throw out.

chapter 12

Crazy. **I'd have** to be plumb out of my mind to fall into a mess like this.

    That is, approaching the noon hour, I was pretty certain I would meet any clinical definition of crazy.

Patti Lea was closing in on crazy right behind me.

And that from a woman who'd started her own business after she'd come home from Valdosta State with a degree in Southern history to find out that qualified her for exactly nothing vocationally except maybe cashier at the Pig. While Dan was off in the Marines and she found out her college degree meant jack in the job market, she went right down to the vocational school and told them to teach her something that she could make a living at. The counselor gave her an aptitude test, and when she scored highest in small-engine repair, she signed up for the full course work. When she got her certificate, and the only lawn-mower repair shop in town wouldn't hire her because she was a woman, she went to the bank. And when the bank wouldn't loan her money to start her own shop, her daddy put a second mortgage on their nice brick house in Country Club Heights and purchased an out-of-business store with a good-size workshop, and her momma ran the books and answered the phone and sweet-talked all her garden-club friends into making their husbands do business with Patti.

Three years later, the other shop closed down for lack of customers, and the owner ended up selling paint at the Wal-Mart. But when Patti was too pregnant with her first son to squat and bend and fix, she didn't just hire the man, she made him a partner. They ran that shop together until he turned seventy-five and retired. Patti threw him a big party, and every year she visits him in St. Pete. And as soon as those two boys of hers could toddle out to the garage, both of them became her students. By the time they hit sixth grade, each boy could take apart a top-of-the-line riding lawn mower and put it back together better than it had been.

"That way," she once told me, "they can major in anything they want in college, and go anywhere they want to live, but still always make a living."

Sometimes I wished Patti had been my mother.

And, given that history, to see her now, this close to the edge, was unnerving.

But before I could figure out what I might do, Dan came whistling back with the news that he had an emergency hearing set for twelve forty-five that afternoon, crashing in on the judge's lunch break, and he fully expected to be Willette's legal guardian by one. Having reported to Patti and me, Dan started hauling out trash and humming a near-tuneless song that made me wonder if the boy was sipping on some high-juice Prozac in his Cokes. Patti, the practical, told him not to get dirty and to please go get her some food before he left for the courthouse. Dan whistled his way on off.

Desperate for some fresh air, I stepped outside and yanked my face mask off.

Then I looked up and saw a pickup truck parked in the front yard, a new one, and a hybrid to boot. That was different, I thought, and watched as a man somewhere in his late fifties or so got out from the driver's side. He appeared to be robust and solid, with a weatherworn face and a Marine's close-cropped hair.

"We been waiting for somebody to come out," he said by way of greeting. "Given Miss Willette's ways, we wasn't sure if we should knock, or what."

I was filthy, hungry, and disgusted, and in no mood to chat with the curious onlookers of the town. "This isn't a good time," I said.

But the man grinned. "By God, if you ain't prettier now than you were as a little gal." He turned back to the man still inside the truck. "Hey, Hank, get yourself out here."

Something about the man began to seem familiar, that is, in a long-ago, faraway sort of way. But before I could place him, I saw a borderline chunky, pleasant-looking man about my age crawl out of the passenger's side of the truck. He had the look of a man who spent equal amounts of time at the gym and at the all-u-can-eat buffet. The buffet was edging out ahead in that race.

"I told you we shouldn't be bothering her," the younger man said to the older and ducked his head, not meeting my eyes.

"I'm sorry," I said. "I didn't mean to be rude, but this *really* isn't a good time."

The younger man looked me up and down, but I didn't think his stare was sexual. The soft light in his eyes when he finally looked at my face was only curious, not rude. "You got me in near to the worst trouble of my whole life," he said. "Fifth grade. You remember?"

"I remember fifth grade."

"You and me got held after class, on 'count we didn't do our home-work. The teacher, old Miss Summerfield, made us wash her car on 'count she said jes' putting us in detention didn't do any good with us."

"I near whipped him good when I heard what he done," the older man said. "Till your grandma told me to never mind about it, it was you put Hank up to it, only we called him Little Toot then. Christian name's Hiriam Williams. Get up here, boy."

"You remember?" Hank asked as he stepped toward me, then looked down at his shoes. "You and me," he said to the ground, "we washed that woman's car with ever one of her windows rolled down and used them big hoses till we near ruint her car insides. I reckon it took her weeks to dry it out."

I couldn't help it, I laughed. My granddad had gotten such a kick out of that stunt he'd had given me a whole shot glass full of home-made whiskey, and we had laughed and laughed. My parents had simply ignored the irate phone calls from Miss Summerfield. Grandmom had cautioned me on the fine art of not getting caught because of being too obvious, and therein laid the foundation for one of the great truths of my life and the art of litigation—sometimes you had to be sneaky.

"Hank," I said, and held out my hand. He took it, but dropped it after a quick but strong shake.

Reminiscing aside, I stared hard at the man, trying to imagine a skinny ten-year-old face in his beefy middle-aged one. Maybe that was the look he'd just given me—looking for the child we'd known each other to be a long time ago.

"Hiriam Williams," I repeated, because it sounded fine to say it.

"Yeah, by God, boy, I told you she'd remember you. You bein' her first boyfriend and all. We call him Hank now, ma'am, he outgrew Little Toot."

While I was trying to remember if I had ever heard Hank called Little Toot, and hoping for his sake I had not, the older man stepped forward and offered his hand. "Jubal Early Williams, ma'am, glad to be seeing you again after all these years."

I shook his hand. "Good to see you again." Truth was, I didn't remember being around Jubal much as a kid, but I had a few memories of a brusque man on his way out the door. Hank and his momma had been a little afraid of him, or at least that's what I remembered my fifth-grader's mind thinking, and my grandmother had warned me not to cross him. In those days, he'd been a logger. And he was still strong and rugged-looking, but I judged him probably too old to still be cutting down trees for a living. While I was studying both the Jubal in front of me and the one way back in my memory, he squeezed my hand like I'd been more to him than I had, just a childhood friend of his kid's. A long time ago.

"Real fine seeing you again," Jubal said, and pumped my hand like he'd been one to take me out fishing or something.

"Jubal Early," I said, and I pulled my hand back. "Any kin to the Confederate general of the same name?"

"No, ma'am, lest not as far as we know. Though my great-great-granddaddy served with him. Four year, and he come home not a scratch on him and then up and died of brain fever that first year home."

Hank edged his father aside and looked at me with the same sweet eyes I remembered from grade school. "Lilly Belle, so pleased to see you again."

Sun-squint lines accented those green eyes now and gray dusted his rust-colored hair, and there were those extra pounds, of course, but otherwise the decades had been kind enough to him.

Hank caught me studying him and blushed out to his earlobes. "You probably don't remember, but I'm not kin to the real Hank Williams. No, ma'am, though I near got all his records. Senior, not the junior."

Given my pressing need for a shower and some organic foods, I didn't want to discuss genealogy, Confederate history, or country music, or play catch-up with my running buddy from grade school. So, I put on my distant, professional expression and asked, "What can I do for you two?"

"We, ah, we got a kind of a legal problem, and we heard you were in town, and, I tell you what, Dan, he's always a-bragging how good a lawyer you are, and . . ." Hank drifted off and took up staring at his feet again.

"I'm not licensed to practice law in Georgia," I said.

"See, what it is, there's this here resort that wants to buy up our place." Jubal stopped and looked at Hank.

"We don't want to sell," Hank said. "Daddy's house has been in our family for over a hundred and thirty years. Since soon after The War. Our family has flat-out owned the property before that, but the original house got burnt down."

"Our family been on that piece of property since Andy Jackson ran the Creeks and the Cherokees out," Jubal tossed in. "A hundred and sixty-five years. You don't run folks with that kind of claim off their land, now do you?"

Well, that depended, I supposed, on who did the owning and who did the running off. Those Creeks and Cherokees Andrew Jackson had dispossessed had a claim that out-dated Jubal's, and if Jubal felt so strongly about ancestral homesteads, maybe he wanted to deed his property back to the remnants of the tribe that still owned a little reservation on the other side of Sleepy Lake. But I doubted this was the time or place for a consciousness-raising session. Instead, I simply said, "So, you don't want to sell. I can understand that." And I did, having tried my best to keep my grandmother's house in the family.

"But we don't have any choice," Jubal said. "That's what the county is telling us now."

"What's the county got to do with it?"

"The resort wants to put in a big lodge and marina, with a fishing pier and boat docks and fancy hotel rooms, and a swanky restaurant, all that where our house and land is."

A resort? In Bugfest? I thought. Well, hell, they put Las Vegas in a desert and everybody knew how that worked out.

"It's all part of this planned development on the lake the county is putting in, damming up Sleepy Creek so that the little lake we're on will be a real big lake. Our place, if you don't recall it, being you been gone so long, is on that little lake Sleepy Creek made, right before it turns and goes on down to the Gulf of Mexico."

I nodded, a little geographically confused.

"Least our place isn't gonna be put under water when they dam up the

creek and make the lake," Jubal said. "All that will be on the north side
of the lake, where the county is trying to gobble up the property, only a
lot of folks aren't happy to sell. They don't want their homesteads being
underwater so rich folks from Florida can go bass fishing."

While Jubal paused to breathe, Hank took over the talking.

"'Cause the county is part of the project, that is, it's the county that's
damming up the creek to make a twelve-hundred-acre lake, and then
they're going to use eminent domain to buy up all the land on the north
side of the new lake. Those folks don't even have lakefront property now,
but they will when the project is done, but the county's gonna take it
from them now, so the appraisal will just show an old dirt farm, what is
cheap. All because of that case out of the Supreme Court," Hank said.
"The one that lets private corporations use a government's power of eminent domain."

"And pay us less, a whole bunch less, though the money's not the
point," Jubal said. "You should hear what little they're offering us, and
telling us we don't have any choice."

"The county said it was the fair market value, but I got a friend who is
a real estate lawyer lady friend, and she says our place is worth twice that,"
Hank said, and blushed again.

Blushing and real estate lawyer lady *friend* probably had a connection,
and, yeah, sales forced by eminent domain were legendary for cheap land
grabs. Also, it being highly unlikely that Bugfest had two lady lawyers, I
figured Hank's friend might also be Bobby's girlfriend's mom and Dan's
new attorney. But right then, I had things other than *small world, isn't
it?* on my mind. I turned over what Jubal and Hank had told me, a few
rotations in my head. So, reduced to the bottom line, the county commissioners were, in effect, proposing to steal Jubal's land and hand it over to a
private resort to build a lodge and a marina.

While all this was terrible, I couldn't help them. "If you have a lady
friend who is a real estate lawyer, then you should be asking her questions."

"Oh, we tried, but she's got a conflict of interest," Hank said.

Jubal made a small but audible rude noise, deep in his throat, and Hank turned and glared at his father.

"Well, then——" I started to say something to smooth over the moment.

"You being a lawyer and all, we figured you'd know that case, that United States Supreme Court case," Hank said, turning back to me and smoothing things over all on his own.

"*Kelo v. City of New London,* yes, I know of the case, of course," I said, though what I didn't know about it was equal to what I did. "But there has to be a public purpose before the county can take your land, and in *New London,* the city appointed a development group to acquire property and develop a riverfront residential and business complex to replace a . . ." I drifted to an early stop in my sentence when I realized that the word I was headed toward might insult Jubal and Hank. The Supreme Court had allowed the city's appointed development group to take the landowners' property through eminent domain because the property being taken was considered a *blight.*

Was their hundred-and-thirty-five-year-old house a *blight*? Truth was, I didn't have exacting standards in fifth grade, which was the last time I'd seen the place. But I stopped before I implied something rude about Jubal's house. Taking a different tack, I said, "If your, er, *friend* has a conflict of interest, have you hired another attorney? One that specializes in land use issues?"

"Well, yes and no. We've got an attorney, but he doesn't specialize in much of anything except being front and center at J.B.'s Barbeque and singing off-key at the Trinity Church. Worse'n that, he's not real optimistic we can fight the resort folks on this one since the county is a part of it," Jubal said. "He says since the county commissioners voted to go in with the resort development group as a partner——"

"The county approved the resort corporation as its development agent," Hank said.

"Didn't I jes' say that?" Jubal asked.

"Then the resort group has the county's powers of eminent domain," Hank said, ignoring his father. "And we are just sunk. They claim the public purpose will be the increased tax revenues to the county, and new jobs, and our lawyer says we're gonna lose our place in the condemnation proceedings if we don't just go ahead and sell now."

"Sure hope you didn't pay much for that advice," I said, though in truth it sounded about right, from what I could remember of the case. "Any chance of changing the county commissioners' minds? Without the commissioners involving the county, the resort can't use eminent domain."

"Commissioners were split right down the middle, even Stephen, for a long time, except for the guy from our district, he held out making up his mind for a while. What with him being the tiebreaker, he waffled this way and that," Jubal said. "Lot of talk in the county against it, old-time folks don't want us to get like Florida. You shoulda been there at the public hearing, you'd've been real proud of my boy here. Spoke up for all us country folks. But then there's a lot of folks wanting this development, folks what can't see past the notion of jobs and money they think the resort and the big lake will bring in."

Well, that was an old story, those who wanted to hold on to what was versus those who wanted something new. Everybody in the county could talk it to death if they wanted to, but I'd seen what had happened in Sarasota, and knew in the end there wasn't any stopping the development. Hell, not even the sheer power of an epidemic of category 3 and 4 hurricanes several years in a row had slowed it down in coastal Florida. The baby boomers were retiring, and the cold, up North places were emptying out of their aging, pensioned-off citizens, and they, by God, didn't want to live in the snow anymore, and were coming south in droves, looking for cheap real estate and mild winters.

And people like Jubal and Hank were just in the way. And apparently more than half of the county commissioners had understood that.

"Who was the tiebreaker," I asked, "on the commission?"

"I think he's an old boyfriend of yours too, that Lonnie Ledbetter," Jubal said.

"Oh no, not a boyfriend of mine," I said, maybe a bit too loud.

"Well, that's right, that's right, he was a boyfriend of that girlfriend of yours, kinda off and on over the years, that Shalonda. That gal sure is a firecracker," Jubal said. "You reckon it's true what they say, that he wrote that song, 'Sweetheart Deal,' about her?" Then, not waiting for an answer, he shook his head. "Well, when nothing else worked out for him, he sure did hightail it home to her, anyways. But here's the thing, that Lonnie's a snake, a real snake to sell us out like that."

So, Shalonda and Lonnie had had something going? Later, I would have to ask Shalonda about this off-and-on thing with Lonnie. And about the song. But before I pondered Shalonda's love life much, Jubal brought me back to the real point.

"It's just a real sorry story, a sure enough sad state of affairs when a company from up North can come down and take away a man's own home place. One that's been in the family for over a hundred and sixty-five years. A sorry, sorry story," Jubal said.

Yes, it was. But Patti Lea picked that minute to stick her head out the front door and positively glare at Jubal, Hank, and me. Given that she is usually both charming and polite, I figured she was pretty much at the end of her rope. Plus, having gotten the gist of it, I didn't want to hear any more of Jubal's sad story at the moment. I had my own, thank you. So, despite Hank's green eyes, I piped up and said, "I'm sorry, but I think my sister-in-law needs some help."

"We thought you might have some ideas of what we can do to fight 'em, legal like, and all," Jubal said.

"I'm sorry, but I am really not licensed to practice law in Georgia," I said, a little sternly, since the first time I had said this apparently went right over their heads.

"Come on, Daddy, I told you—" Hank said.

"Hush, son, I'm trying to pick this here young woman's mind on something. See, Lilly Belle, what the lawyer in town told us was—"

"I'm sorry to have bothered you, Daddy just thought you might could help us." Hank looked me straight in the eyes, then ducked his head again.

"I'd have to do some research, think about it," I said before I could shut myself up.

"Then you'll take our case?" Hank said, and watched me with big, bright little-boy eyes in a big grown man's face.

"No. I'm not licensed to practice in Georgia. I might have mentioned that already? But when I get back to my office in Sarasota, I can do some research, pull some things together and mail them to you. Then you can take them to your attorney here or, perhaps, find another attorney."

"See there, son." Jubal poked Hank in the arm. "I told you she'd help us. You being her first boyfriend and all."

"How's it coming with the house?" Hank asked. "It must be bad the way Patti Lea looked."

"It's horrible," I said, too weary to wordsmith the view from inside. "We have so much trash to throw out, and then there's some good family furniture, antiques, even stuff my grandmother's mother had, that needs to be brought out in the yard and cleaned, and . . ." I drifted off, suddenly overwhelmed with fatigue.

"Lord, then, gal, let me get in there right now. I can lift and tote and clean with the best of 'em," Jubal said, and started jogging toward the front door.

I had to jump to catch him. "I don't think now is the time to interrupt Patti Lea," I said, and literally put my hand out on his chest to stop his forward motion.

"Well, I betcha you ask her, she'd be glad to have me come on in and help out."

"I can help you with the house too," Hank said to me. Then he turned to his father. "Let them catch their breath, okay? We'll make plans to come back later."

"Good idea," I said. "I mean, on the later part."

Hank turned back to me and grinned. "I teach shop over at the high school. And history. And coach the wrestling team."

Wrestling and history, a classic Southern combination, I thought, like whiskey and hunting, remembering my own history teacher had his greater fame as the wrestling coach. But what I said was "So, you're a teacher." I wondered why in the hell I was smiling at him. "You've done well for yourself, then."

Hank turned a bright red I wouldn't have thought humanly possible, and then grinned. "Yes, ma'am. And I can round up a few of those big old sixteen-year-olds off the wrestling team, and we can surely tote anything anywhere you want it toted."

It was, frankly, the best offer I'd had since landing back in Bugfest. Teenage wrestling students, I thought, would be efficient with the heavy furniture, and had good immune systems to fight off the plague germs in the dust and mold. Of course, Patti Lea *was* dead-set against outsiders getting a look at the inside of the house.

"Better let me talk to Dan and Patti Lea," I said.

"I hear you on that," Hank said.

"He's a great teacher. Them boys love him, and they'd do just about anything for Hank." Jubal turned to Hank, then back to me. "Hank never did marry. Dan says you didn't either. Hank's a real forward thinker, talked me into getting that hybrid pickup over there, and got him the first dang Prius hybrid in town, and he's got him a real nice place of his own, just down from my house, the one been in the family—"

"Dad," Hank said, in a tone that highlighted his red face.

"All I'm saying is that Hank's got him a nice house, a good job, and no wife."

"I'm engaged," I lied, knowing my devoted lover, Philip, would agree if he were not five hours away up to his chin in legal details preparing to defend his Cary Grant–like client from commercial spying charges of a grave criminal nature.

"Where's your ring?" Jubal asked, not so easy to throw off the hunt.

"Didn't want to hurt it or lose it, cleaning up this mess."

"Makes sense to me," Hank said, and grinned at me.

"Well, you just let us know. And me and Hank and some of his boys will be right here to help you. I can do it today, but Hank here has got to get back to school, he's just off on a lunch break. I work part-time over to the Tru Blue Drugstore now that I got too long in the tooth to keep logging. You need anything, I'll get you my store discount."

After I watched them drive off, I dashed for Dan's house to shower, check in with Bonita, and eat.

Country singers like to sing about being down to their last bottom dollar, or their last bottle of wine. But what had me worried was how quickly I was getting down to my last box of Save the Forest Organic Trail Mix Bars.

chapter 13

Well, it's all right. It's noon, and I've got two more bottles of kefir.

I sang this to myself, over and over, as I waited for Patti's percolator to perk some coffee. My cell phone peeped, and I picked it up.

"I do not like this situation at all."

"Dr. Hodo?"

"Dr. Weinstein is adamant about keeping the Thorazine dose the same, and refuses to accept me as Willette's psychiatrist."

"Dan will have power of attorney or a guardianship shortly, I'll have him speak to Dr. Weinstein, and put you down as her official physician. And take Dr. Weinstein off the case."

"Speak to Simon McDowell too," Dr. Hodo said.

"That gold-clad guy? What good would that do?"

"Simon runs a tight ship over there at the hospital."

"He does?" I didn't try to hide my surprise. "Are you sure?"

"Absolutely. He's turned that place around since he came on board last year. It's showing a profit for the first time since I've been licensed."

Ah, showing a profit was hardly the same thing as providing quality medical care, I thought, but decided in the interest of diplomacy not to say so. Showing a profit usually meant turning away sick people without insurance. Rather than comment on the ailing health-care system in our country, I stated the obvious closer to home.

"Willette needs to wake up, and eat, and tell us what happened."

"I'm aware of that. You mentioned your theory before. We are working toward the same goal here. But there are medical protocols. And until I have authority as her physician, I will not try to overrule Dr. Weinstein."

I blurted out an inelegant "Yeah, but," when Dr. Hodo cut me off. "Lilly, I don't need to explain the law to you. You need to get that power of attorney and straighten things out with Simon. I'll be back in touch." With that, he said good-bye and hung up.

Damn. Dan already had that hearing set before Judge Parker, but maybe Dr. Hodo was right about speaking with Simon McDowell. After all, if you want something done right, and you can't do it yourself, go all the way to the top person in charge—a lesson honed by living in a world of incompetence. So thinking, I called the hospital administrator, the overly solicitous Simon McDowell, at the number he'd scribbled on his card, and I told him once more that I would personally guarantee paying for my mother's psychiatric evaluation, and the family wanted Dr. Hodo in charge of Willette, and blah blah blah.

I had to question the man's good taste when he asked if I'd come by and sign paperwork to that effect, especially the part where I guaranteed payment, and oh, by the way, would I like to go to dinner with him?

chapter 14

My spine jolted a bit as my little Honda Civic jarred along at a brisk pace over a corrugated dirt road, while Shalonda sang a song I'd never heard before but might have liked if my mind wasn't filled with my own chorus of *hurry, hurry*.

Boom, crash, and we sailed up in the air a tad much for normal bodily comfort after I hit a deep wash in the road.

"White girl, 'less you planning on junking this baby car and paying for me to see a chiropractor, you might want to slow it down."

Slowing down was not something I had any interest in.

Catching the heretofore unknown Judge Parker *was* something I was interested in. I needed to cross paths with the good judge away from the courthouse, as if by accident, in a social setting, where I wouldn't come across as a pushy outsider, heathen lawyer from Florida, but as a dutiful daughter, seeking the man's kind help in a family matter.

And Judge Parker was at Demetrious's barn, checking up on his mule, a dainty little female named Faith. I knew this because Shalonda had told me so, back in the hospital, just moments before I dragged her out of there and we got into the Civic to hurl ourselves toward Judge Parker's last known destination.

As soon as Shalonda had mentioned that visiting-his-mule thing, it had hit me: the perfect plan. Shalonda and Demetrious could introduce me to the judge, say great things about me, allude to the tragedy of my poor mother and her legal limbo and the resulting stalemate with the law and the hospital. Then I'd charm the judge while he was petting his mule, and wheedle him into signing an order appointing Dan as Willette's legal guardian. I had a nice, clean copy of the order sitting on the backseat of my car.

But first I needed to see the judge.

The very judge, I might add, that Dan and his lady lawyer had utterly failed an hour before to convince to sign the same simple order. This, despite the fact that no one objected. When Dan had caught me at his house and told me that Judge Parker had declined to appoint him as his own mother's legal guardian on the spot, I'd bit my tongue to keep from cursing. Reserved ruling, that was what Dan had said the judge had done.

No matter how many questions I had thrown at Dan, I couldn't get any better answer than that he just thought the judge wanted to think about it overnight.

What was there to think about? Frustrated, I had hopped into my car, gone to the hospital, signed those papers for Simon, and popped my head in to visit with Shalonda and Willette.

Not that I was getting any fonder of the hospital, but compared to cleaning out Willette's house, it had a certain appeal. Plus, I'd had the chance to unload on Shalonda about Judge Parker not signing the order. Which was when Shalonda had sparked our current adventure.

"He's just in a hurry to go and see his mule," Shalonda had said.

"His mule?"

"Boards her, Faith's her name, with Demetrious. This is his regular visiting day. Plus, Judge Parker, truth be told, ain't one to make snap decisions."

Snap decisions? He'd had an hour to mull on it by now. He just needed a little push. Obviously, Dan's lawyer might have had the home-court favorite status in a courtroom that I didn't, but she lacked my motivation.

And my persuasive talents. So, how hard could it be to convince this judge to sign up Dan to take over Willette's legal decisions?

And before Shalonda could say "No, thank you," I had her in the passenger side of my Honda, bouncing her along the dirt road to the barn.

We had left Willette temporarily in the care of Patti Lea, who had just stopped by to check on her and pick up a pound cake, and she said seeing as how it was cool and clean in Willette's room, she'd stay as long as I needed her, and for us not to hurry.

Frankly, I think Patti was looking forward to sitting and doing nothing. After all the work she'd done, I didn't blame her, and off Shalonda and I had sailed, to bend the good judge to my way of thinking.

And that's why we were crashing along the dirt road to Demetrious's barn, with Judge Parker the big thing on my mind. Banging my Honda about on the backest of the back roads, I'd just been turning where Shalonda told me to turn. Instead of paying attention to my surroundings, I had been formulating my presentation to Judge Parker. Until a series of canal-size ruts in the dirt road forced me to slow down near a turnoff to an even narrower road with a NO TRESPASSING sign on the gate of a long fence. At once, I recognized the ancient live oak tree with the long, drooping limb that scraped the ground parallel to the roadway. I skidded the car to a halt, and then backed up, Shalonda snapping her neck and giving me the eye like I was a crazy woman.

I jumped out of the car and stared around me. I took in the distinctive sweep of the live oak with its draping branch along the road. Resurrection ferns fanned themselves green in the breeze, telling me it had rained of late and they had unfurled in the showers.

"That's the way to my grandmother's place," I said, and felt like someone had just put their hands around my throat and squeezed.

"Sure is," Shalonda said, having gotten out of the car to stand by me. "I think 'bout her a lot. You and me and Delvon sure had some fun hanging out with her. She was one cool lady."

I thought about her all the time. Sometimes I even talked with her, but

I never mentioned this to anyone. Just a secret between Grandmom and me, this talking. No reason to let a little thing like her being dead stop the bond between us.

"You know who's living there now, don't you, in your grandmomma's house?" Shalonda asked.

Yeah, Lonnie Ledbetter, ex–high school heartthrob, almost country music star, and now the county commissioner that had sold out Jubal and Hank. Ever since he'd bought that house from my mother three years ago, I'd written Lonnie every three or four months, trying to buy the house and property back from him. But without educating Shalonda on that history, I said, "That Lonnie Ledbetter owns it."

"Nope, not anymore," Shalonda said. "He sold it. No more, I don't reckon, than two weeks ago."

"What? Who to?" I asked, shouting so that Shalonda shot me that look of concern again. Then I wondered why Dan hadn't thought to mention this.

"To that Simon McDowell, the hospital administrator," Shalonda said.

"Simon?"

"Yeah. Simon."

It took me a few gulped breaths to get my mind fully around the notion that Lonnie had sold my grandmother's place, even after he had personally and in writing promised to offer it first to me if he ever even just thought about selling it.

Then I had to say "damn" with a few variations, while Shalonda studied me. Then I had to grill Shalonda. "*Simon?* The hospital Simon? What's his story? I mean, why's he want to live out here in the country? In my grandmother's house?"

"You got to ask him." Shalonda shook her head. "Those folks that hired him think we were real lucky to get him to come here and run our hospital, but I'm not so sure 'bout that. Used to be head of the sales part of a drug company out of New Jersey, 'fore he came down here. Now I want to know how that qualifies him to run a hospital?"

But for the moment, I couldn't worry about Simon's resume. I was still working on calming down.

Hellfire and damnation. Lonnie had sold that house not to someone who knew Grandmom and would cherish the property and honor the house as a shrine, but to a former pharmaceutical sales rep who had probably never even lived in the country in his whole life. A damn drug rep from a city up North. He wasn't going to know squat about tending those blueberries Grandmom had prided herself on, or the peach trees.

"You being a lawyer, I want you to tell me, how's selling drugs make that man a hospital administrator?"

Maybe Shalonda had a point about qualifications. Still, I guessed small-town hospitals like the one in Bugfest couldn't be too choosy; I mean, a Harvard-educated M.B.A. with experience running a Chicago hospital probably wouldn't apply for the job. And what did I know about Simon anyway, other than he wore gold and just missed being a good-looking guy because of that goofy hyper thing he had going. Oh, and those unnaturally long arms. Maybe he'd run a few hospitals somewhere after he'd quit peddling drug samples.

So, I jerked my mind away from Simon's track record and back to the main issue, that being my grandmother's place. My quest to regain her house had just been yanked one rung further out of my hands. With Lonnie, I figured I would wear him down, or he'd go broke again and need to sell it in a hurry, and I'd get the house back. Now that didn't seem so likely.

Stunned, I stood, looking down the road to the house where my grandmother had given me the closest thing I'd ever had to a happy family life. I was thinking about the red brick arch on the front porch, and the warm wood floors, and the stone fireplace, and the kitchen where she could cook up just about anything without ever looking at a recipe, and the cool, dark den, with rows and rows of her homemade jellies and jams lining the bookcases. And thinking of her sitting in the living room in the evening, in her low red Naugahyde chair with the matching footstool, when the day's chores were done, telling me stories, Granddaddy sipping his whiskey and keeping time with the rhythm of her voice with his "Un-hum, that's right."

When my grandfather died, years after Grandmom had already crossed over, he left the house and the remaining forty acres to my mother, his only child. And despite the best efforts of Delvon and me, and a real estate agent, Willette had sold my grandmother's house out from under me. Probably out of spite, I'd always thought. And now, damn it all, that Lonnie, that snake, had sold it to a hyper New Jersey guy.

My grandmother's house, in the hands of a carpetbagger.

"You all right, white girl?" Shalonda asked.

How did I explain to Shalonda that the house down that road was the only place I had ever felt safe. "Hey, let's go take a quick look at the old place." I tried to force a chipper quality I didn't feel into my voice. The idea of poking around while Simon was not there to interfere had a lot of immediate appeal.

"I wouldn't mind 'cept we need to get on down to the barn. Judge Parker's habit is to check on Faith, take a quick ride, gossip with Demetrious, and head back for a few more rounds of being a judge at the courthouse."

"Yeah, okay," I said, letting go of the notion slowly. "I guess I can get Simon to show me around later. I've got kind of a date with him."

Shalonda made a rude noise deep in her throat, and I turned to stare at her. "Okay, spit it out. What've you got to say about Simon? Doesn't sound much like you like him."

"I don't," Shalonda said.

"Why?"

"Man got me fired, that's how come."

"Fired? From the hospital? For what?"

"No, I didn't work for the hospital, I worked for the county mental health department. Simon got me fired 'cause he said I 'sassed' him."

"Sassed him? Did you?"

"Hell, yeah, I sassed that man. He came in a patient's room and started telling me how to do my job, and he ain't no doctor and he ain't no social worker, and he ain't no boss of mine."

"And he got you fired for . . . asserting your rights? This is what, 1950?"

"He's a big important white man from up North, and he got my ass fired, okay?"

We got back into the car and I started driving, mulling over this new information in my tired brain. Let's see, *a big important white man from up North*. What was the operative issue there, I wondered. Race? Gender? Up North? I opened my mouth to ask Shalonda, but she said, "I don't want to talk 'bout it, okay?"

"But how did he—"

"Hey, white girl, the old cemetery. You remember?"

Good change-the-subject move by Shalonda. And hell yeah, I remembered that cemetery. Right there, backed up to my grandmother's place. Shalonda knew that cemetery had always fascinated me, and I slowed the car down, stopping this time without hitting the brakes. I had been scared silly of the place as a young child, what with the stories everybody told about the Confederate dead buried there that got up at night and prowled around, looking for Yankees to kill, and the man they hung back in the 1880s, supposed to rise out of his grave on full moons and eat little children.

"Can you believe what the grown-ups used to tell us to keep us out of there?" I said, just a smidgen mad at the recollection of being frightened away from what we later discovered was prime real estate for having youthful indiscretions in.

There was a high fence, and a locked gate around the graveyard now. Things sure change. When I was a kid, nobody around these parts bothered with a fence unless they were running cows. Even then, you were as likely to find a cattle guard across the road as a gate.

Just inside the gate was a battered but still legible sign, which I read out loud: "No burial without permission. See Jubal."

"Yeah, got to watch them unlawful burials," Shalonda said. "I know that keeps the high sheriff real busy."

"Jubal Williams?" I asked.

"Yep. Nobody's been burying anybody here in, oh, I reckon thirty years or more. Not officially anyway. No telling what goes on unofficially in these red hills. But Jubal convinced the county to take care of the place, so he's the caretaker now. That man's purely making a profession off part-time jobs," she said. "Yet, hear him talk, he's not making enough to live on."

"Well, I don't reckon Hank'll let him go hungry," I said.

"Man's got his pride," Shalonda said.

"Well, looks like he's doing a good job," I said. The old place had always had a kind of crumbling gloom about it, what with the Confederate dead and all those rows of tiny stones covered with moss and giving way to the elements, marking the burial sites of the children dead from diverse fevers and the hard lives and hunger of Reconstruction, followed by the more publicized poverty of the Great Depression. But now the old grounds seemed better tended.

"What about the church?" I asked.

"Yep, that church's still down there. Least the building. The county bought out the church and the cemetery last year, now that the church folks meet inside Johnson's Hardware, what went out of business after that big Lowe's opened over to Thomasville," Shalonda said.

As I gave the Honda the gas, I had to ask. "Is the place still haunted?"

"White girl, it's a graveyard, what do you think?"

I laughed.

But as we sped away, I had to wonder if those Confederate haunts could ever find any peace.

chapter 15

As the cosmic forces had surely decreed that I would not meet any of my set goals for the day, naturally we completely missed the good judge.

Demetrious was currying a beaut of a black mule when we drove up, and he kissed Shalonda and shook hands with me. But the judge was gone, he said, and then explained that Judge Parker had been running behind because of an emergency hearing—I figured that was Dan's—so he'd just had time to feed Faith a few carrots, chat a spell, and hightail it back to town.

Well, damn.

"Since you're here, you might as well take a look around," Shalonda said.

"Would you like to take Faith for a little ride, since the judge didn't get to?" Demetrious asked. "I'd go with you, but I've got a lot of work still to do with BB, getting him ready for those blue ribbons at Mule Day."

"Some other time," I said. "It's a nice offer, really, but I left Patti Lea with Willette, and I've got a ton of things to do, and—"

"Sure," Demetrious said, and I had the notion he was relieved.

So, after a quick spin around the barn and a promise to come back and see their house, poof, back into my little Honda car we piled, and I thought, well, hell, that was a waste of time.

Going out the same way we'd come in, I jammed on the brakes again by the live oak that marked the turn to Grandmom's house.

"You game?" I asked. "I mean, now that we're not hurrying to catch the judge?"

Shalonda was definitely up for the trip down memory lane, no-trespassing sign or not. I mean, after all, what's a little transgression like trespassing between friends? Naturally, the gate was locked, and it seemed easier just to park the car and climb over that gate rather than bust the lock so we could drive in.

Okay, yeah, this was sort of like playing hooky. But then Patti Lea was probably still enjoying the peace and quiet of sitting in the hospital room, not having to chat a bit with her mother-in-law or tote out rank garbage.

Walking down that shaded, narrow road, I might have gotten all weepy and weird about being on the way to my grandmother's house, but I was distracted by a loud mechanical noise that roared up from the other side of the road.

Turning toward the noise, I saw a hint of a trail and a woman with a big head of blond hair riding on an ATV. Shalonda said a very loud "oh, shit," and before I could ask her anything, I heard the big-haired woman yelling over the sound of her big, noisy motorized tricycle. She was yelling racial slurs aimed at Shalonda.

I jerked back around to Shalonda, whose face was turning an unbecoming shade of purple.

"That damn Yankee woman with her trash mouth, I can't believe Lonnie married her," Shalonda said. And she bent over and picked up a big chunk of a fallen limb. "You better get you a stick," she said. "A big one."

While I was trying to register exactly what Shalonda could possibly mean by that, a pack of dogs came howling toward us from around the loud woman and her louder ATV. And thrashing through the brush, right directly at me, the innocent bystander on a quest to visit my grandmother's home, were two truly ugly, mean-looking curs.

And me without a dog cookie.

chapter **16**

If a swanky Miami trial attorney had come at me with a scurrilous motion for anything, even disbarment, I would have known precisely what counterattack to make.

If any of my cowboy law partners had come at me with anything even vaguely resembling sexual harassment, I would have known precisely where to kick.

But there I was, on a dirt road, utterly clueless as to the best evasive action to take in the face of two big, mean dogs.

As I scrambled for my own big stick, the alpha dog—a huge pit bull–looking animal—grabbed my left pant leg with such ferocity that I tumbled down into the dirt. Luckily, what Pit Bull Dog had in its mouth was my blue jeans and not skin, but I saw another cur advancing, teeth bared. As I tried to pull free and roll away, I saw I was aiming myself right at a big patch of poison ivy on the side of the road.

Trapped between a pit bull and poison ivy, another dog advancing. There was, of course, in all of this, the perfect analogy to modern litigation with Miami attorneys, but I was too busy tussling around with the mad dog to work out the nuances.

Shalonda, who'd been forward enough in her thinking to have already armed herself, thumped Pit Bull on the head with her stick, and then, for good measure, thunked the beta-dog cur. Sensing, no doubt, a will much greater than their own, the dogs yipped, spun, and ran off.

Shalonda helped me to my feet. "You all right there, Lilly Belle?"

All right being a relative term, I decided to go with the definition that loosely translated into *doesn't need CPR or blood transfusions,* and I said I was.

The mean-mouthed woman, apparently afraid we might have missed the point of her rage toward us, shouted out, "You black whore, get your ass out of here."

But proving herself a coward, the woman called in the dogs and they all ran away.

"Colleen, Lonnie's wife," Shalonda said to me, as if introductions could smooth over the anger. Her face was still purple. "You sure you all right?" she asked me again.

"Are you all right?" I asked right back.

"Yeah. I mean . . . yeah, I'm okay."

"So, what was that about?"

"They, that is Lonnie and that bitch, bought that old Victorian over on the other side of Curtis's place, you know, just a few miles down the big road, not far from here. She likes to roam around in the country like she owns all of it. But I reckon it's better than when we had 'em living practically next door," Shalonda said. "It's still too damn close, though."

"But what was . . . I mean, that woman is vile and contemptible."

"Yep, she's that all right. *Contemptible,* eh? Ain't that a nice lawyer word for *trashy as shit.* You didn't get in any of that poison ivy, did you?"

"So . . . ?"

"This thing with Colleen. See, she hates me."

Yeah, being college-educated and all, I'd pretty much figured that out from the things Colleen had yelled at Shalonda. "Why?" I asked. "You seem like a real nice woman to me, kind of tenderhearted even."

"Well, it's Lonnie. Him and me. We had . . . this thing right after high school. Carried it over to college. But him being this blond future country-music star that was going to run for Congress after his string of hit records and all, he quit me. Truth was, he was aiming for trading up."

"Hey, there weren't any flies on you, and you were headed for the Olympics," I said.

"Well, yep, and I might've got to the Olympics, but, hell, stuff happens. Lonnie and me, that's part of what happened. When that man broke up with me, I got so blue I quit college for a while so's I wouldn't be running into him. I came on home, and we plain lost track of each other."

So far, it sounded like a typical high-school-to-college romance. Only person I knew who had actually married his high school sweetheart was my brother Dan. But the way Shalonda was telling it made me think maybe there was a part of her that had never really gotten over Lonnie.

"And when things didn't work out for Lonnie either in Nashville or up North, he came back, married. Only he didn't bring his wife right off, and he didn't tell me 'bout her, and I didn't know Demetrious yet, and . . . well, you know."

"So, y'all had another little fling, and Colleen heard about it when she did get to town?"

"Yep. And when I found out that man had him a wife he hadn't bothered to mention till she showed up in person, I hit him upside the head so hard she had to take his white ass to the ER."

"Demetrious know?"

"White girl, you forget where you're at? Everybody knows."

She paused, with a dramatic air, and I said, "Okay, what's the rest of the story?"

"That's how I met Demetrious. See, Colleen called the cops on me, and Demetrious investigated. He was a detective then, on his way right up to being the first African-American chief of police."

"He arrest you?"

"Naw, he made one of those police-officer-on-the-street judicial determinations, and told Colleen it was justified, and she's been mean-mouthing us both ever since."

That wasn't all I wanted to hear on the matter of Shalonda's life since high school, but Shalonda looked at her watch. "Damn, we better get back to your car. I've had 'bout enough of white folks yelling at me today, and I'm not taking any chances on Simon catching us hotfooting down his road. That Colleen is just as likely to call him and report us for trespassing as she is to spit on me."

I peered at my own watch. It wasn't even close to five yet. I wondered if Simon would leave work on the word of a vile big-haired woman so he could catch us walking down his gated road. For me, I would have taken the chance; I mean, after all, he wasn't going to shoot us, but something about the set of Shalonda's jaw told me it was time to get back to town.

After a quick jog back down Simon's private road, we jumped into the Honda and roared off toward town.

But when Shalonda didn't go back to singing, I went back to asking questions.

"Have the resort folks threatened y'all with eminent domain proceedings to get your property?"

"Not the county or the resort folks, no. That marina and resort are planned for the eastern shore of what's now Little Sleepy Lake, and will be Big Sleepy Lake. Only they're gonna call it something fancy. Takes in all of Jubal and Hank's place. Then the housing subdivision is set for the southeastern area, where access to I–10 and U.S. 319 is easiest. The flooding to make the big lake will all be on the north shore, so those of us here on the southwestern and western corner are okay. For now."

"So, nobody's tried to buy you out?"

"Oh, yeah. Several times. Folks figure the housing development will spread to us eventually. We keep saying no just as loud and plain as we know how, but they keep sending folks out here. But so far nobody's offered us much, probably because we're off from where the main roads are."

"What about my grandmom's place?"

"Hadn't heard a thing about that. You'd have to ask Simon."

Yeah, I had a few things to ask Simon, didn't I?

chapter 17

Deep in the heart of Dixie lay a deep freeze with jelly eggs.

What the hell was that all about anyway, I wondered, as I steered my ancient Honda into the parking lot of the appliance store that had sent two deliverymen to Willette's house, with something that seemed to have started all this muddle.

And since nobody else was showing the slightest interest in finding out what, Demetrious being all caught up with getting Big Beauty ready for Mule Day, it was up to me to figure it out.

As soon as I pushed my way inside the doors of the store, a short man with a beak nose and a tuft of hair around his round head stuck out his hand at me and asked, "Can I hep you?"

Yes, of course he could, if he knew anything and was loose of tongue. "Do you have anything to do with delivering deep freezes and refrigerators?"

"We can deliver anything to anyone inside the county limits, you jes' pick out what you want, only fifty dollar extra."

"Only? Fifty?" I glanced at the used appliances along the side of the wall and thought half of them weren't even worth fifty dollars. But what

I said was, "Do you know anything about a deep freeze delivered to Willette Cleary's house and left on her porch?"

He frowned at me. "You're not from here, are you?" he asked.

"I grew up here."

His expression suggested he didn't believe me. My expression suggested I didn't care.

"About that deep freeze—"

"I didn't have nothing to do with that," he said, and took not one but two steps backward.

"What about the two deliverymen? Are they available?"

"No, ma'am, they up and quit and took jobs in Valdosta."

"Then I need to speak to the person who was in charge of that delivery."

"He ain't here," Short Man said, taking another step backward. "Ain't a coming back, I don't reckon."

"Who's he?"

"Our assistant manager, Ray Glenn, he's the one that crazy old woman done shot dead."

"Permit me to introduce myself. I'm Lilly Cleary, attorney at law, and the daughter of 'that crazy old woman.'"

At that, Short Man jumped back from me several steps at once. "I don't got nothing to say to you." And he literally ran back into an office and slammed the door.

Well, that was interesting, I thought, and started right after him until I realized he had left me alone and unguarded.

There being no one else in the store, customer or employee, I glanced around a bit, thought things grossly overpriced and over-dusty, and then I rifled in earnest through some loose paperwork on the desk in the corner by a phone. Bunch of bills, delivery orders, but not a single thing with a Cleary name on it. There was a computer sitting right there on the desk, and in no time at all, I was looking at all the accounts receivable. There it was, still listed: Willette Cleary owed them $600 in round figures for a refrigerator, and the store was adding interest weekly. Mentally, I started drafting the threatening letter on my law firm's glossy letterhead, fully intending to scare the pants off the new debt collector.

After playing around some more on the computer, searching inside all the desk drawers, and finding little of interest or value, I figured there was nothing else I could plunder through. I picked up a phone book and I looked up Ray Glenn's address, repeated it a couple of times to myself, and left.

Frustrated, but with my trouble radar on full alert, I drove by the address the phone book gave for Ray Glenn Fussele. The house was one of those fake *Gone With the Wind* things with tacky but expensive pseudo-Grecian columns out front, and a big yard. Even by Bugfest standards, this house didn't come cheap. I pulled into the circle driveway, got out, and pounded on the front door. No one answered—not unexpected, given that the owner was dead and left no family behind, according to the obit I'd hastily read in the local newspaper.

Not one to pass up golden opportunities, I peered in the windows and did a quick risk-benefit analysis of breaking in, but ruled it out for now, because it was broad-open daylight. But I definitely wondered how a bill collector and assistant manager could afford such an expensive house.

While I was still stalking the premises, a big car drove up. I watched as a blond man jumped out of the driver's seat and hustled over toward me, poised as I was, looking in a side window of the big house.

Great. Probably the president of the Home Owners Security Team or something. I busied my mind for the best lie, and then stared at the man gaining on me.

Well, damn, it looked like none other than Big Lonnie Ledbetter himself. That is, if my memory adjusted for twenty years of aging had conjured up the right face.

It was almost karmic, I thought, staring at Lonnie as he stopped right smack-dab in front of me, seeing as how I was definitely interested in yelling at him for selling my grandmother's house to Simon McDowell without first offering it to me per my repeated written requests.

"Liar and double-crosser," I said. "You son of a bitch. You betrayed me."

The man stopped sauntering toward me, and stared hard, and for a moment I wondered if I had just yelled at the wrong person.

But then he flipped his blond bangs out of his eyes in a gesture I remembered, and I noticed he still had the same damn haircut as he did way back when.

"You lied, and you broke your promise, and you betrayed me, you skunk," I shouted.

We glared at each other for a moment.

"I know you?" he asked.

And this from a man I had once had a huge and stupid crush on. I hated remembering my infatuation, embarrassed I'd been caught in the act of being typical, falling for the high school's own version of a future Nashville star, the guy who played guitar and sang a bit like Vince Gill.

Lonnie hadn't much returned my crush, though I had to admit in my memories, he had been nice enough to me. And, as we went round two in our staring contest, I had to admit he was still a fine-looking man, though I could see the soft belly under his knit polo. Still a big, strapping blond, more California surfer than country-western, even if he wasn't keeping up his gym membership. No wonder he could sweet-talk himself into being a county commissioner in no time at all—tall and handsome still gets votes.

Looking at Lonnie now made me remember the last time I had seen him, at my high school graduation. That night, packed in with the other graduating seniors on the football field, all I could think about was this: Getting Out. My parents had not bothered to attend graduation, my grandmother was dead, and Delvon and Farmer Dave were in Atlanta, making a delivery of some homegrown weed. Only my grandfather and my brother Dan had come to the ceremony to see me graduate, and they had to leave early when Granddad had a sinking spell, brought on no doubt by the half bottle of Black Jack he'd consumed to get the energy to go in the first place.

So, while the other graduates threw their hats in the air and made goofy cheers, secure in the bosoms of their family's love and pride, I had glared at the field in front of me, empty as it was of my own kith and kin, and sworn I would leave this town and never come back.

That night, Lonnie had snuck up behind me, grabbed me, spun me around, and kissed me. On the mouth. Our lips had parted, our tongues had flickered, he had fondled my breast and my butt. Then he'd let go of me and said, and I remember it as if I had written it down, "Baby, you're the one that got away."

Of course, later I'd heard he'd copped a feel and used the same line on several girls. But, hey, I was seventeen, and I floated off that football field, and went back to the emptiness of the house I shared with Farmer Dave and Brother Delvon, and I felt like a girl who *had* been wanted by the high school hotshot. The feeling didn't last, but it had felt good for that hour or so it took me to pack everything I owned and hit the highway out of town. *Gone* was all I put on my note to Dave and Delvon.

All those years ago, I thought, and stared at Lonnie as he stared at me. Didn't even recognize me, even with all of my letters to keep my name fresh in his mind.

"Why in damnation did you sell my grandmother's house when you knew perfectly well I wanted it, and you had promised me you'd let me know—"

"Lilly Belle? Is that you?"

"You no-good, sorry S.O.B., liar, why—"

Lonnie grabbed me and kissed me, shutting me up in early rant. Like this stupid dream repeat, our lips parted, our tongues flickered, and he fondled my breast and my butt.

It took me a moment to regroup, but I did. I slapped him and went right back to yelling.

"Oh, baby, I always knew I'd regret letting you get away from me. *You* are the one that got away."

The man was still using the same bull after twenty years? Okay, nobody said country-singers-turned-appliance-store-owners-and-county-commissioners had to be *that* smart, but really? It so stunned me I forgot to slap him again, or to yell at him.

Lonnie rubbed his face and grinned. "I'd heard you were back in town, and I've been meaning to come by, tell you how sorry I am about your momma."

All said nicely, politician-salesman fake-sincere. I nodded on polite reflex, but I was not taken in.

"What are you doing here at Ray Glenn's?" he asked.

"What are you doing here?"

"Looking. Figured it'd be up for sale, and it'll be a good investment. This town is growing, and with that lake and the resort coming in, rich folks are going to start moving in, make us a golden retirement community, like Florida. Boom time, big land boom. Why there's even plans for the Cherokees to put in a casino near that new lake. This place—hey, anybody tell you I'm a county commissioner now?"

"Yes, you, in every letter you wrote after you got elected and promised me you'd give me right of first refusal if you ever wanted to sell my grandmother's place."

"Come here and let me hug you again," Lonnie said.

"You're, you are . . ." I paused, trying to figure out how to approach this, but then I thought suddenly of Jubal and Hank as if they had been real clients. And I wondered if there was any turning Lonnie back, recanting his commission vote on this marina land-grab big-lake-development thing. "Have you thought about what your vote to join forces with that resort is doing to the citizens around that lake, people who voted for you? Any chance you'd change your mind?" Okay, yeah, spank me, totally lacking in subtlety or grace and manipulative ploys, but all that takes time and I wasn't planning on camping out in Bugfest that long.

"Oh, Lilly Belle, that's just business. You don't want to get into that. Come on, let's talk ole times. We had 'em, didn't we?"

No, we hadn't had any old times together, and having a country-boy nitwit dismiss me with "it's just business" pushed a couple of buttons. In other words, I forgot Jubal and Hank's problem in light of my own grievances. I launched again at Lonnie, turncoat sexist that he was.

"I'm a partner in Sarasota's biggest law firm [this is true], sonny, and I routinely handle high-end, complex business deals [this isn't true, but made my point] that you couldn't understand if I diagramed them in red highlighter [this would be true if I weren't lying]. And furthermore, I could sue you for breach of a promissory contract." This was blatantly bull, as there is no cause of action for a plain old-fashioned broken promise, but I didn't figure Lonnie with his degree in failed prior enterprises was likely to know that, and I wanted him as upset as I was.

"Ain't that a shame, you feeling that way about your grandmomma's place," Lonnie said. "But truth be told, Lilly Belle, I got an offer I couldn't refuse." And the idiot grinned big, like he was the first and only person to use that old cliché.

After that, Lonnie bent over backward apologizing, but never explained why he hadn't contacted me to see if I could match the offer, the amount of which he was frustratingly vague about. I began to wind down. "What's done is done" was something my grandmother had often said.

And, I mean, it wasn't like I ever planned to live here again.

So, even knowing Lonnie wasn't sincere in his apologies, I let him off the hook, and said, "What's done is done."

After all, I had bigger fish to catch and fry than this idiot.

chapter 18

There is something about not being in my own bed that means I can't sleep.

Actually, I don't sleep much in my own bed, but at least I know it's an organic, clean bed. I sniffed my oldest nephew's bed—it smelled like Tide. He was away at college, and I was glad I didn't have to crash in a hotel, and I was glad of the Tide, as that meant the sheets had been recently washed, but I wondered what the mattress was made out of, and then I punched the pillows, which were big and puffy. Me, I like a flat pillow.

When I couldn't make these pillows flat by pounding on them, I tried no pillows. But, in thirty seconds, my neck hurt.

I sighed in the dark room, rolled off the bed, clicked on the light, and scouted the bookshelves for reading materials. No way. Not unless I wanted to read my nephew's high school algebra book or any number of his books on football.

I decided to just sit up and worry. After all, I'd been tossing and turning and worrying, so I might as well just go with the flow. Worry is like that, sometimes you just have to sit with it awhile.

So, what I was mostly worried about right then was that Judge Parker had reserved ruling on Dan's motion to be appointed Willette's guardian, and he'd also escaped my plan to snare him into signing the order at Demetrious's barn. Tomorrow, if he didn't sign that order, I'd have to figure out another social setting to just happen to pounce on him—with that spare copy of the order handy, of course.

And so, here we were, I thought, letting the worry out of the worry box to study on it, still without any one of us having a clear-cut legal right to act on Willette's part, the weirdly territorial Dr. Weinstein still in charge and still overmedicating Willette and still absent from my sight, and the question of what to do with Willette legally still hovering, waiting for Demetrious to interview her when she stopped being comatose and psychotic. Had I missed anything? Oh yeah, global warming. When the ice caps all melted and the sea levels rose, Sarasota would be under water and my house would be worth exactly squat times squat.

Okay, sitting in my nephew's bedroom with my worry was suffocating. The outside world seemed to be calling me.

Bobby, being a teenager and all, could sleep through Armageddon, and Patti and Dan were at the hospital sitting up all night with Willette, so I could bang around if I wanted to. Thinking about fresh air and moonlight and stars, I slipped out to the front porch, and sat down on the glider. The cool early-dawn air settled on me, damp and clean, and I inhaled and exhaled, doing my alternate-nostril yoga breathing, and thinking I was getting behind on my exercise and ought to take a long run.

Which is where I was when a blond teenage girl came tiptoeing out the front door and about choked when she saw me.

"Oh, my gosh," she said, by way of hello.

"I'm Lilly, Bobby's aunt," I said, sizing her up immediately as the girl-friend I'd heard mention of and not, say, a hardened criminal intent upon killing us all.

"Becky," she said, and quickly composed herself, offering me her dainty hand. "I'm so pleased to meet you. Bobby just loves you."

I shook her hand, and looked into her face. Just too cute to be real, I thought, plus quick and light on her feet.

"I'm, er, visiting, I mean, Bobby and I were studying, and I, see, I just fell asleep."

"I'm not a hall monitor, or a parent," I said, and smiled. Hell, when I was her age, I was living with a guy and growing marijuana for a living. I try real hard in my life not to pitch that first stone.

Becky smiled back at me, a little cautiously but not in an unfriendly way.

It didn't take long for me to get the story, though we had to work through a few more creative plot lines first. Becky had told her mom she was spending the night with a girlfriend—I mean, really, don't mothers remember these tricks from their own youth? Now Becky had to hotfoot it to her friend's house in time for the girlfriend's mother to feed her breakfast and report to Becky's own mother that her darling daughter was indeed where she was supposed to be.

I promised to keep Becky's secret, and resolved to have my own version of the Safe-Sex Chat with Bobby. But I wasn't going to report Becky and Bobby to either's parents. I wasn't a tattletale.

And I was all for young love.

chapter 19

Life has this nasty way of following moments of pure sweetness with moments of utter hell. I've decided that aside from the natural yin-and-yang thing, this is all about the cosmic forces wanting us to—no, demanding that we—take nothing for granted. And, too, that we must stay vigilant and be ready.

So, yeah, I should have been more *ready*. Here I was, all smiley with the thoughts of Bobby and Becky, teenagers in love, and just how incredibly cute they were. I stood and stretched in the early-morning mist, and decided that rather than jog through the town in the predawn gloom, I'd give that borrowed bed one more chance.

Truly, the bed felt warm and toasty when I crawled back into it. A little drowsy weight started pulling the lids down at the corners of my eyes.

Another minute, I might have nodded off, except I looked at the end of the bed and I saw a ghost standing on the wood floor and staring straight at me.

And not just any ghost. But the ghost of my grandmother.

I closed my eyes. Sometimes stress makes me see things.

After I counted to ten, I opened my eyes.

My grandmother still stood before me. As plain as the pattern of deer on the flannel sheets.

I sat up in the bed, staring at her, my heart banging against my rib cage so hard it seemed to be ricocheting in my head. On a cool fall morning, sweat trickled into my eyes and burned so I had to blink.

My grandmother wouldn't have journeyed over that line we all draw but rarely cross unless something scary was afoot in the small town of Bugfest.

It's one thing that my long-dead grandmother talks to me. But to appear before me, dressed in a flowery housedress, so real I could almost smell the Avon talcum on her, meant something really big was up.

Really big.

"What?" I said.

No sense messing around with niceties when something like that happens.

"Go over to the hospital. Right now. Go. Your momma needs you."

Poof. Grandmom was gone.

I hopped up, tangled up in the sheets, and fell flat on my butt on the floor. From the floor, I scrambled up and dressed in the first clothes my hands touched. I ran out the door, my heart beating like I had drunk two gallons of coffee.

Or like I'd seen a ghost.

I broke a few speed limits on the short trip to the hospital, literally ran past the nurses' station, and dashed past a tiny, ancient man in uniform snoring in a chair outside Willette's room, no doubt the Otis Lee of the Bugfest Police Department's night shift.

I didn't pause to wake him, but shoved open the door to Willette's room.

No one was in the room except Willette. Who, I noted with some relief, seemed to be fine. From the doorway, I watched her chest rise and fall.

I exhaled.

Then I noticed something—a trail of movement around her, on the bed, on her. Dashing into the room, I got to her bedside, and looked closer at Willette, and screamed. I pushed the call button, and then frantically I began to brush her bedding, her face, her body. She and the bed were covered in ants. Fire ants. Red ants. One of the great curses of life in Deep Dixie.

"Help," I screamed, more articulate this time.

Then, for good measure, I belted out a long screech no one could ignore, and I stopped my frantic brushing to pick up the phone and hit 911. I shouted "Tell Demetrious to get to Willette's room now!" and dropped the phone. In a town this small, the 911 operator would know exactly what I meant.

Otis Lee was in the room with me now, and he said a quick, "Lord, have mercy," and set to work brushing bugs off Willette with his fast, thin arms. Then I poured the bedside pitcher of water over her face and, using the edge of a now-wet sheet, tried to wash the ants off her face and arms. I felt something sticky on her, but was too busy knocking fire ants into kingdom come to stop and analyze it.

In a minute or two, or maybe an hour, there were nurses and other people in the room, and after that, things moved fast. They had Willette physically out of the bed, and stripped down naked, and I have to say Otis Lee showed good manners and stepped out of the room while Willette was undressed. Using washcloths and hands, the nurses washed Willette clean of the fire ants, and a doctor was there, and filled her full of antihistamines.

In nothing flat, it seemed like a whole covey of nurses had prodded, tested, checked her blood pressure, and all such things.

"She doesn't have that many bites," a woman who appeared to be the alpha nurse said.

"One bite is too many," I snapped. "She's frail, and she's—"

"Let's move her to the ICU, then, for a precaution," the doctor said, eyeing me sideways, no doubt for my reaction.

While the nurses were bundling Willette up for her transfer to intensive care, Simon rushed in with the second round of the official help wagon, swinging those long arms, and he slipped up beside me, and took my hand, squeezed it tightly with his big hands. "Your mother will be fine, just fine. Just, really, fine."

Oh, not the right tactic.

"What the hell kind of hospital do you run here?" I shouted at him, and snatched my hand back. Also, I wondered who had called him this early.

"Now, Lilly, don't be rude," he said. "I know you are upset but—"

"Rude, my ass, you people have about killed my mother, not once but twice. I'm a lawyer and I'm going to sue the whole lot of you, and I'm transferring her out to a decent hospital, and I will file every complaint known to mankind until I close this rat hole, and I will sue you personally for gross negligence."

And then I stopped. Not because I was acting like a plaintiff. Not because I was running out of steam. But because in the middle of my outrage, I remembered something.

Negligence does, in fact, tend to repeat itself within the same confines; this, being a malpractice defense attorney, I knew for a fact. So, on the one hand, it made perfect sense that a hospital that would allow a patient to practically OD right there in its ER would also allow the same patient to be consumed by an army of small, dangerous insects.

And, yes, bad things happen in threes, so there was yet another shoe to drop.

So, yeah, this could have been just another stupid screwup.

But it wasn't. I knew this as surely as my grandmomma had sent me to save Willette from a terrible death.

Because what I remembered was this: The widespread publicity about the death of a woman in a Florida (naturally) nursing home, from fire-ant bites. The ants had crawled in from a window, and the woman had been too weak to brush them off, and no one heard her cries for help, and she

died from hundreds of bites. I hadn't been able to sleep for nights after I'd
read that story.

Of course, there was a big lawsuit. Of course, her family won. Of
course, there was national publicity.

Given that publicity, a lot of people would know about the case of the
old woman killed by fire ants. Anyone who read the newspaper articles, or
saw a blurb on TV, would know how easy it was to kill someone as frail as
Willette with something that seemed natural, like hundreds of tiny, toxic
bugs. I added this up with the bruises around Willette's jaw, and the near-
fatal OD, and I shook loose of Simon's grip again—can you believe that
man dared to grab my hand a second time? I looked Demetrious in the
eyes as he dashed toward me. "Thank you for coming in so quickly," I said,
my voice low and controlled. "Someone is trying to kill my mother."

A chorus of voices poked at me, Simon's dominating. "It's the cake
crumbs. They're all over the place. The ants—"

"The ants are deliberate," I said. "Someone got the idea from the nursing home case, where the red ants killed an old woman."

Everyone started talking at once. Except for me. I didn't need to talk
now.

Finally, I was calm. I knew exactly what to do: find out who was trying
to kill my mother, and why, and see to it he or she roasted slowly and
forever in hell.

chapter 20

Yeah, yeah, yeah, but I didn't care that nobody could figure out the mechanics of my theory. I mean, as everyone from Simon to the nurses was pointing out to me, murder by fire ants would be a tad tricky. How did the killer-wannabe get hundreds of fire ants into a hospital bed?

"Easy enough," I had snapped. "You go into any yard, any field, any peach orchard, and you dig them up."

"Then where is the dirt? If somebody dug up the ants, then the red dirt of the ant beds would still be with them, and look for yourself, Lilly, there's no dirt," Demetrious said, his voice steady and sensible, and, therefore, irritating.

"The bedding, did anybody check the bedding for dirt?" I asked, an octave or two above normal, polite levels.

"Honey, we were so busy getting that woman out of the bed, and getting the beddings changed, didn't none of us look for dirt," said alpha nurse, her voice equally steady and sensible and irritating.

"It's the damn cake crumbs," Simon said, for about the four hundredth time. "The ants came from around the window—you know they can get

in cracks we can't even see—and were attracted by the crumbs. You know what happens if you leave crumbs, especially sweet crumbs. Especially, very, very sweet crumbs."

"Then where is the trail? Do any of you see a trail of ants from the window to the bed?"

"Honey, we were all so busy saving your mamma, didn't none of us look for no trail of ants," alpha nurse said.

"And why in hell is she so doped up she can't even brush off fire ants, or scream? Look at her. She's like a dead woman."

Everybody turned and looked at Willette. In truth, she did look pitiful and nearly dead. Shallow breathing, and red welts and bites covered in white cream.

"She was sedated," the doctor said. "We've been over this and—"

"Then stop sedating her," I said to the doctor. "And who exactly are you?"

"Dr. Weinstein." He offered a hand and I took it out of reflex, but used the moment to actually focus on him. Short, stocky, trying to hide the balding process by spiking and dying the tufts of hair he had left, but still the man projected a lot of personal energy about him. With a good voice. And a strong handshake.

Okay, Lilly, I told myself, stop evaluating the man like he is your next potential client. Having thus chastised myself, I glared at the doctor as if all of this were his fault, then concluded that some of it—the over-medication, for example—*was* his fault.

"We gave her a good deal of antihistamines to counteract the poison from the bites. That will make her sleepy too," Dr. Weinstein said. "And we can't just stop her other medicines cold-turkey, we need to taper off and—"

"Then taper off. She shouldn't be so doped up she can't even tell she's being eaten alive by fire ants."

"Her dosage is a matter of careful medical deliberation," Dr. Weinstein said.

But what I heard in his patronizingly snide tone was: "What medical school did you go to?"

"I do not need a medical degree to know this woman is oversedated. She needs to come out of this and eat and talk and—"

"Yes, you've made your viewpoint well known," Dr. Weinstein said. "But first, let's get her to ICU and make sure she is stable. Then we will look at reducing her sedation."

Yes, yes, yes, everybody was so very accommodating.

I was being handled, placated, reasoned with, and humored.

But nobody had changed my mind.

I didn't know how the soulless person who had done this had gotten hundreds of ants to crawl in bed with Willette, but I knew as sure as I could spell *res ipsa loquitur* that someone had tried to murder my mother.

"There was something sticky on her," I said. "What if the killer put honey on her hands, arms, and face, and stuck her hand in a bucket filled with red ants? Wouldn't the ants naturally crawl out all over her to follow the honey?"

"Oh my Gawd, honey, I can sure promise you that some of us would've noticed if someone carrying a bucket of ants and a jar of honey passed us at the nurses' station," the alpha-nurse spokeswoman said.

"Well, that's how the Apaches did it in all those B-movie Westerns from the fifties, that is, stake out their victim and pour honey over him," Simon said, thoughtfully, and maybe, perhaps, beginning to lean a little in my favor.

"I always did wonder this, now where did the Apaches get honey in an Arizona desert?" Demetrious asked, and we all turned to look at him a minute.

I noticed that Otis Lee, who had come back unbidden into Willette's hospital room, didn't say anything. No doubt he knew he'd screwed up by falling asleep and was hoping if he kept quiet maybe nobody would fuss at him for that small dereliction of duty. A little bit of malfeasance that might have allowed a person armed with fire ants to glide quietly into Willette's room.

"Honey," I said, turning back to Alpha Nurse and hoping my sarcasm registered in my tone, "it was a long night. Don't tell me y'all didn't take a nap, or visit the john, or all gather around the coffeepot in that little room you hide the food in. Somebody watching with patience could have gotten by you when the desk was deserted." And here, I turned and stared at Otis Lee, who hung his head but maintained his silence.

"That desk is never completely empty," Simon said, and eyed the nurses. "And the nurses do not sleep on duty."

"Right," Alpha Nurse said.

"Right," another nurse said.

"Right," the nurse's aide said.

"My ass," I said.

The three women sucked in their breath at my words. I ignored them.

"Demetrious," I said, my own voice now a model of steady and sensible, "if you would be so kind as to see to it that my mother continues to have round-the-clock police protection, perhaps with shorter shifts so they can stay awake, until I can get her transferred out, I'd be ever so grateful."

He nodded.

"I'll see to getting her transferred as soon as possible, to Sarasota, so that there will not be an undue burden on any of you," I said. "Dr. Weinstein, when will it be medically safe to move her?"

"It depends—" was as far as the doc got before the chief of police asserted his authority.

"There's a matter of . . . jurisdiction," Demetrious said. "She's still in police custody."

"Well, then do whatever you have to do to transfer her to my custody," I snapped.

"Lillian, you are not law enforcement; I cannot do that," Demetrious said.

"There are medical reasons not to move her now, that is for sure," Dr. Weinstein said. "She's very weak, and—"

"And whose fault is that?" I snapped. "First the OD, now this—"

"It will take some time, but we will get it arranged," Simon said, no doubt with his risk-management radar on full alert. "I will see to that myself, coordinating the efforts between Chief Dupree and Dr. Weinstein. We'll have her in a hospital of your choice as soon as it is medically safe for her to be moved and the legal issues are resolved. You just tell me where you want her to go. I will help you. I promise." Simon looked at me, concern evident in his long face.

"I'll rotate the guards outside her door every four hours," Demetrious said.

"Outside of the ICU?"

"Yes, absolutely," he assured me.

"And we will see to it somebody in the family, or otherwise trustworthy, like Shalonda, is with her. Every second," I said, and wondered where in the hell Patti and Dan were, but didn't ask.

And so, there we left it.

With nobody but me understanding that there was a despicable person out there on the loose, who, for some reason I could not imagine, wanted to kill my mother. I mean, it's not like somebody wanted to avenge Ray Glenn, a man everyone apparently despised. Nor was it likely that Willette accidentally witnessed some terrible crime, when she never left her house.

But despite the fact I didn't see any apparent motive for trying to kill Willette, I was already planning to break her out of the hospital if I saw the slightest drop in security.

I mean, how hard could that be? Given the ease with which someone had carted in a bucket of red ants and a pot of honey, I had to figure security at this place was slack.

chapter 21

As the sun rose higher in the sky, I got tired of sitting there guarding Willette, who was sleeping soundly in a cubbyhole room in the corner of the ICU, hooked into a wide variety of little hospital machines. A new police officer had appeared, and he was so earnest about his duties that he wouldn't even chat with me. Or, I noticed, flirt with the nurses.

So, he was serious.

Which made me feel a little bit better, despite the fact he appeared to be all of fifteen.

But he had a gun and a walkie-talkie, and he was alert.

Besides, I told myself, young people can stay awake better.

Meanwhile, Shalonda, having naturally noticed when Demetrious was called out in the early hours of the morning, had showed up, was horrified by the fire-ant story, and took note of not only the bites up and down Willette's arms and neck, but the ones on me.

"Put you some cold vinegar on them," she said.

"I've got some calendula cream back at Dan's, I'll use that. Willette's got hospital stuff all over her, plus a shot of antihistamines."

"You called Dr. Hodo yet?" she asked.

"Fourteen hundred times. He's off at some crisis at a group home in another county, but will call me when he's free."

"White girl, if you need to go find out what's going on, go. Nobody's gonna mess with Willette while I'm here."

Well, okay, I thought. I did need food, a change of scenery, and to find Patti and Dan. Leaving Willette should be all right now, I mean, come on, nobody would try to kill her again this soon, not with all the attention.

But just as I was heading out the door, Patti and Dan came running in.

"Oh, my Lord, my Lord," Dan said. And if that wasn't good enough, he took one look at Willette's sedate but red-spotted face and uttered an anguished, "Oh, my God."

Patti scanned the ICU room in a second, turned back to her very own husband, and said, "There is no reason to blaspheme."

"Where were you?" I said, not trying to keep the accusation out of my voice.

"Where were *you*? Where are you *ever*? Not here, no, not here," Patti said, her tone ratcheting everything up a notch.

"We were, we were—" Dan started.

"You come waltzing in here like some princess, acting like you've been dealing with this . . . this crap . . . and taking over, and ordering Dan around, and now you're, you are . . . accusing me . . . accusing us . . . of some kind of neglect, when you're the one who took off and left us with all this . . . this mess in the first place. You didn't even come to your own grandfather's funeral."

"I was in a trial," I snapped. "I tried to get a continuance and the judge denied it, you know all that damn well, and you need to stop throwing that in my face. Wasn't I the one who paid all the bills for the last few years of his life, and—"

"Whoa, now, whoa," Shalonda said, her trained-social-worker voice in play. "Let's all calm down. Everything is under control now, and you need not be—"

"You might be my friend, Shalonda, but butt out. This is between Lilly and me."

"Patti, come on, Patti," Dan said.

I inhaled deeply, and tried to visualize my calming waterfall.

What I saw instead was the highway out of town.

For a moment, nobody spoke.

Which was good, given, apparently, the direction things had been fixing to go—that is, toward a big family fight.

"We were . . . we were here," Dan said. "But then Dr. Weinstein came by and told us to go on home, that Willette was fine. He was . . . so sure. Said he'd left orders that the nurses were to check on Willette every fifteen minutes, and, you know, Otis was outside the door, and . . . well, Dr. Weinstein was just so sure we didn't need to be here."

"It's bad enough Dan having to take some of his vacation days to be helping out, and him not getting any sleep, and you . . . you . . . just *too good* to spend the night with *your own mother*," Patti said.

"Now, Patti, sweetie, you're being a bit hard—"

"Don't you—" Patti started.

"Whoa, now, whoa—" Shalonda said.

While Patti and Dan snapped at each other and Shalonda whoa'ed and whoa'ed them, I stood in the center of the room, doing my best to ignore them, and added it up.

Dr. Weinstein denied any responsibility for the OD or the bruises, but he was overmedicating Willette and refused to stop at Dr. Hodo's request.

And he sent Patti and Dan home, very coincidentally the same night someone tried to kill Willette.

And he could come and go in the hospital without anyone taking notice or thinking it strange.

So, yeah, means and opportunity, *ding, ding* . . . but what on earth was his motive?

Why would Dr. Weinstein want to kill Willette?

chapter 22

Act normal.

Act like I wasn't suspicious, and wasn't planning on tracking down a would-be killer.

That was my current plan.

Oh, that, and pestering Henry and Bonita both to scour the cyberworld and find out everything they could about the strange Dr. Weinstein. I mean, what good was it having them on my side, what with all the databases the insurance companies had or could access, if I couldn't find out more about the spiky-haired man than from his bio in the hospital pamphlet?

Six phone calls to and from Bonita or Henry later, with rising levels of anxiety and frustration on my part, all I knew was Dr. Weinstein had moved to Bugfest two years ago, from a private practice in New York City, and he had opened an office here and had hospital privileges and no obvious trail of malpractice suits or misdeeds.

So, okay, that didn't mean he wasn't a killer, did it?

And, I'm sorry, but okay, why does someone leave New York City and move to Bugfest? Leave an established practice to start over again in what had to be a whole new environment, political, social, and weather-wise.

Hell, I wasn't even sure the folks in both places spoke the same language. I mean, consider the culture shock alone.

So it was that I was sitting in my car, thinking upon these things, in the hospital parking lot, glaring at my cell phone, when Dan came up.

"Hey," he said.

"Hey."

When Dan didn't say anything else, I ventured a "So?"

"Patti's upset right now. You mustn't take her . . . take it wrong, what she said. She didn't mean anything by it. Patti's just . . . real stressed out."

Oh, and I'm not?

But what I said was "There's no need to explain, or apologize, or anything."

"If we can just get that house cleaned up . . ."

"Forget the damn house," I said. "I need to find out what the connection is between Dr. Weinstein and the deep freeze. Or what the connection is between Ray Glenn and Dr. Weinstein. And we've got to get that judge, Judge Parker, to sign that damn guardianship order. And why . . ."

But then I thought—what if the key to all this is somewhere in the garbage in that house? In all those piles of paper? Good grief, the woman could be hiding the Holy Grail or the Da Vinci code or the stash from a bank robbery or who knows what in there. What if the deep freeze didn't have anything to do with this? I mean, that was just Dan's guilt-ridden theory.

What if all this was about something we didn't even know anything about yet?

Willette's house, and all the mess inside it, suddenly seemed like a big possible clue. Only trouble was, that potential clue was deep in piles of filth I never wanted to touch.

chapter **23**

All **the airborne** toxic dust particles floated around me in a sick halo of something gone terribly, terribly wrong.

I was back in Willette's house. And wading in before me was my sister-in-law, the formidable yet good-souled Patti, with whom just moments before I'd shared our time-tested family version of an apology— that is, we pretended nothing had happened and were pleasant in a kind of tries-hard way.

Confronted once more with all of Willette's stuff, I was frankly rethinking my parking lot inspiration that, potentially, possibly, just maybe, the explanation for this whole blooming predicament was hidden in the rubbish in her house. Nonetheless, we had all converged on it. Patti Lea and I, with Hank and Jubal and a ton of wrestling boys, all of us wearing masks and coveralls, except for the wrestlers, who considered it too weenie-brained, girly-girl to take sensible precautions, and we all dug in to take another stab at cleaning Willette's house. Dan was glum, guilty, and apologetic about having left Willette open to the ant attack—like a soldier who had deserted his post—but ready to work. Patti, straining for a good-behavior medal, had only mildly protested Dan's explanation that he—not me—had invited Jubal and Hank in.

"After all, sweetie," he had said to Patti, "we been knowing them since Lilly Belle was just a babe." I appreciated that Dan took the heat on letting them in the house to help, and I sensed that he trusted them—maybe even Patti trusted them.

But then they also trusted Dr. Weinstein, Simon, Demetrious, Lonnie, and their own teenage son.

Ah, but to quote that very same teenager: "Whatever."

We needed help, and if I kept an eye on everybody, maybe they wouldn't throw out the clue that might lurk under the garbage.

After I commanded the teen squad that no paper with writing was to be thrown out until I had looked at it personally, a task for which I hope God took notice and penciled in some extra-duty brownie points, Patti Lea steered Jubal toward the kitchen, and I trailed him for a moment. But the stench was so bad that both of us soon left. Someone had been bringing her paper plates of food and sacks of takeout. They must have left the food on the porch, but at least Willette had carried it inside. And not eaten much of it. Just piled it on top of other refuse in the sink, until the sink was full, and then onto whatever space she could find.

"Reckon there's a roach colony in here," Jubal said, looking a bit nervous for a rough and robust country fellow.

"Roaches! Jubal, I bet there's a colony of rats in here."

"Well, at least it ain't full of them red ants. Lord, Lilly, I sure was sorry about that. I always hear good things about that hospital, can't believe they'd be so—"

"It wasn't carelessness."

"You don't think somebody did that to your mama on purpose?"

"Yes, I do," I said.

"Now why on earth would somebody want to hurt Willette? She's never done no harm to anybody 'cept herself."

And Ray Glenn, I wondered. Didn't he count? But what I said was, "I don't know. I don't even have a theory. Let's just get this place cleaned up, and maybe we all can think better when we can see the floor."

"Well, awright, but let's get out of this here kitchen, let's let them boys of Hank's take out this kitchen trash. Boys that age don't hardly mind anything if there's good food or money or a girl at the other end."

That made me wonder what Hank had bribed them with, but I readily agreed with Jubal that somewhere other than the kitchen was a better place to be. Especially since I could conceive of no version of any truth in which a New York doctor would try to kill a Bugfest woman over a pile of rotting food.

No, the clue had to be paper.

Of course, as a lawyer, trained as we are to scour through little tiny words on many sheets of paper, I would think that way.

"Reckon her bedroom might be a good place for me to go clear out," Jubal said. "Why don't you just take it easy, go see what Hank's up to, talk with him about things. He's a good talker, knows a lot about a lot, you give him a chance."

With that, Jubal ambled off to Willette's bedroom.

I'd already been there, and wasn't eager to go back, but I caught Patti Lea tearing around a corner and pausing long enough to recognize that I was just standing there, and I put my face mask back on and dashed into Willette's bedroom on the theory that Patti Lea wouldn't approve of Jubal's plan that I go flirt with his unmarried son instead of actually working.

In Willette's bedroom, I discovered Jubal was looking under the bed.

"If you're looking for her jewelry, I already got that out the first day. Family stuff, some from my grandmother. Scattered everywhere, some of it just thrown in with the used Kleenex."

"Lord, Lilly, I wasn't looking to steal no jewelry, jes' getting the lay of the land, trying to figure out where to start."

I hadn't meant to imply I thought he was a thief, I was just expressing my dismay, and explained that to him, and then suggested we start by bagging up the used-Kleenex trash and working our way down to the actual floor. "You see anything that isn't used tissue, you let me look at it," I said.

Jubal eyed the used Kleenex while I watched him. "Maybe I ought to strip the bed, then," he offered. "No telling what's going to come flying out of there. Why don't you go see about Hank? Boy'll overwork himself sometimes."

But instead of going to see Hank, I agreed stripping the bed was a good idea, and we lifted the mattress and pulled off the nastiest sheet I'd ever seen. "Might as well just drag the whole mattress outside, I don't think there's any saving this," I said, when I saw how old and tattered it was.

When we started to drag the mattress off the box springs, the underside of it split wide open along an existing tear, and a bunch of pill bottles spilled out.

There must have been twenty of them. Mostly empty. Some had labels made out to Willette, but, I noticed, most of the bottles were either unmarked or their labels had been pulled off.

Those that had labels were pain pills of the narcotic kind, plus some Ativan, Valium, or other sedatives.

Downers. The same stuff my mother had used when I was a child, only, apparently, judging from the number of bottles, plus her condition and that of the house, the consumption rate had gone up quite a bit.

As I studied the labels on the pill bottles, a little glee club started singing inside my head: Aha, motive! Dr. Weinstein had been illegally overprescribing downers to Willette, and now wanted to kill her to hide his sin. But I was quickly disappointed. Only two of the bottles contained pills prescribed by Dr. Weinstein, and they were standard antibiotics.

Not something anyone would need to kill Willette over, I thought, and pitched the bottles back into the pile.

"We should call Demetrious," I said, eyeing the rest of the stash. "Someone was supplying her with narcotics."

"You reckon?" Jubal asked, picking up, studying, and then discarding bottles one by one. "Could be all her stuff. You know, lawful and all."

"Not this many," I said. "Maybe we shouldn't be touching these. You know, fingerprints of the dealer?"

"Yeah, right, right," Jubal said, and put down the bottle he was holding. "You go call the law if you got to, and I'll see to it none of them teenage boys get in here. Boys that age like to try just about anything."

I stepped out in the hallway to go outside for fresh air and to use my cell phone, but then thought of Patti Lea and her futile attempts at damage and gossip control. And I thought about my brother Delvon and me, supporting ourselves through high school by growing and selling pot after our mother kicked us out of the family nest. I'd financed an entire college career, law school included, off illegally grown marijuana.

The pot calling the kettle black. No pun intended.

The family gene pool. Grandmom's granddaddy had made his own whiskey and sold it for a profit, and her daddy had run untaxed liquor and then illegal rum during the Prohibition. Delvon and me had been the new-age whiskey runners—at least the past tense applied to me. I wondered what Bobby would do, given his gene pool, and shuddered a bit at the thought of poor Patti Lea, with her good Methodist roots traceable all the way back to the Declaration of Independence.

The sister-in-law from the good family, who shamed easily.

Okay, Patti was a tad bossy, and maybe she had some resentment issues, but she and Dan had always been good to me, and they were trying to rise above Willette and Delvon. Rise above me, too, I guessed. Calling the law in to look at Willette's stash wasn't going to help Willette much, and it would sure embarrass Dan and Patti. I headed back to Willette's bedroom, and found Jubal studying the bottles, picking them up and looking at the ones with labels and putting them down. So much for not touching them.

"Maybe—" I started to say, and Jubal jumped.

"Lord, Lilly, you liked to have scared me plumb outta my skin."

"Sorry. But I don't think telling Demetrious about this will help anything."

Jubal nodded. "I reckon you're right."

Now that I wasn't calling in the law, there didn't seem to be any reason not to handle the bottles, and I pulled on my gloves and put my hand into the mattress and pulled out a few more. "This one's about full," I said, opening the lid. I recognized Percocet, and snapped the lid on again. Another one had half a label on it still, no name, but part of the prescription number was still on the label, and the name of a drugstore. That might bear some looking into, and I put the bottle on the edge of the bedside stand.

"Let's flush the pills," I said, though part of me rebelled at the waste. "And bag up the rest. Why don't you go get me some more garbage bags?"

"Can do, can do," Jubal said, and went out the door.

I rifled through the collection, setting aside the bottles that still had drugs in them, so I could flush the contents. The few with scraps of labels with numbers or information on them I slipped into the baggy pocket of my coveralls.

When I fished around for the last time, I found a small notebook, stuffed inside the mattress, and I pulled it out.

Just one of those little books people used to carry around before everything became electronic, something you used to buy at dime stores before dime stores became as obsolete as these little notebooks. I opened it, half expecting a list of her drug transactions, given how precisely she kept records of just about everything else.

But no, it wasn't a list of her narcotic purchases.

The notebook was filled with Willette's distinctively large and clear handwriting, handwriting I recognized with a start, maybe a little pang. Bold and big and neat. Wholly unexpected penmanship from a crazy woman with a drug addiction problem.

I started reading. It was a list. A list of phone calls. Phone calls she had made, or received, with the time and the date, plus the name of the person she had talked with. Dating back three years. I didn't doubt I'd find companion notebooks listing all the phone calls she had made for all the years before that, if I looked long enough.

Because even Dr. Hodo had noted this: Willette was a list maker.

Something I did. Something I did with reason and sense and care—or so I told myself. Lawyer lists I could justify.

Yeah, but here was the truth.

Sometimes I just made lists.

Damn. If there was one thing I did not want to be, it was a chip off the old block.

But there you have it; I made lists of my phone calls too. But I made these lists on my time sheets, to ensure I could bill clients for my phone calls, I hastily told myself. I couldn't imagine why Willette would keep such a careful record of the people she had called.

Curiously, I started flipping through it, looking for the end, thinking maybe there was something in it that might help me find out who wanted to kill her, who brought her the drugs, or why she had apparently killed a man. Maybe this was the clue I'd hoped to find in the garbage.

Mostly she had called Dan.

Plus, Willette had made a few phone calls to Eleanor Spivey, a few to businesses, and even one to Patti Lea. And here was a big surprise, maybe a half dozen calls to Jubal.

Not a lot of phone conversations with Jubal, really, given that the list covered a three-year time frame.

But a lot of phone conversations with a man with whom she personally had no known basis of friendship or kinship. Or at least none I knew about, as I didn't really know squat about my mother's life.

Making a mental note to ask Jubal about this, I kept flipping. Near the end of the book, I saw several phone calls from Ray Glenn listed, no doubt the harassing ones Dan had told me about, the ones where Ray Glenn tried to collect money for a refrigerator never delivered. I turned the last page, but before I could read it, Jubal was breathing over my shoulder.

"What you got, a diary or something?" he said. For a big man, he was light on his feet.

"Just a little notebook, bunch of scribbling. Doesn't look like much," I said, shutting the book then slipping it into my pocket.

"Looked like a bunch of phone calls or something. Your mom, she keep lists of phone calls?"

Jubal didn't sound happy. I made a mental note to check the book on the last few days and see if they had talked recently. But not now, not in front of him.

"Just a bunch of nonsense," I said, and jumped back to work to try to hide my lie.

As we bagged used tissues, and I confronted more evidence of a seriously defective gene pool, I asked Jubal what he knew about Ray Glenn.

"Nothing much. You know, what ever body else knows."

"Did you know Willette? I mean, before all this?"

"Yep. Your momma and me go way back. We went through school together. I kinda had me a crush on her long about senior year, but she wasn't gonna end up with no man got his hands dirty making his living."

"You had a crush on Willette?" This so stunned me I stopped stuffing trash bags with rank garbage and stared at him.

"Well, yep, your momma was a fine-looking gal. And that way she had of keeping off to herself was kinda . . . well, I reckon, kinda mysterious. And she was smart. Made good grades. Her momma kept her dressed real pretty too."

I nodded, trying to imagine a world in which Willette was young and smart and desirable to the young men in the town. Certainly my own father had married her a few months after he'd hired her for his legal secretary.

"Yep, Willette was a looker," Jubal said, sounding nostalgic. "You got to figure you got them good looks of yours from somewhere. Though your grandmother was a pretty woman too. And Willette took her looks after her momma. Why, I remember . . ." But Jubal stopped. "Well, it was a long time ago, you know. And Hank's momma, God rest her soul, was a fine woman, and a good deal sturdier in the mind, I reckon, than Willette."

Before I could explore this further, Patti stuck her head in the door. "Y'all might as well come take a break. Demetrious brought us all some sodas and told us he's been over to the hospital, checking on your mother."

"Thankee, thankee," Jubal said, and I followed him out of the bedroom.

In the den, while everyone sipped from cans of Cokes, I nursed my bottled water, and Demetrious assured us Willette was fine, that is, for a comatose woman. Wearily, I closed my eyes as everyone started talking, and I let the gossip float around my head. Then I tossed out a question that had been bothering me. "Why y'all think Ray Glenn had a big, expensive house? I mean, he was a repo man, right? And maybe an assistant store manager."

"Well, he was pretty much running that store for Lonnie, especially after Lonnie got elected to the commission," Dan said. "I think they made a lot of money off their used appliances, and from their stuff they bought right off the boat."

"Right off the boat?" My ears pricked up at that.

"Ray Glenn was also Lonnie's buyer for secondhand appliances from Miami, Atlanta, and New Orleans. Had him a big trailer, went to auctions and such," Demetrious said.

Hank tumbled in, took a cold Coke from the cooler, and stopped working to gulp it down while he listened to the talk. "Ah, that's the good stuff," he said.

"Yes, Coke's the best," Dan said.

I eyed the cooler of cold Cokes. I glanced at my tepid water. I thought about caffeine and sugar. My tongue curled in my mouth.

Well, hell, when in Rome, I thought, and reached into the cooler, took a can, and while everyone stopped talking to watch me, I paraded into the bathroom, washed the top of the can off with hot water and soap—I mean, okay, but you don't know what's been scurrying across the top of those cans—and then opened it. I sipped.

Damn, it was good. I dashed back to the living room so as not to miss any chatter, already a little rush of energy pulsing into my system.

"What about that right-off-the-boat thing?" I asked, and took a big gulp.

"Ray Glenn also picked up major appliances in Miami, right off the ship too. Saved a ton of money that way, no land shipping charges if he got the appliances right at the dock," Demetrious said.

"You know, they plain don't make anything in this country anymore," Hank said.

"This here Coke is still made in this country," Dan said, a professional pride in his voice. "Right up there in Atlanta."

"Sure hits the spot, don't it?" Hank said, after drinking the whole can in one big swallow.

I held out my bag of plastic and aluminum. "Recycle," I said on reflex, but what I was thinking was: Miami, Atlanta, and New Orleans? The three crime capitals of Dixie? Used-appliance auctions, my ass; Ray Glenn was dealing in stolen property, or worse, no doubt with Lonnie's full knowledge. That big house of the now-dead Ray Glenn began to make a lot more sense to me. Demetrious had to suspect this. I studied his face, his eyes locked on mine, and I saw him shake his head *no* in an almost imperceptible way.

"I got to go," Demetrious said. "I'll be in touch. Just wanted to let you know I'm checking in on Willette, and she's doing fine."

"I'll walk you out," I said, needing some fresh air and a moment alone with him.

"You have a lovely place, and I'm glad to see what you are doing with my grandparents' old pasture."

"It's sure a pretty place. I hope to keep it, but you know, it's going to be rough with that big lake development coming in."

"But Shalonda said nobody was threatening you with eminent domain."

"Nope, not yet anyway. But even if we hold on to our place, what's it going to be like? Eventually, if those damn developers have their way, we'll be surrounded by a bunch of big houses full of people who don't know a thing about our county, and don't care."

"A bunch of big houses," I said. "Jubal just talked about the lake and that marina resort." Though I did remember Shalonda mentioning a housing development, that had gotten lost in the rampant chaos of the last couple of days.

"Jubal didn't tell you the half of it. Those resort development people are planning on putting in a whole subdivision of lakefront homes to sell at a half million and up."

"Half-million-dollar houses? In Bugfest? Who in the hell do they think will buy those?"

"Retirees from up North. That's what they're planning on, now that Florida's full up. Got the idea that what with our low crime, clean air and water, and not but being sixty miles from the Gulf of Mexico, that anybody left up there that isn't already in Florida can come here."

"But there's not the roads, or the shopping, or the medical facilities to support that."

"Damn straight, there isn't. But a majority of the commissioners are for this, like that damn Lonnie Ledbetter. They plan on big high-end shopping malls coming in on the tail of the resort and the big subdivision, then they'll up the taxes and put in the roads, expand the hospital."

"Up the taxes. Yeah, I've seen this before. They'll up the taxes so high that the folks who've been living here and farming for a hundred and sixty years can't afford to pay their property taxes and have to sell out to the developers, and next thing you know, Bugfest is gone."

Like, I thought for a moment with a pang in my chest, Sarasota was all but gone. Like all of coastal Florida was about gone. Like central Florida was going.

"Yep, happening all over north Georgia, in the mountain towns," Demetrious said.

I thought of the gentrification of the poor parts of Sarasota, and the displaced lower-income population forced out to make way for the rich people, and I wondered: Where will these people go? Where would the small farmers go when they were shoved off their land to make way for "shoppes" and people from somewhere else?

"It's a kind of blasphemy," I said, "so-called progress, forcing out the rural folks, off their own lands."

"The real blasphemy, you ask me, is what that big lake will do to those woods on the north side of the lake," Demetrious said. "The commissioners are planning a twelve-hundred-acre lake. That's twelve hundred acres of woods and people's farms that are going under water. Now where are the deer and the fox and the raccoons and the wild turkey in these woods suppose to go live?"

On the north side of the little lake, a wild forest of oak, pine, redbud, and sweetgum grew. I had tromped through every inch of it as a child or teenager. "Yeah, I'd hate to lose that," I said.

"They aren't old-growth forest, none of that's left in this county, but those woods are about as close to old-growth trees as you're going to find around here," Demetrious said. "Damn that Lonnie Ledbetter for voting to bring it all down."

Yeah, damn Lonnie, I agreed. What the hell is a forest full of live things and hundred-year-old trees to a man who just sees them as something to destroy to make room for more money in his pocket?

"The families pushed out will find someplace, not as good a land, but still, a place they can live. But all those deer, turkey, bobcats, raccoons, and such, where are they going to go when that big lake and Sleepy Creek Development takes out those woods?"

"I don't know. Same as in Florida, I guess they just die."

"Yeah, they just flat-out die."

On that sad note, we said our good-byes.

When I stepped back inside, I grabbed up a big bag of garbage to tote to the Dumpster when Jubal looked me over carefully and said, "You know that man seems almost normal, most a the time, don't he?"

"Hush, Daddy," Hank said.

"What? *What?*" I said.

"Nobody told you about his picking up roadkill for the turkey buzzards?" Jubal said, eyeing me like a good audience.

"Daddy, I don't think—"

"He feeds roadkill to the buzzards? Isn't that kind of . . . redundant?"
I asked.

"It's 'cause he saw a bunch of buzzards get hit by a truck once, while
they were picking at a dead raccoon in the middle of the road, and ever
since then, he got him this notion that he'd help 'em out, keep the buzzards from being roadkill themselves, if he fed 'em off the highway," Hank
said, in a tone that suggested he, Hank, thought this was a fine and normal
thing to do.

"Where's he feed them?" I asked.

"Had a place right by his barn, but that Shalonda—she's a firecracker,
ain't she?—made him move it way out back, way from the house and
barn. Said those buzzards spooked her some, hanging around on the tree
limbs, watching her when she worked her garden or hung up her laundry," Jubal said.

As I let that image sink in, Hank took my bag of garbage. "Let me tote
that out for you, you sit and rest a bit," he said.

Before he could drag my garbage sack outside to the Dumpster, a herd
of teenage boys with wide shoulders came thundering into the room,
bringing a rush of wild energy with them. "We got that kitchen done,"
one of them said.

After that, nobody wanted to talk about Demetrious collecting roadkill to feed the buzzards, we all wanted to see if it was safe to go into
Willette's kitchen. So, we trotted into the room, me cautiously in the rear,
in case a flying pan of spoiled food hurled itself at us, and Patti started
oohing and Hank was full of pride over his boys. I tiptoed around them
and peeked into the kitchen. It did look a hundred percent better. Now
I could see the sink, the top of the counter, and the floor. But I wouldn't
eat anything in it.

"Well, that calls for a celebration," Hank said, and steered us all back
to the living room. Hank told all his boys to grab a Coke, toss the empty
cans in "Miss Lilly's recycle bag," and then do whatever Miss Patti wanted

them to do next. With a latent drill-sergeant's talent, Patti Lea soon had them toting salvageable antiques and wood furniture outside into the sunshine, where Jubal, once he'd finished a monologue on the evils of eminent domain, which nobody much cared about or listened to, took a broom and started brushing off four decades worth of dust, soot, and stuff I didn't want to look at close enough to identify. How Hank and his boys had gotten out of school, I didn't know. Frankly, didn't care, I was so grateful to them.

Around noon, I made the executive decision that I needed a vegetarian lunch rather than the Mr. Chick buckets that Dan had fetched for everyone. While Patti Lea was making sure all the wrestling boys washed their hands good, I snuck out and ran to Dan's, where my first order of business was to shower. After I had washed off as much of Willette's house as I could, and possibly my top layer of skin, I fished out Willette's notebook full of her personal telephone history to study while I munched on trail mix bars and apples.

There, on the last page of the notebook, were the three phone calls that Willette had made the day she allegedly shot Ray Glenn. One to Simon McDowell, one to Lonnie, and one to Jubal.

Well, what now? I thought. Whatever could she have had to say to Simon and Jubal? Lonnie, maybe I could understand, something about Grandmom's house, probably.

I puzzled a bit, and then pulled out the pill bottles that had bits and pieces of labels on them, and double-bagged them and put them in my purse, figuring I'd check with the drugstores on the labels and see if I might convince somebody to violate those new federal privacy statutes and tell me whose name might match the prescription number. That person, or persons, might be a good place to start trying to track down Willette's supplier. A couple bottles were from Tru Blue Drugstore, and that made me think I should ask Jubal exactly what he did at the Tru Blue, and if it was within his scope to access its computer, and, maybe, the other pharmacies'.

Then, *bing*! The dust cleared in my own brain as the obvious slapped me upside the face. What if Jubal had been stealing pharmaceuticals from Tru Blue and supplying them to my mother?

After I cussed out loud and let that paranoid thought bounce around in my head a minute, I made myself calm down. The thing was, I liked Jubal, and I didn't want to think him a criminal, and stealing controlled substances from a drugstore would surely be really hard to do. Yeah, I'd have to keep that suspicion in mind, but the man I did not like was the strange and rude Dr. Weinstein. He seemed a lot more likely to be the RX-grade dope dealer. After all, he could write the prescriptions legally.

But even if Dr. Weinstein had been supplying Willette, was that reason enough to kill her?

Maybe, to a man unscrupulous enough to aid and abet prescription abuse in a frail and mentally ill woman. Maybe, to a man who might lose his medical license if he was caught.

Maybe.

I had a big sack of maybes. And five thousand sacks of garbage.

chapter 24

Paper.

Paper rules the world of lawyers.

Paper is how we wage war.

Paper filled with legal words is what we lawyers shoot at each other instead of bullets.

Paper is what offers up clues and tricks and reasons and secrets.

And paper was what Willette's house had been full of, in hosts and hordes and heaps.

So knowing, I also knew I couldn't not look at the important papers from Willette's metal box. My lunch and my pondering done, I grabbed the papers Bobby had been sunning for me, took them to the library—the town being too small for a copy center—and made several copies of the more important ones: the deed to her house, the contract for deed for Grandmom's house, et cetera, et cetera.

When I had asked Dan last night if he had a safety deposit box where I could store these, thinking a little security might be in order under the circumstances, he'd asked me why on earth would he need a safety deposit box? So, there was nothing to do but take the copies back to Dan's, where I shoved one set into the metal box, which I then put up in the hallway closet, behind boxes of who knew what, I mean I wasn't looking. After that, I put the second set of copies into a lockable but unlocked drawer in Dan's desk, and made a mental note to ask him if he actually had a key to it. Then I put the originals in the trunk of my faithful ally, my Honda.

Not completely trusting the new hospital security detail, I went to check on Willette. Outside her new room in the ICU, another young police officer guarded her. He made me show my driver's license and empty my purse before he let me in, and I had to say, irritating as that was, I appreciated it.

Demetrious was making good on his promise of real protection.

Inside Willette's room, I found that Shalonda was gone. In her place sat my old English teacher and Willette's only known friend, the very woman who had force-fed me sweet tea after her peacock, Free Bird, had caused a three-car pileup in the woman's own front yard. After proper greetings, I asked her where everyone else had gone.

"They are all young, and therefore they had things they believed they had to do, and so they left. Shalonda needed to help her husband do something with mules in preparation for Mule Day," Eleanor Spivey, aging, elegant, and proper, explained to me as she paused in her snacking on pound cake and sipping from a bottle of Coke, which she mentioned Dan had been good enough to bring by in a cooler.

"Did he tell you what happened? This morning?" I asked her. "With the fire ants?"

"Yes. And so did exactly nine other people. My phone rang all morning. Are you all right, child?" Eleanor looked at me as if I might burst into tears.

"I'm fine," I said. "Why would anybody want to kill Willette? So, what do you think?"

"I think that Simon ought to make the staff keep a cleaner hospital, and that your imagination is working overtime. There is simply no reason why anyone would want to hurt Willette."

I sighed.

Not even Dan and Patti believed my theory.

"But, nonetheless, Lillian, you need to make your peace with Willette."

"How?" I asked. "The woman is not talking to me." Not, I thought, wholly unlike most of my childhood.

"The Lord will find a way, you just be ready and open for it," Eleanor said.

Notwithstanding my unresolved, and to my own mind, unresolvable, issues with my mother, I was frankly far more interested in what information I could pump from Eleanor, who, oddly enough, launched into a narrative about the virtues of Hank, pointing out he had managed to stay single all these years, but not because the women hadn't tried to catch him. "You two used to be sweet on each other," she said, rather obviously, I thought.

Yeah, sweet on each other in fifth grade. How did that still count?

Instead of pointing out that Hank and I had probably changed our minds about each other in the ensuing twenty-eight years, I told her I was engaged, furthering the half-lie I'd already told, as only Philip believed us engaged. Me, I was keeping my options open.

"Where's your ring?" Eleanor asked.

"Took it off while I was working at Willette's house. Clorox isn't good for gold."

"Well, all I have to say is that Hank is a good man."

"I can tell that," I said. "And he'd be a good catch in all the traditional meanings of the term." Still, I made a memo to my internal file to have Bonita buy me an engagement ring that was fully returnable and FedEx it to me if I wasn't out of this town by the weekend.

"That is well and good about Hank then. Which leaves me with my original point. You need to be ready to make your peace with this woman. She is your mother."

"Uh-huh." I paused, waiting for the next volley. But when Eleanor opted to sip her Coke rather than lecture me, I changed the subject. "What's with all the flowers and the pound cakes people keep bringing Willette?"

"It's the pound cakes that caused those ants," Eleanor said.

"Yes, that was Simon's theory. But why are there so many of them?"

"Ants? Or pound cakes? Be careful of the ambiguous pronoun."

I sighed again. "Pound cakes. Why are there so many pound cakes?"

"I do not mean to sound unchristian, but your mother did this town a favor, shooting that thug, Ray Glenn. He terrorized the migrants, and many other good people, especially people without the resources to hire a lawyer to fight back those ridiculous repossession claims, and there are those among them who appreciate Willette for shooting him. You need never worry about her actually going to jail."

No, I was more worried about her going to the great hereafter.

"What about Lonnie?" I asked.

"What about him? True, he does not have your I.Q., but he is trying hard to make something of himself. You know, he plans to run for state senator next election."

"So it was Ray Glenn, Lonnie's employee, who was doing all the bad stuff? Not Lonnie?"

"That would be the general consensus, I believe. People around here like Lonnie. However, if you want the particulars of his business arrangements, I am not the proper person to ask."

The "particulars of his business arrangements," I gathered, included using Ray Glenn to cheat folks out of stuff that was theirs so that he, Lonnie, could have more stuff of his own. It was, of course, in a shorthand way, pretty much the current American-capitalism concept as it had been processed during this last decade of corporate enrichment, and Lonnie was just doing it on a small-town scale.

"Don't you think if Ray Glenn is a crook, so is Lonnie?" I asked.

"Why no, Lonnie appears to be a fine man. Though I do think that wife of his is a bit . . . overdressed, I guess. Overprocessed too." Eleanor leaned over close to me and whispered, "I do not think she is a real blonde."

We straightened up, and I didn't figure Eleanor would tell me anything too dirty if she had to whisper about hair dye. "Colleen was a beauty queen, a real one, from up North, and I guess she just has to keep up appearances," Eleanor explained.

Before I could point out a thing or two about the vile Colleen, Eleanor changed lanes on me.

"Do you know that a good many fine people in this town have done their best to take care of Willette?"

The look Eleanor gave me seemed to suggest these good folks were doing the job I should have done. Then Eleanor told me how Demetrious had checked on Willette every evening on his way home, standing there in front of the locked door, talking to her, and asking if she was all right, and if she needed anything. Eleanor herself checked on Willette every morning by banging on her bedroom window on her early walk, and Willette would bang back, so Eleanor knew she was still alive. "Sometimes, she would have a word or two to say, sometimes she would just hit the window to let me know she was all right," Eleanor said.

"And a lot of us brought by food, and left it on the back porch. And, of course, Dan dropped off a case of Cokes every other day, and begged Willette to let him in. Soon as he gave up and drove off, Willette would open the door and drag the Cokes inside the house."

"Who brought her the prescriptions?" I asked, thinking of all the narcotic bottles in Willette's bedroom.

"Honey, that is your mother's business, not mine," Eleanor said.

I couldn't help but suspect Eleanor knew more than she was telling on that score, which made her a bit unique in the town, since everyone else seemed generous about sharing what they knew, suspected, or had just plain made up on the spot. But asking her about the pills made me think I needed to prompt Simon to get Willette's hospital transfer done and quick, and oh, by the way, if the invitation still stood, I'd love to have dinner with him. Perhaps after Simon had sipped a few glasses of good wine, I could learn something from him about the stocky Dr. Weinstein, my grandmother's house, and those bruises on Willette's face. Oh yeah, and I needed to bug Dan about that guardianship thing.

All of which led me to ask Eleanor, "Do you know Judge Parker?"

"Why, yes, of course, everyone knows Judge Parker. He is an upstanding man, and a proper judge."

"Can you introduce me to him? Soon? In a . . . a nice, social setting?"

"Why, Lilly? What are you up to?"

"I need to discuss with him, as quickly as possible, why he should sign those guardianship papers for Dan. You know about that, right? But I need to approach him . . . as a, er, daughter, not in a formal, legal setting."

"Lilly, dear, Dan has a lawyer, and she is a fine attorney and a nice lady. You let it be."

So, okay, I guess that meant iced tea and pound cake with the good judge, the errant peacock, and the elegant Eleanor wasn't in the late-afternoon plan. Still, I was going to have to find a way to meet Judge Parker and push this guardianship plan along.

Despite the urgent pull of important things I needed to do, and soon, I didn't want to leave Willette until someone stronger than Eleanor was inside her room with her.

"When is Shalonda coming back?"

"Lilly Belle, don't you go worrying about me. Now that I'm retired, I have too much time on my hands as it is. I volunteer a lot, and nearly every time the church doors open, I'm there. Still, it's hard to fill up sixteen hours a day." She sighed, and I guessed that she was lonely. "I enjoy sitting here with Willette, and should she wake up, I'll be a friendly face."

"Yes, but if . . ." Suddenly I didn't know how to say to Eleanor that she was a tad old to fight off any killers in the night. "How long do you plan to stay?"

"Till later tonight," she said, studying me closely enough to make me nervous. She still had, apparently, an ability to read minds. "Don't worry. I know how to spot an ant, push a call button, and scream. And there's that nice young police officer right outside the door."

That made sense, and Eleanor at least really cared about Willette, which was half the battle. I decided my time could be better spent elsewhere, rather than overseeing Eleanor guarding my mother. As I stood up to leave, she fixed her hazel eyes on me, fierce with that middle-school-teacher glint, and I sat back down.

"There is always another side to every story," Eleanor said.

"Yes, as a litigation attorney, I am more than aware of that."

"But you do not have any conception that your mother has a side of the story too? With you, I mean. You and Delvon."

"You mean, like she's got a . . . a what, a justification for . . ."

"Your mother was never really strong. Unfortunately, she took after her father's side of the family. Her mother dying, and dying like that, broke her," Eleanor said.

"It broke us all," I said, remembering, wholly against my will, the long, agonized death by cancer of the woman who had held us all together.

"No, I beg to differ. In the end it made Delvon, Dan, and you stronger."

"Delvon?" I blurted out indignantly. "Delvon is a—" I stopped. What did Eleanor know about him? That in a small town with limited physical and cultural boundaries, a place where troubled young folks escaped to either substance abuse or Jesus, Delvon was two for two?

"Both of you are strange, like Willette. I don't say that with judgment, but as a fact. But unlike her, you two are strong. Look at you, a successful lawyer. And your brother, Delvon. You think I do not know he has been running his own business since before he dropped out of high school? You think a weak man, a *broken* man, can stay out of jail and year after year turn a tax-free profit?"

I didn't say anything.

"You need to understand, after her momma died, Willette used up most of her daily allotment of energy just to keep herself from becoming one of those poor women who run around downtown screaming and pulling off their clothes."

"I've got to go now." I jumped up, my heart pounding, my hands sweating, and my stomach lurching.

"Stop and face the truth. You and Delvon ran out on your mother." Eleanor looked right at me and said, "Your mother needed you, and she needed Delvon, and you ran out on her."

"My mother did not need us. She had her own father, and my father was still there."

"Not to be unchristian, but did you ever know either one of them to be much comfort to anyone? Your grandfather was a good, dear soul, but he didn't have the backbone to stand up to life, and he certainly was not anyone to lean upon."

"She did not need me, she didn't even like me."

"Willette needed you to keep Delvon around, and she needed Delvon, and you took him away from her. The only thing your mother ever loved wholly and passionately was Delvon, her first son, and from the moment you were born, you took him away from her. And then, right at her hour of greatest need, you had him run off with you because you couldn't stand and face the truth. She didn't even know where you two were. It was like you both slammed some door in her face. That's why she locked you out when you came back."

I shut my eyes, squeezing them against the way that day seemed to rise in front of me like a big-screen TV. The funeral. The suffocating smell of the flowers, already decaying in the summer heat. Women crying, men shaking my hand and saying stuff I couldn't hear, my grandfather so drunk only Dan could handle him, my father in his best suit, reading the eulogy and breaking down in tears—the only time I ever saw the man show any emotion other than a benign bewilderment.

The back of the church was lined with men who stood, in their best Sunday clothes, their John Deere hats in their hands, and their faces downcast, not meeting anyone's eyes, and the backs of their necks brown and wrinkled from the sun, and their hands, spotted with age but still strong. One by one, these men had come to my grandparents' place during the spring and the summer and they broke ground, and seeded, and hoed, and tended the animals, because my grandfather was too crushed and my grandmother too sick to take care of their own little farm. All those good, kind souls, with their shy ways and rough hands, would be gone now, like my grandfather, crossed over to what I hoped was their fair reward, their little farms sold by their city-bound children for the value of the timber.

Their mumbled words of sympathy that day, as they had lined up to bow their heads and take my hand, had been more than I could bear.

Delvon and I had fled. Straight from the cemetery, at the first thud of dirt on the vault with the casket with the body of our grandmother inside. Our eyes had met, and we didn't need words. We ran. For his car. And we left Georgia, spinning our way down to southwest Florida, where we slept in the car, walked on the beach, and tried to find a way to live in a world that seemed so lonesome we could have died ourselves and not cared.

I opened my eyes and looked at Eleanor.

"You ran off when your mother needed you, and then you didn't even come to your own grandfather's funeral. Folks in this town will be a long time remembering that," she said.

Against my will, I remembered Delvon and me, little children, tied to chairs for hours in a room with curtained-off windows, the door locked against curious neighbors.

I was not the villain in this story.

A kind of vicious anger rose up in me at Eleanor, at my mother, at this town, and at all of them.

And I repeated to myself, I was not the villain.

But another voice asked back, *Was I?*

I let my anger cool a moment, and then I walked toward the door.

But in the doorway, I stopped and turned back to Eleanor. "Thank you for loving her." Which was more than I'd ever been able to do.

And then I left as quick as I could move without actually running.

chapter 25

It **turned out** that the nurses in the Bugfest hospital knew how to keep their mouths shut.

So, my afternoon of trying to cajole, charm, or bribe information about Dr. Weinstein or what had happened in the ER the night Willette came in, or about anything else other than the general view that "those were mighty fine pound cakes" had proven to be a big waste of my time.

Oh, except for the fact it kept me from inhaling, ingesting, and absorbing any more of the forty years' worth of black-mold growth from inside my mother's wretched house.

So, there I was, having no doubt, in the eyes of Patti Lea, played hooky all afternoon, imagining how I might explain that in spite of not accomplishing anything worthwhile, I had nonetheless spent a more meaningful afternoon than shoveling garbage and looking for the proverbial needle in all the haystack of used tissues.

Thus, fresh from failure with the nurses, I eased into Dan's house in the dragging hours of the afternoon. Like a sentinel, there sat a weary Patti Lea at her kitchen table, sipping iced tea, her hair wet, no doubt from showering away Willette's house. Demetrious was sitting across from her, sipping tea and eating a slice of pound cake.

"Hello, and hello," I said, looking at each one in turn, and hoping whatever this was wouldn't take too long. After all, I still had to get gorgeous for my sort-of date with Simon.

We traded the usual greetings, and then Demetrious said he had actually come to see me. Patti Lea stood up, announcing she had better check on her laundry, graciously leaving us to her kitchen.

"What's up?" I asked.

"Maybe you can help me, you being an outsider . . . I mean, a visitor."

An outsider in my own hometown? Well, if the shoe fits, I reckon I'd stomp around in it awhile. What I said was, "Maybe."

"You know anything about the illegal importation and sale of exotic meats?"

"That it's illegal?"

"Meat from endangered species, usually from Africa, but a lot from the Caribbean too."

"Uh-huh," I said, my mind beginning to wander toward wardrobe. What was the best dress to induce Simon to tell me his secrets? It couldn't be too obvious, and it couldn't be too staid. Well, damn, I suddenly remembered I was at Patti and Dan's and my wardrobe for dates was limited to a black rayon dress I had wadded up and thrown in my suitcase at the last minute. Nice enough for church and funerals, but hardly the stuff to seduce secrets with.

"Ma'am?" Demetrious asked.

"Hm?" I wondered if Patti had anything that might fit and further the goal of the evening.

"Here, look at these." With that, Demetrious spread before me on the kitchen table some PETA publications on the importation and sale of exotic meats. The pictures were of skinned and gory animals and a large sea turtle with its head cut off, its stumpy neck still oozing.

"I'm a vegetarian," I said. "You don't have to convince me."

"That's why I figured you'd want to help me."

"Help you?"

"Stop this."

Oh yeah, stop an international trade based upon greed and poachers and stupid people who would buy and eat endangered animals because it was some kind of trendy, sick thing to do? Wasn't that a tall order, even for me?

As if reading my skepticism, Demetrious said, "I mean, help stop it locally."

I raised my eyebrows and nodded.

"There's a restaurant called the Deer Den, out in an old country house, halfway between Bugfest and Thomasville, people from three or four counties eat there. Lots of folks come up from Florida to dine there. It's under new ownership and it's rumored to sell illegal beluga caviar, turtle eggs, and occasionally some illegal exotic meats."

"Turtle eggs?" My interest level suddenly jumped. Turtle eggs, like little eggs, like maybe a mentally ill woman could see as voodoo eggs?

"Thought that might catch your attention. What with what Willette said."

"Voodoo eggs. But what—"

"I don't know what the connection is, but I'm trying to find out."

Yeah, between mule-rodeo rehearsals, I thought, but then leaned forward toward him, thinking about Ray Glenn and those trips to the great port crime-centers of Dixie. "You called in the feds?" I didn't mean to imply incompetence on Demetrious's part, but he was a small-town police officer with lots of other things on his mind, like winning a showcase of blue ribbons with Big Beauty come Saturday.

"Tried to. They want more than rumors. Besides, despite federal, even international laws," Demetrious said, "the local federal authorities aren't too interested."

"Well, from what I read, the feds don't mind spying on PETA and Greenpeace and vegan groups, why can't they at least enforce some laws along the way?"

"After 9/11, asking a federal law enforcement officer to sink time in investigating someone for selling turtle eggs or endangered monkey meat is a waste of time unless I can present them with a pretty tight case."

"People eat monkeys?" I asked, disgusted at the thought. But then eating a dead cow is pretty disgusting too, if you think about it.

"Yeah. I can show you the literature on that. You wouldn't believe the price monkey meat brings in places like New York and Chicago. But around here, I think turtle eggs and caviar from the endangered sturgeons are probably what we'd be dealing with."

I nodded, still not past the image of someone eating a monkey.

"Will you help?"

"Yes."

"Good. I don't have jurisdiction—the Deer Den is outside the city limits. I'm just looking to get some evidence. Everybody knows how I feel, so nobody at the Deer Den is going to offer me anything off the menu."

I was thinking about Willette's voodoo eggs again. Turtle eggs in that damn deep freeze could be at the heart of this, after all, and not the elusive stocky little New York doctor.

"Must've been a monumental screwup on somebody's part if they put a deep freeze of smuggled turtle eggs on Willette's porch," I said. "You ever find those two deliverymen that oh-so-conveniently quit their jobs and moved?"

"No, but I've got the police in surrounding counties looking for them."

Yeah, that'd be a high priority, wouldn't it, right up there with turtle eggs?

"You know about Ray Glenn going down to the ports in Miami and picking up so-called appliances right off the ships, right? So don't you think—"

"I think you better be careful who you ask what," Demetrious said. "Smuggling isn't—"

"So you agree with me, somebody tried to kill Willette? With the red ants?"

"Could be. I told you, I'm taking it seriously. She's well protected."

"What do you want me to do? I mean, at the Deer Den. I'm going out tonight with Simon, I can get him to take me there."

Demetrious pulled out a little tape recorder, the kind I sometimes used for dictation. "Can't put a traditional wire on you—we just don't have that kind of equipment—but if you could carry this, and get a recording of someone there offering you the caviar or the turtle eggs. Also, I've got a little camera you can put in your purse. I doubt you'll get a chance to use it, but just in case. The recording is the main thing. Of course, they won't put the illegal stuff on the menu and you'll have to be subtle about it. You can be subtle, can't you?"

I let a slow grin spread over my face. "Yes, I can be subtle." After all, isn't *subtle* just a nice word for *sneaky*?

"Be careful, and take this seriously. You'll be safe so long as you are in the restaurant with other folks, and you don't get anyone suspicious about you."

"Hey, just because I'm a trial attorney doesn't mean I'm into life-threatening behavior."

"Good. The Lacy Act provides up to twenty years in jail and a half million in fines for these kinds of violations, so these folks have something at risk. But the plain truth is there is a lack of enforcement, and lax prosecution. The harshest sentence I've heard about is a man who got forty-one months and a fine for smuggling in beluga caviar from the endangered sturgeon."

Sturgeon suddenly made me think of surgeon, which made me think of Dr. Weinstein. "Does Dr. Weinstein have anything to do with that Deer Den place? Is he one of the owners by chance?"

"Not an owner of record, I've looked. It's owned by a corporation, run by a couple of guys they sent down from up North. Either the corporation is banking on a population boom once the resort is put in, or it's just cleaning up some money. The place does a good business, all right, but not so good a big up North corporation would want to buy it. So I'm figuring it for a money-laundering operation from the smuggling. Or, could be, they're just selling the stuff they can't move quickly up North."

"Money laundering?" That sounded like something Ray Glenn and his trips to Miami might have been part of, and I nodded.

"Why did you ask about Dr. Weinstein?"

Why did I ask, exactly? Because the strange, spiky-haired, stocky Dr. Weinstein was overdosing my mother, ran off Dan and Patti the night someone tried to kill her, and wouldn't let Dr. Hodo intervene until Dan got a court order as Willette's guardian.

How much did I want to tell Demetrious?

"Sturgeons, you say," I said, deciding for now to keep my suspicions to myself.

"Fascinating fish," Demetrious said, taking the bait.

Fascinating and *fish* were not two words I would have joined, but I nodded politely.

"Sturgeons are actually prehistoric, and they can live up to a hundred years."

Wow, old fish, really old fish, I thought, and nodded again. Out of the corner of my eye, I saw Patti flit by and pause, no doubt doubled over with curiosity as to why, in the midst of the great Willette crisis, the police chief and I were discussing historic fish.

"It's because they live so long that taking their eggs—their roe—is so deadly to them. The black market trade in sturgeon caviar is about to wipe them out—imagine, deliberately killing off a species that's been around since prehistoric times."

Yeah, sometimes people suck, I thought.

"Despite all this, enforcement remains lax," Demetrious said as Patti sat down at the table with us.

"Simon is picking me up at seven," I said, eyeing the wall clock and then my sister-in-law, who appeared poised for questions. "If you give me the recorder . . ."

"A recorder?" Patti said, in a hearty tone of curious. "On your date with Simon?"

Demetrious glanced at the clock, then back at me in my grubby jeans. Yeah, I was going to be late or a bit under-groomed if we didn't get the show on the road.

"I'm going to help Demetrious out with a little, er, undercover work," I explained to Patti.

"Wow, really?"

"Now, Miz Cleary, don't you be telling anyone," Demetrious said. And Patti Lea, who'd been known to keep a few secrets, nodded vigorously.

"Let me show you how to use this," Demetrious said, as if somehow I'd managed to have been an adult for all this time, and an attorney to boot, and had never used a tape recorder.

While Demetrious explained the complexity of the on-and-off button, I thought: Life in small towns isn't boring after all. I mean, here I was, a woman with a steady beau going off on a date with a prominent local man so I could spy for the chief of police and maybe help figure out why my mother had to shoot a man over some possibly improperly delivered illegal turtle eggs. Surely all of this somehow would explain why a soulless person had tried to kill her with fire ants.

Tacky dress or not, it should be an interesting evening, I thought.

chapter **26**

Smugglers.

Smugglers who had screwed up.

A smuggler who tried to kill Willette.

And I'm going to help catch them.

In truth, for being so tired, I was actually pretty buzzed over the prospects as I sailed back in to Dan and Patti's kitchen, all showered, spiffed, puffed, and made up, wearing that little black rayon dress. Yeah, it wasn't great, but Patti's collection of what she called her "Sunday-school dresses" had all been one size too big. She did have a pair of spike-heeled black shoes that dressed up my look considerably, and she generously offered them to me. "Dan gave them to me, but they pinched my toes something awful," she explained.

Well, they pinched my toes too, but they were sexy, so I went with them. And a little artful stitchery on the neckline of the rayon dress and basting in a shorter hemline made it less funeral or church, and more like a spying-for-a-good cause dress. Thank goodness my grandmother had taught me to sew.

Still, I was insecure about the overall impact until I sauntered into the kitchen, caught the look Patti gave me, and glanced at my reflection in the mirrored tile above the countertops.

Okay, okay, it was a bit short. Maybe I overdid the hemming. But hey, I didn't spend all that time at the gym fighting the inevitability of gravity and time just to wear a baggy, borrowed dress with a hemline around my ankles. And I wanted Simon to tell me things that he might not want to tell me, and wine and short black dresses generally worked better than cross examination, where men I could not subpoena were concerned.

Patti wasn't alone in her disapproval. Jubal was standing at the kitchen sink, staring out into the backyard, and Dan was boiling something on the stove, which smelled like black-eyed peas. They both turned to greet me, and I saw Jubal take a long look.

"You ought to be going out with Hank, not that Simon man," Jubal said.

I made a mental note to ask Dan and Patti next time we were alone exactly when Jubal had become their new best friend. Just then, the phone on the wall rang.

"Bonita, for you," Patti announced to the kitchen crowd. As I took the phone, Patti Lea and Dan backed out of the room to give me some privacy, but Jubal hung around at the kitchen sink until Patti came back in and led him out.

"Your cell phone is turned off," she said, "and you haven't checked your messages. Are you all right?"

"Fine, fine, just busy. What's up?"

"Your client filed a response opposing your motion to withdraw as his attorney of record."

"Why?"

"He says the usual stuff about prejudice and delay. I've already e-mailed his response to you by attachment. You haven't checked your e-mail either, have you?"

Ignoring the hint of chiding, I focused on the fact that Idiot Client was objecting to letting me go peacefully, as his attorney. Vainly, I figured that he knew my reputation as a great defense attorney, and didn't want to let go of me. Whatever his real reasons were, I had to convince the judge to let me off the case. So, how hard could that be? But I needed to get back to Sarasota and hit the law books for a Lilly Cleary special legal memorandum of law.

While I was thinking all this, I realized Bonita wasn't talking. Her pause suddenly made those damn trapezius muscles clinch into a painful spasm. "What else?"

"He's also filed a suit against Henry and his company for breach of contract and about four other causes of action, and he's asking for punitive damages. He's hired Newly Moneta to represent him in the suit. Henry is in quite a state of mind."

"He doesn't have anything to worry about. Fraud is a clear contractual reason for denying coverage. And I can testi—"

Oops. Suddenly I got it. If I was still Idiot Client's attorney of record, I couldn't very well testify against him under the basic ethical rules of attorney-client privilege. Then it was just Henry's word against Idiot Client's that he had, in fact, changed the relevant medical records. Bonita had not seen the altered records, and, since the attorney-client privilege doctrine extended beyond the attorney to secretaries, she could not testify as long I could not. My guess was that Idiot Client still had enough sense to have completely destroyed those original records and had made a whole new batch, all with no evidence of any fraudulent misdeeds. And poor Henry, with his tendency to all but stutter under stress, would not make a good witness. And the insurance company, though wholly right in this instance, would look to a jury like the corporate Antichrist trying to renege on its contract. And everybody hates an insurance company.

So, my testimony about those altered records was the best—maybe only—chance Henry and his company had of ever winning. If Idiot Client took me out of the picture, he could probably win his suit against his insurer, get his coverage reinstated, and pick up some pocket change in damages along the way.

And Henry's company wouldn't be too happy with Henry.

Or me.

Further, as long as I was technically Idiot Client's attorney of record, I couldn't defend Henry, or even offer him any advice. I'd love to help Henry, and I'd love to take on Newly again in court, Newly having been not once but twice my lover before he left me for my associate, petite Angela, whom he married, somewhat to my public embarrassment.

I had to get out from under Idiot Client. I had to help Henry. I had to beat Newly again.

Right after I solved the case of the attempted murder of my mother.

"I want to see those papers right now, all of them," I said. Damn, and me without a fax. "Scan them in, and e-mail them to me by attachment."

"I already have. And yes, I updated the firewall right before I sent them."

Good for Bonita. She thinks like a lawyer. That being paranoid.

After we said our good-byes, I was nearly overwhelmed with the urge to get out of Bugfest. I needed to get back to my life and my house and my profession.

And to top it off, my date was late and I was damn hungry.

But then the doorbell rang, and while Dan answered it, I went to the bathroom to stuff the mini–tape recorder in my bra.

chapter 27

Blue.

Simon was wearing blue. Blue shirt, pants, tie, jacket, socks, and shoes. At least the shoes were navy, unlike the various shades of bright to royal blue he was otherwise decked out in.

Even his eyeglass frames were blue.

That the man apparently had different-colored glasses to go with his outfits did not endear him to me.

At least he hadn't dyed his gold hair blue.

And then there was the car.

Little. Red. Sporty. Expensive.

A car that shouted out to the world: I'm an insecure middle-aged man in denial.

Whew, I sure hope nobody who knows me sees me with this man, I thought as I crawled into the front seat of the beacon-red car.

I was embarrassed. I was starving. And the mini–tape recorder was cold and sharp inside my bra. And I'd had to remove the push-up padding in one cup to make room for it, and now worried that I had lopsided cleavage.

Not that I was planning on having a second date, so what did it matter?

Upon closer observation, despite his blatant oddities, Simon seemed to be a pretty nice man. His manners were perfect. His concern for Willette and my family and me seemed sincere. His suggestion we go to Annier's Courtyard, where he insisted they served organic and vegetarian fare, boded well. In fact, he so resisted my countersuggestion of going to the Deer Den that I wondered if he knew and was disgusted by the turtle-egg rumors. But gentleman that he was, finally he let me convince him to take me there.

On the long ride through the evening and the countryside, I fully intended to learn one key thing from this man. But "Why did Willette call you the day she shot a man?" seemed way too obvious. So I went at it sideways and asked, in my most friendly, i.e., not lawyer, voice: "Did you know my mother at all? I mean, you're so sweet to her in the hospital, had you met her before?"

Simon took his eyes off the road for a moment to cut them over to me. I smiled my girl-on-a-first-date smile, the one that promises a lot, plus shows off my good dental hygiene.

"No. I heard she didn't get out much," he said, and turned back to the dark country road in front of us.

"True, she didn't. But I'm just learning that she liked to chat with folks on the phone. Why, Eleanor and Dan both said she'd call them up, just to talk. Did she ever call you?"

"Why would she do that?" Simon asked.

Well, yes, that was the twenty-dollar question, wasn't it? And wasn't it interesting that he hadn't actually answered my question yet.

An old lawyer trick is to ask the same question with slightly different wording until you get a better answer. I was usually very good at this. So, I gave it a whirl. "Hm, I think she must have gotten lonely. Maybe she wanted to welcome you to your new home, seeing as how it was the house she grew up in. So, I don't know. She was a strange lady." I paused, hoping Simon would jump in with a suddenly remembered phone conversation with my mother. He kept driving.

"So. Did you ever talk with her? Over the phone, I mean?"

"I don't think she had any reason to call me," Simon said, and then he reached over and put his big hand on my knee. "You know, we have a lot in common. My mother didn't like me either."

"What?"

"Oh, I hear things, but don't worry, that's why we understand each other. My mother thought I was a freak."

"What?" Had my mother thought I was a freak? Had somebody told him that?

"Because of my Marfan syndrome, only a mild case, really, I'm quite healthy; I work out all the time. But she was ashamed of me. Because of the Marfan's."

Ah, Marfan's syndrome, an inherited condition, like some experts thought President Lincoln had. The most obvious symptom being elongated limbs. And being tall, very tall. That would explain Simon's long, long arms. And legs. And his long, thin face.

"It's a genetic mutation, hardly my fault, more like her fault for passing on the DNA. But my own mother blamed me, and despised me for having it. But it gave me something to transcend. Like you. We've both risen above having mothers who didn't care for us. We've both done very well. Very, very well."

I didn't want to pursue either the topic or his hand on my knee. For a moment I just sat still. It was actually pretty hard to transcend having a mother like that. I mean, if the one person in the whole world who is supposed to unqualifiedly adore you despises you instead, then yeah, a hard row of emotional adjustment to hoe lies in front of you—forever. While I still hadn't made up my mind if I liked this man, I was suddenly very sympathetic to him. I didn't reach to take his hand off my knee.

"Did you ever resolve things with her?" I asked, my voice soft.

"No. But I will. I'm going to impress that woman if it's the last thing I do. Right now, I'm the administrator of a little hospital, a good hospital, a very good hospital. But that's not enough for her. She thinks I'm this big failure, this big . . . all because I inherited Marfan's. But see, with all the development and population boom that's coming to this area, that hospital will grow, and I'll be right there, taking it to the top. It'll be the best damn hospital in the whole region, and the biggest. Boom times coming for the community and the hospital. You wait and see."

Before I could figure out how to respond, Simon turned to me and leaned over like he was going to kiss me. But as his face neared my lips, he kept steering straight where the road began a sharp curve.

"Watch the road," I shouted, and he spun the wheel, and after only a little jerk and bump, we were back off the shoulder and on the hardtop again. Maybe, I thought, it'd be in our own interest to wait till he wasn't driving a small car too fast on a dark, curvy road before we made out or delved deeper into our wounded souls.

"Tricky road," he said.

"Well, not if you would actually watch it," I said, our moment of connection gone in a snit. Rather than risk getting back to where we'd left off, that being Simon leaning into a kiss rather than the curve, I asked if I could play his CD, and before you'd know it, we had some jazzman I'd never heard of playing music I didn't much like. But at least Simon kept his eyes on the road.

While I blocked out the music, I thought: Well now, this is interesting. Willette's notebook showed she had called him, and he more or less—indirectly, at least—led me to believe he had never spoken with my mother. However, in a lawyerlike way, he had managed not to actually deny talking with her.

As I was pondering what this might mean, I leaned back in the car and took in the night around us. The stars were bright. No one else was on the road. The car was smooth. The man driving it had opened his soul to me, and had at least some potential if he'd let me renovate his wardrobe and vocabulary. In spite of the dreadful music, this could have been a really good drive on a decent first date—I mean, if Simon had really been my date (at least in my mind), and we weren't going to a horrid place where we wouldn't really eat, and I didn't have a miniature tape recorder poking at me in my bra.

Finally, we arrived at the Deer Den, which was nothing more than a big old farmhouse. Simon explained to me that this place had been a local favorite for a long time. However, just a few months ago, new manage-ment had taken it over when the original owner had sold it. Apparently, the verdict was still out as to whether the new people—*outsiders,* Simon noted without a trace of irony—would run as good a place as the former owners.

I smiled and nodded as if Demetrious hadn't already told me that and more.

As Simon escorted me inside, the tape recorder tried to work its way up from my bra cup, and I turned away from Simon to push it back down. "Lovely view," I said, to explain my sudden turn to the left as I looked out over a big, dark field of denuded cotton stalks. Once the tape recorder was back in place, I thought, all systems go, as Simon led me inside and the hostess took us to a table with a candle by a window. In short order, a young man dropped off a basket of bread and poured water in our glasses.

"You're quite the mystery," I said, and sniffed the water. Chlorinated tap water. Never drink water that smells of chlorine, I thought, and pushed the glass away. "Please, tell me about yourself."

"I really like jazz."

Okay, technically a proper response, but not what I had in mind. Besides, I don't know a thing about jazz.

"Classical," I said, not because it was true but because it sounded impressive. "Now what led you to come down South?"

"I'm passionate about Mendelssohn."

Okay, I had to assume this was a side step about music and not a Southerner he was crazy about. "Uh-huh. Me too." So, was Mendelssohn jazz or classical? Before this hole got dug deeper, I needed to introduce a new, nonmusical topic. "No one seems to want to wait on us. And I'm really hungry."

Simon rose gracefully from the table—gracefully, that is, for a man dressed in bright blue everything and with all those long appendages—and he said, "Permit me to find someone to take our order."

In his absence, I peeked at the rolls—ordinary white-bread things, definitely off the chart on the glycemic index. I pushed the bread basket away and once more poked down the tape recorder.

Simon returned alone. "Someone will be right with us."

Chat chat chat, and the man would not answer a single helpful question, but at least we were no longer discussing jazz versus classical music.

Finally, a blond waitress stood by our table. Sheila, her name tag said, and she was quickly all business. After she rattled off the nightly specials—all some kind of poor dead cow or pig and nothing exotic or illegal—I started hinting about unadvertised specials. Sheila stared at me, not at all taking the bait, no matter how *wink-wink* I was in my inquiry about something "really different, you know, exotic." Suddenly I realized that even if she started rattling off monkey meat and panda filets, I couldn't just turn the tape recorder on while everyone was looking at me—I mean, I couldn't be grabbing my own bra and pushing the on button. So, I said "Excuse me" and crawled under the table, hit the on button, in case the waitress said something incriminating in the next few minutes, and I popped up again. "Slippery napkin," I said.

Simon was staring at me strangely. And this from a guy in a midlife-crisis car and wardrobe-coordinated eyewear.

I ignored his look and went for two more rounds of coy games with the waitress, trying to get her to tell me the "real house specialties" till finally she snapped out something about other customers and stomped off.

Okay, so I hadn't accomplished anything so far beyond irritating the waitress, but the evening was still young. I popped under the table to turn off the tape recorder, as I didn't want to run out of tape. "Really slippery napkin," I said as Simon continued to give me that what-have-I-gotten-into look.

"Do you want to go someplace else?" he asked, his voice the very voice of concern. Or of a man who wanted to get out of the public view before his date did something really strange.

I wiggled around until I was sitting up straight and the recorder in my bra was only poking me a little bit, and I grinned like everything was fine and said, "Why, no. Let's order." As if that wasn't what we'd already tried to do.

Just then, an official-looking manager-type man came to the table. "Sheila tells me you wanted something . . . exotic." He looked me up and down, and then glanced at Simon, who quickly assured him the house specialty—fried chicken—would be just fine for him.

"Oops," I said, and bobbed down under the table again, and pushed the on button on again, and popped back up.

"You guys just have the slipperiest napkins, just won't stay in my lap." Grin, grin.

"Here, try mine, it stays put," Simon said, ever the gentleman, as he handed me his napkin.

Okay, enough with the napkins, I thought, and launched my most mischievous smile at the manager man. "I've heard that for special people, you have some off-the-menu items that are just out of this world. Or out of this country anyway."

"We have some shrimp that's imported from China. Everything else is quite local, I assure you, and quite fresh. Perhaps some of our quail?"

"Quail, eh, why no. I had something . . . *exotic* . . . in mind." Come on, how many times did I have to say "exotic"?

As if Manager Man had been quite well coached in the nuances of entrapment, he said, "Please tell me what you have in mind. Specifically. Then we will see what there is."

I'd watched enough TV over the years to have the gist of entrapment too, and so, instead of saying, look, I want some illegal stuff, I took a different tack. "Hey, Lonnie Ledbetter, who is an old friend of mine dating back to grade school, told me to ask for the off-the-menu specialties and you'd have a real treat for me. Ray Glenn and I were close, real close, up till his unfortunate accident, and he used to brag about your *exotic* meats."

Okay, okay, spank me for being a name-dropper, but Lonnie struck me as the sort that would impress this man, and Ray Glenn sounded exactly like the type of man who would actually eat endangered snow leopard filets. So what if Simon knew I was lying? The man was much too polite to interrupt my quest for recorded evidence to point out to a stranger that I, his date, was, technically speaking, not telling the truth about Ray Glenn.

Still, if our manager guy had had half a brain, he'd have checked my references by calling Lonnie. Instead, he bowed slightly and ran through a couple of nightly specials that included beluga caviar and a rare delicacy—Caribbean sea-turtle eggs.

Hiding my disgust and anger, I swallowed a few times and finally ordered the beluga caviar for an appetizer, and asked Manager Man to check back with us in a few minutes on the main course.

Simon shook his head at the manager, who pranced off totally unaware that I'd just recorded him offering to sell me something in violation of federal and international law.

"I can't believe you would order that," Simon said, and gave me a look that radiated disapproval.

Well, okay, as I'd already admitted, I was not looking for a second date—provided I could learn what I needed on this one.

My first plan had been to order something illegal on tape, then photograph it. Surreptitiously, of course. Maybe even ask for a doggie bag to take it to Demetrious for lab work, or something. But Simon's glare got to me, I had to admit. "I don't want to eat them," I said. "In fact, I don't want to stay here at all."

"Fine. I don't wish to stay here either."

"Good."

Simon stood up to flag down Manager Man, while I crawled under the table to turn off the tape recorder. When we were both eye-to-eye again at the table, he gave me a long, steady look.

"Are you all right? You keep ducking under the table."

"Fine. Good. So." Next time somebody wants me to spy with a tape recorder, I'm putting it in my purse, not my bra.

Manager Man appeared at the table. But before Simon could say whatever he was going to say to him, I said, genteelly, "Oh, please, sir, I was wondering if I might see your kitchen? I've got a kind of cleanliness thing, and I just can't eat at restaurants until I've inspected their kitchen." I didn't want the man becoming suspicious that I was spying for Demetrious, and thought demanding to scrutinize the kitchen an ideal exit strategy. It had certainly resulted in my exit from other restaurants.

Typically so, Manager Man insisted his kitchen was clean, and was equally emphatic that I couldn't see this for myself but would have to take his word for it.

"Well, in that case, cancel my order. We're leaving."

Manager Man cast his eyes at Simon, as if he had the final say. Simon gave me a what-are-you-doing look, and I smiled my sweetest smile at him.

"Isn't that right, Simon?" I asked, in a tone that suggested I wouldn't care for any disagreement.

"Fine," he said, his puzzlement sounding even in that one word.

So, we canceled our orders, Simon left a five on the table for the water and bread, and we huffed and puffed out the front door and back to his spiffy sports car.

"Lilly, what are you up to?" he asked as he held the door open for me.

I slid into the passenger side, and debated bringing him in on the secret mission, but decided not to. Let him just think I'm a bit nutty. After all, he knew my mother's condition and would surely believe I could be weird too.

"Oh, nothing," I said. But once we were both in the car, I had a sudden sense of unfinished business, that being the lack of photographic evidence, and I expressed a need to visit the ladies' room, and got out of the car. Leaving Simon before he could question me further, I trotted back to the restaurant, darted past our former waitress, and barreled my way straight ahead under the EMPLOYEES ONLY sign. In a matter of uninterrupted seconds, I was standing just inside the kitchen, and the salad maker caught my eye. I saw no evidence he had washed that head of iceberg, and he was not wearing gloves.

"You know, you should use romaine, much more nutritional, plus you should wash it, really wash it well, and you should be wearing sterile gloves." I like to be helpful.

Salad Guy stopped chopping iceberg and looked me up and down. "You with the Health Department?"

The words "why, yes" started to form on my lips as I figured that would open some doors here. But a woman who had the look of head chef stepped up to me and said, "I'd like to see your ID."

"Oh, me, I'm sorry, I was just looking for the ladies room." I gave them all what I hoped was a sheepish but friendly look. "The waitress, the blond one, told me it was back here."

"That Sheila," the salad guy said, "doesn't know her head from her—"

"It's back the way you came, first door on the right," the head chef woman said, and crossed her arms in front of her chest in classic defensive mode.

Okay, so this chef knew something in this kitchen didn't bear inspection. Even if it was just dirt.

But now that everyone had stopped chopping and boiling and frying to stare at me, there was nothing to do but turn and head back down the hall.

Only when I got to the first door on the left, where I had spotted a walk-in freezer, I peeked back. Head Chef was watching me, so I continued down the hallway to the bathroom, and ducked in.

After counting to one hundred, I stepped out, and seeing no one staring toward me, I dashed silently back up the hallway, once more boldly ignoring the EMPLOYEES ONLY sign, and turned left into the room with the walk-in freezer. The cosmic gods of sneaks smiled benevolently on me. No one was in this room, and those wide, stainless-steel doors screamed to me to open them.

Within seconds, I was doing just that. Peering behind me toward the kitchen, I couldn't see anyone, and figured that meant no one could see me. In short order, I plopped a bag of frozen peas inside the door to make sure it didn't fully close and lock me in, and I stepped inside, pulling the door mostly shut behind me.

And immediately, I began to shiver.

Violent, whole-body, teeth-chattering, shivering. I mean, this place was cold. Colder than I, a woman with a Deep Dixie childhood and Gulf Coast of Florida adulthood, had ever experienced. I mean, come on, I had never in my life lived where it snowed. In Sarasota, if it gets down to fifty in February, we bitch about the cold. A southwest Florida winter coat is more like a flannel shirt.

Hell, I didn't even like air-conditioning.

But I reminded myself I was not moving in for the night, checked again to make sure the door was still open a crack, flipped on the light, and looked around.

As I took in all the stacks of frozen stuff, all those Jack London stories about men dying in high snowdrifts came back to me in one horrible rush.

chapter 28

I **confess that when** I was in college and taking all those English lit courses they make you take, my efforts focused more on Cliff's Notes than actually, you know, reading the assignments.

But still, I thought I remembered this: Dante's version of hell was cold.

I could be wrong on that, of course. But if Dante hadn't pictured it that way, let me tell you, it'd sure work.

Okay, so just *hurry up,* I told myself, and stop pondering the lost literature of the extreme cold.

Angling around but still standing by the door, I studied stuff closest to me first, on the theory that if I didn't have to walk any further into the freezer, that would be fine with me. Not helped at all by the massed assorted frozen carbs, I felt a little hint of panic kick me in the gut. I checked the bag of peas propping the door open. Still there. I wasn't trapped. And I didn't want to add another phobia to my list: fear of cold. So, I went forth to be useful.

Rubbing my arms futilely for warmth, I pushed myself deeper into the cooler until I was at the meats, and studied them, looking, I suppose, for monkey meat or koala steaks. Alas for both Demetrious and the animals, all the frozen carcasses were some version of cow, pig, or chicken.

But then, I saw an ice chest jammed in the back corner, behind a bunch of dead quail. An ice chest inside a walk-in freezer seemed more than a tad redundant, so naturally, I yanked the lid off.

And there it was: the stash of turtle eggs. Frozen. Clearly labeled.

Within shivery seconds, I had that camera out of my purse and was snapping away.

Got it, I thought, after several shots.

Proud of myself for getting both a voice recording and photographic evidence, I didn't pat myself on the back too long. I had to get out of here before hypothermia set in.

But before I could move from the ice chest of illegal eggs, I heard the clear and unwelcome voice of Manager Man just outside the cracked door. "Nobody goes into the meat locker but us."

I started cramming that camera into my purse like a shoplifter maxed out on cappuccinos.

"Well, she has to be here someplace. This is the only place you haven't looked," Simon, my hero in blue, said.

When they both stepped into the freezer and stared at me, I smiled in what I hoped was a tipsy sort of way, and said, "Oh, hi there."

"What are you doing in there?" they both asked in a weird harmony. I wasn't sure if they'd seen the tail end of the camera disappearing into my purse.

Telling the truth was clearly out of the question. "FDA," I said. "Checking for any dairy with bovine-growth hormones."

"That stuff isn't illegal," Manager Man said. "And it doesn't have to be on labels."

Ignoring the argument that BGH *should* be illegal, I wholly made something up. I snapped out in my most authoritative voice, "The alpha-simulator variety has been recalled, and—"

"Let me see your identification," Manager Man demanded.

Oh, that again.

Time to leave.

Jumping past them both, like a cornered coyote who sees an escape route, I jogged back down the hallway to the dining room. By the time I reached the front door, where the puzzled hostess was staring at me, Simon had caught up with me. "Are you all right?"

So, how many times had Simon asked me that tonight? Poor guy. "Fine, fine," I said. "But we should probably leave."

With that, I turned back to see Manager Man giving me one of those if-looks-could-kill stares. But he made no move toward me, and I sprinted out the door, Simon at my heels.

As I trotted toward Simon's spiffy red sports car, he kept pace beside me. "Lilly, I was worried. You were gone so long. We looked everywhere. I had to insist that man look in the freezer. What were you doing in the freezer?"

"Oh, Simon, how sweet of you to worry, but I'm fine. Still, we should go, right now. I was just checking expiration dates. You wouldn't believe how many places serve expired food."

We jumped into Simon's sports car, and he squealed his tires as he sped out of there.

Simon said something I didn't register because I was studying my rearview mirror. No one was chasing us. But still, I asked, "How fast can this car go?"

"Fast."

"Prove it," I said.

"Can do," Simon said, and punched up the speed and the power, and his little foreign sports car took off, and then, get this: The man laughed.

"What an adventure. I don't care what you did back there. I haven't had to run out of a place with a *pretty* woman, a very, very pretty woman, in, I don't know, years. A very, very pretty woman."

Poor Simon, he probably thought I had been trying to steal a couple of porterhouse steaks or something. So, I let the *very, very* thing slip by.

After all, the man was speeding at my request, and not demanding any real explanation. Maybe I'd ask Eleanor to have a word with him about adverb abuse. And I leaned back in my seat, and I laughed too.

What a particularly generous dose of good karma, I thought, to be on a date with a man who apparently found extreme weirdness attractive. You'd be surprised how rare that is.

chapter 29

S **imon's mother had** a cold, cold heart, okay, I got it. But ten
thousand *very, very*s later, I decided to have a nightcap with the staph
germs in my mother's hospital room rather than with Simon.

It was either that or slap him the next time he said anything with a *y*
on the end of it.

A little wobbly now in my borrowed spike heels, thanks to general
fatigue and an ample amount of wine before, during, and after dinner, I
had trouble at the ICU until somebody finally admitted Willette had been
moved back to a private room. A brief scenic tour of the hospital hallways
later, I wandered past a young man in a uniform, who demanded an ID,
then eyed my legs and my driver's license with equal attention, before I
stumbled into Willette's room for one more good-night bed check.

There, I was surprised to find Jubal and Hank sitting with Willette,
who appeared as comatose as ever, though I noted the red spots from the
ant bites seemed less vivid.

"Hank and me came by to check on your momma, but we could tell
Eleanor was just plain wiped out, so we told her we'd stay till Dan got
over here. Hank's a good man, to do something like that, ain't he?"

"Hank's a good man," I said. And smiled at him just to watch him blush and duck his head. But I also registered the fact that Eleanor obviously trusted Jubal and Hank. Bone-tired or not, I didn't think Eleanor would have left her charge unless she was sure Willette was in safe hands.

Still red-faced, Hank asked if I'd keep his dad company for a few minutes while he stepped outside to get a breath of fresh air.

"It's too late to be calling that lady lawyer, you hear me?" Jubal said.

Hank ignored him and left.

All in all, it looked to me like Jubal could probably handle sitting in a hospital room with Willette by himself. But I sat down on the edge of her bed, and kicked off those damn shoes. "Everything okay?"

"Oh, sure, I mean, good as I reckon it can get. Dan's supposed to come stay the night. Since we been here, she's not said one word, but nobody's bothered her any. And no bugs. She sure seems to be resting easy."

"I'm glad to hear that."

"You have you a good time?" There was an edge to Jubal's question I registered but chose to ignore.

"Fine, thank you," I said. Wanting to change the subject before I got the Hank-as-potential-husband chat, I zeroed in on Jubal's other obsession. "I've been thinking about your property and the eminent domain—"

"You found out anything about that resort and my land?" Jubal asked.

"Nothing specific, I've just been thinking about it."

"Damn that Lonnie. That man promised me and Hank flat-out, time and time again, that he wouldn't vote to go in as partners with the resort, but he'd changed his mind, and now look where we're all at."

Well, we were sort of in the same boat, I thought, and I explained to Jubal how Lonnie had agreed time and time again he would call me first if he ever sold his house.

"And he promised Shalonda he'd up and do right by her, time and time again, you believe the gossip any," Jubal said.

"So I gather Lonnie isn't a man to trust."

"Worse'n that, I'd say."

"So what about this Dr. Weinstein? What do you know about him?"

"I ain't got no use for that man a'tall. He's a low-down skunk, you ask me."

Ah, potentially interesting, I thought, and rubbed my feet.

"Stick your feet over here in my lap, let me do that for you."

That seemed way too familiar, and I shook my head.

"Aw, come on, I ain't getting fresh with you. I know how women torture their feet for the sake of looking good. I had me a wife once, you 'member?"

My feet did hurt, I was a tad tipsy, and yeah, it always felt better when somebody else rubbed my feet. So, I put them in Jubal's lap, and sighed in pleasure at the way he began to massage them, one at time.

We sat quietly for a few moments after that, me feeling better by the minute.

But I didn't want to drop the Dr. Weinstein query.

"So, Jubal, why don't you like him?"

"Man fired me as his patient all 'cause I was going over to the V.A. clinic in Albany. Said he wasn't getting 'nough money from me 'cause of the V.A. I went and saw that lawyer woman Hank's hanging around with—she's not near as pretty as you—and wanted her to sue him. She filed something with some agency, and he got this letter fussing at him, but that was all. I went back to see her about maybe suing him for discriminating against veterans, but . . . well, she got . . . all huffy, and we, um, well it wasn't a good visit, not at all."

So, the Georgia Medical Society had reprimanded Dr. Weinstein for something like wrongful termination of a patient? Perhaps abandonment? Hm? Maybe getting that censure for booting out Jubal explained why Dr. Weinstein was so set on hanging on to Willette. That is, if the doc had already been warned about dumping patients, surely he didn't want to risk sanctions by dropping yet another one.

Or maybe Dr. Weinstein wanted to keep Willette totally in his control until he could kill her.

After plying Jubal with a few more pointed Dr. Weinstein questions, I finally figured he'd told me all he knew about the man, and I was ready to move on. As he massaged my aching toes, I asked, "So, Jubal, did you actually stay in touch with Willette? I mean, after high school."

"Oh, sure, I been knowing her all along. Shoot, you 'member when you and Little Toot"—and he stopped to giggle like a man who'd had more than a nip of sour mash—"Lord, that man hates it when I slip up and call him that—"

"Willette," I said, to prompt him.

"Sure, when you and Hank got in trouble that time, I called her. But, truth is, I didn't really see her none till your daddy moved out. By then, my wife, she'd done crossed over, and I had this notion . . . well, it's silly now. But I had me this idea I might could court Willette."

Court Willette?

That idea was so weird I started to pull my feet out of Jubal's lap, but his big, thick fingers were doing such a good job, I left them there.

"She's a bit odd, but, you know, she's not a bad sort."

Oh, well, yeah, he didn't grow up inside that house, I thought, but kept my mouth shut.

"Your momma would call me now and then, after she got to where she didn't go out at all, to ask me to do odd jobs for her. Mostly picking up packages at the P.O., or getting something from the IGA. Truth is, Dan did most of that for her, but now and again, she'd call me."

So, he volunteered the information and solved the mystery of why those half dozen phone calls to or from him were in Willette's list of phone calls. Even I couldn't make anything too sinister out of a man who up and tells me out of his own goodwill that he used to play fetch for my reclusive mother—all this while easing my aching feet. So, I launched off on the next topic.

"What do you do at the Tru Blue Drugstore?"

"Ever thing. Stock shelves. Clean up. Ring you up and make change. Count out your pills when nobody's looking and the pharmacist is real busy."

That sounded helpful. "You got access to the pharmacist's computer?"

"Yep, especially when nobody's looking."

Two *when nobody's looking*s in sixty seconds. My kind of guy!

"Could you plug in the RX numbers on the pill bottles we got from Willette's, maybe even the partial numbers from ones where the labels were half torn off? That way, maybe we could find out who was supplying her with drugs."

"How's that gonna help anything?" he asked.

"Probably won't. But I'd sure like to know."

"Well, I don't know. I was working up at the U-Save Pharmacy by the hospital—say, you need any prescriptions, now that's a good store to go to—and the pharmacist there, Bill, he's a real nice fella, and just as smart as they come. Only I got let go there and I might not want to be messing around like you ask at the Tru Blue, case I get let go there too."

When I heard Jubal's reluctance, it recrossed my mind that he might have been supplying Willette with drugs from the Tru Blue. Or that he wasn't as free and skilled at the job as he pretended. I didn't want to beg him. But I thought a little trick might induce him to try—unless, of course, he was her dealer.

"What I'm thinking is that Dr. Weinstein is supplying her with those narcotics. I don't see how that ties in with her shooting Ray Glenn, but if Dr. Weinstein is—"

"Yeah, okay, I get it. Could be him, sure, sure. Could be. By gosh, you give me those bottles and I'll sure see what I can find out. Might take me a while, working as I'd be when the druggist is on break."

Maybe I was trusting Jubal too much—not my usual persona, but then I had no other way of finding out this information. And the way he jumped in to volunteer when I mentioned my suspicions regarding Dr. Weinstein made me hope again that Jubal was not Willette's dealer. Maybe whoever had supplied Willette with those pills had also bruised her mouth and jaw trying to force her to take a fatal dose. Maybe not, but I still wanted to know who my mother's dealer was. And Jubal, trustworthy or not, was about my only source. But at least I didn't have to hand the actual bottles over to him. "I don't have those containers with me right now. Let me copy the numbers and bring them to you. When are you working next?"

"Monday, so take your time."

So, there I was, enlisting the aid of a man who wanted to be my step-father and now also to be my father-in-law, with my feet in his lap, when Simon the very, very irritating date danced into the room without so much as a knock.

"Well, Lilly," he said, "I'm surprised to see you here. Very surprised."

And very displeased, I gathered from his tone of voice and the hard look he gave me. Possibly Simon was put out because not more than a half hour earlier I'd insisted I was so tired that I just had to go right back to Dan's and collapse into bed to sleep. This being my response to his invitation to go dancing in Tallahassee or go back to his house for a nightcap. Of course, what I had planned to do was check on Willette in a hurry, then drop off the camera and tape recorder with Demetrious, along with a full report of my evening at the Deer Den, and then collapse at Dan's.

Instead, here I was, having obviously lied to Simon, and with my feet in another man's lap.

Well, I never intended to go on a second date with him anyway.

Before I could think of anything to say, Jubal butted right in. "When do you think y'all can wake Miz Willette up and feed her? She looks like she needs a few good meals."

I seconded the thought, pointing out this was not the first time this particular issue had been raised.

But Simon said that was up to her physician, that she was getting plenty of nutrients in her IVs, that he was administration, not patient care, but he'd sure put in a call to Dr. Weinstein first thing in the morning to find out why he was still keeping Willette so sedated that she couldn't even eat.

That, of course, reminded me that I had to tackle Judge Parker with my concerned-daughter routine and get those guardianship papers done, so Dan could replace Dr. Weinstein with Dr. Hodo.

"Are, by chance, either of you friendly with Judge Parker?" I asked, thinking if they were, they could damn well engineer a gathering in which I could corner the good judge.

But it turned out Simon was too new to the city to socialize in that high a circle, and Jubal did not run much with the business-suit crowd.

After that, we just all strained at small talk about poor Willette. To my great relief, Dan stuck his head in the room, greeted us, then said he was here for the night shift and everybody could go now. A nurse came in and told us it was after visiting hours and only one person could stay, so everyone else shuffled around and left.

In spite of what the nurse had said, I stayed behind to speak with Dan, I mean, I'm immediate family and I was going to stay and talk with my brother if I wanted to, and I dared anyone to try and pitch me outside.

"You've got to get that guardianship, *now,* if we have to go over to Judge Parker's house and drag him out of bed, and we've got to get Dr. Hodo on the case," I said. "We can't wait till Monday. Do you have the judge's home phone number?"

"Nope, his home phone is unlisted. But Judge Parker will be at Mule Day tomorrow, we can talk to him then," Dan said. "He never misses it."

Oh great, petitioning a slow-moving judge at a mule festival. A mule festival I hadn't made up my mind to go to. But if I wanted to get a minute or two with the good judge in a social setting, Mule Day looked like my best bet. Especially since Judge Parker wasn't going to be holding office hours on Saturday.

"I'm going to spend the night, you can go on," Dan said. "I reckon it's my turn, and nobody's gonna make me leave this time. Shalonda can't stay all the time. She's got to help Demetrious get his mules ready for tomorrow. And she's got to sleep. And she deserves some time on her own. She helps us, so we've got to help her."

Everybody was so busy helping everybody, I thought, that maybe they had lost track of the fact some bad stuff was going on.

chapter **30**

While it's true, as Hank Williams sang, that none of us gets out of this world alive, I did hope to get away from the hospital alive. Perhaps that was overly optimistic.

Too weary to be alert in the dim hospital parking lot, I fumbled in my purse, looking for my Honda key, and wondered why a place that charges $20 for a $2 pill couldn't afford better lights.

Before I could quite get my fingers around my keys, someone grabbed my purse off my shoulder, shoved me hard enough that I crashed to the ground, and took off running. Stunned, I sat for a second in a puddle of gravel before I struggled to my feet and shook myself off.

My purse, damn it. My keys. My money. Nobody steals my purse without at least getting a fair fight, I thought, and charged after the shadowy figure, screaming my lungs out. Despite his head start, I would have caught him too, but another man grabbed me. As I tried to fight my way out of his grasp, I finally recognized the voice. It was Hank, and he was trying to calm me down.

"Lilly, Lilly, stop. That man might have a gun. Or a knife. I'll call 911, but nothing in your purse is worth getting hurt over."

Only a man would say that, I thought, and gave one more big struggle before Hank's calming voice and strong grip made me give up.

Of course, my cell phone was locked in my car and my mugger now had my car keys. And of course, Hank didn't have a cell phone. So, by the time he pulled me back to the hospital entrance and dragged me inside, the thief had had enough time to get across the Florida state line, and I was not happy that big, strong Hank had not chased the man down with me instead of stopping my pursuit.

While I sputtered and cursed and voiced my myriad complaints without one whit of reserve, Hank dialed 911. Then practicalities began to surface in my consciousness. I hoped the credit card companies had all-night 800 numbers to report lost cards. Quickly, I did an inventory. Worse than losing my cash and credit cards, the tape of the Deer Den manager offering me a modest menu choice of illegal turtle eggs or illegal fish eggs was in my purse, and now gone. And the camera.

I had officially nothing to give to Demetrious, and nothing to show for a very long night.

Oh, except for a really fine dining experience at Annier's Courtyard, where they had let me inspect the kitchen, and where they did have vegetarian dishes that even I liked, topped off with an excellent wine list. Even Simon's incessant adverb abuse hadn't ruined my meal.

While I was still grumbling to Hank about his utter lack of warrior spirit, Demetrious drove up. No siren. Just a tired, unhappy-looking man. Dragging. I knew the feeling.

All I wanted to do now was get the police thing over with and go home, shower, and collapse into bed. But first we had to go through all that pointless stuff about the purse snatching, I had to confess I'd lost the Deer Den evidence, and then I had to ask Demetrious for a ride home, since I didn't have my car keys.

"Well, let's ride over and check on the car, and then I'll take you home, and we can get a locksmith out here tomorrow. No point calling one this late," Demetrious said, and I had to admire the man for not fussing at me for failing to bring the recorder and camera straight to him, instead of first finishing up my share of a couple of bottles of wine and a fine meal with Simon, plus getting a foot rub.

Hank, who had hovered discreetly enough to pretend to give Demetrious and me some privacy, popped back into our space. He said, since his car was parked near mine, he'd ride over with us for the company. As if we were chipper. As if the parking lot was that vast.

But at my car, a bigger problem presented itself.

Every door to the vehicle was wide open, and the trunk lid was up.

"*Damnation and hellfire,*" I shouted. The thief had quickly put my stolen car keys to good use, and right under Demetrious's nose.

"You sound just like your granddaddy used to," Hank said. "That's what he always said."

Ignoring that nostalgic footnote on my family history, Demetrious said not a word, but got out his flashlight and humped around the car from all directions, as if the thief might be hiding somewhere in the shadow cast by my Honda.

This was bigger than losing my purse. Much bigger, I thought, as I looked into the now mostly empty Honda trunk. The hiding place of the original set of Willette's most important papers.

Just in case I'd missed them in my first look, I grabbed Demetrious's flashlight and I stuck my head way down into the trunk.

But Willette's papers were gone.

While Demetrious took his flashlight back, and asked what was missing from the trunk, I had the satisfaction of thinking: Good thing two sets of copies of Willette's important papers were hidden at Dan and Patti's house.

Then I realized my doubled-bagged collection of Willette's prescription-pill bottles, which I had stashed in the trunk, was also missing. Damn, damn, damn, I thought, now Jubal wouldn't be able to help me find the person supplying my mother with drugs.

For good measure, I rooted around in the glove compartment, discovered my cell phone and lock picks were still there, as were my wet wipes and detailed Honda-maintenance records.

So what was the thief after? Pill bottles, tape recording, camera, important papers—or just my pocket change and my credit cards and whatever might have been in the car and trunk the thief could hock for money?

Uh-oh, like an unmerry little parade, still another unhappy thought pranced toward me.

What if Jubal really had been Willette's drug dealer and just volunteered to help me poke into the Tru Blue computer as a means to hide his own trail? I mean, I know there are regulations, federal, state, and no doubt local, that make pharmacists practically have to take a video of every narcotic pill they handle or sell or dispose of, but there was a cunning criminal element that was very adept at getting the kind of pills they wanted for personal consumption or black-market sales.

Maybe Jubal had a business on the side.

Maybe he didn't want me finding out he was Willette's dealer, and he had been after those pill bottles.

"Where's your father?" I asked, staring hard at Hank.

"Over there, badgering Simon about something. Probably that resort. He's got a bug up his . . . sorry, ma'am. Daddy's just in a snit and he's seeing if Simon, being a nearby landowner, has any ideas."

I looked over where Hank had pointed. In the shadows of the front door of the hospital, I could see two men talking, one waving his hands all about.

If I could see them from my Honda, then couldn't they see my Honda? I mean, why hadn't they noticed someone breaking into my car and done something to stop it? Was the much-touted Southern chivalry dead, or what? "So they were pretty helpful while somebody was emptying out my trunk," I said, possibly a bit more snippy than Hank deserved.

"Simon just stepped outside a couple of minutes ago. Daddy caught up with him after you and Demetrious finished up. By that time, I reckon your purse was already stolen, and the car gone through."

Well, okay, it was an excuse of sorts.

"Let's walk over and chat with them," I said, and started walking.

So, that's what I did, despite the protests of both Hank and Demetrious.

Naturally, neither Jubal nor Simon had seen a thing, heard a thing, or suspected a thing, and both were just really glad I wasn't hurt, et cetera, et cetera. And nobody knew how to hot-wire my Honda so I could drive it back to Dan's house, not even Demetrious. You'd think they'd teach how to hot-wire at the police academy, but *no*.

Thus, after that further waste of time, I let Demetrious drive me home.

After all, tomorrow was shaping up as a busy day. As soon as the locksmith got me new keys to my car, I would have to go to Mule Day to track down and convince the good judge to let my brother make all of Willette's legal decisions for her. Plus all that other stuff I had to do.

Yeah, okay, I was being naive, given that it was midnight in the small town of good and eerie. Sure, it was entirely probable I should have done something more, but as it was, my world had reduced itself to a single, fundamental fact: Get some sleep or die.

So, I went to bed.

chapter 31

As the small towns of the South watched more of each generation of their children move away to the great cities, watched their industries of pickles, paper, and textiles relocate to third-world countries, watched their family farms being crushed by the mega–farm corporations, development, and rising fuel costs and taxes, and watched their place as the butt of the only acceptable ethnic jokes still tossed about the media—redneck being an ethnic group, if you ask me—the small-town Dixie chambers of commerce rallied back.

Damn near every one of them now has some festival, from Swine Time to Mule Day to Rattlesnake Round-Up, into which the civic leaders pour their efforts and their enthusiasm and their hopes.

And so it was that I woke, anxious and fatigued and sore of joint and heart, but with a certain excitement. It was Mule Day.

Despite the chaos and calamity that had clamored down about me of late, I finally decided to go. Hey, it was *Mule Day,* okay? And I hadn't been in twenty years. And, more important, I had to find that judge.

Except, wouldn't you know it, the only locksmith in Bugfest had a mule in the parade, and couldn't come rescue my Honda from its keyless state of inertia. I had to call locksmiths in an ever-widening circle until I found one in Tallahassee, who, for an exorbitant sum of money, would indeed come thirty miles up the canopy road, cross the state line, and do whatever he had to do to re-create a car key for me.

Naturally, this took frigging forever.

Thus, I missed the bulk of the excitement of Mule Day.

I missed the parade, the rodeo, and, more interestingly, the unintended and unscheduled highlight of the day: A big fight between Demetrious and Lonnie and the vile-mouthed Colleen, including cussing, stomping, and out-and-out punching. That is, punching between the menfolk. And though I had missed witnessing this spectacle with my own eyes, pretty much everybody I saw afterward gave me a blow-by-blow description.

But I didn't know about the fight when I drove my Honda with its new and expensive key up to the mule festival grounds just barely in time to capture the apt attentions of one good Judge Parker.

Given the dwindling crowd by the time I got there, I was able to park within a mile of the event, and huffed my way forward in a totally cool pair of tooled red leather cowboy boots that I didn't figure Patti would mind too much if I borrowed from way in the back of her closet.

I found my sister-in-law fixing to chomp down on a fried Oreo cookie. "Wow, you missed it," Patti Lea said. "Colleen cussed out Shalonda and then Lonnie cussed out Demetrious and next thing anybody knew they were hitting each other like schoolboys whose mothers hadn't brought them up right. Demetrious is all right, but a bunch of his deputies had to pull him off Lonnie."

"Is Shalonda all right?" I asked, eyeing the fried trans-fat-and-flour combination in Patti's hand.

"Oh, all right, considering. I had to give her a hug, and a tissue, but at least nobody hit her."

Patti moved the fried dough closer to her mouth.

"You really should not eat that," I said. "That oil in the deep fryer is probably used over and over. It's an established scientific fact that old oil repeatedly heated to high temperatures becomes carcinogenic, did you know that?"

When I annotated my initial warning to Patti on the ill-advised nature of eating such a thing, she gave me a hard look that ended up at my feet.

"Those are Tony Lamas," Patti said, looking at her boots on my feet.

"Oh, I noticed. And they fit me just wonderfully. Thank you for letting me borrow them."

Patti Lea looked me right in the face and took a big bite of that fried cookie.

Well, fine then, you can eat poison-fried poison if you want to, I thought. Just then Bobby and Becky ran up.

"Wow, did you see it?" Becky said. "Demetrious about beat the tar out of that Lonnie, and then when his own deputy men had to pull him off of Lonnie, Demetrious told Lonnie somebody needed to teach him and his wife some manners."

"Reckon Demetrious would teach me to fight like that?" Bobby asked no one in particular.

While Patti started a little speech about the evils of fistfights, I pulled Becky off to the side. "Do you know Judge Parker?" I asked her.

"Everybody knows Judge Parker," she said.

Well I didn't, and Dan hadn't, but I let that slide. "Come on, then, you can help me find him and introduce me." And we started off down the block, leaving Patti pontificating on the value of personal pacifism, while Bobby fidgeted and shifted foot to foot, waiting for his chance to bolt after Becky.

It wasn't, after all, an improper ex parte communication with a judge if I were to tackle Judge Parker into a conversation about Dan's legal guardianship for Willette, since I wasn't the attorney of record, just an anxious next of kin. And how could the judge possibly refuse to chat with me when such a charming young woman as Becky would be introducing us?

"Afterward," I said to Becky, "let's find Shalonda and make sure she is really all right."

"Oh, I think Shalonda and Demetrious might've left. Wow, you should have seen it. Demetrious was just about as mad as I've ever seen anybody get. That Colleen called Shalonda a really bad word. And Demetrious just jumped right in there to her rescue and hit Lonnie right smack in the face."

"You saw this?"

"Everybody saw it."

Well, except me, thanks to the slowness of that Tallahassee locksmith.

"Think Bobby would do that for me?" Becky asked. "Defend me?"

"In a minute," I said, without thinking it through. As it turned out, I wasn't far off the mark.

chapter 32

A **circle of nice,** professional men surrounded the bed of my frail mother, nodding and saying pointless things.

"It's really quite simple," I said, trying but failing to keep the tart out of my tone. "Judge Parker appoints Dan as Willette's legal guardian. No one is objecting. All the paperwork is done." I wisely controlled myself from pointing out Judge Parker could have and should have already done this a couple of days before.

"Is anyone objecting?" Judge Parker asked, as if I hadn't already told him nobody was, and I would have been stupid enough to tell a lie that easily discovered. Nonetheless, we all turned to Dr. Weinstein. If he had the bad taste to say anything, I was prepared to strike him down with my prepared speech, pointing out that he had no standing to object.

"Certainly, it is not my place to object to Dan being her legal guardian, but I insist Mrs. Cleary remain in this hospital until she is stable enough for a transfer," Dr. Weinstein said.

Okay, he'd played his cover-your-ass card, and I turned back to the judge. "As you can see, Your Honor, Willette is not competent, and Dan is her most trusted son, and no one objects, and—"

"All right, Miss Lilly, all right," Judge Parker said.

It was entirely possible *all right* just meant *shut up,* but I took it for a positive ruling and whipped out the paperwork and a pen from where I'd stashed them on Willette's bedside table. "Here."

"This is most irregular," the judge said.

But he signed it when I stood between him and the door out and waggled the pen under his nose, my body language as clear as pig Latin to a ten-year-old.

Dan was now officially Willette's legal guardian.

"Dr. Weinstein, thank you for your services," I said. "But Dr. Hodo is now Willette's treating physician. You got that, Simon?"

"What I heard was Judge Parker appoint Dan, not you," Dr. Weinstein said.

Dan looked at me, then turned back to Dr. Weinstein. "You can go now. Dr. Hodo is going to take care of Willette."

The stocky doctor with the spiky hair turned and left the room.

Finally. Why had I left this to Dan and his lady lawyer in the first place? I verbally kicked myself for half a second for not taking charge sooner, on the well-established principle that the only way to get something done right is to do it yourself. Though, of course, I had chased the elusive judge about town before Becky cornered him for me that afternoon at Mule Day. Becky's mom the lawyer and Dan had just been too damn polite about it, but Becky was a child after my own sense of initiative. All it had taken was my two-minute explanation to Becky about what I was up to, and her sweet introduction of me as her boyfriend's aunt to Judge Parker at Mule Day. First Becky oohed and aahed over the judge's mule winning a second place—second, it turned out, to Demetrious's Big Beauty's blue ribbon in the overall-great-mule category. Then Becky did a sensitive-teen, all-worried-about-Bobby's-distress-over-his-grand-mother thing, and I did my demure, dutiful-daughter persona, a role I had actually never bothered to try on before. In no time at all, we two convinced one Judge Parker to come by the hospital that very afternoon and observe Willette.

After the judge went to fetch his mule as a prelude to coming by the hospital to see Willette, I told Becky she had excellent potential as a future trial attorney, or an actress. She told me my boots were really cool, and could she maybe borrow them sometime, if they fit? We were fully bonded by the time Bobby found us, and I left them to the remainder of their afternoon so I could round up the rest of the happy gang for the transfer of Willette's control over herself to her middle child, Dan, the responsible one.

Thus, through a persistent series of phone calls, and some minor threats, I had gotten Dr. Hodo there too.

And Dan, bloated and green as he was from eating an entire sweet-potato pie from the church ladies' booth at the Mule Day food court, had stood by his mother, nodding and frowning.

Right as Judge Parker had graced Willette's hospital doorway, the ever-vigilant Simon had bobbed in, swinging his arms and offering to help, and shortly in Simon's wake, as if warned by a nurse or a deal with the devil, Dr. Weinstein had also appeared. That was how we had all come to hold a guardianship hearing in a hospital room on a Saturday afternoon.

After Dr. Weinstein left, Dr. Hodo checked Willette's vital signs and her chart, and patted her hand before turning to me.

"I'll taper her off the Thorazine, and we'll get her eating, and then we'll talk to her if she's able," said Dr. Hodo, my father's friend and now officially Willette's doctor of record. "Then we'll make sure she's stable, and transfer her to a rehab center I know in Atlanta. It's the best in the region."

"Fine, then," Simon said, "very good. That's settled. Very, very good. I'm so glad for you, Lilly, that this is working out."

For once, I agreed with the man.

chapter 33

One benefit of my making lists of things to do was the warm, fuzzy glow I felt when I could scratch something off that list.

The bad thing about my making lists of things to accomplish was the cold, nauseous sensation I felt when I couldn't scratch something off that list.

So, there I was, sitting on the glider on Dan's porch, carefully nursing a cup of hot green tea and my last organic apple, letting the good and the bad feelings duke it out inside me.

On the one hand, by finally taking matters into my own hands, I had wrestled the slow-moving judge into our corner, and Dan was now Willette's guardian.

On the other hand, by taking matters into my own hands, I had zip to show for figuring out why Willette allegedly shot a man, and why somebody tried to kill her with red ants.

Actually, the list of failures was a good deal longer than the list of accomplishments. For one, Willette's house loomed full of garbage, and no clue had surfaced yet. Demetrious had called me to say the Fish and Wildlife folks hadn't found anything criminal, or even suspect, at the Deer Den, and had fussed at him for wasting their time. I had no evidence or motive on my Dr. Weinstein theory, and Dr. Hodo said it would take a few hours for the last dose of Thorazine to wear off and for Willette to wake up.

So, we were all kind of waiting around for Willette to come out of her stupor and tell us what had happened the night she apparently shot Ray Glenn, and as I took the last bite of my last apple, I figured I was somewhere between mopey and bored.

Plus I had to get home, I had to figure out how to get rid of Idiot Client so I could testify for Henry, and I had a half dozen cases sitting in my filing cabinets and not getting billed on—I'd have to work till midnight for a month to catch up with the firm's average monthly billing rates.

Thinking of Henry made me think of Bonita. As it was still Saturday, and I wouldn't offend her steadfast rule of honoring the Sabbath, I snatched out my cell phone and, in seconds, the calming voice of Bonita came lilting out of the little piece of plastic in my hand.

"Anything new?" I asked.

"Oh, hello, Lilly. If you can, take a look at the Rules Regulating the Florida Bar. It seems that you have a mandatory obligation to withdraw when a client tries to enlist your help in committing either a crime or a fraud."

Pleased that Bonita was right on that Idiot Client fraud thing, I jumped in too. "So, okay, I should be able to win my motion to withdraw then, right?"

"But the case law and the rules say that you can't testify about the client's fraud because of the attorney-client privilege."

"What?"

"The Ethics Rules require you to withdraw, but forbid you from telling the judge why."

So, okay, what lofty-minded yet reality-challenged fool had drafted that catch-22? Since my client was objecting to my motion to withdraw, I *had* to give the judge a reason, a very good reason. But the same rules that required me to withdraw in the face of my client's fraud forbade me from giving the judge any reason.

"So, okay, would that mean I can't testify against Idiot Client in Henry's case? Even if I withdraw and am no longer his attorney?"

"Lilly, I am not an attorney. I do not know the answer to that. I am just telling you what the rules say."

My stomach knotted in desperation. I had to get back to Sarasota, to my law office, to our law library, to Lexis and Westlaw on a high-speed Internet connection.

Because the thing about the law is this: There is always an exception.

And for Henry's sake, I would have to find it.

We said a few more words. And then we hung up.

My heart was fairly pounding thinking about Henry out there, on his own, without my help, as Idiot Client and Newly ruthlessly ground him and his insurance company into litigation dust.

I wiped my hands on my pants and looked up at the sound of footsteps.

Shalonda came walking up. I hopped up from the glider and stepped out to meet her.

"You all right?" I asked, though it was pretty obvious from looking at her she wasn't. Her eyes were puffy and she was still sniffling. "I looked all over for you after I heard what happened. Even called your house."

"That bitch told Demetrious to keep me off her husband, you believe that? Then she called me a cheating slut and used the n–word."

"Well, don't you worry, we'll get even with her," I said.

"White girl, I already got me a list of 'bout ten–twelve things I can do back at her. I like the way you think."

Colleen might have called Shalonda a slut and a very bad name in front of a Mule Day crowd, and Shalonda's husband might have slugged it out with her ex-lover as a result, but Shalonda was a trooper. I gave her a quick hug and a pat on the back.

"I'm doing all right, not gonna let that little bitch get me down."

"Good girl."

"I hate to ask, but . . ."

"Ask."

"Can you drive me home?"

"Sure. But where's your car?"

"Your mom is still out of it, by the way, but Dr. Hodo left a psych nurse there with her, and she'll call him the minute she starts waking up."

"Oh, good." But that hadn't answered the question I'd just asked. "Where's your car?"

"Demetrious took me by to check on Willette. Then we kinda had a . . . a fight. In the hospital parking lot."

"Not because of—"

"Yeah, because of—"

"I'll take you home, you know that, but don't you think you should call him?"

"I've been calling him. He's not usually a shithead, but he's not answering the phone, so I guess he's still mad enough to leave me high and dry in town."

Yeah, I wanted to take a long drive in the country to end up smack in the middle of this. But what I said was, "I need to get my shoes."

Two minutes later, at the twist of my new car key that had cost me more than the book value of my ancient Honda, my trusty vehicle purred into action, and we were heading out toward Shalonda and Demetrious's formerly happy home.

I didn't ask for any more details about their fight. Once, a long time ago, I'd handled some divorces, complete with all the horrid lies that involves, and I'd developed this highly refined theory about marital discord: Stay the hell out of it.

We drove in a strained silence, and we were not happy, either of us. Mopey had won out over bored, after all, and anxiety was still a player.

"Take me by the barn, please," Shalonda asked. "Maybe Demetrious's not answering at the house because he's in the barn. You know, celebrating with Big Beauty. Everybody forgot BB won that Best in Show, what with all that shit Colleen kicked up."

I wondered how one celebrated with a mule as I parked on the dirt driveway near the barn. I mean, I don't think you'd want to give a mule champagne, so—what? Maybe extra apples? So wondering, I stayed inside the car while Shalonda popped out.

"Something's wrong," she said after glancing around.

Yeah, a number of things were wrong, I thought. But I got out and looked around too.

Two of Demetrious's mules were milling around outside the corral, and Demetrious's truck was backed up to the barn, blocking the door. We didn't see BB in the fenced pasture, and we didn't see Demetrious.

"Why don't you go put those mules up, and I'll go see 'bout Demetrious," Shalonda said, then she ran into the barn.

Catch a mule? Huh. I studied the long-eared animals, who studied me right back, apparently placid enough. But when I reached for one, it brayed, baring exceptionally large teeth, and backed up from me. Okay, frontal attack didn't work, I thought, try gentle persuasion.

While I was trying to sweet-talk the mules into following me into the fence, I heard a heart-stopping scream.

Now what? As it wasn't like Shalonda to scream for no reason, I ran into the barn.

It took a split second for me to process what I saw. A pile of feed. A big pile of feed.

With feet sticking out at one end.

And Shalonda at the other. "Help me."

I processed and jumped at the same time, squatting beside her as the two of us dug away the sweet feed as fast as we could. "Nine-one-one," I gasped, "we need to call—"

"Dig," Shalonda yelled, "damn it, dig."

I kept digging.

How long, I wondered, as I dug, could someone survive with a big pile of sweet feed on top of him?

chapter 34

My own mother, crazy as she seemed to be, with her fear of any air outside her own front door and an apparent tendency, of late, toward psychotic rants, had nonetheless managed to defend herself against one mean bill collector when he burst into her haven.

Or else she had simply shot the man with no provocation other than extreme irritation.

But I much preferred to go with the self-defense theory.

So, there it was, the dominant assumption being that a frail, tiny, crazy woman had successfully defended herself against a big mean man.

She might have been afraid of damn near everything except garbage, but she wasn't afraid to get a gun, point it, and pull the trigger.

Not bad for a ninety-pound woman.

I had to reevaluate my mother's strength.

Especially in contrast to the fact that a man with big feet had apparently stood still while someone dumped a truckload of sweet feed smack on top of him.

One would have thought the man stood a better shot at self-defense.

But the ways of the universe are fickle and weird, or worse. And maybe, unlike Willette, he hadn't had a Saturday night special handy.

All of this was wildly inappropriate thinking on my part, but it distracted me momentarily from the scene that was taking place right in front of me, that being Shalonda and me digging in the waves of feed, digging to create air passages for the man beneath the feed.

Digging.

Until the blue face of one Big Lonnie Ledbetter appeared before us.

"Oh, my God," Shalonda said, and then inhaled and started mouth-to-mouth. "Pound on his chest," she yelled at me between blowing into Lonnie's mouth.

Aside from the fact that Lonnie's chest was still covered in sweet feed, I knew it was too late—the man was blue, and coolish to my touch. A brain dies in ten minutes without oxygen.

It takes longer than ten minutes for a man to turn bluish and cool.

But I didn't have the nerve to stop Shalonda.

Soon enough, she stopped herself.

"You can call 911, now, I guess. Get the high sheriff out here."

I studied Shalonda closely. She seemed all right, steady, and not on the brink of imminent hysteria.

"My cell phone is—"

"Go," she said. "Get the sheriff."

Easing out of the barn and reluctantly leaving Shalonda for a moment with her old lover, I snatched my cell phone out of my glove compartment and called 911. I explained as best I could that Lonnie Ledbetter was dead in Demetrious's barn, and the sheriff himself should get out here as soon as possible. I declined to answer further questions, and tossed the cell back in the Honda.

Lonnie dead in Demetrious's barn. I knew how that sounded. Before the high sheriff stepped out of his car in front of that barn, the rumor mill would have this a love-triangle murder.

I wanted to run into the barn and grab Shalonda and head out for the high hills.

But running away only delays the inevitable. This was one thing my habit of running away as a child had taught me.

So, I lingered outside, giving Shalonda her privacy, and I stared about me, looking for clues as to what had happened.

Over behind the barn, in the trees, I saw a whole covey of buzzards. Just roosting there.

And I remembered what Jubal had said about Demetrious collecting roadkill to feed the buzzards so that they would not get smacked by fast-moving trucks on the road.

Struck with an immediate and intense curiosity, I trotted toward the trees where the buzzards roosted. And came up short in front of a pile of dead something on the ground, a few buzzards lazily circling it. One buzzard looked up, eyed me as if taking my measure, and I flapped my arms. They rose then, awkward and heavy, those huge, ugly heads on top of the big bird-bodies. As I watched, the buzzards finally got their air wings, and rose and rose, and then circled. Graceful in the sky.

Disgusted, I looked down at the mashed mess on the ground, already telling myself to get back to Shalonda.

I'd half turned away when something flashed in my head like a cue card. I turned back.

Crawling all over the fresh carrion were ants.

What looked like millions of them.

Ants. Red ants.

Like the ones in Willette's room, ants without a nest of red dirt, ants on a piece of carrion that could easily have been tossed into a big Baggie and carried into a hospital room, where a little honey on Willette would have enticed them away from the roadkill.

Maybe that was why no one ever found a trace of the red dirt from an ant bed in Willette's hospital room.

Maybe the ants hadn't been scooped from an ant bed but gathered off roadkill.

But now why in the world would Demetrious want to kill Willette?

chapter 35

I t is the nature of love to survive death. My grandparents had taught me that, first by their words and then by their dying.

So it was that Lonnie lying dead on the floor of her husband's barn didn't stop Shalonda from loving him.

This was plain as day as I peeked in the barn and watched Shalonda trace the tips of her fingers along the lines of Lonnie's face, and stop with her ring finger over his lips. Then she leaned over and kissed those lips, and I felt like a voyeur of the worst kind, and eased back out of the barn, letting her sit for a moment longer with the man who, for all his faults, had truly meant something to her.

I was leaning against the fence, watching the mules and cursing the natural forces of evil, when Shalonda ran out of the barn. "I've got to find Demetrious," she shouted, and frantically snatched my cell phone. The sounds of sirens were close now.

Shalonda understood the situation, I gathered. That being it was Demetrious's barn, and he and the dead man had some issues over Shalonda, and had traded punches that very afternoon, with Demetrious threatening Lonnie in front of no less impeccable witnesses than a couple of deputy sheriffs. Demetrious would be a prime suspect, right from the get-go.

"He's not answering up at the house," she said, and closed the phone.

"Is there somebody I can call for you?" I asked.

"We got to find Demetrious," she said. "You stay here, wait for the sheriff, while I run up to the house."

"I think you ought to stay here."

But Shalonda, never one for taking advice, hopped into my Honda and roared up the driveway the half mile or so to the house.

Just on the off chance we didn't have enough people wandering around and messing up the crime scene and getting in one another's way, Jubal showed up a minute and a half behind the sheriff, an ambulance, and a host of cars full of people who seemed to be official but might not have been.

The sheriff, with a stern face and a deep voice, ordered everybody to stay put and not to be traipsing around in the yard. Jubal was, at that moment, traipsing around trying to catch a mule, and the sheriff trotted toward him as if he were an eyewitness or the key suspect.

Since everybody else seemed to be milling around, muddling up any tracks and such, I hotfooted it toward the sheriff and Jubal.

"What the hell are you doing here?" was what I heard the sheriff saying as I got within earshot.

"Helping out, which is more'n you're doing." With that, Jubal grabbed a mule by his mane and stomped off, the snared mule in tow, and the other one following close behind. In a minute, Jubal had them both back inside the corral.

"You want to tell me what's going on here?" the sheriff asked me.

"Jubal just put two mules back inside the fence, and Lonnie Ledbetter is lying in the barn, dead. Beyond that, I don't know." Factual, succinct, the perfect answer. The sheriff gave me a look that said he didn't appreciate it.

"Where's Demetrious?" he asked.

I decided not to answer. After all, I had a right to remain silent, and Shalonda and my Honda had just roared back into the driveway. I turned my back on the sheriff and watched her as she got out of the car and walked toward us.

"Where's Demetrious?" the sheriff asked again, and I kept my eyes on Shalonda and willed her to keep silent too.

"Probably up at his house, minding his own business," Shalonda said, though not five minutes ago, she'd told me that Demetrious was not answering his phone at the house either. "He didn't know Lilly and me were coming from town to the barn, or anything. He told me he had a lot of paperwork to do at the house, earlier, that is. I mean, he told me earlier. That he'd be working at the house. No reason for him to be anywhere near his barn."

I saw the way the sheriff stared at Shalonda, and decided that the first moment he wasn't looking at Shalonda, I would have to give her a quick lesson on the art of lying. She was no good at it at all.

No doubt sensing where the suspicion was landing, Shalonda tried to change the flight pattern. "I'm figuring that barn-burner, Colleen, she's the sort to dump feed on somebody, even her own husband," Shalonda said. "She never much acted like she liked him."

"Shalonda," I said, "you've had a shock. Maybe you should sit down."

And shut up, the words I couldn't speak in front of the sheriff, but I gave her a look that tried to convey to her that now was a good time to keep her thoughts to herself and keep careful watch. After all, her husband was fixing to be the lead suspect in the death of her lover. And it wouldn't take much of a leap to rope her into the circle of official suspects.

And anything you say can and will be used against you.

chapter 36

Patti Lea would not hear for one second any version of an idea that Shalonda should wait at her own house for her own husband all by herself.

So there Shalonda was, in the guest bedroom, sprawled on the bed, stifling her tears for one man and her worry for the other, and sipping green tea, my remedy, laced with Jack Daniels, her remedy, and not a mix likely to make the *Bartender's Guide.*

Patti seemed more than willing to overlook the whiskey and the adultery in light of her friendship with Shalonda, and this from the same woman who had sharply eyed my short dress on a non-date date.

But if Patti could overlook what were, to her, grievous sins, I could overlook the double standard. And we sat, one on either side of Shalonda, patting her hands, listening, and being what comfort we could. After all, a woman who thinks her husband smothered her lover in mule feed needs a little solace.

"Lonnie said he was leaving his wife," Shalonda said.

Honey, I thought but didn't say, they all say that. It's the second biggest lie, right after "Trust me, I wouldn't lie."

"He's like a cool, big old glass of whiskey, and I'm some fool drunk can't say no."

Well, I guess recent events had ended that addiction.

"I don't know where Demetrious is," she said, gulped down some whiskeyed tea, and confessed she had gone back to seeing Lonnie behind Demetrious's back. Maybe she was going to leave Demetrious for Lonnie. Maybe she wasn't. Maybe she loved Demetrious. Maybe she loved Lonnie. The more whiskey she drank, the vaguer she got.

But there were a couple of things not vague at all.

One being the dead man in the barn.

The next being the fact the phone was ringing. Patti and I ignored it. It stopped, then it rang again. And kept ringing.

Patti stood up. "I'll get it," she snapped, as if it were not her house and that somehow I was supposed to have answered the phone.

From the other room, I could hear muffled words but no screams or cries, so I figured at least the body count wasn't going up.

My sister-in-law stomped back into the room, clearly unhappy, and I said, "What?"

"Your mother went crazy."

"I think we all knew that awhile back."

"No, she woke up. That was Dr. Hodo. She woke up from that Thorazine coma, and she just went . . . crazy. Acting out. Seeing things. Screaming. Fighting everybody. He . . . Dr. Hodo . . . called it a . . . a psychotic break. She even hit Dan when he tried to quiet her down."

Frigging great.

Being an obsessive-compulsive agoraphobic wasn't good enough for Willette? She had to become psychotic too? And a violent one at that? The self-defense theory might collect some doubters if she kept being violently psychotic.

"So, what did . . . did they . . . what? Tie her up?" I asked.

"Dr. Hodo ordered a sedative to calm her down. He's hoping to bring her out of sedation slower in the morning, maybe have less of a reaction."

"Is he still there?"

"Yes."

"I don't suppose Willette had a chance to tell anyone why she shot Ray Glenn?"

"No, I don't suppose she did." Patti gave me one of those looks that let me know she was rethinking being part of the Cleary clan.

"I better get over there."

"I'll better go with you," Shalonda said, slurring the words just a hint.

"I'll drive," I said.

"I'll wait here," Patti said. "Somebody needs to be here and field the phone calls."

As I spun my little Honda the few blocks to the hospital, I wondered: Now what do we do with Willette, if our choices are catatonic drug stupor or psychotic rage?

But like a cloak over that worry was a bigger wonderment, one that had been pestering me since I first saw Lonnie's blue face on the barn floor. Okay, so it's not like I'm a specially trained forensic scientist or anything, but even Lonnie wouldn't be stupid enough to stand still while somebody dumped sweet feed on top of him.

chapter 37

Here it was, a bright, chilly morning, the day of the Lord, and all through the town of Bugfest, good folks gathered themselves into their Sunday dresses and suits in preparation for church.

I lay in my bed, like the town drunk, my head pounding and my stomach lurching.

Yeah, I pretty much woke up this way every Sunday in my undergrad days, but that was because I had an unusually stupid learning curve regarding tequila.

This Sunday-morning migraine I could lay straight on the doorstep of the cosmic forces that kept raining down Bad Stuff.

But not on me, per se, but close enough to me that I felt splattered.

I rose on shaky legs and gulped three Advil and four ginger capsules from the stash in my suitcase, and headed to the kitchen. Coffee. Lots of it. Caffeine, along with Advil and ginger, will sometimes knock out a migraine. And if it didn't, I'd weigh the risks/benefits of taking a Zomig.

But the immediate task before me was to consume as much caffeine as I could.

There was a pot of coffee in the percolator by the sink. A carton of ordinary grocery-store milk. Nothing organic. Nothing fair-trade.

I took exactly the time it takes to inhale and exhale to decide: *Yeah, whatever.*

And poured a cup. Added the milk. Added white sugar. And gulped it, burning my tongue.

Hot coffee in the cup versus two in the freezer. No question that Coke had been the beginning of a slippery slope backsliding into regular store-bought food laden with *whatever.* Next thing I knew, I'd be eating pound cake.

Yeah, whatever. I poured another cup and sat down at the table, picked up the Sunday paper, and read this sad story in the local newspaper:

Lonnie Ledbetter, county commissioner and local businessman, crossed over Saturday, probably near evening, when a load of feed fell off a trailer on top of him.

Sheriff Ronnie T. Wyatt said a load of sweet feed meant for Chief of Police Demetrious Dupree's mules fell on the victim.

The incident happened at Dupree's farm on Dead Possum Road. Dupree's prized mule, Big Beauty, had taken the Best in Show award, as well as other first-place ribbons, in the Annual Mule Day earlier on Saturday in Canaan.

In an interview with Sheriff Wyatt, he said no one really knows what happened, all they can do is guess.

"All we know is, somehow Mr. Lonnie got trapped behind the trailer in feed. We don't know what time it happened, exactly, but we took a call in the evening."

"He was dead right there, wasn't anything anybody could do," said a neighbor who didn't want his name put in the paper. "I came running when I heard all the sirens, but there was nothing any of us could do."

At this point, the sheriff says the incident is ruled an accident. Big Beauty, the prize-winning mule, is reported missing. So is Demetrious Dupree, but law enforcement officials refused to comment on this.

Right after I finished reading this story, Dan and Patti, all spiffy in their Sunday-school clothes in spite of a Saturday night straight from the trials of Job, stuck their heads in the kitchen to say good morning before they left for church.

"Shalonda's still asleep, I just checked. You keep an eye on her," Patti said, as if I were too inconsiderate to have thought of this on my own.

"Don't look like you're planning to go to the church with us, so would you run over and check on Willette? Soon as you can? I mean, after you see to Shalonda," Dan asked, as if I were the trained social worker instead of Shalonda, the woman still sleeping off her whiskey and personal tragedy.

I grunted. The vibrations of that sound set off a bouquet of arrows, all razor-sharp and aimed at the soft gray matter right behind my right eyeball.

Apparently, Dan took this evasive grunt as a yes, and ushered Patti out the door. Their car wasn't out of the driveway before Becky and Bobby ducked into the kitchen, making me suspicious that they had been waiting and watching for some private one-on-one time with me.

"We got something we need to tell you," Bobby said.

"We've talked about it. We figure we can trust you. I mean, you didn't rat us out about . . . you know?" Becky added.

A sprinkle of bright lights, some with a hint of blue, popped in my head, then shot past my eyes in a flash, and I stifled a moan. Migraine auras would be cool, actually, if they didn't come with pain and nausea. That Zomig was looking better and better.

Here it was that I had to wonder: Why in the hell was I still in Bugfest?

I could take a Zomig, gather my belongings, and be home in five hours.

I ordered my muscles to lift me up from the chair and go forth to pack. But Bobby and Becky stared at me. Yeah, hadn't they just said they had something they needed to tell me? And yeah, I had to confer with Dr. Hodo this morning about Willette. And I had to keep making sure nobody actually killed her. And we weren't through cleaning out Willette's house. And, as a family, we had to decide what to do with her in the long haul. So, I guess I wasn't running home today in my ancient little Honda. Not just yet. Instead, I steeled myself for teenage confessions. But started on the offensive.

"Why aren't you going to church?" I asked, as another round of ziggy bright lights launched their offensive behind my eyes, each bolt of color zooming through my head, pounding the pain deeper into my brain. About that church thing, I didn't care myself, as I thought God could probably hear any of us anywhere we wanted to pray, given that He could part the Red Sea. But I knew Patti was big on church.

"Oh, we're going, later, the eleven o'clock service, you know, but we got to tell you this thing first, what with everything that's going on, we, er, figured you should know this," Bobby said. "And then we'll ... er ... walk over for Sunday school."

Uh-huh, they were playing hooky—from church. Poor Dan and Patti Lea, having a son that had genes and an attitude more in common with his aunt and uncle.

"We hadn't told anybody else about this," Becky said.

Figuring on a full tree-house confession, I geared up for a Safe-Sex and Anti-Drug antidote to their anticipated admission of sin, but before any of us could say anything more, the doorbell rang.

The three of us lumbered into the living room and opened the door.

There stood Armando, the squat teenage son of my loyal secretary, Bonita, whom I had left house-sitting my place on Tulip Street. Armando had Johnny Winter, his albino ferret, wrapped around his neck.

"What are you doing here?" I asked him. Okay, so, "How are you?" or "Are you all right?" would have been better openings, but after all, this was a surprise, and my head really did hurt.

"I rode the bus all night to get here," Armando said, then glanced at Becky and straightened up his adolescent slouch.

I wondered how he'd convinced the bus driver to let Johnny come too, then I thought to ask him, "Is everything all right? Is anybody hurt?"

Ignoring my question and thereby raising both my already off-the-charts anxiety and the sharp, insistent throbbing inside my skull, Armando said, "I Yahoo-mapped the way to your brother's house, directions right to the door, and I walked from the bus station."

Becky edged closer to the ferret.

"It's kinda cute," she said.

The way Armando looked at Becky told me he thought she was kinda cute. The way Bobby looked at Armando told me Bobby had noticed the way Armando was looking at Becky.

Frigging great, my own adolescent *As the World Turns.*

"What are you doing here?" I asked. "Is everybody all right? Are you all right? Is your mother all right?"

"Mom is going to *marry* that Henry man, and it's all *your fault* and you've got to stop it," he said. He looked like he might hit me.

"Can I hold him?" Becky asked, apparently missing the budding drama and the potential violence, as she reached for Johnny.

"Sure," Armando said, his pugilistic tone wholly mellowed for the cute blond girl, and he unwrapped the wary animal from around his neck as Bobby edged protectively toward Becky.

Wow, I thought, so Bonita had made up her mind. Finally. After a courtship of what? Three years? I was glad, I started to beam, then I saw Armando glare at me again.

"You've got to stop her," he said, the pugilistic tone recaptured.

"I couldn't stop her if I wanted to, and I don't want to. Henry is a good man, a fine man. He's honest, and reliable, and he's—"

"He's not my dad," Armando said.

Johnny curled in Becky's arms, and oonked at her. "What happened to your dad?" she asked.

"He's dead."

"Oh, I'm so sorry." Now draped with Johnny, Becky inched forward and gave Armando an honest-to-gosh hug. Armando had clearly never been hugged by a cute girl, and he froze, rock-still, and for the first time in the many years I'd known this tough little guy, he looked plain old-fashioned scared to death.

"Hug her back," I whispered, but then I saw Bobby jump toward Becky and take her arm and tug on it.

I had the feeling I wasn't going to hear Bobby and Becky's confession this morning.

Becky let Bobby lead her off a few steps before she stopped, and with eyes full of young-blond-girl wisdom, she smiled back at Armando and said, "I've had three stepdads, and it's not so bad. They buy you stuff, and this last one was trying real hard to be my friend. Always asking me about school and what I thought about stuff. Used to come into my bedroom at night and talk about what was going on with me and my friends. Gave me a ruby ring, that's my birthstone. It's a real little stone, but it's still a real ruby. But I reckon he wasn't so good to my momma, 'cause she flat run him off. But I got to keep my ruby. So I think if Aunt Lilly thinks this Henry is a good guy, you ought not to fuss so over it."

Oh wait. When did I become Becky's Aunt Lilly? Was she already considering herself part of Bobby's family? But before I could chime in on that note, Bobby, not to be left out, said, "I don't have a stepdad. But I got a good friend whose real dad ran off and his momma married this new man who drives a yellow Mustang convertible and he's teaching my friend to drive it. Does Henry have a cool car?"

"He drives a minivan," Armando said, the contempt clear in this tone.

"Oh, too bad," Bobby said.

"I bet if you ask him to, he'd trade for something cool and let you drive it. They try real hard at first to get along with you, to the point they'd do stuff like that," Becky said. "You could talk him into getting a cooler car. I can tell you exactly how to. The trick is—"

"Does Bonita know where you are?" I asked, wanting to remind them that I was still there and to cut off Becky's lessons on manipulating adults and especially stepfathers. Henry was already easy enough to manipulate. I knew; I'd been doing it for years. And Becky was kind of scary for one still so young, so I wanted to protect Henry the best I could by cutting her off before she taught Armando the step-by-steps.

"She knows where I am," Armando said.

Yeah, right, I thought. Like Bonita would let you take a bus ride to Bugfest by yourself in the middle of the night so you could enlist me in your campaign to disrupt her wedding. She was not that tolerant a mother.

Rather than challenge him directly, I decided I would just call Bonita. Right then. Besides, all three of the teenagers in Dan's kitchen, and Johnny too, were giving me a kind of *bug-off* look, and my stomach was lurching in step with the migraine auras, so I left them to it. Teen counseling clearly wasn't my calling in this life. Becky was probably going to teach Armando the fine art of manipulating Henry into getting a *cool* car no matter what I did, so I butted out, went to my room, did my risk-benefit analysis on the Zomig thing in the time it took to unwrap the bubble pack around the $20 pill, swallowed it dry, and pulled out my cell phone to call Bonita.

If my heart didn't explode from the Zomig, and my head didn't explode from the migraine, I had a lot of work to do today.

chapter **38**

Bonita's voice over the phone reverberated with an anxiety that
cued me to lead with the news that Armando was safely in the
house of my brother, already adopted by a known pack of teens,
and fast falling in love for his first time.

"Your son, Armando, just showed up at my brother's door. He's fine.
He and my nephew are already friends, and I think he's got his first crush
on a girl, a friend of the family."

"He is not hurt?"

"No, he's fine, really, honest. I wouldn't lie about that."

"I will send Henry for him immediately after Mass," Bonita said.
"They need time alone, just the two of them. They can spend the night in
Tallahassee, and come home on Monday."

So, okay, for a really smart woman, Bonita was missing something
here.

Like, Henry alone with Armando.

First, in a hotel room in Tallahassee. Then, on a five-hour drive. In an
uncool van.

I figured if Armando didn't assault Henry and steal the van the night in the hotel room, they wouldn't make it much past Tallahassee before Armando ran away, or tricked Henry out of the van. I could see it now, all Armando had to do was wait till Henry stopped to use the bathroom, and he could steal the van, leaving Henry stranded. And then sell the van, buy a cooler car, and head for California. Bonita would blame Henry for Armando's disappearance into the great wilds of the West Coast, and they would break up. Armando would get a job as a bodyguard for one of those blond girl-singers. Bonita would marry someone else, and Henry would be left to grow old alone.

I couldn't let that happen to Henry, my friend, the man who fed me malpractice cases and who had taught me, more or less, how to break into buildings using a set of lock picks he himself had selected for me. No, friends don't let friends drive with dangerous teenagers.

"Congratulations on your wedding plans," I said. "I'm really happy for you and Henry." Then I added what seemed pretty darn obvious to me, but then I don't have the mother hormone, "Let Armando stay here, really. You and Henry need some time alone, I mean, without Armando trying to . . . you know, er, sabotage things. Why not let him stay here with me? It's just a couple of days, really, till I'll get all this straightened out and come home. And a couple days away from . . . well, away from you and Henry might do Armando some good."

Bonita no doubt had just flashed on what had happened the last time she had entrusted one of her sons to me. Okay, okay, so I almost got Benicio arrested, not once but twice, and there was that thing with the dead body, but in the end he was a stronger kid for the experience.

But what I said was: "Henry would have to miss work Monday, and it's a long drive. Really, let me bring Armando home. He's cool here. Dan has two empty bedrooms now that his oldest boy is off at college, and they always had the extra guest room. And Bobby is a great kid, and, like I told you, he and Armando have already really hit it off. And there's plenty of room—"

"The girl he has a crush on—"

"Just left for church. She and her mother are close friends of the family. Look, I promise to take care of Armando until we leave. He'll be fine. He can go to school with Bobby, I promise. Really." I left out the fact I was in one spare bedroom and the grieving wife of the missing chief of police was in the other. A kid like Armando could sleep anywhere, and there was a big couch in the living room.

"Are Patti and Dan there?"

"Oh, yes. And they'll take good care of him. You know what a great mother Patti is."

Of course, that was a reach, given that Bonita saw Patti once a year for about two minutes when she and Dan stopped by my office on their way to the beach or Disney World, on their annual trek to visit me and, not incidentally, all the tourist hot spots, but I think I've said positive things about Patti over the years.

There was a long pause. I let Bonita think; I kept my mouth shut.

"Let me speak with Patti," Bonita said.

"Oh, she's at church. I can have her call you first thing when she gets in."

"Church?"

"Oh, yes, and Armando and my nephew Bobby are just heading out to Sunday school and the eleven o'clock service."

So, yeah, in the end, I convinced Bonita to leave Armando in the care of Patti, and that I would bring him home in a day or two.

After I hung up with Bonita, I wandered back into the kitchen, where Armando and Johnny were eating like they'd walked all the way from Sarasota with no food.

"Your mom says you can stay here a couple of days with me, and Dan, Bobby, and Patti, but—"

"Cool," Armando said with a full mouth.

"Cool," Becky said with a big smile.

"Whatever," Bobby said with a look of concern.

"Oonk, oonk," Johnny said with a jowl full of raisins.

After that was settled and Armando and Johnny were done eating, and it didn't look like I was leaving them alone, the kids pretended they were going to Sunday school and would take Armando, ferret and all. I pretended to believe them. The three of them, with Johnny in tow, trotted off down the sidewalk while I watched.

Yeah, yeah, yeah, I know. But I never said I was good mommy material.

chapter 39

One thing about the law is this: it often refuses to make sense.

This is what I concluded as I read case law off an intolerably slow Internet connection to Lexis. On the one hand, I had an ethical obligation to rat out Idiot Client to the judge, because he was planning to defraud the court by submitting falsified medical records in an ongoing medical malpractice case.

That was fraud, no doubt about that, and the case of blah blah versus blah blah held me to a high standard to protect the integrity of the court, a higher standard than that of protecting my client from further trouble with the same court. Thus, not only *could* I, I was in fact *required* to tattle on him.

And, as Bonita had already reminded me, the ethical rules were equally clear that I must disassociate myself from a client who would engage in fraud. That is, that I must file a motion to withdraw.

Okay, so far so good.

But then there was this whole string of cases all holding that I could not violate my attorney-client privilege by ratting him out. That is, I must not tattle on him for doctoring his patient's records and showing me the altered file. I could not even say in my motion to withdraw as Idiot Client's attorney why I wanted to rapidly distance myself from him.

So, what the hell did that mean? I reduced this to the bottom-line query: Could I testify against him or not, in his suit against Henry and Henry's company?

Splitting hairs, which is what most of modern appellate practice is, I decided that I could not testify that Idiot Client had in fact already altered the records. He had completed that act while I was his attorney, and the privilege prevented me from exposing him.

Yet I could testify—maybe—in Henry's breach-of-contract lawsuit that Idiot Client asked me to submit falsified records into his malpractice court proceedings. That is, this was a fraud he was planning to commit, with my help, still in the future.

The little part of my brain that the Zomig had not yet calmed down pulsated behind my eyes like a whole marching band trying to hack their way out of my skull from the inside with tubas. Phrases like *actual fraud, constructive fraud, extrinsic fraud,* and *fraud-in-fact,* with their nuanced distinctions, once would have charmed me for hours as I constructed one of my famously overly detailed and ruthlessly analyzed memoranda of law to prove whatever point I wanted to prove.

Now, I had absolutely no interest in testing this theory of split hairs in a protracted round of litigation in which I might end up a party myself. All I wanted with regard to Idiot Client and his proliferating mess was to be done with him. And to help Henry. Years of legal wrangling and motions and arguing in the circuit court, to be followed with a year or so in the appellate courts, plus fielding complaints against me to the Florida Bar's Ethics Committee, while Henry dangled at the end of a knotted litigation rope, did not in the least appeal to me. I might be up for that kind of protracted legal battle, but Henry was not. Especially not with wedding plans looming.

I had another idea.

If Idiot Client would falsify medical records, he was, at his root core, a fraud.

And a fraud would do other fraudulent things.

And I knew just who could catch him at whatever other fraud was lurking in his personal history.

As much as I hated to pay directory assistance, I did so, and got Philip's Cary Grant–cool commercial spy guy client on the phone. Thank goodness he was home.

The first thing I asked was whether his phone was tapped.

After he assured me he'd swept it that very morning, I spun out my tale of woe in abbreviated, layman's terms. That being I wanted info that would put Idiot Client's lawsuit against Henry under the courthouse, forever. Despite Cary Grant's assurances about no phone tap, I tried not to overtly solicit criminal acts. But I got the basic idea across: triple-check Idiot Client's résumé and credentials, his IRS records, and all bills submitted to either insurance companies or Medicare. Frankly, I didn't care whether Spy Guy had to hack into Idiot Client's computer, his head, or his house. My directive was simple: Find something so bad that Henry could kick Idiot Client's butt out of court, and out of practice.

I hoped this request indebted me only financially, and not for a date or anything, and left the exact payment arrangements for a later, face-to-face moment.

Sure, it was not a textbook example of "zealously representing the interests of my client," which was a key phrase in a paramount provision in the ethical rules. But hey, Idiot Client had started this by suing Henry.

Thus, technically speaking, with a precise eye on the Professional Ethics Code and the criminal statutes of Florida, what I had just put into play was a tad suspect. But when unfounded litigation buzzed inexorably toward my friend, ready to mow down, grind up, and spit him out, I couldn't let a little sissy gray area of the law stop me from saving him.

Henry's interests were crucial to me.

chapter 40

Shalonda **was still** sleeping when I checked on her, and I didn't dare wake her up, though I was eager to start whatever we were going to do today—like find her missing husband, solve a murder, and all that.

I called the police station and asked for Rodney Harrelson, assistant chief of police, the man I'd met while he was protecting Willette. I figured he was in charge now that Demetrious was missing. This didn't fill me with confidence.

In short order, he came on the line, assured me that the whole police department was looking for Demetrious, as was the sheriff's department, and everything would be just fine, and how was Shalonda?

Fine, fine, I lied, and hung up.

As much as I wanted to wake Shalonda up, I let her sleep. She needed her rest. Edgy with my own impatience, I made another cup of coffee, which was just what I needed to calm my nerves, and I made myself ponder my so-called purse-snatching. Given all that was going on, it seemed unlikely that it was random or coincidental. Especially in a town noted for its low crime rate.

A crime rate that was now off the charts, ever since Willette got that damn deep freeze.

So, what did I have that somebody wanted?

The obvious answer was my cash and credit cards.

Another answer, and one Demetrious had favored, was that the Deer Den manager had sent someone after me to steal back the tape recorder with evidence of illegal caviar and turtle eggs.

But, like I'd pointed out to Demetrious, how had they known I had a tape? And how had they known I was at the hospital? Hell, even more basic, how had they even known *who* I was?

No, I didn't buy the Deer Den as purse-snatcher.

Reluctantly, I had to reconsider Jubal. If Jubal was supplying Willette illegally with prescription drugs, then he might want to steal back the pill bottles he'd seen me gather up. Maybe he'd spied on me and seen me put them in my Honda's trunk. Maybe that's why he was hanging around so, waiting for a chance to break in and grab the bottles.

Or maybe it was old Mr. Spiky Hair, aka Dr. Weinstein. Maybe he had somehow learned I had those bottles, and maybe he was the source of them. If he were overprescribing downers to an old woman, he might have risked mugging me to get rid of the evidence.

No, that didn't make sense. There would be records of the prescriptions at the pharmacy. Getting the pill bottles back wouldn't save him.

Maybe it was something in my car. After all, the trunk had been emptied.

Emptied of Willette's important papers.

Papers I had glanced at a couple of times, but not examined with a close, lawyer-trained eye for the basic reason they'd been living in a mold-covered box and smelled bad and I didn't want to touch them.

Ah, but the photocopies I'd stashed in the closet would be relatively clean.

And they had the added benefit that nobody had stolen them.

I hopped up, got the papers out of Dan's closet, and sat down with them in my lap.

So what? I thought, as I whipped through things apparently not worth stealing from my Honda's trunk. But then I paused at the contract Willette and Lonnie had both signed, for the purchase of my grandmother's house and forty acres.

It was not a traditional real estate contract. I had noticed that before, but now I wondered if that meant something I'd overlooked. Rather than the common contract for sale, Willette had Lonnie sign a contract for deed.

Below the contract for deed was an old-fashioned ledger book, in which Willette had carefully noted the date Lonnie had paid her each check, the check number, and the amount. This list stopped, though, nearly eight months ago.

Had Willette stopped recording?

Or had Lonnie stopped paying?

Hm, hm, hm. I rifled through the papers some more, and remembered we had never found her bank book and statements, and didn't know where she banked, or what her accounts might show. But now that Dan was her legal guardian, he could start calling the banks in town—thank goodness there weren't that many—and he could find her account, or accounts, and we could probably figure out what Lonnie had paid her, or not paid her. But not before Monday.

In the meantime, I didn't have any evidence that Lonnie had actually paid Willette the full purchase price for the house. Yeah, Lonnie had moved into the house, but that didn't mean he had legal title. In fact, the whole point of a contract for deed, as opposed to a traditional sale, was that the seller retained title until the buyer had actually paid *all* the money owed. In a traditional sale, the seller tenders title to the buyer, who usually gets a mortgage from a third party and pays the full amount, via the mortgage, to the seller. The buyer then owns the property—subject to the mortgage, of course—but the buyer can certainly resell the property. But in a contract for deed, there is no third-party mortgagor, and the original owner/seller retains title and the buyer cannot resell the property until the original owner is paid off in full.

So, okay, good enough. But who had drafted the paperwork for Willette? Possibly even Willette herself, as she had worked in my father's law office before they were married, back in the days when she was apparently almost a normal person, before marriage and three kids and whatever brain-chemistry trick nature had played upon her.

But maybe my dad had drafted the contract for deed.

Or maybe she hired it out.

It didn't seem likely that Lonnie would have had it drafted, or suggested it, as a contract for deed greatly favors the seller.

In fact, it's not generally a good idea for a buyer.

Unless, that is, the buyer can't get any other kind of financing.

Which made me wonder about Lonnie's life and finances in the Big City Up North, married to Colleen the Big Mouth, before they came back to humble Bugfest.

Maybe Lonnie came home broke. And couldn't get a mortgage, and Willette had agreed to the contract for deed, and then Lonnie had never finished paying on it.

That being so, maybe Willette still owned the property?

Or it could just be that Willette was a sloppy record-keeper, after all, and somewhere in Lonnie's stuff were receipts, and somewhere in a bank his money was collecting interest on behalf of Willette.

But the thing was, Willette was not a sloppy record-keeper. Every piece of paper Willette had touched for forty years was still in her house. Not only still there, but labeled and rubber-banded together in piles. She was, in spite of the dust, dirt, and filth of that house, an exacting record-keeper. She made lists that rivaled my lists. Every bill she'd ever received was in that house, with her precise, bold handwriting noting the date she'd paid it and the check number. Plus, the truly important papers had been carefully collected and saved in the metal box.

And what was in that metal box didn't show that Lonnie had ever finished paying my mother for Grandmom's property.

Which, by the terms of the contract for deed, meant Willette still owned it.

Not Lonnie.

And not Simon.

But why would Simon buy the place from Lonnie unless Lonnie had a deed? I mean, the first step in a title search is, like, you know, making sure the seller has title.

Just to be sure I wasn't missing something, I went through all the copies of the paperwork again. Definitely, no record Lonnie had finished paying Willette what he owed her. From the records in front of me, I calculated he still owed $65,000 on the house and property.

Now, why on God's green earth would Simon buy a house from a man who didn't own it? Simon didn't seem the least bit gullible, just vocabulary- and fashion-challenged. Oh, and that Marfan syndrome. But that hadn't handicapped him in any way, and wouldn't in any event have made him stupid.

I had a sudden and desperate need to check for the deed in the courthouse. Right then. Waiting until Monday wouldn't do.

It was time for Shalonda to wake up.

chapter 41

Of course, Demetrious, being the chief of police in a small town, had a key to the courthouse. And of course, Shalonda, being a good wife—oh, except for the Lonnie thing—knew where Demetrious kept all his extra keys.

Once I got her awake and full of coffee, and past the four hundred phone calls trying to find Demetrious she had to make before she'd even listen to me, she agreed we could borrow Demetrious's key to the courthouse. Okay, steal was what I meant, though if she could get the key back to him before he discovered it was gone it wouldn't be stealing, not in a strict legal technical prove-it-in-court sense. And since Demetrious was officially missing and possibly wanted for murder, we probably had a generous leeway on getting the key back to him.

Which was why, after a side trip to her house to fetch said key, we were in the courthouse, in the property records, and I was ever so glad I knew how to track little columns of numbers in one book to another book and find the recorded deed.

While I was tracking numbers, Shalonda sat dull and morose, and punctuated the air around her every few minutes with some version of the same question: Where was Demetrious?

And yes, it was an interesting and important question. But I didn't see how I was in a position at the moment to answer it, and I was getting just a wee bit tired of hearing it. What I was, however, in a position to answer was the question of the deed. That is, was there a deed that showed Lonnie had actually owned my grandmother's property?

I found the number of the deed-recording book in the index, and pulled the massive book from the case, and flipped through the pages of small print and people's dreams of property ownership.

And there it was, a deed, one purporting to be from Willette to Lonnie, a quit-claim deed.

The rub was this: I saw right off that the signature on the deed was not Willette's. Not unless her craziness had changed her handwriting, which had always been distinctly bold and neat, oddly in contrast to the mess in which she lived.

So, here I paused, then punted. What this suggested was that Lonnie had forged my mother's signature and filed a fake deed. I mean, why not? He had probably judged her—or misjudged her—as too drugged and crazy to object, or to even know he'd filed a fake deed, and the folks at the courthouse do not verify signatures as a matter of course when they record deeds. After all, Lonnie had moved into the house, bitchy wife and all, had lived there for three years, and probably had paid the taxes. To the outside world, it would certainly look like Lonnie had owned that house and the surrounding property. It also crossed my mind that Simon sure had a dandy lawsuit against the folks who did the title search.

Shalonda continued sitting on a stool, in a corner, with that painful, dull look on her face.

"Want to know what I'm doing?" I asked, hoping at the least to perk her up some.

"It gonna tell us where Demetrious is at?"

Well, maybe in the long run. But it wasn't going to be a quick, direct line of causation, so I said no. And she said well, then, no, she didn't care what I was doing.

But talking helps me think, so I explained it to her anyway. That Lonnie had forged a deed to property he probably didn't really own, and then he'd sold it to Simon, who had no doubt looked at the deed, and believed that Lonnie did own Grandmom's place, free and clear.

"Why'd Simon buy something from Lonnie that Lonnie didn't own?"

Okay, Shalonda wasn't paying attention. Grief and worry, no doubt, distracted her from legal details. "I just told you—Lonnie forged a deed. Simon wouldn't have known Lonnie didn't actually own the property."

She gave me that dull look, and I let it go. I wanted to look up Simon's deed, and see what light it might shed on this.

As it turned out, it didn't shed any light at all. Simon's deed looked entirely proper and ordinary. It said the purchase price was $1 and "other consideration," that phrase being a standard devise of Realtors, lawyers, and savvy real estate investors to hide the actual purchase price from the public record. It did not mean for one minute that Simon had paid only $1 for the place—the "other consideration" was most likely several thousand dollars more.

Damn, why was this still Sunday? If only it were Monday morning, I would have filed a lawsuit to determine title by 9:01 in the morning, and, poor defrauded Simon or not, I would get that title to Grandmom's place back where it belonged.

In my hands.

All this, of course, depended upon the unanswered question: Had Lonnie paid Willette for the property?

Okay, if Willette didn't have records showing that he had, or hadn't, paid that last $65,000 on her house, and I couldn't get inside a bank until Monday, where else could I look?

The answer danced in front of me, as bright and pretty as any migraine aura but, in my Zomig no-pain zone, without agony.

That is—we had to look inside Lonnie's house for any records.

And, oh, wasn't it just mighty convenient that Lonnie, being dead, wouldn't be around to disturb us while we looked.

Which left his widow, Colleen the Vile.

I pulled out my cell phone and bugged Shalonda to tell me Lonnie's number, and I called.

No answer. Great!

I called Acting Police Chief Rodney back, and after a bit of a delay, followed by some polite chatter focused on the still-missing chief of police, I asked him if he knew where Colleen was.

"Why, that woman was so struck down with grief, we had to take her to the hospital. They got her up there on the same wing as your momma, sedated. Ain't it a shame?"

Well, no, it wasn't a shame, at least not from my immediate point of view, but I didn't admit that to Rodney.

What I did do was give a quick prayer of thanks to the little demon gods of the B and E crowd, and to a hospital that apparently specialized in deep sedation, and then I went and shook Shalonda.

"Come on. We're going over to Lonnie's house."

She didn't even ask me why.

But she did tell me that before we went anywhere else, we were going to the hospital to check on Willette. Shalonda was clear on that; as a priority, our obligation to my mother trumped breaking and entering. When I protested, even though I had sort of grunted a promise to Dan to do just that, Shalonda took me to task about my mother.

"How do you know that new psych nurse's treating her right? And how you know if that new lawman is awake and guarding her against any more bugs? And what if she woke up with strangers, and had another psychotic fit?"

Shalonda had a point. Thus, eager as I was to get out to Lonnie's for a little sneak and plunder, I agreed to the side trip. Also, it occurred to me to make sure Colleen was still in the hospital and still sedated. Since she was a woman with at least two trained hit dogs, I wanted to make sure she was in no position to sic those dogs on Shalonda and me.

So, we stopped by the hospital. Where we found a nice youth who

looked about fifteen, in a police uniform, sipping coffee outside of Willette's door, and he greeted us as Miss Shalonda and Miss Lilly and assured
us no one had bothered Willette all night, that Dr. Hodo had been in a
couple of times to check on her, and even that strange little doctor from
New York had come by to check on her.

Why the hell would Dr. Spiky Hair have checked on Willette, I
thought, but pushed the question aside for the time being.

We stepped inside the room, where we found Bobby, Becky, and
Armando. Visiting Willette. And not in church. Johnny was stretched out
on Willette's chest, licking up pound-cake crumbs.

"Where's that psych nurse?" I asked.

"On her break," Bobby said. "She said she's legally entitled to a fifteen-
minute break every four hours."

I introduced Armando and Shalonda, and made a mental note to have a
law clerk look up that fifteen-minute-break rule and see if that applied to
psych nurses, and if it did, whether they could just abandon their charges,
and if I had to pay for the break too.

Then I asked Bobby what he was doing in Willette's room.

"I hadn't, you know, ever gotten to see her. Just shouting at her through
the door at Christmas. I wanted to meet my grandmomma."

"It was my idea," Becky said. "A man ought to know his close kin,
don't you think?"

Well, that certainly depended on the kin, but I decided, in the interest
of not belittling Becky's honorable sentiment, not to say so.

"You're a good-looking young man," Shalonda said to Armando, who
puffed out and beamed at Becky. Then, to Bobby, she said, "You get that
ferret off Miss Willette's bed, you hear me, right now. And knock off those
crumbs." Then, to me, she said, "White girl, we are going to find that
psych nurse." And just like that, Shalonda's dullness was gone. But before
we left, I told Bobby what to do if his grandmother woke up screaming—that being call for a nurse and get out of her reach.

Despite a quick hallway patrol, we didn't find hide nor hair of the psych nurse. Shalonda cursed her good and proper for disappearing and leaving Willette with teenagers, saying exactly what I'd been thinking. "They're good kids, but they're still kids, and it ain't right, her getting up and going off like that, leaving poor ole Willette with teenagers that'd let a ferret crawl around on top of her."

Bitch, bitch, bitch, and a renewed and thorough search of the hospital floor and a peek outside for the nurse, and then I stopped at the front desk to ask if Colleen was still in the hospital. She was. However, the nice volunteer pink lady said Colleen was not accepting visitors, which worked out exceedingly well, since I had no wish to visit her but, rather, to explore her Victorian without any impediments.

Back we marched to Willette's room, where we found Simon standing by Willette's bed, having a nice visit with Bobby, Armando, Becky, and the still-sleeping Willette. I noticed that Johnny the Ferret was off the bed and out of sight, and decided not to ask.

Simon, who was dressed all in gold once again, was most gracious to me, even flirty, and I saw Shalonda cutting her eyes at me over this, but then Simon started asking about Willette. He was being so nice about Willette I wondered if he thought she was rich enough to leave them an endowment.

Maybe he was hoping I'd give the hospital an endowment in apprecia-tion for their special care of my mother. Yeah, in a pig's eye. This hospital would be lucky if I didn't sue them. Then I momentarily got tickled with the idea of a lawsuit as a kind of reverse endowment, and studied the intense, long face of one Simon the Hospital Administrator.

Yeah, that was it, I thought—fear of a lawsuit. No doubt, Simon sus-pected the ER had screwed up the night they admitted Willette and nearly gave her a fatal overdose, and there was still that unexplained fire-ant episode. My new guess was that Simon was hoping if he were attentive enough, I, the lawyer daughter, would be perfectly willing to overlook these breaches of the hospital's duty of care.

Still, I was gracious back to Simon's graciousness, and we all just about outdid each other in the *nice* category. But what I was about to do was this: explode. I wanted to get into Lonnie's Victorian and see what I could see, and, all things considered, now was better than later. Just as I was about to suggest Shalonda stay there with Willette and the kids, the psych nurse came back in, fairly reeking of cigarette smoke. Great. That meant a few more smoke breaks in the future.

Before I could fully articulate my unhappiness with her service, her habit, and her abandonment of Willette, Simon did it for me, even threatening to fire her.

"You can't fire me because you didn't hire me," Psych Nurse said.

"No, I hired you and I can fire you," I said, jumping in on Simon's side.

"No, Dr. Hodo hired me, and only he can fire me."

"See, I told you that you should have left Dr. Weinstein in charge," Simon said to me. Then, to Nurse Stubborn, he said, "We are very unhappy with you for leaving your post. This woman needs constant attention. Very, very unhappy with you."

Every *very, very* was costing me precious time in my breaking-and-entering project, and I cut in. "I'm calling Dr. Hodo and telling him to fire you, okay. So you can stay or go, but you are not getting any money from me or Willette. And Shalonda, will you stay with Willette? I'll be right back, as soon as I, er, finish my—"

"Nope, I'm going with you."

"We can stay with Willette," Becky said.

"Yeah, we can stay with your mom," Armando said.

"Yeah, whatever," Bobby said.

"They do seem to be very responsible young adults," Simon said.

Well, yeah, they did *seem* to be so, but sixteen is sixteen, and I knew about the pot in the tree house. Or, at least, I suspected I knew about it. So, no offense and all that, but I called Eleanor, who was just freshly home from church and said she would be right over. She assured me she was glad I had thought of her.

After that, I put in a call to Dr. Hodo's answering service, his answering machine, his cell-phone voice mail, but not, alas, to the man himself. I had to settle for explaining the situation—and huffily, at that—to the various recording devices. With that chore done, Shalonda and I left, with Simon escorting us to my Honda and then hovering about me.

"I would love to take you out to dinner tonight. Both of you, very much," Simon said, gracious enough to include Shalonda, though his look was all for me.

"It's really hectic right now," I said, "what with Armando visiting, and . . . why don't I call you later. When things quiet down." Translation: in the next lifetime.

"Fine, please do." And with that, the man with the long arms and the *very, very* habit leaned over and kissed me. On the mouth. Lightly, and strangely sweetly. Like we'd had a real date. And a real date that hadn't ended with me getting a foot rub from another man right after I'd lied to Simon. Then, making matters worse, Simon hugged me, tightly, crushingly, and I was reminded again of the strength of the man. In a different situation, this could have been sexy. At the moment, it was merely irritating, and I struggled out of his grasp.

"Well, back to work, no rest for the weary," Simon said, shaking off my shaking him off without much obvious embarrassment. And then he walked back toward the hospital.

"You'd be better off holding out for Hank, you wanting to date homeboys."

No, I didn't want to *date homeboys*. I wanted to break into a dead man's house before his wife came to and went home.

chapter 42

Henry had many sterling qualities. I was glad Bonita had finally agreed to marry him.

But I was not sure he was such a great teacher, at least not of the fine art of picking a lock. That is, what with his rudimentary lessons and his cautionary tales, I had apparently failed to learn how to actually pick a lock. I had my lock picks, the ones Henry had purchased specially for me as a birthday present—somewhat to Bonita's disapproval—which my-purse-and-car-trunk thief had left behind. But I could not for the life of me make the damn picks work in Lonnie's locks.

While I was tinkering, Shalonda kept making suggestions, as if she knew something about picking locks. Naturally, I got snappy, and so she wandered off.

Well, stomped off.

And the next thing I knew, the front door burst open and there she was.

Strong and smiling—from the inside of the house of her now-dead former lover.

"How'd you do that?" I asked, a little put out at her for beating me inside.

"Climbed up that big live oak, scampered right into the open upstairs window," she said, apparently over her pique at me for my snarling at her suggestions.

Okay, so she was better at climbing trees than I was, and quick to forgive. Potentially good qualities both, I thought, and turned myself to the task of exploring Lonnie and Colleen's love nest.

I stepped inside and looked around. The first thing I thought was *expensive.*

The place had that interior design–decorated look that costs money. A lot of money. Museum-quality antiques. Paintings and rugs and Victorian knickknacks that didn't look like they came from Target, and window treatments with big pouffy things that definitely weren't from the Sears sale catalog.

"Whoa, you wouldn't think a barn-burner trash-mouthed godless Yankee woman would have this kind of good taste," Shalonda said. "And I know Lonnie didn't care what his furniture looked like."

Yeah, an interior decorator had been through here.

And that meant even more money.

I thought about Ray Glenn's big, expensive house, and now this. Those trips to Miami's ports were sounding bigger than just saving transportation costs on refrigerators. Bigger even than stolen goods.

"Would Lonnie be into smuggling drugs?" I asked.

"No, he wouldn't, and you better not be talking bad about that man. He's dead, you know."

Yeah, I knew he was dead—I'd helped dig his face out of the sweet feed. But hearing Shalonda's tone of voice, I decided to keep my theories to myself for a while, and set out to look for his office, or his desk. Shalonda decided to snoop through Colleen's stuff, and I let her go.

An hour later, I'd covered the downstairs and had decided Lonnie didn't have a desk, safe, or filing cabinet, or anything else interesting on the ground floor. I dashed up the stairs and hunted down Shalonda, who was still studying Colleen's stuff.

"You look at all this shit," Shalonda said. "That woman got more shoes and things than a department store."

I peered into the closet. And into the chest of drawers. And under the bed. And, yeah, Colleen had a whole stash of expensive-looking shoes, clothes, and jewelry. "This clotheshorse habit must cost a whole lot," I said, "plus all the furniture." Translation: drug smuggling out of Miami for sure.

"That ain't the worst of it," Shalonda said. "Look in here."

Inside the shoes inside the shoe boxes, there were several bottles of tranquilizers and painkillers. I picked them up, one by one, studying the label.

"You know this doctor?" I asked, looking at the name of the prescribing physician.

"Nope, and that drugstore ain't even close to local, and there's a good reason for me not knowing that doctor. Let me show you something else." And with that, Shalonda led me to a little den-type room with a computer, one that was up and running. "She didn't even have it passworded or nothing. I went to the bookmarks and found where she's been ordering that shit off of one of those so-called pharmacy sites on the Internet. You know the kind I'm talking about?"

Yeah, the kind of pharmacy site that charges a person a large sum for a so-called consultation with a doctor, who writes the prescription, and then the Internet drugstore mails the drugs to the person. "Yeah," I said, and looked at my old friend with expanded respect. Wow, Shalonda had a talent for this sort of thing. Then I looked back at the computer screen for a minute or so, hitting buttons and satisfying myself that if I didn't mind spending a ton of money, I too could have pharmacy-grade—or at least that's what they claimed—drugs mailed to me.

This drugs-for-money scam would put the black market and the street dealers out of business if it wasn't so expensive.

I wondered if this was the source for Willette's own stash. Not that Willette had a computer, but that someone had used a site like this to get drugs for her. Had Lonnie been supplying Willette's own habits?

But before I could get too caught up in wondering about the pill bottles, something wholly new caught my eye.

A locked drawer on the computer desk.

One that had recently been busted open.

"You do that?" I asked.

"Damn straight, it was just a toy lock, didn't even need them lock picks you so proud of. You know, that woman's been calling me names since she hit town. You think I owe her anything?"

"Not a thing," I said, and pulled open the drawer.

"Yeah, you gonna want to look at some a that stuff."

Yes, I was. There it was, the Big Clue. A deed, backdated three years, for the transfer of title of my grandmother's house to Lonnie.

The only thing was, the line for Willette's signature was blank.

chapter 43

Obviously it had never seriously occurred to either Colleen or Lonnie that anyone might go through their house.

Or else they were stupid.

Or both.

No password, no serious lock on the desk, no especially clever hiding places, and no safe.

Instead of a safe, they used a picnic basket.

Like a crook, or a snoop, wouldn't think to lift the lid and look inside.

Of course, Shalonda and I thought to do just that, and there it was. Cash money.

A lot of it.

We stopped plundering through the upstairs of poor dead Lonnie and vile but sedated Colleen long enough to count it.

Sixty-five thousand dollars.

Exactly the amount Lonnie had owed Willette under the terms of the contract for deed.

Well, hell, what had Lonnie been up to? I mean, even if there were angels of coincidence floating around, that was just too much coincidence not to have some specific meaning.

"We've got to take this," I said, pondering theories of coincidental versus true clue.

"No we don't, that'd be stealing," Shalonda said. "Why'd you want to take it anyway?"

There was an old maxim around in my courthouse crowd, that if someone offers you money, you take it, and who was I to argue if the cosmic forces offered up a picnic basket with exactly the amount of money a dead man probably had owed my mother. So yeah, it wasn't precisely like someone had offered it to *me,* not in person or anything, but the cosmic forces certainly had offered it up for grabs in my general vicinity. Close enough, you ask me.

But Shalonda, not being a lawyer and therefore not trained to follow the money (or keep it, I guess) wasn't going to buy that explanation. So, I tossed her another explanation.

"We need to make sure this money is safe," I said.

"What makes you think it's not safe right here? 'Sides, we broke in to find out who killed poor ole Lonnie, not to steal his money," Shalonda said.

"Well, he's dead, so that makes it Colleen's money. You want her to have it? You think it's safe to leave it in her hands?"

Shalonda had to think about that a minute. "Well, it's not our money, is all I'm saying."

"I'm not taking it to keep it, I'm taking it to protect it."

"What do you mean?"

"Until we know what's going on, I don't think we should trust Colleen with this money. It's material evidence. What if somebody killed Lonnie for this money?"

"Then how come they didn't take it?"

"They might not know where it is, or maybe they're coming for it later."

"What do you think this has got to do with Demetrious running off?"

"I'm not sure."

Also, I wasn't sure Demetrious had *run off.* I didn't like the feeling I was getting over the possible fate of Demetrious now that I knew money was at play. Money and drugs, and smuggling stuff out of Miami, and now two dead men. This wasn't some heartbroke love triangle we were dealing with.

And Demetrious hadn't struck me as the kind of man who'd run away.

But I didn't want to worry Shalonda worse than she already was by voicing any of this.

"What we need to do with this money," I said, "is take it now and put it someplace safe."

"Nope, we ought to call Rodney, he's in charge now that Demetrious is . . . gone off. We'll have Rodney take it into protective custody."

Forcing myself not to sigh, I tried to explain: Rodney could not just take the money into protective custody. Not without warrants and all that. It was stupid but not illegal per se to have $65,000 in cash in a picnic basket in your closet under some winter coats. "So, see, Rodney has no legal right to the money."

"Oh, and we do?" Shalonda snapped at me.

"Look, I'm not going to go buy a gold Lexus with it, all right? I'm just keeping it safe."

Bicker, squabble, argue. *Mierda,* but people with inflexible moral codes about stealing are tough to break and enter with.

Finally, Shalonda said we would take the money, but only if we delivered it to Rodney for safekeeping. I pretended to agree.

But once we had it in the Honda, and were speeding away from the dead man's Victorian, I tried to reason anew with Shalonda about the wisdom of telling Rodney we had this money.

"Because technically, in a purely . . . you know . . . technical sense, we stole that money. We took the money after we illegally entered the house and that makes it a crime, and I don't think we want to tell Rodney that."

"He won't arrest us," Shalonda said.

Well, not her anyway, as arresting your boss's wife probably wasn't a good career move, even if that boss was currently missing in action. But I was outside that protected zone and not at all interested in finding out how flexible Rodney's professional code of conduct was.

But Shalonda had stopped worrying about the money, and was back to worrying about her husband. "Give me that cell phone, white girl, and let me call ever body again and see if Demetrious showed up yet."

As it turned out, he hadn't.

chapter 44

T**he mournful sound** of Patsy Cline lamenting about walking after midnight greeted us at the door.

The door to Willette's house.

Where we'd gone because Shalonda got Patti on the cell phone and Patti said we should all meet up there, and she had some questions for me about this boy from Sarasota, like why he thought he was moving in with her and all.

What we found at the house of Willette was not Patti and her questions, but Armando and Johnny Winter, happily hanging out in the den, with Armando playing a Patsy Cline record on a truly ancient but obviously functional turntable, while looking through some old records as if they were museum pieces, which I guess they were. In short order, Armando told me Becky and Bobby were outside in the tree house, and Dan and Patti had gone for food, and he was fine, thank you, he liked it here, and maybe he'd just stay in Willette's house as there seemed to be some question about whether he was staying at Dan and Patti's.

Not wanting to argue with him, especially since he was discovering real country music—and apparently for the first time in his deprived, child-of-rap-music life—I left him to it.

Shalonda started looking through the records and found an old Stevie Wonder, and when Armando said *who,* nothing would do but for her to play it for him.

Perfect. The world around us had gone to hell in a handbasket, and the grieving survivor of a love triangle and perhaps a drug-smuggling/land-fraud scheme was teaching a teenage boy she'd just met all about purely American soul music.

Go figure.

Leaving them to lessons of early Motown, I went in search of a proper place to stash the sixty-five thousand, that is, somewhere other than my Honda, seeing as how somebody who didn't mind stealing stuff had my stolen key to it. Plus, with Shalonda at least formerly all fired up to confess our crime and hand the money over to the acting police chief, relocating the cash seemed like a decent idea. Once that picnic basket was relocated, Shalonda couldn't turn it over to Rodney if she didn't know where it was. Simple enough.

It took me a few minutes to figure out the safest place to hide the picnic basket was probably the kitchen, especially since Hank's high school boys had cleaned it up so nicely. So, I crammed the basket in the cabinet over the stove.

Then, without further interrupting Shalonda and Armando's school of soul, I stuck my head outside and looked at the tree house. And sniffed the air. And followed my nose through the faint path in the high grass of Willette's untamed backyard, right up to the tree-house ladder, and right up into that tree, into the house where my nephew and his girlfriend had recently been engaging in an indiscretion.

In the tree house, Becky and Bobby were sitting with pleasantly blank expressions on their faces, no doubt having been warned by the sound of my climbing up the homemade ladder to compose themselves for adults on the prowl. But despite their blameless little faces, the evidence of recently smoked marijuana hung, diffused but potent, in the air. I mean, there is just no way to hide that scent.

"You need to be way more careful about doing this," I said.

"Doing what?" Becky asked, her face wholly the sweetly composed face of an innocent.

"I can smell the pot all the way down at the back door."

Nobody admitted anything, and I sat down on the sleeping bag, and waited.

"Aunt Lilly, Becky and I do need to talk to you. Alone."

"I think we are alone," I said.

Bobby looked around as if he didn't believe me. Becky continued to smile at me with that sweet, innocent grin.

"So?" I mean, I didn't have all day for teenage confessions.

"We . . . er, Becky and me, we were . . ."

"See, we were up here in the tree house, the night your momma shot that Ray Glenn man."

I perked right up at Becky's statement. This was way more interesting than what I'd expected. "What did you see?"

"I'm not . . . we aren't, really, you know, sure," Bobby said.

"Well, I'm sure," Becky said. "We heard a noise, I guess it was the shot, and so I got up and looked down at the house, and then this man came running out the back door, you know, the kitchen door?"

"Who was it?"

"It was Lonnie Ledbetter," Becky said. "And he was carrying a picnic basket."

Whoa, Lonnie was there, inside the house, the night Willette shot Ray Glenn? With a picnic basket?

Or the night Willette was accused of shooting Ray Glenn. Maybe Lonnie shot him?

"Why didn't you tell Demetrious? Or Dan? Or somebody?"

Yeah, I sounded a bit like a parent there, but it was an obvious question, and somebody needed to ask it.

"We talked about it," Bobby said. "We were . . . but, you know, Mr. Ledbetter was a big, important county commissioner, and we figured he'd just say we were lying, or something, and everybody'd believe him and not us."

"Yes, ma'am," Becky added, "and, you know, we're just kids, and then we were . . . you know?"

Yeah, I knew. Smoking pot.

I could see their point.

Stoned teenagers accuse a popular county commissioner of fleeing the scene of a shooting.

It wouldn't have played out that well for Becky and Bobby no matter who believed or didn't believe them.

"You know how Momma is," Bobby said. "We had already told everybody we were studying at the library, so we knew we'd get in trouble if we told anybody we were up here in the tree house."

Well, yeah, as it turned out, they'd called that one pretty good on the getting-in-trouble part, but not exactly in the way they meant.

chapter 45

Folks who go where they are not supposed to be often learn things they would not otherwise necessarily have the chance to know.

This had been, and no doubt would continue to be, a rationale behind my improving skills at breaking and entering. Okay, okay, I need to practice more on the lock-picking thing, and maybe learn to climb trees better. But look at what just one illegal tour through Lonnie's house had brought me: An unsigned deed and a picnic basket with precisely the amount it appeared Lonnie had owed my mother on the purchase price of my grandmother's old home.

And now, with this added information, that being Lonnie fleeing the scene of the Ray Glenn shooting, surely I could figure out this big frigging mess.

I mean, how hard could it be? If, as it now appeared, Lonnie was definitely a bad guy smack in the middle of this circle-melee, and Lonnie was, shall we say in Bugfest-ese, pert near dumb as a post, then it stood to reason his fellow conspirators might be equally challenged in the detail-planning aspects of attempted and actual murder.

I was close. I could taste it.

I needed to act upon this new knowledge.

Instead, here I was, sitting in a tree house with two teenagers who were supposed to have gone to Sunday school and church rather than mellow out on a cool autumn day with a little marijuana.

"Come on," I said.

"Where?" Becky said.

I didn't know yet, so I didn't answer, but just climbed down the tree and jogged back into Willette's house.

When we paraded into the den, we found Shalonda teaching Armando how to dance cool to some old R&B records. Becky immediately joined them in dancing, and Bobby stood by like somebody who didn't have any rhythm.

"Get in there," I said, and shoved him toward Becky. "Just grab her arm and shake to the music."

But Bobby shook his head no, and slumped his shoulders and glared at Armando.

I needed to run all this newfound information by Shalonda to try to figure it out via the old-fashioned method of talking. But I wasn't going to interrupt her dance lesson for Armando.

Becky, I noted, needed no dance lessons.

So, I went and slumped next to my gloomy nephew. And looked around the living room. Yeah, it was a lot better than when we had all started cleaning it up, but I still didn't want to hang out in the place—there were some nasty rooms and nasty memories both. Patti had pretty much cleared out the valuable antiques and family heirlooms, which made me think she was pretty sure ole Willette wasn't coming back to this house and nobody would fuss about the fact Patti helped herself to Willette's good stuff. I knew I wasn't going to make an issue out of it, figuring Patti deserved every stick and piece of furniture in the house if she was willing to put up with all the Cleary weirdness.

The Motown concert came to an end when the record stopped, and I jumped in to get the kids somewhere else so Shalonda and I could concentrate on figuring out what was going on. After all, she knew Lonnie way better than I did, maybe she would have some insight as to why he might have gone to Willette's with Ray Glenn, and why, ultimately, this had led to both Ray Glenn's and his own death. As this was not a discussion I wanted Armando, Bobby, or Becky listening to, I had to shepherd them somewhere else, where I could keep their ears all innocent and sweet so they could concentrate on lying about church and smoking dope.

"We need to go," I said, looking straight at Shalonda in a way I hoped suggested private talk.

"But Dad's bringing Mr. Chick for all of us," Bobby said, in a way that suggested adolescent munchies.

Oh, yeah, great, that's a big help to me, I thought, and wondered how much longer I could live on bottled water, coffee, Save the Forest trail mix bars, and organic apples. The only decent meal I'd had since I got here was courtesy of Simon and Annier's Courtyard, and I wondered in passing if they were open for Sunday dinner.

"Yeah, I like Mr. Chick," Becky said. "They have really great food."

At the sound of *Mr. Chick* repeated, like a summons from the Fried Dead Bird Netherworld, Shalonda, who had been too grief-stricken and worried to eat any breakfast, cocked her head toward the door. "Reckon I could eat too," she said.

Frigging great. Dead and near-dead, mayhem and possible drug smuggling and land fraud, plus the missing chief of police, and we were going to have to stop for a damn picnic in a dirty house.

chapter **46**

Hiding in the tree house from the snare of the seductive smell of fried chicken, my own stomach gnawed by hunger, I tried to marshal my inner resources and to think this through.

So, here's what I had so far: As soon as Simon offered to buy Lonnie's house, Lonnie had hotfooted it into the courthouse and filed a forged deed to show he owned the place. Simon or his title-search company didn't know Willette's signature from Adam's house cat, and so had not suspected anything with the deed when they did a title search, and poor, tricked Simon had purchased the property from Lonnie without discovering Willette's signature was forged. Then Willette phoned Lonnie and Simon on the same day—it'd probably be a good bet that call was about Grandmom's house. That evening, after Willette's phoning set something in motion, Lonnie and Ray Glenn had gone over to her house. Given the unsigned deed and the sixty-five thousand we found at Lonnie's, maybe he had gone to pay off the last of what he had owed Willette, and to get her to sign the quit-claim deed.

So, like, maybe this didn't have a thing to do with the damn deep freeze?

Maybe Ray Glenn was just Lonnie's muscleman?

Maybe this didn't completely add up.

Still, the idea that Lonnie and Ray Glenn had gone to Willette's to pay her what Lonnie owed and then get her to sign that unsigned deed kept playing in my head, as steadily as Stevie Wonder had been playing on the old turntable.

If everything had gone right, Lonnie would have had ample opportunity to substitute the new quit-claim deed with Willette's real signature for the one he had forged. After all, he had been a county commissioner, who naturally would have spent time in the courthouse, and no one would have thought it odd if he'd stepped into the property records office.

Yet something had gone wrong. Here I was purely guessing, but it looked like a good wager that Willette had refused to take the money and sign the deed. Given her refusal, maybe Ray Glenn, being Lonnie's henchman, had tried to force her. And, of course, if they had tried to force her to sign the new deed, *perhaps,* maybe, they had tried to kill her, possibly by forcing a bunch of pills down her throat. Pills Lonnie might have brought with him. That suggested strongly to me that Lonnie was the source of Willette's downer collection.

But wait a minute, that didn't make good sense. Why bring the cash to pay off his debt to Willette if he was planning on killing her?

Maybe Ray Glenn had a different agenda?

Maybe the bruises around her jaw happened in the ER? Like, maybe, someone had tried to OD her there, and not in her own home? Which made me remember the strange saga of Dr. Weinstein and his steadfast refusal to give Willette over to Dr. Hodo's care.

And then there was the missing Demetrious, who had access and means to pull off the death-by-red-ants attempt, though no motive, as far as I could see.

Whatever guesswork was in all this, and whatever Lonnie and Ray Glenn had planned for Willette, one thing was for sure. Somebody had shot Ray Glenn, and things had gone quickly downhill from there.

No doubt, Lonnie had run out the back door instead of hanging around to explain to Demetrious why he was there with cash in a picnic basket, an unsigned backdated deed, and a dead man on the filthy carpet.

But wouldn't Willette eventually straighten up enough to tell Demetrious what was going on the night she shot Ray Glenn, including the fact that Lonnie was there?

Oh, yeah, okay, that would make Lonnie the lead suspect in the question of who tried to kill Willette, first with dope and then with ants. Being practically a neighbor, he probably knew about Demetrious's roadkill and buzzard haven and could have siphoned off some red ants. And his motive would be obvious enough from my theory.

Okay, so that pulled Demetrious off the hook for the attempt on Willette.

But here was the thing that wasn't obvious at all: Who had killed Lonnie?

And why?

Okay, so I was fuzzy on the details here, but the ground work was being laid out nicely. First thing, though, I needed to check in on my mother and her round-the-clock psychiatric nurses and child police officers.

I climbed down from the tree house and eased back into Willette's living room, where the Mr. Chick picnic was winding down, and I looked about me, taking stock of my helpmates: the stoned, the indignant, the worried, and the merely puzzled, plus one albino ferret. While I stared at them, the thought that hung itself out like a bright red flag against a blue sky was this: There was still a dangerous person out there somewhere, and I didn't have a clue who it was.

chapter 47

Becky was a show-off.

 I guess it wasn't good enough to just be sixteen, and blond, and cute, and a good dancer, but she also had to be the smart one, the one that knew secrets, the drama queen.

So it was that with their bellies full, and Patti trying to organize an antique-moving party with the available strong backs, Becky noticed Armando and Bobby were no longer vying for her attention. While Becky was noticing this, and Patti was organizing, Shalonda had cut everybody slices of pound cake from one Patti brought from the hospital. Nobody even pretended to listen to me when I tried to point out we didn't know who cooked it, what was in it, and how clean the kitchen from which it had come had been. The fact they were eating on paper plates on the floor in the living room of Willette's house suggested that cleanliness issues didn't concern anybody but me. Still, I had to try.

"Armando," I said, trying to sound like a stern mother, or maybe a hired nanny with good-behavior issues, "don't let that ferret eat off your plate."

"Oh, let me get him a plate," Becky said, sweet as if it were Eleanor sitting on the floor with her face in Armando's plate, and not a strange white cousin to a polecat. And before I could object, Johnny was standing in his own plate and eating pound cake.

Then everyone went back to ignoring Becky in favor of making excuses to Patti.

So, naturally, Becky had to drop the big one, rather than let Patti have center stage.

"You know Simon paid Lonnie four hundred thousand for your grandmomma's old place," she said to me in a fake stage whisper.

Lonnie sold that place for $400,000?

"Not possible," I said.

"I don't think so," Shalonda said.

"No way," Patti and Dan said, in concert.

"Is too. I saw the paperwork. My mom is a real estate attorney and she handled the sale for Mr. Ledbetter. I work over at her office sometimes after school and she had me making photocopies of all the paperwork on the sale."

I gave Becky my best trust-me smile, and started my cross-examination.

"Was it the final contract for sale you saw? Or an offer? And, when was it dated? And, tell me again, what was the price?"

Becky, the teen vixen, gave me one of those blank-slate-but-pleasant stares perfected by seasoned witnesses. And didn't say a word.

Uh-oh. Too eager on my part. Breathe, smile, relax.

"I bet you're just remembering someone else's contract," I said, trying too late to fake a certain nonchalance.

"That's an awful lot of money for that place," Dan said.

"Mom did say no little piece a land, with part of it wet, and no house that old, what with it just being a two/one, was worth that. Even with all the fruit and nut trees," Becky said, turning her head slightly toward Dan.

Part of me took umbrage at Becky's mother's dismissal of my grand-mother's place, and I didn't care if she was a trained professional—it was forty acres, and it was only wet when we had a major storm or hurricane, which of course nowadays, with global warming, was four or five times a year, but hey, those serial monster hurricanes hadn't impacted Florida coastal property prices. Plus, Grandmom's house was solid brick with hardwood floors, a giant front porch, a blueberry patch, a dozen pecan trees, and a small peach orchard. And it backed up to Little Sleepy Lake, and had a good clay private drive leading down to the house from off a county road.

But even I, seeing the property in its most positive terms, had to remember it was located just outside Bugfest, in a rural county. In Bugfest terms, old farmland without saleable timber still went for $3,000–4,000 an acre, and an older brick house with only two bedrooms and one bath, no matter how nice, rarely sold for more than $100,000.

Older country houses in Bugfest just didn't go for that much. One reason so many people from up North were eyeing the county for retirement was our cheap real estate. So, no matter how you cut it, Simon had seriously overpaid—that is, if he had paid $400,000 for the place. I figured quickly in my head that the top price for Grandmom's place would have been $260,000. And that would have made that sale a real sweetheart deal.

So, if there was any truth to Becky's tale, that certainly explained why Lonnie had used the "one dollar and other consideration" phrase on the deed to hide the real sale price from the nosy eyes of anyone who knew how to look up public records.

So, what gives, I wondered.

"Are you sure—" I started to ask.

"I'm sure," Becky said. "I have an excellent memory."

And no reason to lie about it that I could imagine. Still, Becky might be mistaken.

I aimed another round of questions at Becky, quickly abandoning my previous pretense at nonchalance. But she stuck to her original story. Yet even in her center-stage stoned zone, my shooting twenty questions at her must have signaled her that she'd crossed a line in blurting out that original story. While Becky didn't back off the $400,000, she wouldn't tell me a thing more.

But maybe she'd told me enough, I thought, and rocked back on my heels on the floor, and stared at her cute little face. So, Becky's mom had handled the sale between Lonnie and Simon? That might be the conflict of interest she had mentioned to Hank. I mean, if Lonnie was her client and a county commissioner, she could hardly represent him in a sale and then turn right around and represent Hank and Jubal in an eminent domain lawsuit, where Lonnie and the other commissioners would be front and center on the opposing side.

Well, very ethical of Becky's mom on that conflict-of-interest thing, but apparently she had not impressed firmly enough upon her offspring the legal and ethical importance of keeping a client's secret.

And if Becky was telling the truth, then her mother, as a real estate attorney, knew Simon had overpaid for the property.

Of course, as she was Lonnie's attorney, it wasn't necessarily Becky's mom's place to tell Simon he was being an idiot, but she still might know something about *why* Simon had overpaid. And she might know if Lonnie had, in fact, ever actually finished paying my mother for the property.

"I'm going to go find out if he really paid that much," I said. "It sounds like up North prices, but surely Simon realized he wasn't up North anymore."

"How?" Shalonda asked.

"How did he know he wasn't up North anymore? You'd think a trip to the IGA would show him that. You think they sell pigs' feet in a jar at the grocery stores up North?"

"No, how are you going to find out?"

"I'm going to go ask Becky's mother."

Becky protested, but I figured I was holding a few secrets on her behalf, for which she owed me, and I wouldn't mind pointing this out to her in private if she made a big deal of my seeing her mom. Further, this overpayment might possibly be related to why Lonnie was dead, though I could hardly imagine how yet, and Becky would just have to take her chances once her mother knew she'd blabbed important client secrets to a relative stranger.

I gathered up Shalonda, the kids, and Johnny, who had cake crumbs in his whiskers, leaving a protesting Patti behind with only poor old Dan to move antiques for her.

We all piled in the car, and Becky reluctantly told me how to get to her house. When we pulled up outside, I rolled down the windows, turned off the car, and told Bobby and Armando to stay put while I ran in just long enough to chat with Becky's mom. Becky, swathed in Johnny Winter, and Shalonda followed me.

I thought the yard a tad overly manicured, and the house itself a bit too cluttered with decorative stuff. But it was all a nice, clean contrast to Willette's, and I wasn't afraid to inhale.

Inside, Becky made the introductions, and I could tell right off where Becky got her cute; her momma was Cute with a capital C, with big blue eyes, a pert nose, a wide mouth, and what appeared to be a wholly natural and not artificially enhanced but still rather nice body, despite a little early-middle-age pear-shapedness coming to it. If she asked, I had one word for her: StairMaster.

Her name was Rebecca, and I thought it was cool that she had named her daughter after her, but when I said so, she didn't seem to care.

With Becky talking a mile a minute by way of introduction, including an explanation about how, being the manipulative devil that I was, I had conned her into telling me about the sale price on Lonnie's land, Becky's mom was not necessarily warming right up to me.

She and Shalonda greeted each other friendly enough, though, and that gave me some hope.

"Why are you wearing a fur scarf?" Rebecca asked Becky.

As if he understood Rebecca, Johnny perked up and oonked.

"Her son ran away from home, and brought this guy with him," Becky said. "He's a ferret and his name is Johnny Winter, after some old rock guy. Her son is waiting in the car, but let me take Johnny for a while."

"He's not my son," I said.

Before we got farther off track, I shooed Becky out of the living room, but not before Rebecca gave her a scolding look. Becky offered a repentant postscript: "I'm sorry but she tricked me."

Rather than explain that Becky had volunteered information while in a pound-cake-and-pot zone of reduced mental capacity and a hot need to be the center of attention, I started asking Rebecca about the sale price on Lonnie's house and forty acres. Shalonda took the opportunity to stand awkwardly around. My best-phrased questions netted a single, simple reply.

"I think it's safe to say that is none of your business," Rebecca said.

Of course, I hadn't for one moment really expected Rebecca the grown-up to verify what Becky the teenager had told me, but I was a good student of watching people's faces, and the oh-no look on Rebecca's face when I tossed out the $400,000 figure told me a lot.

Not as much as, say, looking at the sales contract would have, but one works with what one can get. But, at the thought of the sales contract, I suddenly looked around at the windows in Rebecca's fine little house and tried to remember the kind of lock on the front door, and then realized copies of the paperwork would be at her office, and I need not plan on breaking into her house. I did, however, need to find out where her office was, and figured asking Shalonda later would be less suspicious than asking Rebecca where her office was and then breaking into it within the same twenty-four-hour stretch.

All of this pondering on my part created a pause in our conversation, and when I finally filled it, I did so with a side step. "What about with all the new land speculation? All the new and proposed development?" I asked. "Hasn't that driven land prices way up?"

"Yes. And, see there, you have answered your own question."

Not quite. What Shalonda had told me suggested otherwise for my grandmom's former farm. Plus, I still didn't buy for one minute that a piece of property that had sold for $180,000 just three years ago, and at best could have appreciated another $80,000 or $100,000, could reasonably sell for $400,000. In Florida, yes, with one of the hottest real estate markets in the country, but not in rural southwest Georgia.

While I was doing math in my head, the front door slammed and Bobby and Armando came tromping into the living room. "It's too hot to wait in the car," Armando said. "And it's boring."

"Hi, Miss Rebecca," Bobby said. "May we come in?"

Rebecca smiled at Bobby in a way that told me she wholly approved of him as dating material, and I wondered if she suspected about the tree house and the marijuana, but wasn't about to rat out Bobby or Becky. Instead, I introduced Armando, who, to his credit and Bonita's, knew the polite responses.

Becky materialized out of the back of the house, Johnny perched on her shoulder, and took each young man by the arm, pulling them together in a way they didn't seem to like.

"We will go into the kitchen while you two finish talking," Becky said to her mother and me. "I'll serve them Coke and pound cake. I'm going to use the gold china." And she flounced out of the living room, toward the kitchen.

Whoa! Three transformations in fifteen minutes, from stoned heartthrob drama princess, to contrite daughter, to Junior League hostess. This girl had serious lawyer potential. I made a mental note to stay in touch with her in case she needed extra mentoring.

"Use the blue china," Rebecca said. Then, eyeing me, she explained, "It's the everyday china."

"We do need to get those boys back to Dan's," I said, ignoring the insult that we only deserved the everyday stuff and figuring this was as much as I was going to learn from Becky's mom. Also I did not want to spend the afternoon at a tea party with teenagers, regardless of the china pattern.

Following Rebecca, I peered into the kitchen, where the kids had gone, Johnny in tow, and decided from the looks of things that Armando was pretty much planning on moving in with Becky and Rebecca, and that Becky was, indeed, using the gold china.

Rebecca apparently decided not to make an issue of it, and offered Shalonda and me some iced tea. While we were declining on the basis of needing to make a quick escape, Johnny untangled himself from Becky and scampered across the floor straight to Rebecca. She picked him up and he did a ferret swoon when she cuddled him on her generous chest.

"Why, he is just a little sweetheart," Rebecca said.

All this time, I'd thought Johnny didn't like women. Turns out, he just didn't like me. Or maybe he had a thing for blondes. He wouldn't be the first male if he did.

Putting aside the ferret's peccadilloes, I looked at Shalonda. "We've got to go."

"Bobby and your son are welcome to stay. Don't worry, I'll be home all afternoon and will look out for them," Rebecca said, in a tone that suggested she figured me for child-neglect issues at the best.

"He's not my son," I said.

"Leave 'em here," Shalonda said. "They're having fun."

Oh, yeah, whatever. So, after I made Armando promise to stay with Bobby, and to keep an eye out for Johnny, Shalonda and I left them.

How was I to know they were going to cross paths with a person without a soul?

chapter 48

A **few years back,** my junior associate had stolen Newly, my boyfriend, and before that, a much-younger nurse had vamped away a doctor I'd imagined I'd loved. Given that history, I was sensitive on the issue of women being dumped.

So it was that when Rebecca followed Shalonda and me out to the Honda and revealed her own paranoia in this direction, I was a great deal more tolerant of the fact she was wasting my time than I might otherwise have been.

Just as I had been about to hop into the driver's side of my car, Rebecca said, "I'd like to speak to you, if I may."

Oh, nice and polite. "Talk," I said.

"She means alone," Shalonda said, and got in the passenger's side. "Don't be long, I got to be calling around and seeing if Demetrious has showed up."

"Cell phone's in the glove compartment, help yourself," I said.

Curious, I followed Rebecca off to the side of her front yard.

"I know a lot about you," she said.

"I doubt that," I said.

"Look, it's a small town, I've been knowing Patti and Dan ever since Bobby and Becky started dating. I know you're one of those people who went off to law school planning to be Atticus Finch and you're all high and mighty in Sarasota saving the downtrodden and all."

Not even close, on either point, I thought, but if that was the spin Patti Lea had put on my legal career, it wasn't my place to correct her to her friend. Besides, I wanted to let Rebecca have free range to express herself so I could see where she'd end up.

"Well, I'm not. That is, not one of those people who wanted to be Atticus Finch, see," Rebecca said. "I grew up here, *younger* than you, of course, but I didn't figure I was going to marry any of these local guys and I didn't want to end up working in the bank, handling everybody else's money. I wanted my own money. So I went to law school, and I went off to Atlanta to get rich, but now I've got Becky to think about, and you can just forget about coming in here with your perfect hair and skinny ass and taking Hank away from me."

On reflex, I started to say thank you. I am proud of my hair. I should be, as I pay enough to Brock, my hairdresser, to keep it a perfect, long, black pageboy. Then the romance angle hit me. Hank? That was what this was about?

"He'll be a good father to Becky, not like that . . . that last one," Rebecca said.

I assured Rebecca that while I doubted she was that much younger than me, she could relax on the Hank matter, as I was engaged to a perfectly nice man, who, by the way, was a world-class criminal-defense attorney and damn good-looking and rich as sin. (So okay, I was exaggerating a little, how exactly was she going to check all that out?) Further, I assured her that Hank and I were old friends, nothing more, and I appreciated her directness, and I left.

Despite Rebecca's concerns, as far as I could see, the only one dead-set on Hank and me getting married was Jubal, and if I couldn't outwit a matchmaking old ex-logger, then I had no business being a lawyer.

chapter 49

My next goal was to drive by Rebecca's office and scout it out for a late-night return so I might tour her files, looking for that sales contract between Lonnie and Simon.

Shalonda wanted to go home and look for signs of her missing husband.

Naturally, that trumped my making plans for a jump back on the B and E wagon, so, after I finagled directions to Rebecca's office for future use, off we went to Shalonda's house.

Demetrious was not anywhere around, but the yellow crime tape by the barn and the deputy sheriff snooping around the house put us both in a dark, gloomy mood.

Shalonda collapsed at the kitchen table, while I hoped she wouldn't cry and decided to make tea for both of us. After checking the inside of the teapot for mule hair or worse, I boiled the water, and found the tea bags—Luzianne—in the cupboard, and made hot tea.

Shalonda sipped, and looked less like she might cry. "When Demetrious comes home," she said, "I'm going to tell him about that money."

With that pronouncement, Shalonda pulled out a pound cake and cut off a piece. "Want some?" she asked, and I shook my head, wondering what kind of security Rebecca might have for her law office.

This being Bugfest, a low-crime zone, maybe Rebecca had no security, and maybe a cheap lock, I hoped.

"Sure?" Shalonda asked, waving a piece of pound cake right under my nose. While I inhaled the buttery smell and whimpered, I tried to counsel Shalonda on her diet.

"Would you shut up about food. You got the two college degrees, you need to be figuring out what in the hell's going on, and who killed Lonnie, and where Demetrious is. And what this has got to do with Willette."

Good points.

"Stop daydreaming and get to work," Shalonda said, and shoved the last of her pound cake into her mouth, and then smacked me lightly across the top of my shoulders with her napkin.

Okay, yeah, right, I was suddenly all for doing something rash right now, especially since I'd have to at least wait till midnight to try and get into Rebecca's filing cabinets.

But even rash needed a direction. Where did we go from here?

Rather than run around in circles, I decided the thing to do was gather more information. Starting with the source in front of me.

"So, tell me about Lonnie."

Shalonda sniffed a bit, a real sad look coming into her eyes. "He was not a bad man. Not really."

Well, okay, so far you could have fooled me on that "not a bad man" thing, but then lovers see the object of their lust differently than the rest of the world does. The lawyer in me took over. "Let's talk facts, not emotional supposition," I said. "What was he doing up North before he came back here?"

"Well, you know he was in Nashville for a while. Long time, and he had him that hit song—" and she paused to hum the chorus. "You know he wrote that song 'bout me, don't you? Used to call me up and tell me I was his own, true sweetheart."

"Yeah, I know that song. About you, wow, that's so cool," I said, but I was thinking Lonnie probably told that to every woman, like his infamous "you're the one who got away" line.

"Yeah, it was a great song. But after that, I don't know, nothing seemed to happen for him."

"I heard he'd never got anywhere after that, and he left Nashville," I said. "Dan and Patti used to tell me stuff about him, time to time, like when he went up North to run his own business."

"Yeah, he did. Ran a little sporting goods store. He was part-owner."

"Where?"

"In Minnesota."

Minnesota? Where they had snow? Serious snow? No wonder he failed, he was too cold to think. Why did a man from the semi-rain-forest heat and humidity of Bugfest, Georgia, go to the land of deep snow to make his way in the world?

I asked Shalonda just that.

"'Cause that stuck-up woman with the foul mouth he married was from up there. He followed her home, then married her." Shalonda shook her head, her beaded hair lifting and circling. "She's his whiskey, I reckon. They're not happy far as I could tell, but, Lord, that man was drunk on her."

Shalonda paused for a moment, and the look on her face was sad. "I reckon he needed me 'cause a man needs a little softness, some tenderness."

Being an attorney, not a relationship counselor, I merely nodded, then went straight back to the cross-examination.

"What happened to the store?"

"It went broke."

"So, when he came back to Bugfest, he didn't have much money, right?"

"I don't know 'bout that. I didn't ask him 'bout his money."

"But soon after he came back, he got him the appliance store, right?"

Perhaps he got local financing on the basis of having been almost the next Vince Gill, but I didn't figure Shalonda would know where he got his money to start another store. So, I went with what she would know. "Where was he living? I mean before he bought my grandmom's house."

"He and that bitch wife were renting a little old house downtown. I don't think she was real happy about it."

"So then three years ago, Willette sells him my grandmom's place for $180,000. Right? And then Simon buys it from him two weeks ago for $400,000? That is, according to Becky."

"Yeah, well Lonnie never said nothing to me about getting no $400,000 for your grandmomma's place. You can bet I'd've mentioned that to you."

That amount being so fishy, I could understand why Lonnie might not have told Shalonda or anyone else. Of course, understanding why Lonnie wasn't bragging about the sale price didn't explain why on earth Simon so overpaid for that property.

Maybe Lonnie was blackmailing Simon somehow. But with Lonnie being the one who was probably dealing in stolen goods, defrauding poor people, maybe supplying Willette with drugs off the Internet, and maybe having a hand in some smuggling, it seemed more likely that Simon could be blackmailing him.

"When did Simon come to town?" I asked.

"Can't give you an exact date, but 'bout a year ago."

"When did the county start planning on damming up the creek and making a big lake?"

"Oh, they been talking 'bout that near two decades. You come home now and then, you'd know these things. Corps of Engineers approved the plans 'bout a year ago. Maybe a little more than a year."

"What about the resort and the marina?"

"That's new. I mean, compared to the lake plans. But once the county's plans got approved, talk 'bout a resort and a marina just started springing up everywhere. Lot a stories in the paper, going back maybe ten months or so."

"So, roughly speaking, the county's *real* plans to make a big bass lake and the resort's plans to develop a marina all date back to about the same time Simon came to town?"

Shalonda looked at me, narrowing her eyes, maybe sensing some kind of trap for Lonnie, though he was well beyond police jurisdiction now. Then she said, "Yeah, 'bout the same time. But Simon, he runs the hospital, he's not developing the resort."

As far as we know, I thought. Often, though, big developers liked to fly under the radar so they could buy up the locals' inheritances at cheap land prices. One standard trick was to send in different buyers to grab up key chunks here and there before word got out and the prices soared.

So, yeah, maybe Simon was an advance scout. And Lonnie one of the targets. Maybe my grandmother's land was destined to be some big, but as yet undisclosed, part of this bass-lake project. And Simon just paid a high price because he knew he could ultimately resell it for a profit to the resort.

But even as I thought this, I knew it didn't make a lick of sense.

The resort corporation wasn't into overpaying for future lakefront property. They were into stealing it from folks at a lower value through eminent domain. I mean, hadn't I been listening to Jubal's discourse on that from my second day in town?

So, what was Simon up to?

Poor weird Simon, with his long arms and legs, who wanted his momma's respect. Poor Simon, who wanted to be the administrator of a big hospital, a big, important job that would catch his momma's attention.

Poor Simon, who just wanted his momma to like him.

Then the sensation of an electrical shot went through me, and my brain pulsed with a vivid color behind my eyes.

This wasn't a migraine aura. This was an inspired-idea aura.

"Lonnie came back to town when? Exactly?" I asked.

"He came back a good five years 'fore Simon showed up. You can't go tying him up with Simon in no land scam," Shalonda said, still defensive of the man she'd had a thing for, dead under suspicious circumstances though he might be.

"Yes, I think I can," I said.

But before I could explain, the phone rang, and Shalonda snatched it up, but after listening a moment, she said, "Oh my God," and thrust the phone at me.

It was Rebecca.

She was sobbing.

Someone had broken into her house while she was taking a shower, and the kids were gone.

chapter 50

Children run away.

Lord knows Delvon and I had done just that often enough. In fact, Delvon made his first bid for freedom and greener pastures when he was still wearing diapers. Just days after his second birthday, he'd climbed out of his crib, opened the unlatched screen door, and toddled off. He'd made it seven blocks from the house before the postman caught him and took him to our father's office.

I made my first break right out of first grade, during recess on the first day of class, having tired quickly of being trapped inside and talked at by a teacher woman with a humped back and plenty of stupid ideas. Delvon, who had been running to third base during the same recess, saw me heading around the corner away from school at a fast trot, and ran straight off the softball field to join me. Despite the attention Delvon caused, we made it to the corner drugstore, where Mr. Gainey gave us each a fountain Coke and a pimento-cheese sandwich before he called our grandmother.

After that, we refined our running-away skills somewhat, getting farther and farther afield. Until my mother hit upon an idea to stop us. Every time the postman, or a neighbor, or a peanut farmer on the edge of town caught us and brought us home, Willette tied us each to a separate chair. We were still small enough that she could overpower us.

The two of us, tied to our chairs, in a room with the curtains drawn against the curiosity of town folks. Hour after hour. Willette would untie us when she heard my father's car in the driveway. We never told our father, or anyone else, what she was doing.

I guess, in retrospect, Delvon and I were supposed to figure out that if we stopped running away, then our mother would stop tying us to chairs in a dark room.

But what our little children's minds had come up with instead of that cause-and-effect paradigm was this: If we kept running away, sooner or later we would actually *get away*.

Accordingly, we spent a good part of my first- and second-grade experiences tied to chairs in a room with the curtains pulled, entertaining each other with increasingly outlandish made-up stories. In a strange way, it was ideal training for law school and personal-injury litigation.

While Delvon and I were honing our imaginations and our bladder control, my grandmother came over one day unexpectedly and found us tied up. She cut us loose, and without a word to my mother, she took us home with her, where we lived for three of the happiest months of my childhood. Grandmother cooked real food for us, she listened to us, and she asked us questions about what we were doing and what we thought of this and that. And we slept in clean beds, with sheets of white cotton, which had dried on the clothesline and smelled like sunshine. Someone always took the garbage out. Our grandfather let us sip from his whiskey, and ride in the back of his pickup when he fed the cows in the evening. Grandmom taught us how to hug and to trust, plus the rudiments of gardening, cooking, and sewing. Even Delvon can make his own clothes to this good day.

The only thing Grandmom asked us to do in return for our stay in this heaven for kids was to stop running away.

We stopped running away. The boredom and confinement of school was a minor price to pay for the comfort of sitting at the kitchen table after school in my grandmother's clean house, eating her homemade ice-box cookies and telling her in great detail about the stupid things our old teachers had done that day.

Then my father came and shut himself in a room with both Grand-mom and Granddad, while Delvon and I paced nervously outside.

When our father came out, he took us home.

In short order, Delvon and I backslid to our former bad habit of un-secured flights. But now, when somebody found us alongside a road or in their barn and brought us home, our mother didn't tie us to chairs. She ignored us. She ignored Dan too, and he kept busy staying off the radar and out of everybody's way.

Thus, as much as a form of recreation as of political protest, Delvon and I kept running off as children and as teenagers. Eventually nobody came after us. We had finally *gotten away.*

So, with my own history firmly in mind as I listened to a sobbing Rebecca over the phone, I tried to reassure her that since the missing young people were teenagers, and therefore both wild and irresponsible by definition, the kids had just taken off on an adolescent frolic.

Rebecca made a strangling noise.

"I'm sure, knowing Bobby, they've just . . . run away. Just for a little while," I repeated, trying to quell my own rising panic and to comfort Rebecca.

"No," Rebecca said, followed by a clear sobbing noise. Then she appar-ently regrouped. "I was in the shower, and I heard noise, you know, like crashing and blamming, but by the time I got my robe on and got down-stairs, the kitchen was a mess."

"That doesn't necessarily rule out running away," I said. "Maybe—"

"They put up a good fight," she said, a tone of pride cutting through her panic. "They didn't run away."

"Did you call 911?"

"Yes, yes, of course I called 911, and the dispatcher was going to find Rodney and the sheriff, and I've called just about everybody else, but I need to talk to Dan and Patti. Now. When I couldn't get any of you at Dan's, I figured you might be at Shalonda's. And you needed to know, because of, you know, that other boy, of yours, er, your son."

"He's not my son, but I'm glad you told me. Dan and Patti are over at Willette's house," I said.

"Well, go and find Dan and Patti and tell them what's going on, now," Rebecca said, and slammed down the phone.

Shalonda and I looked at each other, and I had the overwhelming urge to scream or throw up or both.

"Somebody took them kids," she said. "And it's got something to do with how come your momma shot that man, and all this mess happening since then."

I nodded, unable for once to talk.

"Whole county'll be looking for them," she said, apparently trying to reassure herself.

"We've got to look too," I said, and jumped up from the table. If I didn't move heaven and earth, and everything in between, to find those kids, I'd never forgive myself. "We've got to find those kids."

"Rodney could use some help, I reckon," she said, and stood up. "And I got me something to help us look."

We rushed off to Demetrious's room to gather up Shalonda's weapon of choice.

And it wasn't pound cake.

chapter 51

Ten minutes before my cell phone made that irritating and idiotic metallic ring, I wouldn't have thought it possible for things to go from bad to worse.

You'd think by now I'd know better.

So, when I heard my phone, deep inside the purse I'd borrowed from Patti, who has really good taste in accessories, I snatched the cell out like a happy idiot, fully expecting the reassuring voice of someone telling me the kids were all safe and sound and somewhere eating pound cake.

What I heard instead was the voice of Dr. Hodo, finally getting back to me after my hundred and twelve messages.

"This is not a good time," I said before he finished the second syllable of *hello.* Shalonda and I were whirling through space in my ancient Honda, and reception was iffy on the cell, not to mention my fraying nerves.

"Someone is giving your mother flunitrazepam," Dr. Hodo said, ignoring my opening as he flung another scoop of disaster into the head winds.

"What?"

"Rohypnol."

"*What?*"

"Lilly, it's a drug. Rohypnol is the brand name. It's a pill prescribed in Mexico, South America, Europe, and Asia. It has not been approved for use by the FDA in the United States. It's illegal in this country."

"Let's save the history for later, okay. What's it do?"

"Heard of roofies?" Dr. Hodo asked.

"Yeah, date-rape drug, right?"

"That's the street name for flunitrazepam. But it's all the same drug, Rohypnol, roofies, or flunitrazepam."

"Someone is giving Willette roofies?"

Who in their right mind would want to date-rape Willette?

But, yeah, well, who in their right mind wanted to date-rape anyone?

"It's a sedative, a sleeping pill, really," Dr. Hodo said. "And effective. Memory loss is a bit of a troubling side effect—"

"That's why she's . . . so comatose?"

"Yes. It's a potentially dangerous drug on its own, but mixing it with Thorazine is not a good idea. An especially not good idea."

"Damn, it's a wonder she's breathing."

"Lilly, it gets worse."

No, it couldn't get worse. That was scientifically impossible. But what I said was: "What? How?"

"Somebody also gave her LSD. The thing about LSD is that it wouldn't routinely show up on the tox screen. I got suspicious about her psychotic reaction when I tapered her off the Thorazine. She acted out as if she were hallucinating, and nothing in her history suggested either that or her psychotic behavior. But it took a while to get the test results. And that's when the lab found the LSD and the roofies. The thing about the roofies is that they would have shown up in the tox screen, so it's new. Or else the tox screens from before were wrong."

"Or someone altered the results?"

"That's possible too."

"Dr. Weinstein," I blurted out.

"Is arrogant and aloof, but he would not do something like this," Dr. Hodo finished.

But I stopped listening to him.

"Meet me at the hospital," I shouted at Dr. Hodo, and hung up.

Someone with free run of the hospital was trying to kill my mother, and that told me that she definitely knew something worth being killed over.

And that told me that I had to get her out of there.

Now.

But, oh, and that would be before or after I rescued the kidnapped trio of Bobby, Becky, and Armando?

And how did you break someone out of the hospital when they were guarded by a young, earnest police officer?

chapter 52

On the spot, I would have made a deal with the devil himself if Delvon could have been transported to Bugfest in the flash of my eye. Delvon would know how to get Willette out of the hospital.

And when she woke up, he would be there to comfort her.

Delvon, the creative one. The only one Willette had ever wanted, if Eleanor was to be believed.

But I didn't really think I could make a deal with Satan, and that meant it was up to me.

As Shalonda and I sped to the hospital, I babbled forth what I hoped was a coherent summary of Willette's plight. Most of it she'd picked up from hearing my side of the phone conversation.

I was on a mission, and I had no plan, no painfully researched and excessively detailed legal documents, and no court order. I was neither dressed in my warrior colors, i.e., lawyer gray, nor backed up by a whole law firm with an army of law clerks. All I had was anxiety-fueled adrenaline, and a strong sense that immediate, direct action was necessary.

And Shalonda.

The police chief's wife. Maybe that would count for something.

So it was that after a squealing-tire parking job, Shalonda and I bailed out of the Honda, sprinted past the nurses' station, and plowed smack into a young police officer whose face seemed familiar. He spoke to Shalonda in a tone of respect, and eyed me like I was a crazy disheveled woman bent on breaking some hard-and-fast rules. In other words, he seemed to see me for what I was.

"She all right?" I asked.

"Of course. Miss Eleanor is in there with her," Young Lawman said.

Eleanor, Shalonda, and me. Not the typical SWAT team, but one thing I've learned in this life is this: You use what you are given.

So thinking, I dashed into the room, Shalonda right behind me, and I exhaled. Sure enough, there was Eleanor Spivey, sitting in a chair, knitting a long, brightly colored something.

"My word, Lilly, you look—"

"Someone is trying to kill Willette. Dr. Hodo found roofies and LSD in her blood, and enough downers to kill a normal person."

Okay, so maybe a broad interpretation on the "kill a normal person," but Eleanor was one of those unflappable, slow-to-action sorts, and I wanted her adrenaline to pump.

"I'm sure you are—"

"She ain't lying," Shalonda said, and stuck her head right down into Willette's face, as if she could discern some valuable piece of information a half-inch from Willette's nose.

"She's still breathing," Shalonda said.

"Why, of course she is. All that equipment, and—"

"Somebody in the hospital, some doctor maybe, is trying to kill her and they might have done something with the equipment," I said, nearly snapping at Eleanor.

"I assure you I would notice if Willette died," Eleanor said, and put down her knitting and stood up, advancing on Willette as if to test her own words.

"We've got to get her out of here. Dr. Hodo is on his way, but I'm not waiting, not another moment."

"I'll get a wheelchair," Shalonda said, and fairly ran out of the room.

"I don't think they will let you just take her," Eleanor said, slipping her fingers down on Willette's wrist and taking her pulse.

"Watch me." I mean, come on, how would they stop us? Young Lawman wasn't going to shoot us, and between Eleanor, Shalonda, and me, we could probably whip him in a fair fight.

I started yanking wires and IV lines and sticky things out of machines, and plugs out of walls, and a whole caterwauling of beeps and flashing lights rewarded me for my efforts. I left the ends of the things attached to Willette as they were, and left the IV in her arms, not wanting to mess with needles in her paper-thin skin, but was careful to make sure the IV was disconnected from the hospital paraphernalia. Then I lifted Willette's body out of the bed. She was that light. But though I could pick her up, I didn't think I could carry her all the way out of the hospital, especially if irate nurses and a possible murderer chased me.

Shalonda, my hero, whipped back into the room with a wheelchair.

With an angry-sounding nurse on her tail, yelling at her to stop, or some such nonsense. Followed by a young nurse, no doubt tracking the bells and whistles on the monitor I had ripped asunder.

That brought in Young Lawman, who tried to bring order by talking louder than Shalonda and the nurses. Soon enough the yelling-begets-yelling rule was at play.

Eleanor and I decided to ignore them all, and I put Willette into the wheelchair, where she slumped as if she would fall out of it. While I held her, I scanned the room, searching for something to tie my mother into the wheelchair. But then Eleanor pulled the scarf she was knitting around Willette's waist and tied it in a bunch at the back of the wheelchair. "Ought to be good for something," she said, and patted Willette's hand as if somehow Willette might know what was going on.

I got behind the wheelchair and started pushing and had Willette in the doorway before this registered on Young Lawman, Younger Nurse, and Yelling Nurse, all of whom turned in force on me, shouting orders, telling me things like I couldn't take Willette, I couldn't take the wheelchair, et cetera, et cetera. Ignoring them, I kept pushing, turning around only once and quickly, to make sure Young Lawman wasn't pulling a gun.

To his credit, he didn't pull out a weapon. But he was quick and nimble, this cop, and he pulled me away from the wheelchair and spun me around and said, in pure cop language: "Stop. This woman is in police custody."

I tried to snatch myself out of his hold, but he was strong.

But there is no more determined force on the face of the earth than a retired schoolteacher with a mission of saving someone she loves, though why Eleanor would love Willette remains as much of a mystery as what happened to the Lost Colony of Roanoke. Which is to say, Eleanor popped in behind the wheelchair and gave it a mighty shove and got clean out into the hallway, what with me holding up Young Lawman and Shalonda holding up Yelling Nurses.

Eleanor had that wheelchair a yard past the nurses' station by the time Young Lawman broke loose of me and took off running after her. Shalonda and I ran after him. The Yelling Nurse Duo apparently decided the better part of valor was to abandon the field, and they went off in another direction, possibly looking for Security.

Young Lawman, being barely more than a kid, had a physical advantage over Eleanor, highly motivated though she was, and he jumped past Shalonda and me, blocking Eleanor and the wheelchair that contained Willette. "Y'all stop now, damn it," he said, flushed and no doubt a tad peeved.

Eleanor shoved the wheelchair another inch or two before he grabbed her arm.

"Don't you grab that woman," I said.

"I'm the police chief's wife," Shalonda said, "and in his absence, I'm ordering you to let that woman go." She made a commanding presence.

Young Lawman let go of Eleanor and stood still, looking like a puzzled puppy caught between a shoe he wants to chew and a memory of what happened last time he chewed one.

"As the chief of police's wife, I command you to let Miz Willette go," Shalonda said, her voice and posture equally bold.

"You're not . . . I mean . . . you can't . . ." Young Lawman stammered.

Well, exactly, I thought, though I admired Shalonda's sudden claim to being the acting police chief solely by virtue of her marriage vows.

"Young man," Eleanor said, "didn't I teach you to respect your elders?"

"Yes, ma'am," Young Lawman said. "And I appreciate to this good day all the help you gave me when I was foolish enough to take that Shakespeare course over to Valdosta State, but I can't be letting you steal this woman."

"You have a fine mind, young man. You just let the idea of Shakespeare intimidate you."

"Yes, ma'am. Everybody sure was surprised when I got a B in that course, me most of all. But be that as it may, I can't be letting you just take Miss Willette out of here."

"Yes, you can, young man, I wouldn't lie or trick you, any more than Mrs. Dupree here would. We need to get this woman transferred to another facility. Now. It is an emergency." As she talked, Eleanor eased away from Willette, forcing the still-puzzled-looking police officer to back up. I saw at once what Eleanor was doing, as did Shalonda, who marched in beside Eleanor and both of them kept pressing the zone of personal space about Young Lawman, who kept backing up.

Every step they backed up left more and more leeway around Willette. In a second, I whipped into that empty space behind the wheelchair and started running and pushing.

When Young Lawman tried to run after me, Shalonda flat-out tackled the man.

I saw this out of the corner of my eye as I ran, glancing back while pushing the wheelchair in front of me, and I made the front door, where I nearly collided with Dr. Hodo, who, bless his heart, didn't bother to ask questions of medical protocol this time but took over pushing the wheelchair while I bent over, gasping momentarily to catch my breath. Then I followed him to his car, where we laid Willette out in the back seat.

"You trust me?" he asked.

I stared him in the face, taking his measure. For a moment, I had my doubts. What if Willette had known something about him, some valid reason to ban him from our house all those years ago? I had to ask. "Why did my mother run you off?"

Dr. Hodo looked at me, then gazed off in the distance for a minute before he turned back to me, staring into my own eyes with his intense blue ones.

"Every year I get a Christmas card from a convicted pedophile," he said.

What the hell did that have to do with anything, I wondered, and opened my mouth to protest this digression.

"That man, I could help. And I did. And he thanks me, every December, in that card."

"So what in the name of—"

"But I couldn't help Willette. Or your father."

Oh, I thought, and considered the weight this man's profession laid on his shoulders.

"Your mother was jealous. Jealous because your father and I went fishing. She took offense at any time he took away from her."

Like she was jealous of me, because Delvon would rather hang out with me than her. Yeah, okay, it fit. It fit, but it was also too easy, his explanation, and I stared back at him with my own intense blue eyes. "What else?"

"I tried to suggest to her that she and her father both needed some professional help. He was drinking too much, and she was taking entirely too many tranquilizers and painkillers. You do know there is a strong family history of manic-depressive behavior on your grandfather's side? Sometimes this can manifest itself in substance abuse."

I sidestepped my faulty gene pool and asked, "And she refused your help?"

"Yes, to put it mildly. Then I compounded my sin. I told your father he had a problem."

A problem with his wife.

My father's friend from long ago. A compassionate, trained psychiatrist. Wanting to help, and being turned out of the family and the friendship as his reward. It fit what little I really knew about Willette.

It also fit one of the first lessons of my life: You don't talk about it.

Don't tell anyone what goes on inside. Don't let anybody know. Bar the door. Drape the windows. Hunker down and shut up.

But mow the grass and paint the house and wear a clean white shirt to the office so everybody will think it's all just fine.

On the surface, everything's all right.

So, naturally, my father let Willette run off the proffered help, and covered up the mess.

I felt a sharp jab of anger at my parents. Then I shook my head to clear the feelings. And I turned back to the question at hand. Did I trust Dr. Hodo?

For a fleeting moment, it occurred to me Dr. Hodo probably had access to roofies and LSD and red ants. And that he could come and go in the hospital.

But I could conceive of no motive. And I could conceive of no evil in this man. And his story rang true to me.

So, in the end, after looking into his blue eyes, I said, "Yes, I trust you."

"Then go help find those kids, and let me get Willette to a hospital in Thomasville."

"Call me," I said, already turning back to my own car.

I left Shalonda, Young Lawman, and Eleanor to sort it out among themselves.

But I had the notion that Young Lawman wasn't about to arrest the missing police chief's wife or his former English teacher.

He did seem like a nice young man.

chapter 53

It **was simple,** really: Who had killed or tried to kill whom and why no longer mattered.

We had to get the kids back.

That was all that was important. Especially now that the endangered Willette was presumably safely on her way to a hospital where someone wasn't trying to kill her, and where, properly detoxed from LSD, roofies, and Thorazine, she might finally tell us what had happened the day she allegedly shot Ray Glenn.

So, why was I thinking about this story in a newspaper about a congressman who had sold his house in a desirable city to a big oil lobbyist? No big deal there. But then, within a year, the lobbyist sold it at a loss—an $800,000 loss. Which was unheard of in the middle of this country's biggest housing bubble, where the inflated prices of real estate in certain cities and states were creating both a false wealth and a growing class of the newly homeless.

And, naturally enough, the congressman had voted in favor of Big Oil in every vote since that lobbyist had purchased his house.

That the lobbyist had bribed the congressman by paying much

more than the house was worth eventually got them both in some trouble.

Being a busy lawyer with things like billable hours, clients being sued, and expert witnesses to worry about, I'd more or less forgotten that story.

Till now.

Bribery. And the missing kids. If I could find the connection, maybe I could find Bobby, Becky, and Armando.

So, with connecting the dots in mind, I called Rebecca from the phone in Patti and Dan's kitchen. Halfway through the first ring, she answered, her voice breathless and scared. "Becky?" she asked.

"Lilly," I said.

"God, do you know anything?"

"Not about the kids, but—"

She hung up.

I called her right back.

"Listen, this is important. I've got to know this to help find Becky."

This time she didn't hang up.

"Did Simon really pay Lonnie four hundred thousand for that property?"

Pause.

"How is that—"

"I think Simon was bribing Lonnie for his vote on the resort, and somehow Simon figures Becky knows something." Okay, the condensed version.

I could practically hear Rebecca's brain working. "What's Simon got to do with it?"

"I don't know exactly, but something. Maybe he's a cover for—"

"The resort."

"Yeah."

"Let me go check something," and *bam,* she hung up again.

What was she checking? The ethics code for whether she could break a client confidence to save her child? I could give a quick answer on that—loosely translated, hell, yes—and if the Georgia Bar disagreed, screw 'em, and I dialed her number again.

"Becky?" she asked.

"Lilly."

"Don't call me, I'll call you." *Bam,* she hung up on me again.

Twenty minutes later, when the phone rang, I'd already chewed a hole in my lip trying to use Westlaw on my laptop, with Bobby's slow-speed dial-up, to find the connection between Simon and the resort. "What?"

"Rebecca here. The CEO of the resort is a man named Davis Pombo."

"So?"

"He started out as a salesman for the same drug company as Simon. They would have known each other."

So, there it was.

Simon and the CEO of the resort, both fledgling salesmen in a pharmaceutical company as they started out on their lives of greed and crime.

"How did you find that out?"

"I've got Simon's résumé, from being on the hiring board. And I did a Lexis news database search on the resort, got Pombo's name, and researched him, and found a feature article on him that gave a bio."

Wow, Rebecca was good.

"So, did—"

"Yes, Simon paid four hundred thousand to Lonnie for that place. I told Lonnie it wasn't worth it, and I . . . I worried about fraud, but I didn't think of bribery."

Okay, Rebecca wasn't that good. "Gotta go," I said.

"Wait, I forgot to tell you, your son's ferret is missing too," and then, *bam,* she hung up again.

Now I had to explain to Shalonda why we needed to go to Simon's place.

Naturally, Shalonda and Eleanor had talked their way around Young Lawman, and Shalonda had come back to Dan's house, and so, here we were again.

Sitting together in a room, with trouble writ large around us. The grown-up version of all those hours we had spent in after-school detention.

The first thing I did was tell her what Bobby and Becky had told me: that Lonnie was inside Willette's house the night Ray Glenn got shot, and had run out. She took a long time digesting this, but to her credit, didn't try to pass off Bobby and Becky as liars or mistaken.

"I'm sorry this is happening to you," I said.

"We got your momma safe, and we're gonna find those kids, and Demetrious is gonna have a real good explanation when he comes home, you just wait and see."

Optimistic people make me nervous, so I plunged ahead into my theory. Here's what I told her: Simon had bribed Lonnie. Pure and simple. That purchase of Lonnie's place, aka my grandmother's home, was a bribe that had somehow led to attempted murder, real murder, and kidnapping.

"I don't get it," Shalonda said. "Why bribe Lonnie?"

That Shalonda didn't understand why Lonnie was a great subject for a bribe suggested she still refused to see him for who he had been.

A spineless, greedy politician on the make.

Possibly a redundancy in the labeling, I thought, as I set out to explain the broad principles to Shalonda. With as much gentleness as I could, I told her that Lonnie had been a cheat all the way around.

Lonnie was the swing vote on whether the county would appoint the resort corporation as the county's agent for development, and without his vote, the resort couldn't use the county's power of eminent domain. And eminent domain was, finally, the key, quite simply, to stealing Jubal and Hank's place under the government's power to take land for the public good, as Jubal and Hank had the misfortune to own what apparently was the gem of the future lakefront property. Eminent domain was also the key to cutting out inflated selling prices for many of the other property owners, and the cure for any other balky landowners. Especially the ones

who didn't live on lakefront property now, but would when the county
finished damming up the creek and making a big lake. If the county got
their property now, under eminent domain, it would be purchased at the
modest, rural-farmland prices, not at lakefront prices. Given the many
hundreds of acres at issue, this would make a huge difference in the cost
of doing business for the planned development. No telling how many
other property owners around Sleepy Lake, or north of it, where the
county planned to flood twelve hundred acres, were in the same boat as
Jubal and Hank.

So, yeah, there was a passel of property to be had, and having it at
the cheapest price was the goal. That being using the county to help the
resort gobble it up at the government's idea of the fair-market value, plus
being able to force out those like Jubal and Hank, who did not want to
sell. But in order to use eminent domain under the new Supreme Court
decision, local government needed to side with the resort and the developers, and offer at least some pretense of a public purpose. That meant
convincing the commissioners to vote the way of the resort, and thereby
become partners with it in the grand development scheme—and offer
up increased tax revenue and new jobs as the public good. Overlook-
ing, of course, that the highest-paid jobs would come from outside the
county and that the increased taxes meant the locals' own property taxes
would increase.

And into this picture of greed and grab, there boogied good ole
Lonnie, county commissioner and failed country singer, holding on to
that key vote.

Till Simon hit the right asking price.

A $140,000 bribe.

And how better to bribe someone without leaving an obvious trail?

There were a congressman and a lobbyist who'd already figured
this out.

Pay the bribee more than his house was worth, let him pocket the
money, all fair and square. Shoot, Lonnie wouldn't even have to pay capi-

tal gains tax on it if he had a CPA with a brain bigger than a pea, since that place had been his home for more than two years and would fit into the tax-exempt category.

It was actually a very clever plan.

But it was a plan that required that no one looked too closely at the transaction.

Thus, except for one small misstep and Willette's good aim, it probably would have worked out just dandy for Lonnie, Simon, and the resort corporation.

The screwup was that Lonnie might possibly have forgotten to mention to Simon that he didn't actually, you know, *own* the house and property, because he, Lonnie, the big shot, might possibly have forgotten, you know, to actually pay Willette the rest of the purchase price because he had expensive lifestyle issues. I mean, from Lonnie's point of view, why pay a drug-addled and crazy old woman the last $65,000 when you could just fake her signature on a deed and count on the fact that she wasn't leaving her house long enough to realize what was going on and to raise a stink? And maybe Lonnie had thrown some extra drugs her way to up the addled quotient.

What Lonnie hadn't counted on was Willette's contact with the outside world via modern telecommunications. And her phone list. And the fact that she wasn't really that crazy after all. Just reclusive. What had Dr. Hodo said? Agoraphobic and obsessive-compulsive disorder. A gene pool with manic-depressive DNA. But, contrary to general appearances, not actually crazy enough not to notice when she was being screwed over *in land and money.*

Someone—Jubal the errand boy, Dan the dutiful son, Eleanor the friend—probably picked up on some rumors about the sale and the price, and they'd called Willette. More than likely, she'd called Simon and Lonnie. I mean, I had that phone-list notebook that showed she'd called Simon the day Ray Glenn got shot. Once she was detoxed enough, we could find out for sure, but for now, my money was on guessing Willette wanted Simon to pay her the same $400,000 that he had paid Lonnie for the house she still legally owned.

But, being the recluse she was, obviously she wasn't a county commissioner with the power to swing a vote, and there was no reason in the world for Simon to pay her $400,000 for a place with a fair market value of no greater than $260,000.

So, obviously, Simon would want Lonnie to get clean title, and to shut Willette up.

I tossed out my theory to Shalonda.

"So, Simon's in on it. No doubt," Shalonda said, agreeing. "But Lonnie—"

I had held back some of my suspicions before, out of consideration for Shalonda's feelings for Lonnie, but the lives and mental health of three teenagers were at issue now. Not to mention the missing Demetrious, mule, and ferret.

"Someone, like, say, an irate Simon, must have impressed upon Lonnie the need to get a real deed with Willette's real signature on it. Simon had to be afraid Willette would raise a stink, and sue to get title back to her place. Everything gets put under a microscope in a trial. At the very least, it'd go into the public record that Simon'd overpaid and raise ugly questions," I said, as Shalonda nodded.

"You don't want to shine too much light on a bad thing, do you?" Shalonda said.

"Exactly. The way I figure it, Lonnie went with Ray Glenn to Willette's that night, planning to get her to sign a deed he'd prepared and backdated," I said. "He carried that sixty-five thousand in cash with him. I mean, he had the money now that he had Simon's bribe, and Lonnie probably hoped he could just pay Willette what he owed and get her to sign the quit-claim deed. He could get that substituted for the fake one easy enough. I'm not sure how Lonnie figured to keep Willette quiet about all that, but it doesn't matter now. Something went wrong, and Willette shot Ray Glenn, and Lonnie ran away. But Bobby and Becky were in the tree house and saw him run out."

"And Willette was too upset to tell Demetrious what'd happened. No way that woman was able to tell him anything. Way he told it, she was just a-screaming and a-screaming."

"Yeah. No doubt." It also occurred to me that this whole experience had probably gone a long way to validate Willette's rule that nobody was allowed inside her house in the first place.

And somebody—like Simon the hospital administrator with a prior employment history that included a thorough knowledge of prescription drugs—was able to see to it she never could tell Demetrious what happened that night. All he'd had to do was augment the Thorazine with a few roofies. That is, just long enough to buy him the time to kill her with red ants so it would look like a horrible accident and not murder. When that failed, and Simon heard Dr. Hodo was going to bring Willette out of her drug stupor, no doubt he'd had a chance to slip her some LSD, enough to make her seem psychotic and to force Dr. Hodo to sedate her all over again.

And keep her sedated until he could figure out how to kill her while she was under guard by both police and her own kith and kin.

"But how did Simon know Becky and Bobby saw Lonnie run out from Willette's while they were sitting up in that tree house?" Shalonda asked. "And how come that would even matter?"

"I don't know. But I can sure guess that Simon didn't want Lonnie getting caught by the law because he was sure to try and talk his way out of trouble by pointing the finger right at Simon. So Simon's the one probably killed Lonnie."

"Praise the Lord, then, it was Simon and not Demetrious," Shalonda shouted, and slumped with relief. And then she brought herself back to the really important thing: saving Bobby, Becky, and Armando. "So those kids are another loose end for Simon, 'cause they tie Lonnie into the mess and raise some questions that get back to Simon."

"That's what I'm thinking. Once Ray Glenn got killed, the stakes jumped pretty high. Under the felony-murder doctrine, Simon is as guilty as if he shot Ray Glenn because he set it all in motion."

"Yeah, I got it," Shalonda said.

"I say the place to start looking for Bobby, Armando, and Becky is at Simon's."

"Yeah, but we're going to tell Rodney first," Shalonda said.

Neither of us could stand to give voice to the great fear that it might already be too late. But Shalonda understood when I said, "Time is of the essence."

"I can call him quick. Have him get out there to Simon's place."

"He might need to get a warrant or something, but you call him for backup while we drive." Actually, I didn't have a clue as to whether Rodney would need a warrant or not where the lives of kids were involved. Hey, I'm a medical malpractice attorney, not a criminal defense one, but I didn't want to take the time to call Philip and ask. What I wanted to do, very badly and right then, was to go find my nephew and his girlfriend and Bonita's son. Yeah, and the damn ferret too. I mean, he was a weird little guy, but he had once saved my life.

"Use my cell to call Rodney while I drive."

"Well, let's go then," Shalonda said.

There was no argument on my part over Shalonda's company, especially since she had already dug around in Demetrious's closet earlier that day and pulled out a traditional .12-gauge shotgun, which she had left stashed in the trunk of my faithful Honda.

"You know how to use that, don't you?" I asked when she pulled it out of the trunk right before we set off to catch Simon and rescue the kids.

"It's for show, white girl, I can bluff with this thing better'n I can shoot it."

I wanted Shalonda to load the shotgun, but she said, "Lord says, you live by the shotgun, you die by the shotgun. I ain't taking no loaded gun with me."

Even in the face of Shalonda's stubbornness, I tried again to convince her that a couple of loads wouldn't hurt. I mean, the list of the known dead stood at two, and the list of the missing was growing by the hour.

But Shalonda would not budge. She was not loading that shotgun.

Even as we sped away to Simon's place, I was pretty sure we were going to regret not putting shells in that .12-gauge.

chapter 54

Well, damn, I thought as I smashed in Simon's window, there being, in my mind at least, no particular reason to try to hide this B and E. I sure hated that my first visit back inside my grandmom's house had to be under these circumstances.

But at least I was too busy looking for kidnapped teenagers to get mopey or nostalgic.

And too in a hurry to fool with those damn lock picks.

The good news was that Simon was not at home to get in our way as we ransacked the house he probably didn't really own.

The bad news was that we found nothing of kids or clues as to where they might be.

I did find something very interesting, though—Willette's missing bank records, plus her monthly statements from her stockbroker. No doubt Simon had broken into her house the night she shot Ray Glenn and taken them in an attempt to hide the fact Lonnie still owed her $65,000 on my grandmom's house, and therefore didn't own it when he sold it to him. Simon must not have had the time or the skill to find her gray metal box full of important papers, with the contract for the deed. But I took a quick glance through the paperwork he had stolen, and could easily trace the deposits from Lonnie. Yep, they definitely stopped long before they should have, like $65,000 short. As for her stock account, even I was momentarily impressed by her portfolio. Hmm, I thought, I'll be able to get Dan to reimburse me for anything I might have to pay that psych nurse or Dr. Hodo. Then I reprimanded myself for thinking about money while the kids were still missing.

Missing, as in not in the house. But there were the outbuildings and forty acres yet to search, and we headed out to the barn and the pump house.

Even with the fearsome-looking though unloaded shotgun, I was edgy about Simon—what if he drove up? I'd made a passing effort to hide my Honda in the middle of a long row of well-spaced blueberries. I mean, if nobody walked through the blueberries, the car was probably hidden. But hidden car or not, the busted window in the front of the house was pretty darn obvious, and if Simon showed up, he might kidnap us, or he might freak and hurt the kids.

If he hadn't already.

No, I told myself, put that thought out of your head.

Besides, we had backup coming just any minute now.

Shalonda had left word over a broken cell-phone connection with the 911 dispatcher to tell Rodney and the high sheriff to get out here. If Rebecca had good sense, and she seemed to, she'd also called the sheriff about Simon. A small army of armed uniformed officers had to be on the way, right?

So, while Shalonda toted her shotgun, and I relied on backup arriving any minute, we searched all the outbuildings.

Nothing.

"No kids and no Demetrious," Shalonda said, sounding weary and forlorn. She wandered off briefly back to the garage to make sure we hadn't missed any trap doors or some such thing.

"Come on, let's walk along the lake, make sure . . ." I paused. Make sure what? There weren't bodies floating in it? Children chained to trees?

Shalonda and I galloped down to the shoreline and studied the lake. A blue heron was wading along the eastern shore, looking for its supper. A small flock of wood ducks floated mid-lake, and on the other side, I saw the sloping, green hills of a cow pasture, a few Black Angus grazing in the sun. Beyond that, as far as I could see, were dense woods of old oaks, pine, and sweetgum.

In the center of the lake, a small island stood, surrounded by submerged logs, covered in the olive-colored sliders—the lake turtles named for their habit of sliding into the water at the approach of anyone. In the early spring, I knew that island would turn yellow from the woven vines of Carolina jasmine, and as the jasmine faded, the pale pink and white of the wild azaleas would take over until the island became a dense, green thicket by summer.

Closer to me, a couple of small egrets with their big yellow feet patrolled the edge of the lake. I'd grown up calling those egrets "cow birds," because they mostly followed the herds, literally standing on the cow's back, catching and eating the bugs the cattle naturally attracted.

Watching the lake, I was hit by a wave of grief almost as overwhelming as my fear for the kids. Damn Lonnie, damn the commissioners. This stable, healthy lake would be submerged into a big, fake monster-lake. The island, the pasture, and the woods would all be underwater soon. And the sliders, the egrets, the ducks, and the herons would have to cope with crowds of bass boats and kids on Jet Skis. The trees would be lumbered before the damming and the flooding, their pulp sold to paper mills. And all those creatures that lived in those woods would drown, or die from loss of habitat.

The native landscape of my childhood was going to be nothing more than a weekend resort for city folks who didn't know, and didn't care, what life they had killed to get those few days on a big-ass man-made lake.

But I didn't have time to waste on getting angry. I had to find Bobby, Becky, and Armando. So, I gave the lake a last, careful study, and Shalonda and I ran around the edges calling out names and getting no answer. We poked around in deep bushes, shoving aside poison ivy and Virginia creeper, finding nothing but more vegetation. Even in the cool of the autumn day, we worked up a sweat before we looked each other in the face, in defeat.

Satisfied we were not going to find the kids along the shoreline, we walked back to the barn we had already fruitlessly searched. Had we missed any possible hiding places?

While staring at all the nooks and crannies, I noticed an electric meter on the side of the barn. The wheel in the meter was whirling around like a windmill on amphetamines, and I wondered why Simon would need that much power in his barn. But when I looked closer, I noticed that the line ran away from the barn and cut through the woods.

Well, that was interesting, I thought, and grabbed Shalonda. "Let's follow that power line, and see what's at the other end."

Thus, we went running off into the woods, leaving my only marginally hidden Honda and a busted window as a calling card for Simon, should he come back to the house he paid $400,000 for but still didn't own.

chapter 55

There's nothing like a brisk jog through the dense brown, orange, and green woods of the red hills of Georgia in the fall to make one appreciate the virtues of good shoes, bug repellent, and a machete.

Too bad what I had were my sister-in-law's boots, not even a bottle of citronella, and a high school girlfriend with an unloaded shotgun.

Which is to say, I had a few bites, the gnawing suspicion that the boots didn't really fit so well after all, and scratches from the thick limbs and scrubs that didn't give way easily as we followed beneath the overhead power line. The whole time we were shoving our way through brambles often stronger than we were, Shalonda kept wondering out loud why on earth the Rural Electric Co-op people hadn't cut beneath the line. "They're always cutting the trees under the lines out to our place. Look at this mess here, come any old kind of storm, and there's gonna be a tree down on this line."

Me, see, I didn't care if the mystery power line crashed and burned so long as Armando, Bobby, and Becky were not under the tree when it fell.

But we both stopped short, and shut up with our litany of what was in the larger sense minor complaints when we saw where the power line went.

To the old cemetery. The one with the glorious Confederate dead, the ghost of the hanged man, the relatively new fence, and rows and rows of people who could finally answer the question of what lay on the other side.

"Dead people need electricity?" I asked, testing Shalonda's concept of the rhetorical question.

"There's that old church in there," Shalonda said, "the one you asked about. I guess they ran the line off of your grandmomma's place way back, being the shorter distance, to save money instead of putting up a whole new line out there. She was pretty smart to make 'em get their own meter."

"Yeah, but you said the county bought that church and nobody uses it or the graveyard anymore."

"Well, then let's go see." Shalonda hoisted up the shotgun on her shoulder, scampered up the slatted wood gate, and hopped over. I followed.

Sure enough, the power line went into the old church on one side, but it also extended beyond the church, into the center of the graveyard, where a clump of trees, newly expressing themselves in red and orange, blocked our view.

First things first, I thought, and tried the front door to the old building in front of me.

The church was locked, of course.

"Now, see, if you'd put shells in that gun, we could have blasted our way in," I said, after yanking on the padlock and finding it secure. "Guess we'll have to bust a window out and crawl in." I was aiming a rock at the front window.

"You ain't busting up any of this old stain-glass," Shalonda said. "Not when we can get in from the back."

So we huffed our way around to the back, busted out a plain old glass window, picked the shards out of the way, and crawled into the dark church through the window.

I flicked on a light switch, and no illumination came forth, and I cursed myself for not bringing the flashlight from the Honda, and double cursed the quaint church-building notion that semiopaque stained-glass windows and dark interiors would please God. I mean, God made the sun and the bright blue skies, so it seemed to me He'd appreciate some of that shining through into His house.

Feeling my way in the gloom, I found a breaker box inside the church, and fingered them till I could figure out all the breakers were switched off. But that power meter on the barn had been twirling around like that line was responsible for air-conditioning all of southwest Georgia.

Right now I wanted light, and I didn't care if I ran up some church's bill. I switched all the breakers back on, and then we went through the church turning all the light switches on. Fortunately, a couple of bulbs still worked, and we got a meager light.

The church seemed eerily like it had the last time I was in it—when I was sixteen, on a mission I'd rather not disclose at my current age. Preserved, like a museum piece, with the old wooden pews and the rough-hewn altar. Even the smell was the same—a cross between ladies' Avon talc, musty hymnals and prayer books, and clean human sweat. The place had never been air-conditioned.

In the dim light, we searched high and low.

No sign of the kids, no sign of Demetrious, and no sign of Simon.

In fact, no sign anyone had been inside the church in years. Dust lay ghostly on all the surfaces, and the only footprints in the sand and dust on the floor were our own.

"Come on. Nobody's in here, let's get outside and keep looking," I said, as if Shalonda couldn't have figured that out by herself.

We crawled back out the window, this time dislodging an impressive spiderweb with a late-season golden orb about as big as a pet hamster. "Now ain't she a beauty," Shalonda said, staring at the spider.

She was, but I was in no mood to admire a big banana spider. "Nobody's been using this place. Not for a long time. We got to trace that line to its end."

Just beyond the church, front and center at the beginning of the grave-yard, a battered sign read: WE'RE GROWING. JOIN US.

"Reckon they meant the congregation, or the cemetery?" I asked.

"Not the church," Shalonda said, "judging from that spiderweb."

And not the cemetery, since Shalonda said it wasn't used anymore.

Just an old leftover sign. With a leftover church.

And a power line to something else.

We trudged along, under the power line, until we were deeper into the old graveyard.

Deep into the part where the hanged man's ghost reportedly ate chil-dren and teenagers.

Okay, I was a long way past believing that old nonsense, passed down by grown-ups who didn't want kids horsing around and smoking rabbit tobacco or marijuana among their dead family.

But I knew ghosts were real.

I'd seen one pretty darn recently.

So, I stepped forward through the freelance thickets and huckleberry bushes with a tingling sense of unease running up and down my back.

chapter 56

My brother Delvon likes to tell me that I need to relax, that God will provide me with what I really need, when I need it.

In theory, I believe this. In practice, relaxing and trusting are not my things. I like to keep my fridge full, my cupboards fuller, and my tools sharp. I'm the kind who doesn't need to rush to the store when a category 4 hurricane is coming: I've been hoarding batteries, dried fruit, brown rice, and bottled water for Armageddon for a long time.

Still, despite my tendency to over-prepare, wouldn't you know it? I didn't have a chain saw with me when I needed it.

But there, under a tarp, on the ground, exactly where and when I needed it, God put me a chain saw, one that worked.

And gave me a woman who knew how to use it.

Thus it came about that Shalonda and I, in our quest through the graveyard, searching for kidnapped kids, in short order had found a small shack, apparently used to house lawn mowers and such, from the look of the garden tools scattered outside of the building.

"Looks like somebody emptied it out," Shalonda said.

We looked at each other a second when she said that, then ran like jaguars after prey toward the shed. Naturally, the plywood door was locked.

And there were no windows to break out.

And my lock picks were back in my Honda.

While I gave voice to this, figuring I'd have to run back through the woods after the lock picks, and not looking forward to that, Shalonda nosed around in the scattered lawn tools and pulled up a chain saw from under a tarp.

"I reckon if it'll cut through trees it will cut through this old door," she said, and tossed me the shotgun to hold for her. "Got to be careful with these things," she said, and pulled on the cord.

Well, yeah. Careful being an understatement. If a chain saw would cut through trees, it'd cut through arms and fingers and hands pretty quick too.

The chain saw did not start. Shalonda yanked at the cord again.

"I cut up some trees ever winter for wood for our fireplace. How 'bout you? You put up any wood for winter?"

"Shalonda, I live in southwest Florida. We don't have winter." Which sounded better than admitting that hurricane-preparation queen that I was, I was still afraid of chain saws.

"Well, I got right handy with chain saws the last few years, what with all those hurricanes coming up at us from the Gulf. Picks up the pace some for the Electric Co-op boys if you can clear up your own downed trees."

Not wanting to discuss the use, or nonuse, of chain saws much further, I hoisted the shotgun and pretended to use it while Shalonda gave that cord another hard tug. The chain saw roared to life, and Shalonda said something I couldn't hear over the racket, and she grinned.

I took a play shot at the door of the shed. Practice at making believe you could use it, I told myself, in case you need to use an unloaded gun to fake out a bad man—and when I looked back at Shalonda, damn if she didn't have a hole cut through that door. Of course, she had also made enough noise to wake up all the glorious Confederate dead and, not incidentally, warn anybody lurking in the woods that we were around.

After enlarging the space some, Shalonda turned off the chain saw and stuck her hand through the hole, messed around with the door handle, and the next thing we knew we were inside the shed, and she shut that door behind us as nicely as if we were visiting at Eleanor's.

What we found inside was not the kids, not Demetrious, not Simon, not a mule, and not a ferret.

What we found instead were deep freezes.

A room plumb full of deep freezes. I counted them—four deep freezes. And they were all just humming away, keeping whatever was inside icy-frozen. As the church didn't even have a garden, no one in its congregation needed to be putting up peas or corn for Jesus.

"Why you reckon somebody dumped all those good garden tools outside to make room to put these deep freezes in here?" Shalonda asked.

A good question, and one I figured we could answer by opening the deep freezes and taking a look.

But we stood right where we were, frozen on the dirt-and-straw floor.

My guess was that there were about four choices for what was in those freezers. Dead teenagers. Dead Demetrious. Dead human body parts. Or illegally smuggled exotic meats, turtle eggs, and caviar. Some version of the same idea must have hit Shalonda too, from the way she was dragging her feet.

Okay, sorry, PETA, but I was pretty much hoping for turtle meat and sturgeon eggs.

"Damn, we gotta look," I said, and each of us took a few steps forward.

Shalonda the Bold then jumped at one of the freezers, snatched it open, and cried out, "Eggs. Little eggs. What would a graveyard want with freezers of frozen little eggs?"

We checked all the freezers. Two had turtle eggs, one had beluga caviar, and the fourth one had turtle meat. All with nice labels, including the date frozen, the country of origin, and what it was in the wrappers.

I slumped in relief against a cobwebby wall, and exhaled.

Wherever Becky, Bobby, Armando, and Demetrious were, at least they were not frozen in parts in a shed in a graveyard.

"Amen on that thought," Shalonda said. "Now get back here, and let's study on this."

"Willette's voodoo eggs," I said, easing off the wall toward the freezers and picking up a package in clear plastic. "Shalonda, you know anything about sea-turtle eggs?"

"Sure, Demetrious told me 'bout them. I mean, the sea turtles are protected from poachers and smugglers. He was pretty hot 'bout hearing rumors on that kind of smuggling passing through here."

It occurred to me suddenly Shalonda didn't know about my Deer Den adventures. So, Demetrious had kept a secret from Shalonda—he'd never said a word to her about my acting like his spy to try to close down the Deer Den. 'Course, neither had I.

But Demetrious keeping secrets from his wife was more important, I thought, because it opened up the idea he might have kept other secrets from her.

Of course, she kept secrets from him. Like that seeing-Lonnie thing.

I wondered if all husbands and wives kept secrets. Did it go with the territory? Was it the inevitable cost of living day in and day out with someone?

But contemplating the secret lives of husbands and wives was something I needed to save for a saner moment.

"Yep, Demetrious told me something about the smuggling he thought was going on around here, or through here, I guess," I said. "I think this stuff was bound for the big cities, but maybe just being stored here temporarily. Maybe a little of it was sold around here. Who knows?"

"Oh, yeah, don't even get Demetrious started on stuff like that. Bad enough that man thinks he's gotta feed the damn buzzards in the backyard, like they ain't got the God-given sense to find their own roadkill. But get him started on the Caribbean turtles and those Russian fish, and he gets plain worked up."

Then she stopped and looked at me, and little tears puddled up in her eyes.

"He's a good man, a mighty fine man, and here I didn't . . . appreciate him. Loving all the little things, like he does."

And loving you, I thought but didn't say. We didn't have time to get mopey. And maybe Demetrious was all right and would come home with Big Beauty and a good explanation. I switched gears so I wouldn't have to calculate the odds on that. "What'd Demetrious tell you about stuff like this?"

"There's a big illegal market for the shells, the meat, and the oils, and people are just so mean and greedy they don't care if they're wiping out a whole species. All so rich folks can have a bunch of stuff they don't even need. I mean, you really need a tortoiseshell comb? Isn't wood or plastic good enough?"

Well, at least there was no monkey meat in the freezers, I thought, though, of course, who was to say that a turtle was any less deserving of being saved from extinction than a primate.

"How about the eggs?" I asked.

Before I could answer, the sound of the chain-sawed door dragging across the floor made us both jump, and we swung around to the sound. Shalonda was quick on the uptake, shifting the unloaded shotgun into a menacing stance.

We had company.

And it wasn't Becky, Bobby, or Armando.

chapter 57

When you break and enter a building in daylight in search of a murderer and kidnapped kids, it is best not to stand around chatting with your girlfriend.

I made a mental note to add that to my list of rules to live by.

Assuming I got to continue living.

Shalonda and I had been so busy breaking into the freezer shack, we hadn't heard Jubal come up behind us, not until he pushed the big, heavy door across the rough floor.

But evidently he had heard us talking.

"Easy smuggling," he said. "Feds so busy looking for cocaine or terrorists with nuclear bombs that eggs and turtle oil and meat slide right on through. Poachers sell 'em to smugglers who bring 'em into Miami. After customs is done with our appliances, Ray Glenn'd meet the smugglers down near the Everglades, load the eggs up in the deep freezes with dry ice, and haul 'em back. I let him use this old place to store 'em. He'd hold some here till the folks next in line sent trucks for 'em. Most of 'em make their way to New York and L.A., but a tiny bit stays right 'round here. Ray Glenn give me a cut for letting him use this place, and helping him drive to and from Miami. Easiest money I ever made."

"Jubal, damnation," I said, and got that sick feeling in the pit of my stomach that I'd screwed up, that I'd been chasing the wrong man.

While I was listening, Shalonda had been pointing that shotgun, the one I sure did wish actually was loaded.

"I ain't no killer, and I ain't no kidnapper," he said, nodding toward Shalonda and her weapon.

"What're you doing here?" Shalonda said, and jabbed the shotgun toward Jubal till it was pointed right at his gut.

"I'm looking for those kids, same as you. That boy's Willette's own grandson, and I'm not aiming to let anything bad happen to one of hers."

"Really?" Shalonda said.

"Swear to God."

Shalonda put her weapon down, but I reached over and snatched that shotgun up, and pointed it back at Jubal. After all, I'd been a lawyer for a long time, and I expected people to lie to me. Given Shalonda's love life with Lonnie the low-life liar, you'd think she would be less trusting. But there she was, willing to take the word of an admitted smuggler's assistant that he only wanted to help.

I shook the gun just in case Jubal had missed my point in snatching it from Shalonda and pointing it at him.

"No need of that," Jubal said. "I told you, I'm just looking for those kids."

"Well, let's get to looking," Shalonda said, and cut her eyes over to me like I was being rude.

"Those kids being gone, it doesn't have anything to do with this," Jubal said, and kicked one of the freezers. "This was just Ray Glenn and me. Lonnie weren't no part of it. With Ray Glenn outta it, I'm waiting to sell this load sometime next week."

"But there can't be that much money in it?" I said.

"You'd be surprised. Folks'll buy that exotic meat and them eggs at upscale restaurants in New York City and Atlanta and L.A. It's all trendy, and then there's those who think they're aphrodisiacs. One restaurant in Atlanta gave Ray Glenn five dollar an egg if they're fresh. Frozen ones go for less, but it all adds up, 'specially what with the aphrodisiac buyers."

Couldn't they just eat oysters or take Viagra, I wondered, and leave the turtles alone?

"Man'll do just 'bout anything make his dick stand up," Shalonda said.

"But not enough money to kill anybody over," Jubal said, and shook his head. "I'm sorry I let him talk me into this, but Ray Glenn needed a safe place to run the freezers. Couldn't be having the freezers just sitting there in Lonnie's store, all full of illegal meat and eggs."

"So Lonnie wasn't in on this," Shalonda said, and gave me a triumphant look.

"Nope, he wasn't. He could've been, but Ray Glenn thought his boss was too dumb to deal in. Lonnie's been . . . that is, he was planning on running for state senate. Then on to Washington. Man needs a lot of money for that, but . . ." Here Jubal stopped, but I could have sworn he had something else important to say.

"But what?" I said. "You might as well come clean now. Maybe you know something that'll help find Bobby, Becky, and Armando."

"I'll help find those kids, even if it means me going off to jail awhile," he said, and looked first me and then Shalonda in the eyes.

It was a good show, but I didn't drop the shotgun.

"That man, Lonnie, made some money out of his store, sure, but mostly 'cause of Ray Glenn. But Lonnie kept angling for getting more money. So when Lonnie up and sold that house of your grandmom's for four hundred thousand, Ray Glenn and me figured he and that Simon were up to something big. Ray Glenn and me made a good profit right there," he said, gesturing toward the freezers, "but Ray Glenn was anxious to get in on whatever else Lonnie had going."

"How'd you know about the four hundred thousand?" I asked.

Jubal shook his head. "Ain't I supposed to protect my sources?"

"Only if you're a reporter protected by the First Amendment," I said.

"Stop your yammering," Shalonda said, "and get to the point. We got the kids and Demetrious to find."

"Jubal?"

"Well, awright. Truth is, nobody exactly told me. I kinda found out when I went to see that lady lawyer about a legal matter, and she left me alone in her office for a couple of minutes. And I, er, snooped."

"So you found out Simon overpaid on that property. And that's how Willette got in all this, isn't it? Through you?"

"Yep. And I feel right bad about all that. We had to keep the freezers at the store for a little bit, after we got 'em back from Miami. They were in the back, out of sight, jes' till I could move 'em out here at night. And some idiot deliveryman took the wrong freezer to Willette's. Put it on her porch full of turtle eggs."

So, she hadn't been hallucinating when she complained the freezer that mistakenly landed on her porch had been full of voodoo eggs.

"And, look, I done got too old to cut trees for a living, but I ain't old enough to be living off that boy of mine. And all that part-time work don't add up to spit. I wasn't no kind of daddy to that boy when he was little, so I aim to leave him enough to go and see the world, I do. Me, I ain't never been more than five hundred miles from where I was born, and even that's only 'cause Ray Glenn needed me to drive them old trucks. I'm going to do right by Hank, make it up to him. Boy smart as he is ought to get to see Paris. Or at least California."

I didn't think Hank would want the money once he knew where it came from.

But Jubal looked so beat down, I didn't say so.

"I swear, I messed up real bad, I did," he added. That, plus the sheer weariness, and maybe the shame in his eyes, finally made me believe him. I put the shotgun down, but I didn't let go of it.

"What else?" I asked, but my voice was softer now that I suspected Jubal would be his own worst punishment.

"I shouldn't've told that Ray Glenn about the four hundred thousand. That got him real worked up. See, Ray Glenn figured somehow Lonnie was blackmailing Simon and he set out to find out why, so he could blackmail him too. But what I did, was call up Willette and tell her that Simon had bought that house of her momma's for four hundred thousand."

"Why'd you do that?" I asked, thinking Jubal had pulled Willette into not one but two big, dangerous messes, and Ray Glenn was just one of the common threads.

"Hell, I thought the woman ought to know." But Jubal cut his eyes away from me.

"Tell me the real reason." I took a step toward Jubal, and he backed up.

But after a few seconds of wrestling with his demons, he looked back at me and said, "See, I was your momma's legs when she needed something she didn't want Dan to know about."

Like her narcotics, I thought, but kept my mouth shut, letting Jubal finish his story.

"She had me do some photocopying for her when she sold that place off to Lonnie. So, naturally, I took a look at what it was I was copying at the library. I saw she was using a contract for deed, and so I asked that lady lawyer what that was, and she told me. This was way back before Simon came to town, when she and me was getting along okay. 'Fore, you know, she caught me snooping through her stuff and got all ugly to me."

Shalonda said, "Y'all need to hurry this up so's we can get back to looking for those kids."

"I'll finish quick then," Jubal said. "When Lonnie paid your momma monthly, I'd take the money to the bank for her, and . . . pick up her some . . . supplies."

Yeah, I knew what at least some of those supplies were.

"But then he stopped paying her. I didn't ask her about her business, I just did what she needed me to do. So I didn't know what she was going to do about it. But I did know from what that lady lawyer explained to me, that if Lonnie didn't pay up, your momma still owned her momma's place."

"Why'd Willette keep quiet about him not paying her?" Shalonda asked.

"See, that's 'cause Lonnie took over getting her some of her . . . supplies. I was having some problems at the . . . Tru Blue, and I, er . . . had to slack off some."

"So you told Willette that Simon paid Lonnie four hundred thousand for a house he didn't own, that she still owned, right? And you were thinking that she might get some money out of Simon to hush up about things while he and Lonnie got it all straight, and Willette would give you a . . . a what? A finder's fee?"

"Yep, that's it, the whole sorry story, least the parts of it I know."

"Not quite," I said. "Lonnie took the money he owed Willette to her house that night, money he got from Simon's payoff, and he wanted Willette to take the money and sign the deed. Only she wouldn't. Ray Glenn went along to force Willette, right?"

"I didn't have nu'thing to do with that, I swear. Ray Glenn knew how I felt about that woman, and he didn't tell me nu'thing about him planning to go over there. Why, I wouldn't a hurt a hair on that poor woman's head, not ever, not for no money."

"You didn't know about the sixty-five thousand? You weren't just helping us at Willette's house so you could look for it?"

"I don't know nu'thing about any sixty-five thousand. How come you know so much about that money?"

I ignored his question and wondered, so, maybe Jubal had just been helping us out of the goodness of his misguided heart? Or he was lying about the money.

Money that was now resting quietly in a picnic basket in a recently cleaned-out kitchen cabinet.

But before I could take it any further, Jubal reminded me of why we were all standing around in a shed in a graveyard.

"Well, damn it to hell then, let's find those kids," Jubal said.

chapter 58

There are cultures that believe a person has an animal guide in life, or an animal talisman.

It's a lovely idea, and, if I were asked to select my animal guide, I'd pick something totally graceful and cool, like, say, a Florida panther or a deer. Or something totally smart and mischievous, like a dolphin.

But it seemed the animal-guide matchmakers had something else in mind for me.

As in an albino ferret.

Go figure.

All of which is to say that as much as I'd like to tell the tale so that either Shalonda or I were the heroine, it turned out that Johnny the Ferret once more saved the day.

We were thrashing around in the graveyard, not even sure if the kidnapped trio was there, and, if so, where among the tombs and the graves they might be hidden, when a white flash dashed up to me, oonking like the end of the world, and dancing about like the ground was on fire.

Johnny.

And it didn't take my law degree to figure out that where Johnny was, Armando wasn't too far behind.

While Johnny spun and oonked around me, I took comfort in knowing we were close to finding those kids. "Where are they, Johnny? Take me to them," I said.

"Whoa, that thing ain't Lassie," Jubal said.

"Go, Johnny, go," Shalonda said.

And Johnny did an especially big oonk, and spun in a half-circle and started scampering. We scampered right after him.

To a mausoleum, with an inscription dating back to 1897, and an angel guarding it, and the green, lichen-coated door, cracked partly open.

It took the three of us maybe as long as it takes to inhale to get the damn door all the way open, and for Jubal to stick his head in. "Becky," he cried out. "Bobby, you all in here?"

Thump, thump, thump was our answer, the sound of someone alive hitting the ground with their feet.

The operative words were "someone alive."

I pushed Jubal aside, jumped in, and shuddered. When the smell of the half-underground mold and ooze hit my nose, and I saw pieces of skeletons, I thought Willette's house really wasn't so bad after all, and then I ran toward the prone, tied, and gagged forms of Bobby, Becky, and Armando. Johnny oonked and jumped up and down on Armando, and Jubal pushed me aside and pulled out a big pocketknife, and Shalonda stood at the door and shouted encouragement and questions.

The kids were spiderwebby and dirty, but when we got them untied and outside, we could see they were still healthy. Not a one of them had been cut or shot or hit.

Becky did a head-spinning version of a damsel-in-distress routine, while Bobby and Armando tried to out-cool and out-alpha-male each other in order to attend to her. But I didn't think any of them were nearly as scared as they should have been. Armando was the first to announce he needed to "take a leak," and did so, a little too close for privacy, and then Becky took my hand and insisted I go with her behind a bush, but "don't look."

Becky was a spunky little thing, and, in no time at all she didn't need me to hold her hand, and she started blabbing forth, somewhat incoherently, about their adventures.

Simon had busted into her house, she told me in little breathless snippets, and he had a gun, and some rope and some tape, and, yes, they fought, and, oh, but Bobby hit and punched so heroically to protect her, while Armando tried to knock Simon down by butting him in the back, and they were so very brave. Bobby and Armando did their best to fight for her, Becky said, beaming with pride at her boys.

Still, I understood why Simon maintained the upper hand. He was a man who worked out seriously in a gym, who had probably learned to fight tough against taunts on the schoolyards of his long-limbed childhood. And he had a gun.

Guns usually trump teenage boys.

So it was, Becky admitted, they were all afraid of the gun, and finally Simon marched them outside into a paneled van he had parked in the backyard.

Where exactly were the neighbors, I wondered. "Nobody saw him? I mean, saw him taking you and the boys?"

"It's Sunday, everybody was at church or Mr. Chick's," she said, using a tone that suggested she thought I was pretty dumb.

"He told us he'd shoot us, and go back and shoot Momma, if we didn't do what he told us, and, even so, Bobby tried to duck out and run, so Simon tied him 'round the neck, and gave him a big shot of something that put him right out. While Simon was fighting with Armando, Johnny jumped into the van. I don't think Simon saw him, what with Armando kicking and stuff."

Good for Johnny, I thought.

"We woke up, all tied up and with nasty old gags in our mouths, right in here," Becky said. "And I got a headache, I reckon from the

drug Simon gave us. And I sure am thirsty, but I think I'm okay otherwise."

They needed water, and food, and to get the hell out of there. And, by
the way, just where was all that official law enforcement backup?

Simon the soulless man was around somewhere, and I didn't like the
fact we were acting like we were on a family Fourth of July campout,
peeing in the woods and telling tales. While Bobby finally broke down
and used the outdoor facilities, I dialed 911 from my cell phone, which
I'd tucked into my pocket for just such an emergency. But we were too
far out and couldn't get service, which made me think I needed to write
that can-you-hear-me-now guy a nasty letter.

"Come on, we got to get," Shalonda said.

"It's all my fault," Becky said.

"Tell us about it on the way back to town," I said.

"I'm so sorry," Becky said, and then hugged both Bobby and Armando.
I saw the way Bobby swelled with pride when she hugged him first.

"It wasn't your fault," he said.

"Let's get," Shalonda repeated, though no one seemed to be paying
her any attention.

"We were, that is Bobby and me, we were talking in Willette's room,
you know, at the hospital. I mean, she couldn't hear us, and I didn't think
anybody else could, and so I was telling Armando all that had been going
on, and then we were talking about what it meant that Mr. Lonnie went
running out of Willette's house. And if that had something to do with
why Simon paid too much for that house of Mr. Lonnie's."

"Damn it, we got to get," Shalonda said, raising her voice.

"Damn straight," Jubal said. "You can walk and talk, can't you?" With
that, Jubal gave me a little shove. "My truck's out front, on the road."

"Simon came into Willette's room, and we didn't think he'd heard
us, you know, talking about him and Lonnie. I mean, he acted real nice,"
Bobby said. "But I guess he heard us all right."

"Faster," Jubal said, and pushed me again.

I turned around and glared at him. "Watch that shoving."

Just then, Johnny, who'd been resting in Armando's arms, saw a squir-rel on a low limb, doing that little squirrel-tease dance they like to do with cats when they know full well they are out of the cat's range, and Johnny shot down out of Armando's grip, and hit the ground running. The squirrel hit the ground running too, and then, instead of dashing up a tree in a squirrel-sensible escape, went zipping into the undergrowth of the woods on the other side of the fence, at the edge of the graveyard, Johnny on his tail.

In a blink, both squirrel and ferret had wholly disappeared, eaten up by shadows and scrubs of the dense Georgia piney woods.

"Well, damnation, come on," Jubal said. "Leave the little guy, I'll come back and get him later."

"I'm not leaving Johnny," Armando said, and before anyone could grab him, he dashed away into the darkening woods, climbing and jump-ing over the fence in a split second, and compounding the ferret-squirrel disappearance act.

"I'm not leaving without Armando," I said, and started moving toward the spot where he'd disappeared.

"Whoa, there, white girl," Shalonda said, and grabbed my arm. "Hold on."

While I tried to pull out of Shalonda's grip, Jubal showed us a calm head. "Boy, you drive a stick?" Jubal asked Bobby.

"Yes, sir."

Jubal rattled his hand around in his pocket, fished out the keys, and tossed them at Bobby, who caught them. "Stay right on this path till it hits the road, and my truck's right there. Only pickup out there. Get you and that little gal out of here, go straight to town, and get the law. Tell 'em ever thing, you hear? We'll get that boy of Lilly's."

Bobby turned and looked at me.

"Do it," I said, "and don't dare stop that truck for anything but a red light, and then only if something's coming in the cross street."

I gave Becky my cell. "Keep trying your momma till you get her. Then have Bobby call Patti Lea."

Becky and Bobby might still be young enough to expect the happy ending as the norm and to believe they were immortal, but their mothers surely knew better by now. And I wanted Rebecca and Patti to know their children were found and safe.

"I know these here woods better than y'all. I'll go get that boy and that critter. You two get back to your car and get it out of Simon's yard, come back here on the road, pick me and those two up."

"We should stick together," I said, not liking one whit the fact that Jubal was suddenly giving me orders.

But Jubal didn't wait till I finished my objection, he had already started jogging toward the woods.

And *poof*, just like another man down the bunny hole, he was gone too.

"He's right. Let's get that car and get it out of that man's blueberries 'fore he comes home and sees it."

"No, I'm going after Armando," I said, and ran to the edge of the woods before I realized that in the absence of a trail, the barrier of the scrub and the undergrowth and the trees made one spot look pretty much like the other. "Where'd they go?"

"He'll find 'em, come on. Jubal been knowing these woods longer'n you and me been living," Shalonda said.

But I was studying the limbs and leaves, and the ground, looking for some trace of evidence to say that a ferret, a boy, and a man had dashed in there somewhere.

And that's exactly what I was still doing when the last person on earth I ever wanted to see showed up.

chapter **59**

Never let your guard down, not even when poking in the bushes looking for some track or trace that a wayward teenage boy and his equally errant ferret have passed that way before.

Which is to say, I had my head bent down about two feet off the ground, studying a bowed stem on a low-lying scrub, trying to discern if it grew that way or got bent by Armando's mad dash after his pet, when Shalonda let out a yip and I jumped straight up so fast I got dizzy.

There stood Simon the Soulless.

And Simon was not alone.

He had his spiffy, new-looking shotgun with him.

A shotgun, no doubt, that was loaded, in sharp contrast with Shalonda's strictly-for-show gun.

"You left a trail through the woods any idiot could follow," he said.

Okay, so spank me, I'm not a Native American hunter trained to pass without a trace through the underbrush.

"Oh, hello, Simon," I said, first-date perky, on the extraordinarily remote chance I was a hundred percent wrong about everything and he was just out with his shotgun, taking the evening air and not intent upon wiping out three generations of Cleary folks in one week.

Shalonda didn't play that long shot. She jerked up her own shotgun in a hurry.

Simon matched the bet and raised it, pointing his shotgun right at Shalonda's gut, then swinging it back at my own stomach, which had taken that inopportune moment to squeeze and flip so hard I thought I might possibly throw up.

"Where are those kids?" he said, in a tone as menacing as the gun then traveling a path between my stomach and Shalonda's.

Okay, so the good news was I hadn't been wrong about him. And the bad news was I hadn't been wrong about him. Time to punt.

"They're gone. Back to town. We've already called 911. You might as well give up."

Shalonda pointed her shotgun right back at his gut. "You surrender to us, and we'll see you get back to town safe and sound."

"Get real," Simon said, and laughed.

"I know how to use this thing," Shalonda said, not a girlish quiver anywhere in her voice. "And Lilly's got her a .38."

I jerked my hand behind my back as if I could possibly be holding a gun in it out of sight, but I knew Simon would not be tricked.

A man who tries to kill old ladies with ants and LSD and binds and gags children in a crypt is not a man afraid of two unarmed women with a mouthful of bluff.

At least that would be my instant assessment.

Nope, right then, I figured our best, maybe only, hope lay with Jubal, and I started my risk-benefit analysis on screaming out for Jubal's help.

"Shoot him, Lilly," Shalonda said. I guess her plan was that Simon would turn to me and she'd knock him over the head with her empty shotgun.

But it occurred to me his most likely response would be to spin and shoot me, so I threw myself on the ground as quick and hard as I could, and rolled into a tiny ball behind the nearest bush. I've been shot at before.

While I was playing roly-poly, Simon was playing Action Man, and in one quick and vicious lunge, he knocked the unloaded gun out of Shalonda's grip. Shalonda aimed her body low to tackle his legs, and I unrolled and launched myself at the empty shotgun on the ground, thinking maybe I could use it, baseball-bat-like, to bash Simon's head in.

Before I could get a good grip on the damn thing, Simon brought down his gun on top of Shalonda's head with a heart-stabbing crack, and she splayed out like a drunk or a dead woman.

I tried to swing the empty shotgun for a weapon, but I didn't have a good grip on it, and the next thing I knew, Simon had kicked it out of my hands. I sure wished I had hold of that chain saw, but even that might not have done any good, because I saw something now I hadn't fully appreciated before: Under those gaudy business clothes he'd worn, Simon was strong. Very, very strong. And he was angry. Very, very angry.

In an embarrassingly short time, he wrestled me into at least temporary submission.

Physically, Shalonda and I had simply been no match for him. But at least I was not knocked out, unlike poor Shalonda, and I made sure I kept my mind and my eyes open.

"Your car's still at my place, so those kids are here someplace," he said.

When he said that, I realized Simon didn't know Jubal was around. Why would he, after all, since Jubal's truck was already hightailing it back to town, and Jubal had disappeared into the forest before Simon pounced upon Shalonda and me.

So, okay, Jubal, I thought, rescue us. Now would be good.

And don't get Armando or that damn ferret hurt.

Pretty tall order for an ex-logger-turned-smuggler.

Still, I had hope. I also realized it had been stupid times ten to have left my Honda parked at Simon's, especially since there was no mistaking that busted-out window in Simon's house. It wouldn't have taken him long to add up my calling cards, and, as he'd mentioned, find our trail through the woods to the graveyard. So, if I ended up dead, which seemed to be a good bet at the moment, it would be my own stupid fault.

That didn't make me any more resigned to my fate.

"And I don't aim to be fooling with you two while I look. I get rid of them, and I get rid of you two, then nobody is going to connect me up with that idiot Lonnie, especially now that I've got that damn contract for deed out of your trunk, so nobody will know he didn't buy that place from your mother."

Aha, so he was the one that had broken into my Honda and stolen Willette's important papers. Not that this detail particularly mattered at the moment.

"I sent that fool Lonnie," Simon said, "to Willette's to get her to sign that backdated deed, then he and Ray Glenn were supposed to kill her, make it look like an OD. That man couldn't even do that right. He decides, all on his own, to take cash and pay her what he owed her. He planned on walking out of there, with her still alive, once he got her name on the deed."

Ah, not a bad man, just like Shalonda had been saying. "So, he couldn't kill her, could he?" I said, on the theory that conversation with Satan's sidekick was better than getting shot.

"You know, if you had just minded your own business, we could have had a good time together. A very good time."

Minded my own business? Like keeping my mother alive wasn't my business? But a tart response didn't seem like the proper life-saving response, so I kept quiet and waited for a miracle or Jubal to save me.

"Stupid hick country boy, Lonnie, way he tells me later, he figured seeing all that money in cash would turn her head, and she'd take it, keep quiet, and sign the deed. After selling me a piece of property he didn't even own, that man didn't understand why we had to make sure she never talked."

I didn't either, really—I mean, not to the extent of killing Willette. Up to that point, it was just bribery. Assuming Willette had called in the *Atlanta Constitution* and documented the whole story, bribe and all, the most that probably would have happened was that she could have reclaimed the property in a suit to quiet title, and Lonnie would have had to pay back Simon's money. And maybe Simon got tagged for bribery, and lost his job running the hospital, and Lonnie got booted off the commission. But even with the generally low value placed on human life these days, killing Willette to keep the bribery a secret seemed a bit of an overreaction.

Besides, bribing public officials—the only crime I could figure Simon for until he began to engage in the sport of real and attempted murder—was hardly even a crime anymore, just a routine cost of doing business. Hell, in the next few years, Congress will probably pass a law making bribery of public officials a tax-deductible business expense.

But then I remembered: Simon was trying to prove to his mother he wasn't a worthless freak. Losing his job for bribing a public official would have just proved her correct in her assessment of him.

Plus, I could hear Shalonda when she had said earlier, "White girl, you remember where you're at."

I was in Bugfest, not in Washington, D.C. I was in a county full of people who still believed that right was right, people who posted the Ten Commandments on signs in their yards and believed that was the way you ought to act. A taint as real as a big bribe of a county commissioner in a county this honest and God-fearing would have rippled through the community like real sin. The repercussions would have upset all the resort's development plans—Lonnie, as a corrupt bribe-taker, would have been kicked off the commission, there would have been a new vote by the governing board, and those commissioners would have bent over backward to avoid the appearance of bribery or bad dealings. Meaning that the commissioners would have voted against joining ranks with the evil, bribe-offering resort.

Without the commissioners as their partner, that resort would have had to buy the land at whatever asking price the sellers wanted, which would, of course, be hugely inflated now that everybody knew what was going on. That is, if they would even agree to sell it. And if Jubal and the others held strong and refused to sell, without eminent domain to force them off their land, it was entirely probable the resort, the marina, and the half-million-dollar homes could not even be built.

Further, if the casino rumors were to be believed, that meant all that gambling money could be lost too.

The whole land-grab scheme, based as it was on cheap land, eminent domain, and a friendly county commission, would have tumbled down in no time at all.

And there was Lonnie, dimwitted enough to sell a piece of property he didn't own as part of accepting a bribe for a favorable vote. What did you expect, I thought, from a man stupid enough to use the same pick-up line for two decades? *You're the one that got away,* my ass.

"So Lonnie ended up being a loose end," I said, thinking aloud.

"Not anymore," Simon said. "After that fight he and Demetrious had, I saw how I could kill Lonnie and keep his mouth shut, and everybody would figure it was Demetrious who killed him."

"Where is Demetrious?" I asked.

"Where he can't help you."

Uh-oh. That sounded like dead and buried someplace nobody would find him.

Poor Shalonda, losing Demetrious and Lonnie both. Not that it hugely mattered if Simon killed her—and me. Which I intuitively surmised was his current plan. And after us, no doubt, he planned to sashay by the hospital and give Willette a triple dose of deadly downers, except that Dr. Hodo had spirited her away to a safe haven in Thomasville.

I wondered if it would buy Shalonda and me any advantage to point out to Simon that Willette was out of his reach now, and so there was no reason to kill anybody else as she would eventually wake from her roofies vacation and sing a song that would implicate Simon in a host of things that wouldn't impress his mother. Or, for that matter, Official Law Enforcement.

While I was debating the pros and cons, Simon, apparently talked-out at the moment, raised his shotgun to my head and told me to "hold still."

But I didn't particularly aim to go gently into that good night. I bunched my muscles to run or jump or spring or do something, but when I did, Simon swung his shotgun against the side of my head like a baseball bat, and I went right down on the ground in a huddle with Shalonda.

When I tried to work my mouth so I could tell him about Willette, the pros seeming suddenly to outweigh the cons, I found I couldn't talk. I pretty much figured this was it, that I was fixing to die with a shotgun blast, and I briefly worried about what an ugly corpse I'd make, but before I could say my prayers, Simon grabbed my arm and pricked me with a needle. I hoped it was a clean one, and then I was out.

chapter 60

Someone was butting me in the stomach.

"Get up, get up, this house's on fire. I ain't going to burn up," Shalonda was shouting as she frantically butted me awake with her head.

Groggy, with an intense headache, but coming back to consciousness, I looked around me and saw that I was in my own mother's house. Everything was pitch-black night.

Except for a glow of red coming in around the cracks under the door. A red glow accompanied by the acrid smell of smoke.

Oh, mierda. Shalonda was right. The house was on fire. Smoke roiled up under the door, though there were no flames in the room where we were tied up. But the idea that the main fire was still on the other side of the door only encouraged me for about a half-second. Terror replaced that feeling in a blink.

Shalonda and I were both bound up, with ropes around our ankles and our hands tied behind our backs, our butts on the uncarpeted floor.

"Armando, my God, is he in here? Jubal? Are they here?" I shouted.

"I don't think so, that nasty man dumped us in the car 'fore he even looked for them. I wasn't all the way out till he stuck that needle in me in the car."

Shalonda flopped over on her side, and lifted her hips off the floor just enough to pull her tied hands under her butt, and then in front of her. Then she rolled and squiggled until she could shove her bound wrists in front of my face. "Use your teeth and get me untied," Shalonda commanded.

I tried my best, but the rope was too thick, or my teeth too small. "Wait a minute," I said, and followed her lead on rolling on my side and lifting my butt till my hands were in front of me. But with my fingers limited by the rope ties, I couldn't untie her hands either.

Though I was gasping now, and scared nearly beyond reason, I thought of that big plate-glass window behind the curtain. And wondered, just how thick was it?

"Shalonda, the window. It's a plate-glass window, nothing but a big sheet of glass. No bars or cross ties or—"

"Get up," Shalonda said.

"I'm trying," I said.

We flopped around on the floor trying to stand up, until finally I found that by rolling once more to my side, I was able to work my feet under me, and push myself up. Shalonda quickly followed suit.

We were standing, but we were standing with tied feet and tied hands.

In a house that was on fire.

More smoke was filling the room and taking the place of the oxygen we needed to be breathing. Flames would soon eat away the door between us and hell.

"I bet I can plumb get through that big ole plate-glass window all tied up," Shalonda said. "And, white girl, you bests be right behind me 'cause I ain't coming back for you." With that declaration, Shalonda hopped, her feet still tied at the ankles, toward the plate-glass window that was the barrier between safe outside and burned-alive inside.

Holding my breath now against the smoke, I gathered all my strength for a life-or-death hopping contest with the agents of the devil.

Shalonda hopped toward that window with amazing speed, her head down like a charging bull. With her fingers, she dragged the curtain to the side, went into a three-point stance like a football player, and lunged, leading with her broad, swim-competition-tough shoulders. In a loud minute, she shattered her way through the window.

Perceiving no reasonable alternative, I followed her, though I have to say that hopping with my ankles tied was pretty damn hard, but then I was pretty damn motivated. Lunging through the busted glass, I went careening down from the window on top of Shalonda, who was cursing the idiot who planted roses under the window.

Old roses, I thought. My grandmother had planted them once as a birthday present to Willette, who never much cared about gardening. Idly, I wondered who had tended them all these years, and then I rolled off Shalonda and decided we should put some distance between us and the house. I discovered I could still do a somersault. And with my hands and feet tied.

But then Shalonda showed me up, doing a series of somewhat crooked somersaults past me in the grass, but making excellent time, and screaming obscenities as she rolled.

Behind me, I felt the heat of the fire, and in front of me, I saw Eleanor running screaming toward us. Watching Willette in Thomasville must have gotten old, I guessed, as Eleanor pulled us to our feet. An older man who seemed vaguely familiar came running up beside her.

Now that I wasn't consumed with terror at the thought of burning to death, I was consumed with terror that Armando and Jubal might be fixing to burn to death.

"There might be somebody else in there," I cried. "Jubal and a boy."

"Lord, have mercy," the older man said, and I turned and really looked at him in the glow of the streetlamps, and recognized the very same man whose car I had hit on the way into town, the one who proudly declared himself a member of the Greatest Generation and a veteran of the Great War, who was for some reason with Eleanor this night. But before I could say "Call 911," this man took off and dashed inside the burning house. Another old man—this one I recognized as Rodney, the acting chief of police—took off after him, lickety-split.

I didn't think that was a good idea, letting old men dash into a burning house, but then how else was anyone going to find out if Armando and Jubal were inside.

Eleanor went screaming after the two of them to be careful, and I figured the veteran, having survived the Great War, probably had "careful" down about as pat as a man who rushes into a burning building could get it.

Eleanor stopped on the porch, and switched from shouting "Careful" to screaming "Hurry." I doubted Mr. Veteran or Rodney needed to be told that.

Another neighbor came running up, made a quick assessment of the situation, took out his pocketknife, and cut Shalonda and me free of our ropes. And ambulances and fire trucks and official vehicles with loud sirens converged upon us like gnats at dusk.

Just as trained firemen began working at their hoses, Rodney and the veteran of the Great War came staggering out the same door they'd gone in, and between them, they were half-holding and half-dragging Demetrious, tied up and half knocked-out.

"Found him in the kitchen," said the veteran, and the entire collection of EMTs in Bugfest rushed to the men as they collapsed in the ill-kept yard.

"With a can of gasoline right by him," Rodney said, gasping between his words. "But his hands's all tied up. So I know he didn't start no fire, but somebody sure 'nuff wanted us to think he started it, that can of gas sitting right there."

Yep, somebody had wanted everyone to think Demetrious had started the fire, after killing Lonnie, and taking me and Shalonda out with him. The *why* would be a puzzlement—was it an accident, a suicide-murder, a love triangle with me as the innocent bystander, or what? My guess was that Simon assumed that folks would be so busy trying to figure out a rhyme and reason for all the bodies in the fire, they'd naturally *not* conclude that he had a thing to do with it. Then, after he OD'd Willette and covered it up as a natural death—why, he could just keep right on helping the resort cheat people out of their homesteads.

Except for Bobby and Becky, who could connect Lonnie and Simon with bribery and murder.

"Where are Bobby and Becky, did they get back safe?" I shouted.

No one around me knew.

But in no time at all, old Otis Lee, the second acting chief of police, pulled up in a police cruiser. Like Rodney, he moved right brisk for an older man, and before I could ask him anything about the kids, Patti and Dan drove up—I figured in another minute pretty much the whole town would be here—the door to Patti's car burst open, and Bobby and Becky and Rebecca all stumbled out and made a beeline right for Shalonda and me.

Apparently almost getting killed together was a real bonding experience for the kids, and they started hugging and kissing us. Pretty quick, everyone got in on it. Of course, I noticed Rebecca kind of hung back on hugging me, though Patti and Dan took hold of me like they weren't ever going to see me again in this lifetime and this was the last great hug. Then Becky and Bobby had another round hugging us like we'd saved them from a burning house.

Well, maybe we had. Maybe Simon meant to burn us all up.

It didn't matter too much now, I thought, and grabbed an extra hug from Bobby.

"I best get you gals to the ER, get you looked over," Rodney said. "And that was a bad thing y'all done, stealing your momma out the hospital. If you'd just called me and tolt me what was—"

"Wait, what about Jubal and Armando. Where are they?" I asked.

My reward for having asked an entirely appropriate and important question was another round of nobody knowing.

But they were safe, weren't they? Maybe lost, but surely not in Simon's hands.

I started babbling forth my fears and theories to Rodney and Otis Lee, till out of the corner of my eye I saw a battered Demetrious, one eye swollen shut and a gash on his lip surely needing a stitch, break from the paramedics and limp toward Shalonda. I turned to watch them.

They studied each other, wary and no doubt exhausted, for a long moment. Just as I was about to give up on the happy ending for them, Demetrious held out his arms toward Shalonda, and she went to him. After a long embrace, Shalonda backed out of his arms, looked up at his battered face, then pulled his head against her chest and sobbed.

It was too private to watch, and I turned back to Rodney and Otis.

"I hadn't seen hide nor hair of that boy of yours, not of Jubal either. But we found that place in the graveyard with the freezers and we got law scattered all over the place around Simon's and the graveyard, and about ever place in between. The kids done tolt me what happened and I got ever body, even the off-duties and the retired law, out there looking," Rodney said. "What for, you reckon, caused that man to go on a killing binge like that?"

It was a long story. And I didn't want to take time to tell it. I wanted to find Jubal and Armando. Oh, and Johnny too.

Shalonda had finished her cry and finished hugging her still-living husband, and she came up beside me and said, "We need to get Demetrious to the ER."

But I ignored Demetrious's need for medical attention for a minute, and I asked her, "What woke you up?"

"Lonnie. I seen him big as day, he shook me till I woke up. He told me to get my butt out a that house 'fore I burnt up. Said being dead's better'n you'd expect, but he wanted me live so I'd kill that sonabitch Simon."

I would have laughed out loud at that, except my worry box was filling up again. Because it wasn't over. The last we'd seen of Jubal and Armando and Johnny was them dashing off into the darkening woods.

And Simon, the man without a soul, was still out there.

chapter 61

Poor old Rodney had done just about all the reassuring he could do for two women who'd been through what Shalonda and I had been through, and finally I said I wanted to lay my own eyes on Jubal and Armando, and I was going back out to the woods behind the cemetery and staying there until I, or somebody, found those two.

"Hadn't I done finished telling you? We got ever body already out there," Rodney said. "Besides there's still a bunch of stuff I don't understand and I need you to explain it to me."

"Armando is missing. Find him. Simon is the bad guy. Get him," I said, wondering why the fine details mattered at this point.

The radio in Rodney's police car squawked to life, and he ran toward it like he wasn't an old man, and Demetrious limped toward it faster than he probably should have, given the beating he had obviously taken. I turned to do a visual check on the continuing safety of Bobby and Becky, and saw, to my surprise, on a day I didn't think I could be surprised again, that Eleanor and the veteran of the Great War were still hugging. Long, long past the breakup of the group hug.

I stared at them, yeah, yeah, it was rude. But so what.

And then they started kissing. And groping.

While I was watching Eleanor make a public spectacle of herself for what was surely the first time ever, Demetrious let out a whoop—a good noise. I turned back to the crowd at the police radio, hoping Jubal and Armando had surfaced.

"BB," Shalonda said to me. "One of the deputies found him in an old orchard of sand pears on the back ten of Lonnie's land. Finishing off the last of the fall pears. Deputy reports he's fine."

After that piece of good news, we turned back to the burning house only long enough to see it was still burning despite the efforts of the firefighters, and then back to Eleanor and the Great Veteran, who were still making out. Watching Eleanor was more fun than looking at Willette's house burning to the ground. "Reckon we ought to get the firemen to hose 'em off," Shalonda said, and then giggled. The old Shalonda giggle.

But before that giggle died on its own, there was a terrible noise. The loud bang and clank of metal against metal, machine against machine. The reverberation of a car crash.

"Oh, Lord, now what?" Rodney asked, and we all turned toward the sound of the accident as if we could see through the houses and the trees and the nighttime. The accident sounded close, but not close enough that we could see it. Maybe a few blocks away.

In no time at all, the police radio squawked again, and Rodney and Demetrious both leaned into the car to listen.

I didn't see any reason why Shalonda and I couldn't stick our heads in as close as we could, so I tugged on her arm and we pressed into the men by the police car.

"Bad accident over to the hospital," Rodney said. "Come on, Demetrious, let's get, and I can drop you off to the ER."

I was about to lose interest in the car wreck, when the radio squawked back.

"Damn if it don't look like it's that Simon McDowell, the hospital guy," the radio dispatcher said. "Some guy in a blue Honda hit him a good one."

A blue Honda? *Mierda*, I shouted, thinking about my blue Honda, last seen in Simon's blueberries, with Armando, Johnny, and Jubal somewhere in the general vicinity.

"What about Armando?" I shouted at the radio. "Was there a kid and an albino ferret in the wreck?"

But the radio didn't answer me. Shalonda and I looked at each other, and I could tell she didn't like this any better than I did.

"We're going with you," I said to Rodney, who uttered some sort of something that loosely translated to he couldn't take us in a police car, and I shoved past him and crawled into the backseat, Shalonda right behind me. Demetrious jumped into the driver's seat, and if Rodney hadn't been way quicker than he looked, he'd be left standing in the driveway of a burning house.

chapter 62

Those not as fast as Shalonda, Demetrious, and me had to settle for riding in Dan's or Eleanor's vehicles, and we all went like a parade of the nearly insane to the intersection in front of the hospital, Demetrious running with sirens and light, Rodney working the radio, and Shalonda and me holding hands and saying a little prayer together for Jubal and Armando.

There it was, the wreck, already drawing a crowd. A team from the hospital was rushing over, and I didn't think the accident looked too good. Simon's big-ass American car had been plowed into, on the driver's side, by my ancient blue Honda. I recognized my own car with a pang—a pang for the car, but a larger surge of fear and anxiety over who might have been in it. Who might still be in it, crushed or trapped or both or worse.

I jumped out of Rodney's vehicle and ran toward my car, praying as I went that Armando and Jubal were not inside it.

And there, on the other side of the Honda, staggered a stooped and dazed Jubal and a stocky Armando, complete with Johnny Winter around his neck. They had already extracted themselves from the wreckage of my little car, which looked pretty much like it was dead on the road for all times.

Armando actually grinned at me and said, "Hey, *Tia* Lilly."

Jubal didn't speak, or even look at me, but he advanced on Simon's car until he stood, a bit wobbly, at the driver's-side window, and stared in. Shalonda and I rushed over to peer in too, but Demetrious came up behind us pretty darn quick for a man who'd recently had a serious licking and was limping to beat hell. "You two get out of the way," he said, not endearing himself to me at all at that moment. Then paramedic types pushed at him to get out of their way.

I gave way to the officials once I got a good look. Trapped by his airbag, Simon had not stumbled out like Jubal and Armando, and, in fact, he didn't much move.

After I moved to let the firemen and EMTs do their thing, I turned to Jubal and Armando.

"Are you all right?" I asked, stifling an urge to hug them both but afraid of further injuring them.

"I done hit him to stop him getting away," Jubal shouted, and then stumbled back from Simon's car and sat down, with a sudden thud, into the soft grass in the yard in front of which he'd killed my car stopping a bad man's escape.

"That was so cool," Armando said, heading right for Becky, who had jumped out of the back of Dan's car. "Did you see that, Becky? Did you? Was that cool or what?"

I peered at Jubal, then at Armando. Teenage boys bounce back better than an aging ex-logger was my conclusion, and I moved over toward Jubal. "Are you all right? Do you need me to get an EMT?"

Shalonda plunked down on the ground beside him and took his pulse, and asked him how many fingers she was holding and who was the vice president, and then declared that he didn't appear to be in immediate danger.

"They teach you that in social-worker school?"

"I watch *ER* and those Discovery-channel shows."

"I stopped him, didn't I?" Jubal asked.

"Yes, you did. What happened?" I asked.

"Armando got that little white critter, and then I found 'em and we went right back to where we left y'all, but you were gone. We started looking around and found that shotgun of Shalonda's—"

"He knocked that thing right outta my hands like I was some sissy little girl," Shalonda said, shame evident in her tone.

"Well, looks like he beat the crap out of Demetrious too, so I don't think you ought to be too hard on yourself," I said.

"You want to know what happened or what?" Jubal asked.

"Yeah, what?" Shalonda said.

"After that we found where there looked like a fight, signs in the dirt and all, so we hightailed it back to your car, looking for y'all, and nobody was at Simon's house, so we called 911—"

"That'd be about the four-hundredth 911 call today," I said.

"Yeah, that's sorta what that gal said who answered. Said we'd set a record for 911 calls in one day. Anyway, she told us to stay put, deputies were already on their way. But I didn't see that we should stay put when I figured Simon had you and Shalonda off somewhere. Then Armando told me he'd seen a bunch of gas cans in the trunk of Simon's car when Simon was getting extra rope to double-tie him, when he was putting them in that crypt thing. He's the one thought Simon meant to burn y'all up in a house."

I glanced over at Armando then, who was talking to Becky and Bobby with possibly more animation than I'd ever seen from him, and I thought how proud Bonita would be. I mean, you know, if we ever actually admitted any of this to her.

"Anyway I didn't figure you'd mind too much if I hot-wired your car and went off to rescue you."

"So you do know how to hot-wire a car," I said, remembering he had denied this skill the night Simon stole my purse and keys, and left me stranded with a car I couldn't start.

"Yep, but you didn't want me admitting that in front of Demetrious, did you? I do that and ever time somebody gets his car stole, that man'd be coming after me. Now, you want to hear what happened or not?"

"Yes, please."

"We first figured Simon was gonna burn y'all up at Demetrious's house or barn, and we went off there. When we didn't see anything there to make us think you two were anywhere around, I got to thinking maybe he meant to burn down Willette's house, so we were rushing there when I come around the corner . . . and . . . er, there was . . . there was Simon, see, and I could tell he was getting away, and wasn't no way else I could stop him, and so"—here Jubal paused ever so slightly and rubbed his hands on the grass—"see, I just plowed right into him so's he couldn't get away."

Uh-oh, I'd been a lawyer long enough to recognize basic Lying 101 signs.

"Okay, what really happened?" I asked. But before Jubal could answer, Rodney and another police officer came over and shooed me away, and that was that.

By the next day, the official side of the story came down that Simon had not been able to find Becky, Bobby, or Armando, and figured his game was pretty much up, and, wisely discerning that he would not much enjoy life in a Georgia state prison, he had loaded his car in a hurry with all the essential things he needed to start a nice new life in another country, no doubt one without a strong extradition treaty. The only thing that stopped Simon from if not a clean getaway then at least a prodigious head start was Jubal's gallant decision to put himself in harm's way by crashing my car into Simon's. To block his escape.

Of course, we all overlooked that he'd put Armando at risk. Honda cars are tough, but there wasn't any guarantee Jubal and Armando wouldn't have been hurt. But Armando couldn't have been happier about being in a big car crash and walking away with full bragging rights.

And, of course, the only two people who knew what had really happened, that being Jubal and Armando, kept quiet about it. Until later. Jubal was the one who finally told me, while I was bringing him some fried tofu in his jail cell.

The thing was, Jubal had swerved my car going around the curve because Free Bird, Eleanor's peacock, had run out in the road slap-dab in front of him. It was just pure instinct that made Jubal swerve, and just happenstance or cosmic intervention that Simon's vehicle was what Jubal swerved into. Jubal kept saying he was just "real, real sorry" about my car. The peacock got clean away.

In truth, Jubal hadn't known Simon's car from Adam's house cat.

But when he crawled out of my Honda and looked in the window of the car he'd smashed into, he recognized Simon. And Jubal was a man with a good imagination and a fast tongue.

That night at the jail, after he'd confessed his hero status was purely accidental and due to an errant bird, I told Jubal that all in all he'd done a terrible thing helping Ray Glenn with his endangered-species smuggling. But Jubal was doing his best to redeem himself, and even Patti Lea agreed God doesn't ask or expect much more than that. I promised Jubal that I'd have Philip Cohen see if he could be temporarily admitted to practice in a Georgia court and defend him, or, failing that, find Jubal a good Georgia criminal defense attorney.

And, we all learned after a careful investigation by Demetrious, that Simon had fled down that road because he'd had to get a few things from his office at the hospital, like a quarter of a million dollars of bearer bonds. In a less than well-thought-out manner, Simon had stored these bearer bonds in a safe in his office at the hospital because my grandmomma's house did not have a safe.

But all this we were to learn later. That night, while we were staring at the car wreck, against the backdrop of a deep indigo sky darkening with the rising smoke from Willette's burning house, everybody figured Jubal for a hero, and I kept my doubts to myself.

And while Jubal, shaky as he was, and Armando had walked away from the wreck, Simon had not. As we watched, the EMTs loaded Simon onto a stretcher bound for the hospital that he had once ruled.

But I only spent a minute or two watching Simon. I turned my head back in the direction of my grandmother's house, the one that should have been mine, the redbrick house with the porch, resting in its haven

among the blueberries, the peach trees, with the living fence of chestnut
and pecan trees, all backed up by the little blue lake with the great blue
herons and white egrets. Though I couldn't see the house from here, I
could feel it—like the cool breeze on a hot day, which my granddaddy
always thought was his beloved whispering to him.

Well damn, if I couldn't wrestle a quit-claim deed in my name for
Grandmom's place out of all this, I would personally renounce my law
degree and hang up my shingle.

chapter 63

The $65,000, what with all the general excitement, had slipped my mind until late night, when I woke with a start and realized all that cash was now ashes somewhere in the eastern corner of what had once been Willette's house.

I kept that thought to myself when Dan, Patti, and I walked over after coffee the next morning to stare at the pile of charred timbers and soot that had once been the house Dan and I had grown up in, but which, tried though they might, the firemen could not save.

"Good thing we got all her important papers out," Patti the Glass-Is-Half-Full said.

"Reckon we don't have to worry about cleaning any more of it up," Dan the Practical said.

I had my mouth open to wonder out loud what sort of toxic mold smoke we had inhaled, when Shalonda pulled up in her car and got out.

"Ain't pretty, is it?" she asked by way of greeting.

Then everybody had to hug everybody else, and as soon as that was over, I pulled Shalonda aside and whispered that I'd put the cash in Willette's kitchen for safekeeping.

"Good plan," she said.

"Well, we couldn't've kept it anyway," I added. "Just means Colleen is short that $65,000."

"Lord works in mysterious ways," Shalonda said, and grinned at me. "And good thing I never told Demetrious or Rodney about you taking it. Reckon we ought to leave it be. I dang sure don't want Colleen suing me for that money."

While I absorbed the wisdom of that, Patti put her arm around Dan's shoulders. "I'm sorry about the house, but at least we got the antiques and the money out."

Got the money out?

"What money?" I asked.

"Willette had $65,000 in cash—in *cash,* mind you—stuffed inside a picnic basket in the kitchen," Patti said. "Can you imagine that?"

Yes, I could, and looked at Shalonda with an expression that dared her to say anything.

"We just don't have any idea where she'd come up with that kind of cash money. But let me tell you this, we can sure afford to get her in the best detox center in all of Georgia. Plenty of money to pay for it now," Dan said. "And you wouldn't believe the money she's got in a stock portfolio. That Scott fellow works over at the stockbrokers' sure gave her good advice. Going to start investing with him myself."

Shalonda was the first to laugh. I knew then she wouldn't be telling her husband anything at all about that money we took out of Lonnie's Victorian. Later, when Colleen never reported its theft, we figured that Lonnie had never told her about the cash. Her attorney and Simon's attorney and the state's attorneys and the IRS all locked themselves into a tizzy of a battle over the funds Simon had paid Lonnie, and frankly I don't care how that turns out, so long as Colleen the Vile doesn't get it.

And yes, Simon had been friends with the CEO of the real estate development corporation, and they'd both had these checkered careers, all told, and when the CEO asked Simon to "grease" the resort-development process, Simon had taken it *totally on his own* to bribe Lonnie, the holdout county commissioner, or at least that was what all the resort people said. Nobody much listened to Simon's side of the story. But when the money tracers finished proving that the money Simon paid Lonnie came from the resort's own corporation, and there were some suspicious deposits in Simon's stock portfolio strongly suggesting the developers had been generous to Simon, the state and the feds jumped in to investigate.

As for the resort itself, aside from fraud and bribery criminal actions hovering out there over them, once the story about Lonnie's bribe came out, the rest of the commissioners naturally decided to rescind the vote to join forces with the resort, and redid the vote—well after Lonnie's replacement had been appointed. Shalonda stepped up to the plate and, in no time at all, Bugfest County had a brand-new commissioner, the county's first woman, and in a unanimous vote, the good commissioners of Bugfest decided to have nothing to do with the resort, and to put on hold its plans to dam the creek and make a big lake out of a small lake. So, at least for a while, that resort and any others will just have to wait.

Jubal, whose only legal sin was finally summed up as aiding and abetting a conspiracy to smuggle, will get out of jail in plenty of time to enjoy quite a few more years on the property his family had owned for one hundred and sixty-five years.

Dan felt a great sense of relief upon learning that Ray Glenn had not gone to Willette to collect the bill for the refrigerator he had ordered, but had gone there with Lonnie with the full intention of getting Willette's signature on a backdated deed, and then, at least from Ray Glenn's point of view, to kill her—per Simon's orders to Ray Glenn.

Between what Willette told Demetrious as she was coming off her drugs, and what Simon told Demetrious as he was going under his drugs in the ER, Demetrious pieced it together nicely. Lonnie was slow-witted enough that when Simon offered him $400,000 for my grandmom's place, instead of explaining the truth to Simon and paying Willette off, he just signed Willette's name himself on a deed and snuck it into the courthouse. So, when Simon looked, there it was—a forged deed. And when Jubal found out what Simon had paid for the property and called Willette, she'd promptly phoned Simon and explained that, legally, she still owned that house but she'd be glad to sell it to him for $400,000.

Naturally enough, Simon came unglued after that, and cornered Lonnie with a demand that he get Willette's real signature on a back-dated deed. Simon was in no mood to deal with Willette, a lawsuit to quiet title, public knowledge about the inflated sale price, or any of the rest of the can of worms Jubal had unleashed with his snoop and disclo-sure moves.

But, as Grandmom would have said, "once burnt, twice careful." That is, Simon didn't trust Lonnie not to screw up again. And there was Simon's new best friend, Ray Glenn, anybody's bad man for hire. They'd met when Ray Glenn had started sniffing around Simon, looking for an angle to get some of that big money floating between Simon and Lonnie. In a classic example of takes-one-to-know-one, Simon had spotted Ray Glenn for the evil soul he was, and hired him to dispose of Willette after she signed the backdated deed. But when Willette refused to sign the deed, and Ray Glenn started stuffing pills down her throat, aiming to kill her, Lonnie tried to fight Ray Glenn off to save her life. And while the two men were fighting, Willette got a gun out of the end table. When Ray Glenn shoved Lonnie aside, and started back after Willette, she had simply shot Ray Glenn to death.

Shalonda takes great comfort in this story, and has repeated to me a hundred times or more, "See, I told you he wasn't a bad man."

Willette herself had shipped out to a detox-and-rehab center in Atlanta, right after she transferred title to Grandmom's place to me for its fair market value, minus what Lonnie had already paid on it. Detox and deed transfer were both arranged by her legal guardian, Dan, while she was still mentally incompetent. Her prognosis for regaining her mental and physical health is uncertain, given the long years of drug abuse and bad nutrition. But Dan remains optimistic and speaks of bringing Willette home to live with him and Patti Lea, an idea that Patti Lea considers on a par with Armageddon.

The only things my mother asked for was for Delvon to visit, and for plenty of cold Cokes. Delvon showed up with his girlfriend, Lenora the Saint, and they prayed her through the worst of the detox. And none of the official law came from Bugfest with warrants for Delvon's arrest, though we remained nervous about the state boys while Delvon stayed in Atlanta at the detox clinic.

The only things Willette said to me when I visited her after detox was that she damn well wasn't going to live with me, and she wanted her own house rebuilt, by God, and plenty of Cokes. Oh, and don't any of us be coming around too much.

I agreed I wouldn't be coming around *too much*.

Because, just as I'd figured, Willette remained unrelenting.

She wanted no more to do with me than I wanted to do with her. Whatever sin, real or imagined, I had committed in my childhood—even if it was only that Delvon had preferred to play with me rather than his mother—was unforgivable in Willette's troubled mind. Having never expected anything better, I was not disappointed. That Eleanor wanted me to make peace with my mother was, after all, achieved, though not in the way that Eleanor had probably envisioned. Our peace, that is for Willette and me, was that we would simply go our own ways.

Willette had saved her own life once, and I had saved it a second time, and whatever she made with the rest of it would be without me playing any role in it.

There was, in all of that, a kind of a truce.

So, I wouldn't be coming back to Bugfest to see Willette. But I'd be coming around enough to visit Shalonda and my own family. And to fix up my grandmom's old farmhouse, down by little Sleepy Lake, a house that Armando wants to move into as soon as he graduates from high school, thus escaping the odious task of making friends with his soon-to-be stepfather. Armando and I, on the drive back to Sarasota, decided that it would be in everyone's best interest, especially our own, not to tell Bonita he had been kidnapped and imprisoned in a tomb and narrowly escaped bodily harm in a car wreck while in my care. And there is nothing like a shared secret to bond two people together. So, Bonita still lets him ride shotgun with me when I drive up to Bugfest.

Armando has painted my old bedroom at Grandmom's house a shade of gray only a teenage boy could like, and figures it for his room when he graduates. Living in my grandmom's house would put him closer to his first love, the ever-charming Becky. I don't know that this will come to pass, but it's a lovely-sounding plan for the time being.

Back on my own home front, my own beloved, Philip, tangled his Cary Grant–cool client's jury up in befuddled knots to the point where they couldn't reach a verdict, and the judge had to declare a mistrial. Not too long after that, I got a notice that Idiot Client had dropped his lawsuit against Henry and his insurance company. My theory that he was an across-the-board fraud was right on the money. Incredibly enough, the man had never actually graduated from chiropractic school, not to mention his little problem with the Medicare fraud division breathing down his neck after a well-placed phone tip from a reliable source, followed up with an anonymous e-mail with an attachment proving his years of cheating.

Idiot Client, now a man with state and fed officials after him, grinding his miserable life to shreds, did not have any chance of winning that lawsuit against Henry and his company. That I had brought about a just result by somewhat suspect means troubled me for a while, but then I put it out of my head. I'd been a trial lawyer too long to ruminate on stuff like that.

Alas, my faithful Honda was declared totaled by my insurance company. But I bought it back from the junkyard, and Hank has a crew of high school shop boys doing their senior project trying to rebuild her. We'll see. In the meantime, somewhat to the chagrin of my uptown law partners, I am driving Jubal's pickup. After all, he wrecked my car, only fair he should give me his. And, being a hybrid, it gets almost as good mileage as my Honda did.

Oh, and about that gun Willette had used—after much fussing over it, I finally found out that her loyal, protective friend and neighbor Eleanor gave it to Willette years back, right after everybody but Willette moved out of the house. The occasion for learning this was my trip back to Bugfest, to bring my new best friend and future tenant, Armando, to visit Becky, and to attend the wedding of Eleanor and the survivor of the Great War. Her first marriage, his third.

When I asked Eleanor why she had given my mother a gun, she said, "A little woman like that, all by herself, I was afraid for her. The Lord works in mysterious ways. But it does not hurt any to be well armed."